I SEE A RED DOOR

I See A Red Door

AYNA MEPPELINK

Ayna Meppelink

YELLOWBACK MYSTERIES
JAMES A. ROCK & COMPANY, PUBLISHERS
ROCKVILLE • MARYLAND

I See A Red Door by Ayna Meppelink

is an imprint of JAMES A. ROCK & CO., PUBLISHERS

I See A Red Door copyright ©2007 by Ayna Meppelink

Special contents of this edition copyright ©2007
by James A. Rock & Co., Publishers

Front and Back Cover Photos ©2007 by Ayna Meppelink.

All applicable copyrights and other rights reserved worldwide. No part of this publication may be reproduced, in any form or by any means, for any purpose, except as provided by the U.S. Copyright Law, without the express, written permission of the copyright owner.

This is a work of fiction. Names, characters, places and incidents either are the product of the author's imagination or are used fictitiously. Any resemblance to actual events, locales, organizations, or persons, living or dead, is entirely coincidental and beyond the intent of either the author or the publisher.

Address comments and inquiries to:
YELLOWBACK MYSTERIES
James A. Rock & Company, Publishers
9710 Traville Gateway Drive, #305
Rockville, MD 20850

E-mail:
jrock@rockpublishing.com   lrock@rockpublishing.com
Internet URL: www.rockpublishing.com

Paperback ISBN: 978-1-59663-778-8

Library of Congress Control Number: 2006937878

Printed in the United States of America

First Edition: 2007

To the memory of my mother,

Avis May Farnsworth-Meppelink

and my father,

Reinder Meppelink,

and my Opa and Oma,

Gerrit and Ina Meppelink-Brasz.

With love and respect.

ACKNOWLEDGMENTS

My thanks to Bonnie, reader of the first draft, who had her first blowout in twenty years after reading the first chapters (one of many such coincidences) and who corroborated details I *knew* I had made up; to Bill Hawke, who shared his extensive knowledge about gold mines (in relation to a real-life case) and who first pointed out that I was seeing through the eyes of the victims; and to Donna Seebo, psychic medium, author, and talk show host, whose insights and kind encouragement were much appreciated and who first identified the seeing and said, "You have a rare gift. You are a *medium*." (h ⁓ = me, after falling off chair)

Special thanks also to Sheriff Steve Moore of San Joaquin County, California, who good-naturedly interrupted his busy schedule to provide me with correct investigative and procedural information (which I then proceeded to embroider upon with my own fabrications).

My loving gratitude to my brother, Bert, for his feedback on an early draft, of which he asked, "Is this real or is it séance fiction?" (the answer is *both*); to my brother, Gary, for his input during the final stages and for thinking I'm funny (often when I'm not trying); to my friend, Annie Shebanow, for never thinking small and for cheering me on and for her enduring friendship; to my aunts and uncles, for feeding me spaghetti when I was hungry, whistling in the back alley, teaching me the importance of education, giving me my very first book, and so very much more; and to my nieces and nephews, for keeping me updated and for respectfully refraining from laughing at my rusty Dutch and, simply, for being adorable.

Author's note: All chapter titles are lines
from Shakespeare's *Hamlet*.

I could a tale unfold whose lightest word
Would harrow up thy soul, freeze thy young blood,
Make thy two eyes, like stars, start from their spheres,
Thy knotted and combinèd locks to part
And each particular hair to stand an end,
Like quills upon the fretful porpentine.
But this eternal blazon must not be
To ears of flesh and blood. List, list, oh, list!

—William Shakespeare, *Hamlet* (I, v, 15-22)

Chapter 1

Oh, my prophetic soul!

Rotting leaves. Broken twigs. Crushed walnuts. A whorl, like the gnarly face of some prehistoric animal, on the trunk of a tree. A gray-speckled pebble touching a curly strand of hair. And water. Rivulets of muddy water in the soft, dark soil. Around an arm spread in a motionless wave. Around a cold hand, fingers fanned out. The polished nails on those fingers, jewels in the mud.

Soundlessly, the vision imploded. Darkness swirled in the air before my eyes. Then the road appeared again in the headlights. I took a gulping breath. Bracing myself against the back of my seat, I swerved into the nearby turnout and stomped on the brakes. For a few seconds, I sat quietly and listened to the idling car, waiting for the inevitable disruption of the dead calm inside my head.

And it came—silently, yet screaming and roaring—to bring with it a mass of disarranged details of what I'd just seen in that flash, rushing around between my temples. My heart pounded. I shook my head firmly to stop the onslaught of information. To my surprise, this worked. I could think again.

"Oh, my God, she's dead," I thought. No, I *knew*.

Breathing deeply, I closed my eyes and called the vision back. My mind's eye drifted over the scene. Again, I saw all the various bumps and pits that formed the primitive face in the whorl, the shape of each decaying leaf, every shade of gray on the speckled pebble. But now that I could gradually take in the details rather than have them force fed to me, I was able to make inferences: the moon was missing, and if I could notice that the moon was missing, it must be night; the pale circle of light on the ground, like the hazy negative of the iris of an eye, was cast by an artificial source located behind me.

Carefully, my attention moved along the arm toward the hand. *Her* hand. Bruised and scraped. White knuckles. That color of nail polish, what had she called it? *Amazing Magenta.* "Looks more like fuchsia," I had said. Now, the Amazing Magenta was badly chipped, her nails torn.

Knowing that if I let go, I wouldn't be able to bring this image back so vividly, never again see all this so clearly, I hung on a few moments longer, waiting for more information. But this second look offered nothing new, and I was left with the many useless details of twigs and walnuts, a missing moon, and Amazing Magenta fingernails.

My consciousness shifted back to inside the car. I bit my lip, then let out a deep sigh. Pulling the seatbelt away from my chest, I rolled down the window and stuck my head out. I would have sat there like that for the next hour, had not a speeding truck hit a large puddle near my car. I jerked my head back in, grabbed the tissues from the passenger seat and wiped my face, too stunned to utter any of my customary maledictions for rude drivers.

The giant headache that usually develops after one of these psychic broadcasts pushed on my forehead, poked at my eyes. I checked the side mirror, turned on the blinker, and shifted the car into drive.

Back on the road, it took a few moments before I remembered where I was going. I was on my way to Modesto, to a meeting—one of those where drunks go if they have an earnest desire to stay sober. I'd better keep heading in that direction.

It was the last Saturday in January, just after the final stray Christmas cards had served as annual proof of life. As usual before a gathering of kindred ex-lushes, I had felt mellow, even slightly serene. Wandering through the corridors of that day, my thoughts stopping here and there, I'd been searching for nothing in particular when I'd accidentally opened the wrong door. This is when Knowledge sneaks in, when I'm relaxed, my guard is down, and my conscious mind doesn't filter information.

Holding on to my steering wheel as if it were a deflating lifesaver, I couldn't help thinking, "Why me?" Of course, I immediately realized it was far worse for the person I'd seen in that vision. How terribly selfish. What was wrong with me? I had a long list of shortcomings handy, most of which had nothing to do with this occasion, but if I were going on a guilt trip, I might as well visit all the old familiar places. After a few miles of self-flagellation, I reminded myself that I am neither as wicked nor as virtuous as my imagination allows me to be. My very next thought was not for me but for the dead woman.

I was angry with her. I wished I could have saved her, but I was angry. And when the tears began streaming down my face, I wasn't sure if I were crying out of sorrow or fury.

Why didn't she listen to me? How did she get herself killed? Get herself killed? Sounds as if she conspired in her own murder. *All right then, how had she been murdered?* Only a sweeping hush answered that question. Was it the wrong question? Was she even a victim? She must be. I'd never had this kind of vision about anyone who had died of natural causes. Where exactly was she? I tried to let my mind float out of focus, but I couldn't stop thinking, *thinking*, and nothing could come in.

If I just reject this vision, it won't be true. But denial, always an integral part of my first-response routine, could change nothing about what I'd seen. My only recourse was to pray that unsophisticated prayer I'd used so often during my drinking days: *Oh, God, please no!* It's not much of a prayer. As far as prayers go, it pretty much stinks, because I'm always saying it after the shit has hit the fan.

By the time I got to the meeting I'd calmed down and renewed the promise—to my infinitely higher Self—to find help with my abilities. Ignoring them, in the hope of getting rid of them altogether, certainly wasn't working. I'd find a guide, a kind of psychic sponsor. How, I had no idea.

The greeter at the door said, "Hi, *Lizzz!*" I grimaced in response to his goofy smile. I wasn't in the mood for his Liz Taylor joke. I knew for a fact—well, I'd read somewhere—that Ms. Taylor prefers not to be called *Liz*. Besides, I suspected he only called me Liz because he'd forgotten my real name. I couldn't remember his either. I scanned his face to check again if he looked like anybody famous so I could reciprocate, but all I could come up with was Alfred E. Neuman, and that wouldn't do.

I snuck into the bathroom, took one look in the mirror and shouted, "Oh, crap!" Behind me a toilet flushed. I wasn't alone after all.

"You look great, Fae!" The woman, short and rotund, walked to the sink and began fanatically washing her hands as if this sanitation would last beyond the doorknob. I was trying to remember her name—Lisa? Linda? Something with an L. Shirley? Shirlene?—when she looked over at me and sweetly asked, "Did you forget my name again?"

I nodded, biting the inside of my cheek. That was two in a row. There definitely wasn't a psychic TV show in my future: they'd laugh me out of the studio before I got through the alphabet.

"It's *Karen*," Karen said with a kind smile on her round, peach-cheeked face. "You did something new to your hair!"

I did? I looked in the mirror again. My coiffure still looked like a cluster of underwater plants. "Not on purpose," I said and raked my fingers through my weeds, but then, thinking better of it, looked for a real comb, which was in my purse somewhere.

"Well, it looks nice. Shows off those Delft-blue eyes." She dried her hands, wrinkled her pug nose at me, and left the bathroom before I could protest too much. "Oh, no, that's my new eye shadow," I said to the door.

I combed my hair, wiped the mascara smudges from around my eyes, which were decidedly more denim than Delft in my opinion, then sat down on the straight-back chair and thought for a while about what passed for Delft blue nowadays on eBay: German Delft blue, Belgian Delft blue, lots of Japanese Delft blue. Also, the tricky "blue Delft," to confuse the gullible. Less than half seemed to be *Delfts blauw* from the city of Delft in the province of South Holland in the Netherlands. True Delft blue.

By the time I came to what was left of my senses, I was late for the meeting. I looked around to see if I could spot my best friend and sponsor, Kate. I needed to talk to someone about what had happened, someone who knew me better than to think I was crazy. But Kate was nowhere to be seen.

I poured myself a cup of coffee and parked in the nearest empty chair. Chain smoking and unable to focus on what was being said, I fidgeted throughout the first half of the meeting, changing seats each time I got up to get more coffee. When someone called on me to talk, I claimed I would rather listen, which happens about once every two decades, and I hadn't been sober that long. A few of the regulars raised their eyebrows in mock concern.

My attention flitted across the room. We had several out-of-town visitors. My eyes fell on one of them.

She was sitting quietly, looking straight ahead of her, hands in her lap, palms up. Waist-length, jet-black hair framed her oval face. Long, curving lashes shaded her large, dark brown eyes. Twin moons shone in those eyes. A soft smile played catch with the corners of her shapely mouth. She was one of the most beautiful women I'd ever seen. I saw sorrow and joy, doubt and faith, pride and humility in her face, and I could tell she wasn't at all paying attention because her mind was somewhere else.

I looked away for a moment, feeling like an intruder, as if I'd secretly been reading her diary, but then something compelled me to stare at her again. I knew this woman, recognized her somehow, although I was sure we'd never met.

Suddenly, she turned her head and gazed back at me. Feeling caught, I tried to look away again, but our eyes locked and her mouth widened into a deeper smile. Then, she winked at me.

I practically had to sit on my hands for the rest of the meeting, so badly did I want to talk to this woman. She paid me no further attention but focused on whoever was sharing.

After closing, she moved through the melee and was gone before I knew it. I was about to run after her, but a bulky shape with a crew cut stepped between me and the door. "Hi, Beautiful! Give me a hug," he said, faking the leering look of some misguided thirteenth-stepper.

"Oh, Bill, I have to run." I tried to point past his beefy arm at the door, but instead my finger aimed at the ceiling.

"Get out of her way, Bill," Karen said, walking up. "Can't you see she's in a hurry?"

"Well, hello, Beautiful!" Bill said to Karen. And I made my escape.

I was afraid the woman had left, but I almost ran into her because she was standing right outside. "I need your help," I blurted out.

She turned and smiled at me. "Yes, I know. I was waiting for you."

We moved to a corner of the parking lot, away from the others who were hanging out to chat after the meeting. I'm usually careful not to be overheard when I talk about these things, since there are always people lurking about who think that admitting you have a strongly developed sixth sense is tantamount to confessing you don't have much sense at all. *Catagelophobia*? Fear of being ridiculed? Hardly. It's more a fear of being annoyed.

"I'm Fae Nelson." I held out my hand.

"Gwendolyn Blackwaters. Gwen." She shook my hand. Hers felt cool and light, almost fragile.

"I have these visions," I said. Gwen nodded.

I was all set to unload my psychic woes on her, but as soon as I opened my mouth again she held up her hand to stop me and asked, "When did this begin?"

Startled, I answered, "Tonight."

"I mean, when did these *phenomena* begin? Any of it." She rearranged the purple shawl around her neck. It was cold despite the cloud cover.

"I'm not sure. For as long as I can remember I've known things about people. Good things, bad things, secrets they wouldn't want others to know, or things about their future they themselves wouldn't want to know, such as that they'd die soon. I usually keep these insights to myself. If it is something bad, I always hope I might be wrong. Though, I can't remember ever being wrong. I don't mean *me*, of course, I mean the information I am receiving. *It* was never wrong. I call it *Knowledge*, with a capital K. But even as a kid I knew people would think I was weird. And, I didn't want to be weird."

Gwen nodded and smiled. "Sounds familiar. It's funny how nobody thinks twice about the gifted in other areas. Our gift should make us no weirder than someone who can go beyond simple algebra to do complex mathematical calculations, or someone who can go beyond Chopsticks to play Chopin to perfection. I've never met anyone who outright claimed never to have had an intuition or premonition. But if your abilities go beyond that, they act as if you belong in a Stephen King movie, just because not everyone can access this sixth sense to the same extent."

"I think we all tap into that great pool of Knowledge, the universal mind, if you will," I said, a bit uncomfortable with the new-age lingo.

"What's the first significant incident you remember?"

"A dream I had when I was nine years old."

"Tell me about that," Gwen said.

Even after so many years, I clearly remembered. I'd dreamed the world was dark, lit up only by exploding grenades and smoky fires. Large coils of barbed wire divided the countryside, dead bodies lay in pools of blood, buildings had been bombed to ruins. I was stumbling around, crying and getting snagged in the wire, searching for my mother and my father and my four brothers, because somehow we'd gotten separated. I was just about to give up and lie down on the blood-soaked soil, when suddenly a beam of light—the kind you see in the circus, but much, much brighter—shone from above, surrounding me like a protective cylinder. Then a mighty voice boomed from heaven, "You shall be together." I remember noticing that God spoke Dutch. This surprised me, because I'd expected God to speak English like my mother. Then, gradually, all my family members appeared. And I woke up.

"It was so vivid. Not just what I saw, but how I felt. Lost and terrified. For the longest time, I was convinced we were about to have another big war. It scared the hell out of me."

"That *is* quite some dream for a little girl to have," Gwen's voice was full of compassion. "Where do you think this came from?"

"A mixture of different factors. Growing up in post-war Europe, the Netherlands. The stories about the Nazi terror during the Second World War. Then there were the conditions at home, in the Van Dalen household. I think all this melted together and projected itself into my dream."

Gwen raised her eyebrows, indicating I should elaborate.

"My father, who wasn't even sixteen when the Germans invaded in 1940, joined the Dutch Underground. He was one of a small, elite group of saboteurs, a weapons and explosives expert. My dad rarely talked about the things he had to do. Most of the stories I heard came from my grandmother, who probably didn't know the half of it. But he seemed to have never lost that war-time mindset. He lived hard, drank hard, disappeared for long periods at a time. He came from a conservative Protestant family, but I'm not sure if he believed in anything. My mother, on the other hand, was an American born-again Christian of the kind who put a strong emphasis on *Revelations*, the tribulations, the end of times. So, while my mother tried to pull down little parts of heaven, my father was always raising hell. They had a lot to argue about, to put it mildly."

"What happened when you told them about your dream?" Gwen asked.

I smiled. "Oh, boy! I remember that *very* well." I related to Gwen how my parents had reacted. My mother hadn't seemed to be the slightest perturbed about the terrible destruction I'd seen, because to her my dream foretold the inevitable redemption of our whole family, including even my father. She'd waived her hands above her head and said "Praise the Lord" a few times, her face radiant with a rapturous glow of pride that her middle child, her only daughter, was a veritable prophetess. Though my experience had scared me stiff, I was glad my dream pleased my mother so, mostly because my new status set me apart from my four brothers, none of whom had ever shown even the slightest inclination to being a prophet, but also because I was keenly aware that my mother had so little to be happy about beyond anything to do with her faith. My father, who happened to be home for once, had listened while trying to hide an irreverent smirk. Every so often, he'd said "*Echt?*" Really? But I could tell by the look on his face that he *really* didn't believe a word I was saying. He thought I made the whole dream up just to please my mother.

Gwen smiled. "It's significant that you remember this event so well, in such detail. Sounds like your parents' opposite reactions laid the foundation for your ambivalence."

Had I said anything about being ambivalent? I glanced at Gwen. "Of course, this was years before I had the vocabulary to put into words what I felt, but I remember being hurt and annoyed by his skepticism. And yet, I recognized fear behind his rejection. I knew he somehow *had* to disbelieve me, and that he was making a number of faulty assumptions to accommodate this need to disbelieve. Assumptions about me and my integrity. I found this insulting, but still, I began to question my experiences. Stopped talking about them. Started to ignore them."

"But what about your mother?" Gwen asked.

"She told me that second sight—only, she called it the Gift of Prophesy—ran in her family, sort of the way some families have a mean streak running through them, I suppose. She said it had come in through our Cherokee ancestry. Both her parents had Cherokee grandmothers."

Gwen looked at me with a smirk on her face. "So, your great-great-grandmothers were Cherokee princesses?" There was no sting in her words.

I snickered. "I doubt that, but we were extremely proud of our Cherokee bloodlines."

"It may be why your mother was able to validate your experiences," Gwen said.

"She did, but it was very confusing. I wasn't sure how she could be right, because according to my Dutch grandparents, only born-again Christians and those people who had been long dead so their names could appear in the Bible were supposed to be able to prophesy. And then only in a general way. Any other foretelling was of the Devil and should be avoided at all cost on the threat of burning hell and eternal damnation.

"I knew I had to wait a while to be old enough to become born again and that I didn't qualify on account of the other stipulations. I was in a real bind, especially since God spoke fluent Dutch. I was receiving information I wasn't supposed to be receiving. My grandparents' strict views on these matters made me so petrified of my gift that I hid it from them and the rest of my extended family."

Gwen shook her head. Then she gazed up at the clouded sky. Somewhere, there was a moon.

I studied her as she quietly stood there, apparently absorbing what I'd just told her. She looked about my age, somewhere in her late-forties. She dressed nothing like some of the women I'd mistakenly sought help from in the past, the fakes and flakes who claimed to be far more psychic than closer examination proved them to be. I noted she wasn't wearing a speck of black and her attire was devoid of jewelry except for a pair of dangling, turquoise-and-silver, bear-paw earrings. No gaudy amulets or window-decoration-sized crystals hung around her neck. No spooky make-up. Perhaps this was part of why I felt so comfortable talking to Gwen: she looked normal.

I grabbed one of the coffee cans that were spread around the perimeter of the parking lot and put it near my feet. Gwen waited as I searched in my black-hole purse for my cigarettes and finally found them. I lit a cigarette, took a deep drag, and pushed the coffee can around with the toe of my boot.

"How have you been coping?" Gwen asked, her forehead wrinkling in concern.

"I often feel like Alice, tumbling down that rabbit hole on her way to Wonderland. I never know what I'm going to see or know. It comes when I least expect it. It's been my Pandora's box: I've been afraid to look into it. Afraid I'll find something really, *really* terrible. So far, it's only been terrible for others. But most of it's been good. What has come to me for myself has always been helpful. Just last week, I was told to back off from a truck that had just entered the freeway in front of me. I did, and before the next exit, large sheets of plywood came sailing off the back of that truck. Had I not slowed down, one of those would have gone right through my windshield."

"It saved your life."

"Yes. I have no doubt about that. It's just that, certain aspects, they're scary. I don't know how to control it, what to do with this ... *gift*." I almost spat the word out. I needed some real help from the beautiful Gwendolyn Blackwaters.

She sighed. "Well, I have a sense of where your head is. You want to tell me about what happened tonight?"

I sure did, and in one long, drawn-out sentence without punctuation I complained about my latest vision, telling her what I'd seen, but leaving out the identity of the victim. She nodded once in a while as I rattled on. "I don't walk around having visions all the time, seeing things. They're rare. This type of vision has always been about women, murder victims whose bodies have been hidden by the killers." I took a deep breath. "But this vision, it was different. She was out in the open, not hidden. And, up until now, the victims were all strangers, women who lived nearby but who I'd only read about in the paper or heard of on the news. This time, I *knew* the victim."

Gwen pursed her lips but said nothing.

"Why don't I know where they are exactly? In a flash, instantly, I get an incredible amount of information. Minute details. I just taught myself to call a vision back, so I can describe all those details in a linear way, through language. Sometimes, pages of writing and drawings come from this one blink of an eye. But I only see the immediate surroundings. What's the use of showing me something that's of no use? It's not as if I can go to the cops and point at a spot on the map." I waved my tobacco-free hand around. "But then, some time later, they find these women exactly where I saw them. In a cave, an abandoned goldmine, a shallow forest grave."

"Your gift will develop despite your qualms about it."

That much I had figured out. "It's as if someone jams one of those View Masters in front of my nose, only the picture is a live feed: water flows, leaves blow in the wind, things like that. This time, those leaves and twigs seemed to be touching my face. And the hand, it was right in front of me. But, I didn't see the body." I frowned. "Actually, I never do see the body. I just *know* the body is there and who she is." It had never before occurred to me, but this seemed strange suddenly.

Gwen glanced away for a moment before she looked me straight in the eyes and said, "That's because you're seeing things from the point of view of the victim."

It took a few seconds before I figured out the implications of what she'd just said. Then, an electrical current seemed to run through me, raising the hair all over my body. I felt dizzy. "You mean, I *become* the victim?" My voice was hoarse.

"No, the victims are showing you what you see. They are somehow able to contact you."

"You mean, I see what they're staring at with their dead eyes?" I whispered.

Gwen nodded slowly. "You have a very rare gift, Fae. You're a medium."

I wanted to cry out, "No way!" but could barely breathe. I felt overwhelmed, out of my own league. A storm raged inside my head. But it was a short storm, because, in its apparent chaos, I suddenly clearly saw how what Gwen just told me connected with my experiences.

"What should I do?"

"You mean about what you just saw—that vision." It wasn't a question.

I nodded.

She looked at me with something akin to pity in her dark eyes. I ground my cigarette to shreds on the inside of the coffee can.

"It's *Time*, Fae."

I looked at my boots to stop feeling as if I were falling from a great height. I swallowed hard. *She can't help me either.*

But she calmly continued. "The problem is that time doesn't exist the way we think of it here. In the realm of eternity, what you just saw has already happened, even if for us, here, it happens tomorrow. There's nothing you can do but pray and hope for the best."

Just pray and hope for the best? That's it? I had expected her to come up with something better than that. "There has to be *something* I can do!" I croaked.

Gwen now spoke to me as if I were a petulant child. "I'll help you develop your abilities, Fae. But in this particular case," she hesitated, "you can only pray and hope for the best."

Not again? But meekly I said, "I know." Nothing she'd said was news to me. I'd just been hoping she'd tell me something different. "Can you help me shut this off? Close the door?" I firmly believe that for every problem, there is a solution, and for every question, there is an answer.

"No," Gwen answered.

I realized it wasn't quite rational, because I'd known the answer beforehand, but I was still extremely disappointed. I already knew I wasn't in charge of the universe, but I should at least be able to choose *when* I would have these visions and *what* I would know, sort of like changing the channel on a television or zooming in and out with a camera. Unwanted Knowledge shouldn't be able to creep up on me without my conscious cooperation and informed consent. And, I couldn't get rid of the sneaking suspicion she was holding something back. Not that I had any idea of what this *something* was.

I waited, hoping she had a trick or two up her sleeve she might share with me. But her silence confirmed what in my unquiet heart I had already understood: acceptance was the golden key to serenity.

Acceptance—being a key—is often lost to me. I had half a mind to begin a discussion about free will versus predestination, but with the other half I was aware that Gwen didn't make the rules of this universe, she only reported how she experienced them.

Silently, I said a facetious *Thank you very much!* to the creator of all this, rolling my eyes up at the sky, though sure God wasn't floating around up there, but old habits die hard.

A soft rain had started to come down as we were talking. Gwen glanced at her watch. "Fae, it's getting late. I have a project to finish this weekend, but we should talk more this coming week. Will you call me tomorrow?" She handed me a business card.

I looked at it. Underneath the acronymic company logo was her name with the titles, "President and CEO Engineering Department." She was an engineer? Maybe I should ask her to help upgrade my computer.

"I wish I could tell you something different," she said as she pulled me to her and gave me a hug.

"It's OK," I said, though it wasn't. "Thanks, Gwen." I watched her walk to her car. Then I turned and marched to my own car, thinking, "This universe *sucks!*" I backed out and drove out of the parking lot, all the while wearily repeating, "Just pray and hope for the best." But by the time I reached the first red traffic light, I had simmered down enough to have the sense to stop until it turned green and, despite my misgivings, to follow Gwen's advice. For a few miles I prayed with zeal, hoping to ward off as much evil as possible.

Chapter 2

**I could a tale unfold whose lightest word
would harrow up thy soul.**

    I stared at the road ahead. Lightning flashed in the northern sky, twelve seconds later followed by a slow and powerful roll of thunder. The heathen god Thor on the warpath again, tossing his battle-axe through the inky heavens, riding his chariot to his dark, unholy home. The slight drizzle of rain that had caressed the land earlier suddenly turned into a vicious downpour and then just as suddenly abated. I hated this California version of rain that compelled me to keep playing with my windshield wipers. After a few miles of indecisive precipitation, it finally began to pour down in a respectable manner. I switched the wipers to high speed, my attention immediately divided between their rapid movements and the hazy lines that marked safe passage. Mesmerized by the millions of flickering lights reflecting from the wet blacktop, I blinked hard every so often to become focused again.

    As the road began to wind into the lower foothills, I decided to distract myself even more by turning on the radio. On my old rock 'n' roll station that had gone country the year before, someone with a twangy voice sang a warped version of Barney's song. *I love you, you love him, he loves her.* Conjugation, in more ways than one. I pushed the button of my favorite rock station to hear only squeals and crackles. Searching past a few random-noise numbers, I finally settled for a static *Riders on the Storm*. At least someone was on the ball, or maybe just a related roll.

    I hoped that Hal—my other but not necessarily better half, though unquestionably the better pyrotechnician of us two—had built a fine, big fire. He'd been putting together a triple-decker lasagna when I left. A huge chunk of cheesy pasta would help me get my feet back on the ground.

I hoped the power lines would hold up in the storm. At some point during even the slightest rainfall the magic of electricity inevitably failed, and we'd drag out our large collection of candles, storm lamps, and flash lights. You'd think we were deathly afraid of the dark. *Achluophobia.* What would it feel like to suffer from *autophobia,* a fear of oneself? How would that manifest itself? Could you never go window shopping?

I rolled my head around to loosen up my neck and shoulder muscles. This had been a strange day, starting with this morning. When *she* had come to visit.

A loud bang and unseen hands tugging at my steering wheel suddenly ripped me from my reveries. I had no time to think but automatically slowed down and steered over to the side of the narrow road, coming to a stop a few yards from a soft-shoulder sign. I turned the motor off, fumbled to find the hazard switch and pulled it out. The arrows on my dashboard began to click and blink, *click and blink.* I stared at them for a few moments, my mind blank. Then I groaned, because I realized I'd had a blowout, and that meant my marriage was in trouble.

Hal had told me I needed new tires on my Saturn. And now he would tell me that he told me so. I'd never hear the end of it as violins would be playing haunting melodies.

So, here I was. I'd never changed a tire before, though Hal had insisted I watch him once, years ago. He'd made it look so easy, and since I suspected he did this on purpose, I had stood there the whole time, watching him with a look as if he were showing me something particularly distasteful.

If I hadn't been too worried about my tires, it was his fault for making everything look so easy. I'd figured I'd just call roadside assistance, or Hal, tire-changing *Wunderkind.* I could, if I'd still had a cell phone, but I'd had it disconnected after making the mistake of giving my number to my students. *How many paragraphs? What's a topic sentence again? When is the essay due?*

I banged my hands on the steering wheel in frustration. I should have just *changed* the number. Now I'd have to change the tire. What if the nuts were stuck? I vaguely remembered hearing about nuts being stuck from some guy whose nuts had been stuck. What if I jacked the car up too high and it rolled over on its side? On top of me? This would mean of course I'd quickly have to run to the other side after jacking up the car, but still. I was trying to think of a few more problems, possible and impossible, that would keep me safely sitting in the driver's seat. I clearly suffered from a fear of changing tires. *Something*-phobia.

I flipped the overhead light switch on and then off again, which wasn't helpful at all. I needed to acquire a more positive attitude. I closed my eyes and visualized myself cranking up the car and changing the tire in a few fluid motions. I fervently hoped this would work.

The rain seemed bent on breaking the windshield. I wrapped the collar of my coat tightly around my neck and opened the door, halfway expecting the downpour to be a powerful illusion I'd conjured up through negative thinking patterns. A gust of wind grabbed the door, sweeping it outward until the hinges shrieked.

No car lights moved along the road in either direction. No kind, helpful Samaritans. I lifted the trunk lid and hefted the instrument-of-death flashlight, which Hal insisted I keep with me at all times, out of its case. Shining the light downward, I began to circle the car clockwise until I reached tire number four, at the right-rear, one step from where I'd started my research. It was as flat as a crêpe. I kicked it hard, only partly to make sure it was indeed as flat as it looked. Then I stared at it for a while. Perhaps it would miraculously inflate itself—the mind being a powerful thing.

When I tried to move again, to get the jack, my feet were stuck. I aimed the flashlight downward and saw that I was standing in a slight depression filled with water. My brand-new, black suede boots were sinking deeper and deeper into the thick, sucking valley clay. My unhappiness increased a few degrees.

And then I noticed it: I was being watched. Not by just one person, but by a crowd, a host of ... No, it was just all the coffee I'd drunk at the meeting. The leaded kind often causes me to experience a mild but undeniable paranoia. Nothing more than how most women feel in a department store's fitting room. Nothing really all that crazy.

I began to extract my left foot from the mud. It took a few wiggles and hard tugs. Since I had to put all my weight on my right foot, I had to work a little harder to liberate that one. Then the left foot again, and so on, until I was doing the hokey-pokey in slow motion.

I figured I'd better keep moving so I wouldn't sink away in the muck altogether. They'd find the Saturn and no Fae. I'd be gone but my failure to buy tires not forgotten.

Awkwardly, I walked the length of the car back and forth a few times, trying to think of some clever way to get out of changing the tire, only to discover that the fertile San Joaquin Valley soil was now layering itself under the soles of my boots. I was quickly becoming almost as tall as I'd always wanted to be.

No sooner had I made this observation, or—*Oh, Alice!*—my arms flailing, I slid down the sloping ramp of the ditch that ran between the road and the orchards beyond. Trying to regain my balance, I let go of the heavy flashlight, which fell with a smacking sound in the mud. And so did I, landing on my rear. Unable to stop myself, I continued to slide further down to the center of the ditch.

I uttered some ancient Dutch curses. (My mother had once washed her little prophetess's dirty mouth out with soap, the old-fashioned, lime-colored kind with the strong lye smell, but her crude aversion technique resulted only in my buying better-smelling soap; I could now do profanity in six languages and was still learning.) I was sliding around, trying to locate my feet, when suddenly my eyes were caught by a mass of blue material illuminated by the flashlight.

Just an old discarded raincoat.

I wanted to look away, but my eyes wouldn't let me. I wanted no part of this, yet I compulsively peered into the darkness. Beyond the circle of light, I spotted a pair of rubber boots lying at an awkward angle to the coat.

My heart rose in my chest. My gut felt punched. I had to make a conscious effort to get air into my lungs. And then, I saw the face of a prehistoric animal on the trunk of a nearby tree. I crawled over to where the collar of the crumpled coat was.

There, long strands of mud-caked curls were spread in a messy circle among last year's walnuts. A gray-speckled pebble touched a strand of hair. Rivulets of muddy water flowed around an arm, around a cold hand, waving a final goodbye. Polished finger nails. *Amazing Magenta.*

As if to awaken this woman from her deepest sleep, I carefully placed my hand on her shoulder. I meant to gently lift her head out of the mud, but I just couldn't do it. Instead, I closed my eyes and raised my face up into the rain.

A wailing sound came from far outside somewhere and escaped through my wide-open mouth. For the third time that evening I desperately prayed to the God of my understanding.

I didn't need to turn her to see who she was. She'd sat at my kitchen table that very morning. It had been upon her my lingering thoughts had stopped when I'd inadvertently opened that door. It had been her Knowledge had shown me in that unmerciful vision.

I had prayed and hoped for the best.

But Lani Pochard was definitely dead.

Chapter 3

Affection! Pooh! You speak like a green girl …

That Saturday morning, as soon as Lani Pochard had arrived, Hal had reluctantly broken off his weekend routine of reading the paper back to front while drinking a full pot of muddy coffee. As Lani had seated herself across from him, he'd jerked up his head, stared out the window for a few seconds and then produced a look on his face as if he'd suddenly remembered something of vital importance.

It was such a bad acting job that I'd been tempted to boo him off the stage, which he must have sensed because he avoided looking at me during his entire performance. He quickly put on his boots and rain slicker and, mumbling something that sounded like complete gibberish to me, he'd stepped out the door, giving me a surreptitious smile as he turned to close it. He knew I'd be stuck for a while and was gloating. I heard him load up his truck and drive to the back of the property.

Lani, who regularly watched soap operas, seemed to have noticed nothing peculiar about Hal's behavior. She always appeared a little more dizzy than usual when he was around, and I suspected she had a bit of a crush on my husband. Something about her body posture, the fluttering of her eye lashes, inflection of her voice.

"So, what do you think?" Two hours after Hal's departure, Lani was still sitting at my kitchen table, sipping her fifth, or so, cup of his real coffee. She tilted her head to give me a better view of her new hairdo, a frizzy perm that looked like the result of a misguided experiment in species crossover.

If she'd asked before she renovated her head, I might have taken her request for my opinion more seriously. I gathered the manuscript pages I'd been pretending to edit for the last hour and tapped them on the table into a neat stack. Since my ploy hadn't made her disappear, I might as well quit. I looked at her, frowning slightly to give my face a studious look, and thought about how diplomatic my answer needed to be.

Rita, my ferocious all-or-nothing cleaning aide, was mopping the floor, sighing heavily as she came near Lani's feet to indicate that they were in the way, but for the rest completely ignoring my guest.

Lani turned the back of her head to me. "Well? What do you think?" she asked again.

I wish people wouldn't ask me that particular question. More often than not, it causes a struggle inside my head between Honesty and Kindness, which manage to make everything betwixt them seem like a lie. I'm not a very good liar, because lying requires slyness, good memory, and a certain indifference about being found out. It seems like hard work. And, even the whitest of lies makes the conservative church bells ring throughout my being. Maybe I'm simply too dumb or lazy or scared to lie. Nevertheless, I decided to make an effort.

"It's very curly," I said carefully, deliberately adding an upward lilt to my voice to sound positive. I pretended not to see Rita, who—behind Lani's back—opened her mouth wide, stuck an index finger in, and made a few gagging motions.

When she noticed I was ignoring her, Rita raised her eyebrows and pulled her mouth to one side. When she acted like this, which was frequently, I had to remind myself that she made far more fun of herself than of others, and rightly so, being a short, scrawny woman with a face like a piece of reassembled pottery, pepper-colored hair sprouting out of her head like cropped pampas grass, and her hazel eyes squinting behind thick, horn-rimmed glasses.

I looked Rita up and down. As usual, she was in her uniform of pull-on stretch jeans and checkered flannel man's shirt—for summer, she had a stack of the short-sleeved variety—that gave her the shape of an upside-down, double-stemmed, skinny pear. Her feet were shod with the same pair of horrid flatboat sandals she wore all year long, the kind that screamed for *Lederhosen* and some earnest knee-slapping, Teutonic dancing.

Apparently unaware of the silent exchange that was taking place between Rita and me, Lani patted the top of her hairdo as she scrutinized my face. "You don't like it!" she exclaimed with a sullen look.

I had nowhere to hide my lying eyes. "I didn't say that!" I hate it when people first ask what you think and then argue about what you say you think.

"You didn't have to." She pulled a strand of hair in front of her face and secured it between her nose and upper lip by puckering her mouth in pouting position.

I wanted to remind her to act her age but suspected she had lied about that too, as she did about most anything else, so I had come to discover.

Rita meaningfully wrung her hands as she sidled out through the swinging door into the living room, no doubt to continue her work where she could freely express herself in the serene presence of her nineteen-year-old daughter, Sarah. On occasion, Sarah would come along to keep me company while Rita cleaned (neither one of us was allowed to interfere with Rita's intricate and incomprehensible cleaning system), but today she was hiding out, reading a stack of magazines I'd handed her when Lani showed up.

"I just think I like your natural hair better," I cautiously tried again. I thought no such thing. I hadn't the faintest idea what Lani's "natural" hair looked like, because she changed it about every other month. Since we had met a little over a year ago, I'd known her as a curly blonde, a wavy redhead, a straight platina, and now, since too soon in the morning, a frizzy brunette. Neither did her eyebrows give a clue as to her original coloring, because she had savagely plucked them into non-existence and penciled in two thin arches, giving her that look of perpetual surprise so in vogue mid last century. God forbid Lani should ever ask me advice on her eyebrows.

I had a disclaimer posted on my refrigerator door as a reminder—mostly to myself—of my Berkeley days, when I had drunken aspirations of becoming a guru, a delayed reaction to my youthful experiences as a prophetess. "Take my advice! I'm not using it," it said, clearly visible to all who entered the sanctuary of my kitchen. I now looked at it pointedly. Lani didn't seem to notice.

I thought she was going to argue some more, but instead she leaned her head on her hands, smiled hazily in my general direction, and said, "Oh, well." She sighed dismissively.

If I hate it when people ask me what I think and then argue about my answer, I hate it even more when they ask me what I think and then dismiss my answer as inconsequential. I almost snarled at her.

"I can always straighten it again," she then suddenly said, as if she'd had time to think it over.

She could shave her head, for all I cared.

But she made no such offer. She spread her hands in front of her face, nails outward, and wiggled her fingers. "Amazing Magenta," she announced proudly, her voice all of a sudden squealing with delight.

"Looks more like fuchsia," I said spitefully. *Flabbergasting Fuchsia*. I wondered if she'd done her toes to match but then was dismayed to find I'd moved on to yet another one of Lani's body parts. Her extreme preoccupation with her exterior still baffled me, because she was quite a good-looking woman, having a slender figure and a pretty face—remarkably unlined considering her lifestyle—with a slightly upturned nose and generous mouth. In fact, during her blonde period she'd vaguely reminded me of Brigitte Bardot.

Silently, I said the first line of the Serenity Prayer, and not for the first time since Lani had arived. It seemed God was deliberately misinterpreting my petition by giving me the opportunity to *practice* patience instead of making an outright grant of it, which would save so much time and misery.

I glanced at Lani. Her lips were moving, but I didn't hear a sound as if I were underwater. Was there such a thing as hysterical deafness? Perhaps, but she was just chewing on one of my coconut wreaths. There was a piece sticking between her beautifully capped front teeth.

Restlessly, I let my eyes travel along the rows of fussy little cupboards. I'd never actually counted them. Suddenly, I wanted to know how many there were. No, I didn't. I looked around my large, square country kitchen. Here, surrounded by my fifties cherry furniture and eclectic collection of Delft blue, was where I usually visited with family and friends. But here was Lani, who, especially lately, didn't fall into either category.

Desperate now, I got up, grabbed the copper colander off its hook, and tossed all the dark-red apples from the fruit bowl in it. I'd busy myself with peeling apples. I had no idea what I'd do with them once they were peeled, but I hoped this invented chore would inspire Lani to think of something equally domestic to do at her own home.

When Lani had first entered my life, her twisted sense of humor had seemed funny, her exaggerated tales charmingly amusing. She could turn what must have been the most painful episodes of her life into hilarious entertainment. Only die-hard drunks can do this so flawlessly. In time, though, after the same stories—different versions— had been told and retold, it began to dawn on me that her talking was only a way to keep old miseries alive, that she was keeping her past a current event so she could stay sloshed, and that I had been her unwitting accomplice. I would emerge drained, squirmy, and resentful after any prolonged contact, and all contact with Lani was prolonged.

For the past month, I'd been able to restrict our communications to the cordless phone, which allowed me to go about my chores, putting in an occasional *Uh-huh*. A week ago, however, when I had finally hung up after one of her tirades, I'd heard a piercing whistle in my ear. To boot, when I tried to straighten my head, my neck seemed irreversibly crooked to one side as if I were still clamping the phone there. I knew it was time to reclaim control over my life. I successfully cut short the last few calls she made and had just the evening before congratulated myself on my progress in setting appropriate boundaries, when she had hounded me down to my cozy kitchen.

My back to her, I rummaged through my wildly miscellaneous drawer longer than was necessary to find the peeler. After two hours of Lani's unrestrained chatter about Lani's clothes, Lani's hair, and Lani's nails, I was beginning to feel homicidal from Lani's Lani-ness. I wanted to smack her over the head with my colander. But instead, I sat down again across from her, colander on my lap, and retreated to that quiet space within.

How do I get rid of her? I could kill her when nobody's looking. Nobody is looking. They're all somewhere else. With what? The colander is out. The peeler I'm holding? Nobody will suspect me, because I'm so good. Not that good, if I'm contemplating homicide! I'll just pretend she's not here. I'll sit and peel apple after apple. A is for Apeirophobia, *fear of infinity, an infinity of having to listen to Lani. Her heaven would be my hell.*

Pandemonium had broken out in the advisory committee's room upstairs in my head. Anger argued with Patience, Spite sneered at Mercy, Guilt and Self-pity seemed to have morphed into one, while I peeled faster and faster.

I had yet to hear the sound of Hal's chain saw. I supposed his mumbling, as he had walked out the door, could have been about the live oak trees near the creek on the back of our property. One of his main ongoing projects had been to clear them of the large clusters of mistletoe, the kiss of death. But he was probably just sitting in his truck, reading John Mack's *Abduction* for the umpteenth time, smoking whole cartons of cigarettes, waiting for little gray men to carry Lani off.

"I told him it doesn't bother me." Lani briefly met my uncomprehending gaze, but then she shifted her baby-blue eyes to a point behind me.

I must have missed something. I poked at a rotten spot in the apple I was holding to hide the fact that I had paid no attention whatsoever to what she'd been saying for the past few minutes.

"After all, nobody ever guesses my age." She was serious and sixty-two, at least.

I hazarded that she was talking, once more, about the age difference between her and her thirty-eight-year-old boyfriend, a topic she could endlessly explore with a kind of perverse, shameful enjoyment.

"Well, time will tell!" I knew the pun would fly right over her hairdo.

"It's just that he's too sensitive. I've told him that." She leaned forward, looking at me expectantly, waiting to be cast more pearls of wisdom to trample upon.

I wanted to scream at her, "Sensitive, my foot!" After a few beers, this "sensitive" type felt the need to knock Lani around, a fact she had recently shared with such an eerie stand-by-your-man pride in her voice that I myself had wanted to slap her some more.

When, a couple of months earlier, she'd brought Steve Krieger to our house, I'd been instantaneously overcome by an intense dislike. Briefly, I'd wondered if my antipathy could be based on his looks alone—he had beady eyes with no noticeable space between them, a nose that overshadowed most of his face, and was missing both an upper lip and a real chin—when I noticed that Mab and Dooley, our normally slobberingly sociable dogs, stood some yards away, suspiciously eyeing Steve Krieger. No, I was not being superficial: there was something off about the man's energy.

We'd stood in the cold, under the three naked beech trees on the grassy field next to the house. As I'd pulled my jacket tightly around me and stomped my feet against the chill, Mr. Krieger had repeatedly spat on the ground as if marking territory or showing his contempt for us women. When Lani informed him that I taught English at Sandhill College, a curious look appeared in his eyes. It happened so fast that I wasn't sure it had been there. But then his use of double negatives increased in such a way as to become quite ludicrous.

I knew he was aware that I could see right into his dark mess. All during the conversation, he'd sent me sneaky, angry glances when he thought I wasn't looking. I caught these in the corner of my eye, but when I'd turn my face toward him, he'd look right past me. Though, a few times, he had the temerity to smile at me as if that last angry glance had never been there. What was Lani doing with this creep? To my relief, I'd been spared repeat encounters with Steve Krieger.

Now, as I looked over at Lani, brightly back-lit geometric shapes, like stained-glass Gothic windows, appeared in my peripheral vision. I felt the migraine headache coming on, its large, rough hands placing themselves around my skull, pressing on my temples, wrenching my pate out of its socket.

As if on cue, Rita bustled in, her sandals slapping the wooden floor like enormous duck feet. Unceremoniously, she plopped down on a chair and relit one of the foul-smelling cigars she'd left in the ashtray. "What you do to that hair o' yours?" she croaked, pretending to just have noticed the metamorphosis. She took her glasses off and craned her neck forward to take an even better look, horror and curiosity mixing on her face as if she were gawking at a terrible accident. I watched closely, ready to encourage her to buzz off.

Only on rare occasions did Rita address Lani directly. Rita wasn't in the habit of throwing her pearls before the swine. She usually introduced herself by her first name only, no matter where she was. "Hi, I'm Rita," she'd say in her raspy voice, and at meetings she'd proudly add, "I'm a drunk and a dope fiend." After going through the heartbreak of losing three children to alcoholism, she'd become wary of those who kept finding excuses to go out and drink. "People die from those excuses," she'd say. But despite her gruffness, I'd seen her tenderly bully the most hopeless drunks into sobriety.

Anyway, who was I to berate Rita? After all, hadn't I just felt like bumping Lani off—with my peeler? *Mea maxima culpa.* My *culpa* was much more *maxima* than Rita's *culpa*.

Rita's sudden attempt at social interaction was causing Lani to nervously study the copper lamp over the table.

I cleared my throat to call Rita back to order.

"Sarah wants to know you got any books she can borrow," she said without looking at me, passionately puffing on her cigar between every other word.

Sarah must have finished that entire stack of magazines. Were whole continents being divided while Lani sat at my table, jabbering on?

"Sure, tell her to go into the library and take whatever she wants," I said, hoping Rita would take her stinking cigar and attitude with her as she went to give Sarah my reply. But she immediately hollered through the closed door, "Fae says, *Take it all!*" and then smirked at me. Clamping the cigar between her teeth, she leaned on the table with both hands while hoisting herself out of her chair. Nonchalantly, she picked up Lani's coffee cup and, before I could stop her, she'd put it in the sink and then sat down again.

Lani couldn't seem to keep her hands off her hair: it was beginning to look like a flat-top.

When Rita began to imitate the patting gesture, I cleared my throat a couple of times again to make her stop. "You got a cold or something?" she irritatedly inquired.

"Something," I answered and tossed her an apple.

She had to quickly stop her Simon-says game to catch it, glaring at me for spoiling her fun. But then she immediately turned back to Lani. "So? How's the *boy*friend?" she asked, heavily accenting the *boy* part of the word, chewing on the tattered end of her drug of choice, which mercifully had extinguished itself. She peered over her glasses at Lani's head in another deliberate show of disbelief at what she was seeing.

"He's fine." Lani's voice was barely audible.

I bet he is. He'll make sure of that. I dug around for another unpeeled apple. When I looked up, Lani and Rita were holding a glaring contest.

The standoff was cut short when Sarah, carrying a stack of books, came in and immediately improved the atmosphere in the room. "I left these on the library table last time I was here. Is it OK if I borrow them, Fae?" She swept her long, honey-blond hair from her face and began reading off the titles.

"That's fine," I interrupted, always glad when anybody wanted to read anything.

Sarah placed the books on the table. "When did you get that new dog?"

"What new dog?" I asked absentmindedly. I stared at the mix of rapidly browning apples and peels in the colander on my lap.

"She ain't got no new dog," Rita answered for me as she got up.

"Mom! I know what I saw! It was a black Labrador. I just saw it going upstairs when I came out of the library." Quiet and thoughtful, serenity incarnate, Rita's youngest always delighted me when she spoke up to her mouthy mother.

Rita gave me a dark double-dare look.

I sighed as if capitulating. "It's just Bluebelle," I then said quickly and took my turn to smirk at Rita.

Sarah's soft, hazel eyes grew even larger. "You mean I saw Bluebelle, the dog who died ten years ago? So, she *is* real! Mom told me you have a ghost dog, a dog that has followed you from one house to the next. But she said you must … " She stopped, an embarrassed look on her face.

"Be crazy? What else did she say?" I snickered and winked at her. A slight blush colored her cheeks as she looked accusingly at her deceitful mother.

Rita shrugged. "So what? I seen that dog a hundred times. Pain-in-the-ass spook!"

Both Sarah and I now gaped at the scowling Rita. *No-nonsense, rough, little Rita, seeing dead dogs walking. Who would'uv thunk it?*

All the while, Lani sat at the table, dumfounded, her head jerking from one to the other, a deep frown making her painted eyebrows dip over the bridge of her nose so they looked like two toppled question marks.

Sarah shivered and hugged herself.

"There's nothing to be afraid of," I assured her. "Bluebelle is absolutely harmless."

"It's not that. I'm just a little cold." Sarah rubbed her upper arms.

"Didn't you bring a sweater or coat?" I asked. She was wearing one of those short-sleeved shirts Rita must have picked out for her.

Sarah peered down at her shirt as if she'd forgotten what she was wearing.

I went over to the coat rack and grabbed my turquoise jacket. "Here!" I handed it to her. "Keep it. I've outgrown it." I patted my stomach, arching my back to make sure the full extent of my mythical weight gain would show.

"Are you sure?" Sarah asked, looking at the intricately quilted jacket.

"I've got at least thirty upstairs." I wasn't lying, although, *thirty* might be a bit of an exaggeration.

"Thanks!" Sarah said, and she put the jacket on. "Neat!" She turned to her mother, twirling around. Then she took her stack of books and retreated to the living room.

"Well, I better get on!" Rita smashed her cigar in the ashtray so hard that its shredded remains spilled onto my nice Persian tablecloth. "Break's over!" She marched to the back Lani's chair. "Got to polish the woodwork, you know!" she yelled in Lani's ear and promptly began to polish the chair Lani was sitting on.

Lani winced and shook her head, but she didn't move.

I felt sorry for her. There was more than enough wood to polish in this house besides the furniture we were sitting on. Just the ornately carved stair railings could keep Rita busy for hours. "Huh, Rita," I said, jerking my head slightly in the direction of the door to the hallway.

Stuffing the large polishing rag in her apron pocket, Rita took off, habitual scowl firmly in place.

Lani frowned at my tablecloth and smoothed out some imaginary wrinkles with the flat of her hand. "It's really nobody's business," she said in an even voice.

I blinked hard a few times. *Is she still talking about Steve?*

From upstairs, Rita bellowed, "Hey, Fae? I sure need help! Can you come up here? Tell me what you want done with this here mess!" It sounded as if she were calling all the way from the attic, which being my art studio had a right to be a mess. What had happened to the urgent care of the woodwork? She must have run straight up there, determined to play her version of guardian angel.

I decided to play along with her, because I feared Lani was about to enter into another one of her reiteration modes. "I'll be right up!" I hollered back and then, as an afterthought, I yelled, "Don't touch anything!" I could just see her reorganizing my art supplies as she'd done a few weeks earlier, by color, mixing up my oils and gouaches.

"Lani, I need to go upstairs to help Rita. I'll see you tonight at the meeting?" I put the colander on the counter and wiped my hands off. *Did I double-peel the apples? They look awfully small.*

Lani hesitated, "Steve's coming to pick me up. We're going to the movies." She wasn't making eye contact again; her pants were on fire.

I wanted to ask, "What movie?" but decided to let it be. Waving a hand through the air, I went upstairs.

A few minutes later, I heard her car start.

I didn't know this had been the last time I'd seen Lani alive.

But Guilt, my faithful companion since childhood, had followed me all the way up to the attic.

Chapter 4

Stay illusion! If thou hast any sound,
Or use of voice, speak to me.

For how long I sat next to Lani's body, I couldn't say. As the rain came down in gusts of wind, time seemed to stretch and shrink and stretch again while I looked down at her, my hand resting on her shoulder. My thoughts chased each other around until they were like a jumble of wool.

I tried to move but felt paralyzed by a disturbing energy around me. My mind went numb. Then the numbness turned into a strange buzzing sensation, and my heart began to flutter like a captured bird.

Some unseen evil hovered nearby. "It's just your caffeine-induced imagination," I said to myself. But I had all too often second-guessed my sixth sense and been sorry for it, so I looked around.

I saw nothing. Nothing I could distinguish from the dark that surrounded me beyond the hazy circle of light cast by the torch. And yet, whatever I felt was there, close by.

Nausea crept up from the pit of my stomach. I sniffed the air and realized that some of my discomfort was caused by the strong alcoholic fumes wafting up from Lani's body. After I quit drinking, I became quite sensitive to the smell of alcohol, and what I used to inhale and call *bouquet* now made me want to throw up. I swallowed hard a few times to stop the gagging.

I took my hand off her shoulder and moved away a little, my knees scraping against the rough debris in the ditch. I wanted to get up, go back to my car, get help somehow. But how could I leave her here in the mud, so cold, so alone? I leaned forward again to touch her back.

She's gone. There's nothing I can do for her.

Suddenly, the rain stopped. Out loud, I coached myself to crawl out of the ditch to the side of the road. Heaving, I staggered toward the car and leaned on it, hands flat on the hood as if in position for a police search. My hazard lights blinked their inappropriately joyful red like the leftover Christmas decorations we hadn't seen fit to take down yet. When the nausea finally subsided, I stumbled over to the driver's door.

To prevent a rising panic from taking over, I deliberately kept my mind on the mundane details of minimizing further damage to my material possessions. I took off my muddy coat, turned it inside out, rolled it into a bundle, and placed it on the backseat. Sitting sideways in the driver's seat with my legs outside, I peeled off my ruined boots, shook them out, and carefully set them on the floorboard in front of the passenger seat. Then I swung my legs in, shut the door, and moved the seat back to its farthest position to give myself more breathing space. I wanted to breathe now. Deeply.

I sat and waited—inhaling, holding, exhaling, counting four seconds for each, the best I could do. I looked down at my hands that only moments ago had touched Lani's cold and lifeless body. The image of those brightly lacquered, broken fingernails seemed burned into my corneas. *Think about something else.*

I thought about one of the strange ideas that had tumbled through my mind as I was kneeling next to her. *What if I can make her spirit return?* Could somewhere inside me be the latent Gift of Healing, some resource I hadn't accessed, dormant deep in the divine center of my being?

The Gift of Healing was by far the most mysterious of my childhood. Many reports of miraculous healings did the rounds, and my mother was always sure to let us know when she'd heard of yet another heavenly intervention in this department. No small miracles, either: the lame didn't just walk, but their formerly missing legs grew back and they won national skating contests; the blind didn't just see, but they became the eagle-eyed who saved the country from raging floods, no small feat when one-third of the land lies below sea level. Although I'd never personally witnessed an actual healing, my mother's faith had created a world that never lacked hope. Hope had been the main staple of our spiritual nourishment. In Camden's *Britannia* I'd found the old English proverb "Without hope, the heart would breake." But didn't hope also break hearts?

I peered at the rearview mirror. The only cluster of lights seemed miles away, on the flatlands I'd just left behind, a scattering of farmhouses where people were warm and safe—and alive.

I took my cigarettes from my purse and slid one out of the pack.

It took three tries to light it. I dragged on the filter with short puffs and tipped the yet-unformed ashes in the soda can, my makeshift ashtray. I should have ordered an ashtray with the car; I hadn't quit smoking after all. I'd *hoped* I would, but hadn't done so yet. *Any day now. Stinking habit.*

Guilt slipped in to chastise me, *You shouldn't be thinking about ash trays while Lani is lying dead in a ditch nearby.* I argued back, *What should I think about when a friend has just died?*

Friend? She was—had been—more an acquaintance. I hadn't known her all that long. Friends take years to make where I come from.

There were more ways than one to emotionally distance myself from the woman in the ditch. Nevertheless, I was disgusted by my own coldness of acting on my need to do so and decided to edit out all thoughts that weren't kind and compassionate.

What the hell was she doing on the side of the road, so far from her home? What ... ? Two lights on high beam approached rapidly. I wondered if I should get out of the car and jump up and down, do a scissor wave or so, but then pictured myself run over and flattened out on the road and decided against it. I dropped my cigarette in the soda can. A plume of concentrated smoke escaped from the opening.

A truck pulled up on the wrong side of the road, swerved around the soft-shoulder sign, and suddenly came to a full stop only a few feet from my Saturn. Lights were dimmed to low beams.

"Close call, Hal," I said out loud, for it was my lawfully wedded husband. Relieved, I rolled down the window.

Hal stepped out of his truck and meandered over, hands casually in the pockets of his jeans, his tall, broad frame outlined by the headlights.

Leaning on the door, he bent over and stuck his head in until his nose almost touched mine. His thick, silver-flecked hair stood up in places, and I had to suppress the urge to run my fingers through it to straighten it out. Instead, I nervously grabbed my cigarettes again. Hal pried the lighter out of my shaking hand and lit my cigarette. "What are you doing here?" he then finally asked without much curiosity in his voice but with his dark green eyes watching me. He straightened himself, took a step back, and looked away before I could answer.

"What are *you* doing here?" My efforts to appear calm fell a bit flat, because I swallowed a mouthful of smoke and began to cough.

"I came out to see what was keeping you. You're late." He stared at my face, then let his eyes travel down my clothes. "You look like a mess."

"*You* look like a mess." Which wasn't true at all, but sometimes Hal and I had whole conversations—if that's what you'd call them—that sounded as if we were afflicted with a strange form of echolalia. I began to sniffle.

He frowned. "What's wrong?" Alarm in his voice.

"Hal," I said and paused, trying to keep the weeping at bay that was flooding into my voice. "Lani's dead. She's down in the ditch—over there." I pointed over my shoulder.

He rubbed his beard and looked at me intently as if he were trying to figure out why the outcome of one of his research experiments didn't match his theories. Then he coughed a polite little cough, covering his mouth briefly, and bent over to me again. "Are you OK?" He searched my face for signs of ... *mental derangement?*

"No, I'm not! Hal, just go look!" Sobbing, I grabbed the door handle. He stepped away from my car. "She's over there. She's dead, Hal! Dead!" I almost spelled the word out for him.

"Are you sure?" Why was this normally bright scientist looking at me as if I'd just told him the world was flat after all?

Speechless, I stared back at him. For an instant, it was as if my mind were trying to erase what had happened because it was too shocking to contain. Perhaps his question was making me doubt my short-term memory. I needed to put it all into words, speak it back into reality, for his sake as well as my own. I told him what had happened, beginning with the blowout.

As soon as I finished, Hal walked over to the ditch and picked up the flashlight, which was still shining, a little less brightly, in the mud. Against all reason, I found myself hoping all this would turn out to be just a bad dream and he'd momentarily come back and assure me there was nothing, no one. But I could soon tell this wasn't about to happen. He did a quick search of the area by letting the light slide along the length of the ditch, pausing at where I knew Lani's body was. Then he went down into the ditch. I could still see his head and shoulders until he must have crouched down beside Lani's body. A little later, he reappeared and climbed out of the ditch.

He turned and aimed the light over into the walnut orchard. A jack rabbit shot from behind one of the walnut trees and leapt for the cover of darkness, sailing through the air except for a few brief touchdowns. A screech owl let out an angry cry, its wings making a swooshing sound as it took flight. Then it was dead quiet again.

For several seconds, Hal stood utterly still. Then he turned once more and walked back to me, a grim look on his face. He didn't speak but lightly touched my cheek, wiping at the traces of my tears. His gesture made me want to cry again.

I thought of asking if Lani were still there, but it occurred to me that she couldn't have gone anywhere in her condition. I thought of saying something about trampling a crime scene, but then it occurred to me that I myself had actually rolled around in the crime scene, and maybe I was wrong after all and it wasn't a crime scene but the scene of an accident, though I really didn't think so.

Before I could say anything, Hal walked to the rear of the car to check out the tire. I watched him in the right-hand side mirror as he sat on his haunches for a closer look and stood up again. Then, he kicked the tire. That made me feel better, somehow.

Leaning into my window, he said, "Yes, it's flat!"

I put my muddy boots back on, got out of the car, and stood on the road, shivering. Hal took off his jacket and wrapped it around my shoulders.

He grabbed the jack and, with the same fluid motions I'd imagined myself doing this, he changed the tire in less than ten minutes. No nuts were stuck and the car didn't topple over on its side. I wondered if he secretly practiced visualization. If he did, it was working better for him than for me.

"We'd better go home and call the sheriff," he said as he put the jack back into the trunk. "I'll follow you. Your spare doesn't look too good either."

I felt faintly proud of him that he hadn't said, "I told you so!"

He opened the door for me. "You'll need to get a new set of tires, like I told you."

I stood there, looking at him, until he put his hands on my upper arms and pulled me to him then gently pushed me backwards into the driver's seat.

I drove slowly, so it seemed to take forever to get home. Hal had turned on the Christmas lights before he left, but since it was definitely past the season to be jolly, I pulled the plug. After acknowledging Mab and Dooley's exuberant welcome, we left them on the porch to dry out their muddy paws. The kitchen was warm and smelled of Hal's lasagna, but I didn't think I'd ever want to eat again. A musty wine-cellar odor of fermenting fruit also drifted into my nostrils. I'd forgotten all about my apples, having left them on the counter to rot. Hal must have tossed them in the garbage; the colander was hanging from its hook.

I went to the bathroom and scrubbed my hands with the nailbrush until Hal knocked on the door to check on me.

He poured coffee while I leafed through the phone book and found the sheriff's department. With stiff fingers I dialed the number. After one ring the phone was answered.

"I want to report a body." I wasn't quite sure how to go about this.

"Is this an emergency, Ma'am?" an adenoidal female voice inquired.

"I'm not sure. I just found a dead woman." *Should I have called 911? Once a person is dead, is it still an emergency?*

"Just a moment, please?" she said pleasantly, but without waiting for an answer she put me on hold. I thought Henri Mancini would come on as if I were calling a doctor's office, but I was made to listen to a lack of music. Hal placed a mug of coffee on the table in front of me and then stood behind my chair.

"This is Detective van Zand. How may I help you?" Bobby van Zand's deep, business-like voice interrupted the silence.

"Bobby? I just found Lani Pochard at the side of the road in front of her orchards. She's in the ditch. She's dead!" My voice broke so that I wasn't sure if he'd been able to understand me.

But he had. He waited a few seconds, allowing me to catch my breath, and then asked several questions about the exact location of Lani's body.

Lani's property consisted of three separate orchards, each roughly thirty acres, planted with cherries, almonds, and walnuts. Another ten acres around her house were fenced for horses she never had. I gave as accurate a description as I could, mentioning the soft-shoulder sign and the walnuts in the ditch. He said they'd check things out and then he'd come over. After a moment of silence, he asked carefully, "Is Hal there?"

I answered in the affirmative and offered to put Hal on. "No, that's all right. Just take it easy. I'll be over in a little." He hung up.

Hal and I quietly moved into the living room to wait for Bobby to show up. We sat down on the large couch, facing the open fireplace where several oak logs burned, the flames reflecting off the walls, flickering on our faces. Neither of us turned on the lights. Holding the mug in both hands, I sipped my coffee, grateful to be home.

Our fluffy black cat Moon, so named for one white spot shaped like a waxing moon on her chest, lazily stretched and then curled up again in front of the fireplace. After a brief glance she paid us no further attention. But Mellow, Moon's black-and-silver-striped mate, jumped into my lap. I petted him absentmindedly, finding comfort in his contented purr.

I looked past Hal, out the French doors, at the vague outlines of the old almond orchard behind our house. Mab and Dooley were watching us from the porch with eager let-me-in faces, their noses drawing wet doodles on the glass. I gave them the *down* sign with my hand, but they only got more excited by this show of attention and smeared another layer of snot and slobber on the small windows.

After a while, Hal got up and poked around in the fire, for no reason as far as I could tell but to be busy. When he sat down again, we began to talk in muted tones about what could have happened to Lani.

At this point, I didn't know much more than Hal. I told him about my vision and why it made me suspect—I deliberately avoided using the word *convinced*—she was murdered.

He was thoughtful enough not to voice his doubts about my sixth-sense experience, although for a few minutes he seemed to be talking to Mab and Dooley on the other side of the French doors, and then somehow our conversation moved on to other things: taking down the Christmas lights, repairing the back porch, my preparations for the upcoming semester.

It wasn't until we were on this third subject that I realized we had changed topic because Hal had subtly steered the conversation away from my observations about my vision. He didn't want to deal with anything originating from the psychic realm. I stopped talking in midsentence. It was difficult enough to come to terms with my abilities *without* his disdain. We then sat in silence and stared into the fire.

A fearful thought that had been gnawing at the edge of my consciousness suddenly came into focus. *Have I gone through some kind of gateway to another level of experience? Gwen said that my gift was developing. But developing into what?* Before I knew it, the committee grabbed the opportunity and was off and running. *Will all my murder visions from now on be of people I know? Am I going to find all sorts of bodies? Who will I find next?* This went on until Hal, who must have sensed something was wrong or simply felt guilty for having been an insensitive ass, lightly patted me on the back. "Hey!" he—a man of few words—said.

Exhausted from my imaginary exploits, I leaned against him and shut large portions of my brain off by thinking about interior decorating, a diversion that worked wonders as long as I didn't think about pastels—pretend-colors.

A couple of hours after my phone call, Bobby arrived, his swarthy face looking even darker with solemnity, his gray-blue eyes weary.

I'd known Bobby and his family for years, since long before we moved to this area. His parents, Bert and Janny van Zand, owned a large dairy farm about halfway between town and our place, a few miles past Lani's farm. Their Dutch cheeses were sold at farmers' markets and fairs all over northern California. Forty-two-year-old Bobby, still a bachelor, was the oldest of nine children. Several of his much younger brothers and sisters were taking classes at Sandhill College.

I squinted when Hal turned the overhead lights on in full glory.

Bobby took off his navy trench coat and sat down on the mauve love seat that stood perpendicular to the couch. He looked at Mab and Dooley, who had returned to their vigil on the back porch after welcoming him at the front door, as evidenced by the paw prints on his nice coat.

Hal brought in coffee for us all. Bobby took a few sips from his mug, pulled a pen and pad out of his jacket pocket and turned his attention to me, his face wiped clean of all expression.

I waited for him to say something conventional such as, "Spill the beans, Fae," but apparently his gaze was to be the only indication he wanted me to talk.

So I told him about finding Lani.

Scribbling with the pad on his knee, Bobby interrupted me frequently, asking questions to fill in the gaps he thought I was leaving in my story. After a while, I wondered if he might be suffering from receptive aphasia, being unable to decode the words he was hearing, but this seemed an unlikely disability for a police detective and I had never noticed it before.

How did you come to stop right there? I told you, I had a blowout. *Why did you go down into the ditch?* I told you, I *fell* into the ditch. *How did you know where to find her?* I told you, ... what? *So you went down into the ditch?* No, I did not *went*, I *fell*. I slided. No, I mean I *slid*!

Halfway through my narative, I was tempted to tell him to just shut up and let me finish, and I would have, had he been there as Janny's son and not in the capacity of investigator. This must be how they'd taught him to question people in Detective School: to pretend that everything a person had done had been done on purpose, to keep rephrasing every question to trip up the guilty (and the not-guilty), and to mirror each answer so it retained only the remotest resemblance to the original statement.

To my consternation, I noticed how much I sounded like Hal, which meant, since he was sitting right next to me, I'd forever lost the moral high ground from which I could point out his smart-aleck way of talking.

When I finally came to the end of my story, Bobby, unperturbed, looked over his notes, shook his head, and thoughtfully tapped his pen on the paper.

I could almost hear him think. He sensed I'd skipped over some details he hadn't been able to pry out of me with his convoluted questioning, and now he was looking for a way to get to them. I couldn't very well tell him about my vision, could I? I'd already gone out on a limb by telling Hal. Why would Bobby need that information? So what if I'd seen where she was before I found her? Telling him would only start another avalanche of questions.

I thought he'd given up and was finally done with me, but then he suddenly asked, "When did you last see Lani?"

"She came over this morning ... for a chat." *Chat?* She hadn't shut up for three hours straight, and I'd gotten so mad I'd wanted to clobber her with my colander. I felt my face becoming red at the shameful memory of my exasperation with Lani. Had it been a coincidence that someone else had actually killed her? Had I been picking up someone else's intent? Or, even scarier, had someone else picked up my energy and done the deed for me? Had I killed her after all—by proxy?

Lucky for me, I said none of this out loud. I wondered where this came from.

"Did she say anything?" Bobby asked.

This so generally phrased question caused an awkward silence. According to Hal, Bobby knew Lani from several run-ins on the road, years ago, when he was still in uniform, one of them quite literal when she'd rear-ended his police cruiser.

The three of us cast furtive looks at each other. I didn't know what to answer. *She just talked about her hair? Showed me her fingernails? Bragged about her crazy boyfriend?*

"I mean, did she say anything about what she planned to do today?" Bobby broke the impasse.

"She told me she was going to the movies with Steve Krieger tonight. Why?"

"She had some large bruises. Of course, we have to wait for the coroner's report." Bobby stared at me while writing something down. I wondered how he could write like that, without looking, and suspected he was doodling on his pad and not taking proper notes. But as I craned my neck to confirm my suspicions, he placed his hand on the pad, covering up the evidence.

"They're taking her to the county hospital morgue," he said.

I began to giggle, a high, silly sound that echoed off the walls in the otherwise quiet room. Disgusted with myself, I put a hand over my mouth as if that would stop them from hearing me, but then my whole body began to shake with what was quickly becoming a bout of hysterical laughter.

Bobby and Hal glanced at each other in surprise and then looked back at me, disapprovingly.

Not sure if I should explain my outburst, I demurely fixed my eyes on the rug. Should I tell them that Lani had once said she wouldn't want to be found dead at the county hospital? But it wasn't funny at all, not then and especially not now. *Lani at the county morgue. Found dead.*

"It's nothing," I stuttered. Those two were really making me nervous, sitting there, looking at me like a couple of court-appointed psychiatrists. I thought of enlightening them by stating the well-known fact that tragedy often uncontrollably affects the funny bone.

Bobby cleared his throat and—with one eyebrow raised higher than strictly necessary to show what he thought of my nervous hilarity—asked where Steve Krieger might be found.

As I shifted my attention to answer his question, the hysteria subsided. "I think he lives on the other side of town. He moved here last year from out of state." I wasn't sure, because I'd listened to less than half of what Lani was saying when she'd been going on about him. It seemed Bobby should know far more than I about Steve Krieger.

"All right. If you think of anything else, give me a call." He got up, a puzzled look on his face.

Hal let him out. I could hear them whisper in the hallway, though I couldn't make out what they were saying. *Fae has lost her mind? I'll keep an eye on her?*

"What was *that* all about?" Hal wanted to know when he returned.

"Just something Lani once said—that she wouldn't want to be found dead at the county hospital."

He didn't seem to think it was very funny either. To cover up my embarrassment I made a lame attempt at explaining the concept of irony to him. "Yeah, yeah," he said impatiently when I began to elaborate in full teacher's mode.

Well, that shut me up. I let Mab and Dooley in, rubbed them down with an old towel, and gave them each a dog biscuit to reward their unconditional acceptance.

It was nearly two o'clock when we went upstairs, to bed. I fell asleep almost immediately. But a short while later I awoke from a dream so startlingly vivid, it took me some time to realize I'd been sleeping.

In my dream, Lani had appeared, dressed in a red gauzy muumuu, her hair straight and gray. She was walking—practically floating—along a bright, sandy beach. I had the strange sensation that she was aware of my watching her, that she was putting on a show, especially for me. A secretive smile veiled her face.

At the water's edge, she bent to pick something up. Her back was to me now, and I couldn't see what it was she held in her hands. Facing the ocean, she continued to hover along the water line until she reached a red door that suddenly appeared out of nowhere, hanging suspended in the air. As the red of her muumuu blended with the red of the door, Lani faded until she was gone.

I lay awake for a while thinking about what the dream meant, picking it apart and storing each facet so I'd remember in the morning. But by the time I dozed off again, the only conclusion I'd drawn was that there mustn't be any decent hair salons where she was now.

Chapter 5

**Beware of entrance to a quarrel, but being in,
bear't that the opposed may beware of thee.**

Through the half-closed curtains the sun played a game of catch on the quilt. I watched the patches of light run across the reds, greens, and blues of the Rolling Stones pattern. My head felt thick and heavy, and I had a bad taste in my mouth. I stuck out my tongue to let it air out. This was as close to a hangover as I ever hoped to get again. I squinted at the clock on the night stand: the little hand was near the ten, way past the decent time to rise and shine.

As I lay wondering why I'd slept so late, a sense of doom slowly infiltrated my mind. My muscles tensed. Something was terribly wrong. Something irreversible had happened, but there was an empty space when I tried to remember what it was. The remnants of sleep still acted as a buffer to reality, a tug of war was going on inside my head.

I rolled to the edge of the bed, brought myself in a semi-upright position, and carefully placed my feet on the fluffy, aubergine rug. The events of the night before now slowly filtered in until the memory of what was causing my uneasiness was complete. It knocked the wind out of me. What little energy I had was sucked out, and I wanted to crawl back into bed, pull the covers over my head, sleep for a long, long time. I put my hands over my face, the tips of my fingers pressing on my eyes. But then I dropped my arms to my sides, took a few puffs of air as if I were getting ready to run a marathon, and got up. I went over to the balcony doors and opened them wide. The chilly morning air washed over my face, seeped through my nightgown.

Millions of luminous, white flowers reflected the bright morning sunlight. The almond orchard had come into full bloom overnight. A sea of life. My gloom ebbed away as I stepped out onto the balcony and stood quietly gazing at the blossoms, bathing in their sweet comfort of beauty, peaceful perfection.

Our children of the dog variety, Mab and Dooley, were frolicking on the lawn, creating crop circles in the young grass and practically uprooting the beech trees each time they slammed into them. Amused, I watched their roughhousing.

They were like a reversed set of *The Lady and the Tramp*. Mab—with her rough, dark-gray coat, floppy ears, bushy tail, all tell-tale signs of a French Briard ancestry—had been our pick of a litter of Humane Society refugees left on a dirt road in 105 degrees Fahrenheit, dehydrated and starving (Hal and I had wanted to erect old-fashioned stocks in the center of town for the jerks who'd done this). She now stood twenty-five inches at the shoulder, had filled out nicely, her playfulness a sign of robust health.

Dooley, a purebred Newfoundland with the luxurious, jet-black coat native to his breed, had come from a long line of aristocrats. Though he was a few inches taller than Mab and outweighed her by forty pounds, he good-naturedly allowed her to boss him around and always let her go first. Quite the gentleman. I sensed these two loved each other beyond measure.

As I watched them rearranging the plant life in our backyard, I felt an intense, canine-like gratitude for the mutual guardianship bestowed upon us. That reminded me: I should wipe the snot and slobber off the French door windows so I wouldn't have to listen to Rita's bitching.

Music poured out of the open barn doors: Peter Gabriel's *Sledge Hammer*. Hal was splitting logs under the blooming, gnarly almond trees. Synchronicity? He seemed totally absorbed in his chopping chore, but then suddenly he looked up and waved his axe overhead like a victor in combat. I smiled and pointed at the trees, forming an admiring O with my lips. He missed the point and slammed the axe down on the innocent piece of wood in front of him.

Behind me, the phone on Hal's night stand rang. I walked over and picked up the receiver. "Hello?" No response, only a clicking sound, followed by an echo-like stillness as if someone were calling long distance. Perhaps one of my brothers was trying to reach me from the Netherlands. I hung up, standing by, ready for it to ring again momentarily, but it remained silent.

It's too soon for this to be starting. In the corner of my eye I saw something move, a dark blur near the doorway. I turned my head just in time to see Bluebelle leave the room. *Maybe it has started.*

No matter. It was time to get on with my day. I took a quick shower, wriggled into some available underwear, pulled on a pair of jeans, and shoved a t-shirt over my wet head as I went downstairs to the kitchen.

Moon was sleeping innocently on the Sunday paper, which was spread all over the kitchen table, shredded parts spilling onto the floor. I poured myself a cup of coffee, nudged Moon from her comfortable position, and sat down to scan what was left of the local news section. Nothing about Lani, but I hadn't expected to see anything because it had all happened quite late in the evening.

"Who was that on the phone?" Hal asked as he entered.

"Nobody. Hung up." I looked at his boots. He'd laid down a trail of zigzag-patterned mud prints. Maybe I should get him a pair of wooden shoes. Mud doesn't stick to those, because they're smooth and wide at the bottom, a perfect shape for the water-logged lands they were designed for. Besides, they are religiously left outside near the doormat before entering a home. On the other hand, they hurt like hell until a buffering layer of calluses builds up in a few places. There's the rub. Maybe I shouldn't force the contraptions on Hal. Hobbling Hal.

"Hey, could you take those boots off? Please? Rita just mopped the floor yesterday."

Hal pulled up one boot at a time and checked underneath. Convinced they were clean now, since all the mud was on the floor, he made no effort to rid himself of the offending foot gear but sat down, stretching his long legs out under the table. Hopeless. Easier to mop the floors again than to put in any further effort to show him the error of his ways.

"What's that in front of the barn?" I asked. I'd noticed a new rusty piece of junk near his Harley when I was standing on the bedroom balcony.

"What?"

"That heap of rust."

"It's a barbecue," he said, looking insulted and in a tone of voice conveying I should have known what it was.

I hadn't recognized it as a barbecue, but then I didn't recognize a lot of things Hal brought home. The barn was full of strange and wondrous *objects d'inutilité*. "Don't you already have four barbecues?"

"Yes, but none of them work." He stretched his arms over his head.

"Does this one work?"

"No."

I lifted the shredded comics page to cover my face, rolled my eyes, and read *The Far Side*. I didn't get it.

"I can make a couple of good ones out of them, maybe."

"Maybe?" I mumbled behind the paper. There must be some method to his madness.

That's just what he needed: more projects. The year before, we'd bought the house and the forty partially wooded acres that came with it from Lani, who'd inherited the property from her aunt. The old lady hadn't been able to keep up with the care: the house needed quite a bit more than a paint job and the land had grown into natural disarray. I'd thought it all rather charming, romantic, *Wuthering Heights* and such, but Hal proclaimed it a big mess. He'd pointed out that the house would soon need a new roof and predicted that, even sooner perhaps, depending on the vigor of the next rainy season, the back porch would break off and become a free-floating ferry. The storms that had blasted through the area in the past decade had neutralized most of the fencing and felled quite a number of oak trees; many of the surviving trees were being choked to death by mistletoe. It had taken all of my powers of persuasion to convince him this would be *Home*. I succeeded only because the price was right: Lani had been eager to sell.

He'd only recently stopped complaining, probably because he was too busy to do so. There were indeed plenty of projects, and Hal had to do most of them on account that I wasn't so good with a chainsaw while he had no such excuse. But despite Hal's protestations, our home was quite comfortable. It was a three-story, solid, red-brick house built early last century. The porch, which ran on the west and south side (until we had unprecedented rains and that last section turned into a ferry), and the shutters flanking the windows were painted white and trimmed in a cheery periwinkle blue. Because it didn't require a chainsaw, I was in charge of the painting and that gave me the right to pick the colors (Hal would never have picked periwinkle). Since most of the major projects were still ahead of him and he kept adding new ones, I figured things weren't quite as urgent as Hal had projected.

"Why don't you just buy a new one?" I asked.

"A new *what*?" He frowned, at a loss what I was talking about.

"Barbecue!" I put the paper down on the table. Were the comics becoming less funny or was I losing my sense of humor? I looked from the dirty floor to the broom closet, but quickly overcame the temptation. "I think I'll go to town. Do you need anything?" Shopping's a sure-fire way to ward off the compulsion to do housekeeping, and thus my outright-but-unrepented betrayal of the stereotypical Dutch cleanliness and frugality. But then, of course, I'm only half Dutch.

It's funny to be half something. When people say (because they're not really *asking*, I finally figured out), "How are you today?" California Fae just answers, "Fine, thank you," but Dutch Fae really wants to tell them, even if it's not *fine*. Dutch Fae feels like a liar when she answers *fine* if things aren't absolutely *fine*. Dutch Fae thinks people shouldn't ask questions without wanting to hear an honest answer. They should just wish her a good morning or afternoon or evening. California Fae thinks Dutch Fae takes matters too literally, too Calvinistically correct. But then, Dutch Fae thinks California Fae is an airhead.

"Are you going to Modesto?" Hal asked as he plucked our joint shopping list from the fridge and handed it to me.

"No, just to Londen." I perused the note and interrogated him about a couple of items which, in my opinion, we definitely had no need for. We already had a drawer full of D, C, AA, and AAA batteries, enough to last us through a number of antarctic winters. And canned string beans? Since when did he eat canned string beans? "For a casserole I want to make," he said. As always, he won the short debate that followed, so I added a few nonessentials of my own. A jacket and a pair of shoes later, I was happily on my way.

Londen, a thirty-minute drive from our home on Blackberry Road in the lower Sierra Nevada foothills, lies in the flatlands of the San Joaquin Valley. The town is surrounded by pastures teeming with solid milking cows that placidly support the local dairy farms and orchards that produce a variety of fruits and nuts while serving as main indicators for the change of seasons. The locals usually put the adjective *little* in front of the town's official name as if it might otherwise too easily be confused with the original in Great Britain. Londen, spelled with an *e*, as it is in Dutch, was named so as a pun on the treacherous theft and renaming of New Amsterdam by the British in 1664. (The Dutch are forgiving, but who could forget that if the British hadn't done what they did, this whole continent would be speaking Dutch today.)

Most houses in this area are stubbornly built of the same red brick used everywhere in the Old Country, where earthquakes are a rarity. During the fifties, droves of Netherlanders made a new home on these familiar-looking lowlands, leaving their crowded fatherland behind while simultaneously bringing it with them in their language and social customs. Aspects of the Netherlandic culture soon blended with the American, the Dutch being a highly adaptable and practical people. Some even planted tacky little windmills in their gardens, which they wouldn't have been caught dead with in Holland.

For the first years after my return to the country of my birth—in the decade of the advent of the microwave oven and the Pet Rock—it was sort of my sacred mission to dispel the myths about the Dutch that pervade American society. Number one is, of course, that Holland is not the capital of Denmark. Number two and three are that, just as not all Irish are drunks and not all Italians are in the Mafia, so do not all Netherlanders wear wooden shoes and have indiscriminate sex. Not all the time, anyway, and especially not simultaneously. I surprised people by telling them that during my twenty-one years in the Netherlands, I never saw a Dutch barn, tasted a Dutch apple pie (except the ones my American mother made), or heard the story of Hans Brinker. This could be because the barns are German, the pies English, and the story of Hans Brinker was cooked up in New York City. I'd finally pooped out on my mission to educate my fellow Americans. It proved all too overwhelming a task, and since I was trying to blend in, it seemed an un-American activity. Besides, nobody was thanking me for setting them straight. People usually responded by looking at me as if I were just trying to stir up shit. Which I usually was.

I suddenly realized I was driving kind of fast for someone with a funny looking spare tire on her car and slowed down a bit. As I drove past Lani's orchards, my eyes were compulsively drawn to the site where I'd found her. Yellow strips of printed plastic were strung around stakes and bushes. I now remembered every detail of what had happened the night before, of course, but it still felt unreal, as if I'd made it up and the not-so-holy ghost of my father would suddenly appear and inquire, "*Really?*"

I stepped on the gas, exceeding the speed limit despite the spare tire, wanting to get as far away as fast as I could. I kept my mind on my shopping list, mentally adding a few more items, and sailed into Londen about fifteen minutes later, feeling as if I'd walked all the way.

Londen on Sundays resembled a ghost town. Although most stores were open, few people did any shopping on the Day of Rest. The town was basically one wide main street intersected by a few smaller streets, all named for long-dead Dutch painters. I parked in front of the bakery on Jan Steen Street, the thoroughfare.

Every self-respecting Dutch town has a center, a heart. In Londen, our small library-cum-community house, fulfilled that role. Set back about a hundred feet from Steen Street, it had a wonderful garden in front, grandly named Vondel Park for Joost van den Vondel (one of the most prolific Dutch poets and dramatists of the seventeenth century), or maybe for the large park named for him in south Amsterdam. I wasn't quite sure.

The deep purple irises hadn't stopped blooming all winter; clusters of narcissi and crocuses scattered in the grass were just starting to show their petals. Near the front door on the edge of the lawn, a couple of ornate, cast-iron benches offered a place to sit and watch the flowers grow, and to admire the statue of *Zwarte Jan* (Black John) that stood smack-dash in the middle of the unreal green.

Supposedly, this Jan van Delderen had founded Londen some time during the Gold Rush. *Supposedly*, because a number of locals harbored reservations about the historical verity of this man's existence, probably the same people who had formed the somewhat secret society that occasionally circulated petitions to have the statue removed. To them, *Zwarte Jan* was an abomination, a blot on the clean sheet of Londen's *true* history, a Rorschach they'd rather not identify.

Now, if I got the story right, Jan was indeed a little wild, even for the rather tolerant Dutch. Sprouted from a family whose nobility was more in their heads than in their pedigree, Jan's main problem had been that his Calvinistic environment was too restrictive for his exuberant personality, or perhaps he was truly wicked and licentious, as his own father claimed when he publicly denounced Jan as a thief and a gambler in an attempt to keep his erring offspring's relationship with several ladies of the red-light district from the boy's mother. To no avail, because when one day Mevrouw van Delderen visited the butcher (or maybe it was the baker), a neighbor, imbued with the traditional Dutch self-righteousness, let the feral cat out of the bag. Jan's mother was literally mortified by her son's whoremongering: she dropped dead on the butcher's doorstep and became the only person in recorded Dutch medical history to actually die of shame.

His mother in Heaven, Jan's behavior became possibly even more wanton. His next arrest was for drunk and disorderly conduct at his mother's funeral. When he was let go, the distraught father slapped some money into his son's hand, pointed at America, and gave Jan the parental wooden shoe. Alas, Jan van Delderen appears to have been an early example of *Wherever you go, that's where you are.* He fell into bad company after he landed in San Francisco, and while some bad company was undoubtedly worse than others, Jan and *his* bad company were reprehensible enough to be run out of even the City of Sin. And that's how Jan van Delderen ended up on the flatlands, as a statue in the middle of Vondel Park. Despite the numerous stories of his amorous escapades, I can't think of anyone who claimed him as an ancestor. Today, Jan looked a bit more pooped on than normally, his head and shoulders covered with large gobs of pigeon droppings. Not that it had wiped the rakish smile off his face.

On one side of Vondel Park, spreading good news several times a day, was Ben's Warme Bakkerij, which I was about to enter. On the other side was the cozy coffee shop, Full of Beans, painted in an unbelievable array of browns, so that from a distance it gave the impression you were looking at the representation of giant, square turd. All summer long coffee drinkers, sitting under poop-colored parasols, usurped the sidewalk for a terrace.

Across the street from the park was our only grocery store. Here, we could buy imported Dutch foods: chocolate syrup, chocolate paste, chocolate hail, chocolate flakes, coconut slices, apple syrup (all for on bread), licorice in one hundred varieties, smoked mackerel, salted and pickled herring, almond-paste-filled cookies, crispy rusk, rough rye bread, kale, cumin-spiced cheese, and numerous other edibles we refused to do without.

Next to the grocer was a large shop, aptly named House of Variety, because it carried a large and rather peculiar assortment of furniture, knickknacks, household goods, and objects of unknown origin or purpose. I seldom visited town without a good browse here. My best buy was a one-dollar twig basket that defied classification but was very useful as a distractive tool. It looked like the top half of a bird or an oriental fish trap or maybe an angel, *sans* halo, in flight. If guests were rattling on, I'd let my eyes wander to my halo-less angel and gaze at it until their eyes would follow mine. They'd ask what it was and I'd say, "I have no idea," because I didn't, and smile enigmatically. Some then smiled too, others looked totally confused because everything *has* to be something, a few true conservatives frowned in silent disapproval of the frivolity of buying something that is nothing. But all had finally shut up (except Lani).

A notice on the door of the bakery announced "Open Sunday, Closed Monday," a sure sign Ben and his wife Sandra had indeed left the *vaderland* far behind. A shrill bell rang as I entered. The delicious fragrance of crusty breads and pastries immediately engulfed me. I stopped in the middle of the store and inhaled deeply, my empty stomach rumbling, saliva flooding my mouth.

Sandra was just filling a rack with steaming hot baguettes. *Oh, yes!* I swallowed my drool and asked her to bag one for me, inserting "Hi, Sandra!" somewhere in the middle of my request. I added a few dinner rolls, a loaf of whole wheat, and a crunchy almond roll I intended to tear into as soon as it would be polite to do so.

While Sandra took her time to put my purchases in a large, paper bag, I stood at the counter with an imploring look on my face. Sandra took her time about everything. She was a sturdy woman with a pleasant face surrounded by tight dark curls, which I imagined she set every night with painstaking precision. Her blue eyes missed little of what was going on in the world around her.

I'd used my basket on her once when she'd tried to entice me to become a member of the Dutch Club. She'd been on to me immediately, emitted a loud, snorty laugh, and said, "I think that's a Dutch conversation stopper." Blushing, I'd signed up for the club. April 30th, I'd have to attend the Queen's birthday celebration, wearing not-my-color orange. I still had a few months to brush up on the words of the national anthem, *Wilhelmus van Nassouwe*.

Sandra carefully put the receipt on the counter. I tried to see what the total was so I could pay her, but she placed her chubby hand on top of the paper. "Are you all right, Fae?"

"Pretty good," California Fae answered, waving a few bills in the air as bait. *I would be if I'd get my almond roll.*

"You look pale." She took her hand off the receipt and lightly slapped one of her puffy, red cheeks. No one would ever call her pale.

"I'm just hungry." I wasn't sure if I should tell anyone about Lani, and I *was* hungry.

After she finally took my money, I practically stumbled outside, shamelessly ripping into the delectable, buttery roll until my mouth was almost too stuffed to chew.

I had just opened the trunk of my car to stash the bread, when a voice right behind me hissed, "You bitch! Who the hell do you think you are? Bitch!"

I don't care much for being addressed in this manner and was therefore inclined to ignore the source—also because my mouth was still very full—but my head had already turned involuntarily.

Steve Krieger was crowding my space, his long face contorted, his squinty eyes black puddles of anger.

"Hi, Steve!" I said with a joviality I certainly didn't feel, pretending I hadn't heard him call me the B-word. I swallowed to empty my mouth.

"Hi, Steve!" he mimicked, his voice rising to a squealing pitch, his eyelids fluttering so rapidly I feared they'd detach themselves and take flight, and his whole body wiggling in an obscene imitation of someone female. The guy was fruity! But I didn't think this was the time to tell him so.

"What the hell did you tell the cops?" His face was now only inches from mine. The stench of a night's heavy drinking almost knocked me out. For a moment, I wondered if he was aware of how truly bad he smelled and if I shouldn't at least enlighten him on this point, so he could perhaps make some friends, other than me. I wasn't able to step backwards, because the car was there, so I moved with careful little steps to the side walk, still holding my bag of bread.

"What did you tell them?" He insisted, moving in the same direction as if we were dancing.

"They asked me if I knew what Lani's plans were, and I told them she was supposed to go to a movie with you. Why? What's the problem?"

"What's the problem? What's the *problem*?" Again, the fluttering eyelids, those loathsome gyrations. He was really getting on my nerves. "She's dead! *That's* the problem!"

I could see his point but suspected Lani's death had been less of a surprise to him than the swift appearance of the sheriff on his doorstep. "I know, Steve. I found her. What happened? Did you disagree about what movie to go to?" I kept my eyes on him as I put the bag down and then raised myself to my full height, just under five feet, four inches. Planting my feet a little apart and resting my hands on my hips, I assumed the don't-mess-with-me stance I'd so often used when I was still teaching sixth grade.

It occurred to me that something was definitely off in my flight-or-fight department: I should be afraid of this guy, especially after what had happened to Lani. Instead, right knee twitching, I was fully ready to do some painful damage. I wondered if I weren't a little crazy and hoped this wasn't as impossible as being a little pregnant.

"She was *fine* when I left!" Steve spat the words at me, complete with real spit, some of which landed on my Moody Blues T-shirt.

Well, well, he must have asked her how she'd been doing. How considerate! I looked down with disgust at the spit on my shirt.

Suddenly, he quit wiggling and became very quiet. For a few seconds, he returned my glare. Then he blinked and focused on a point between us on the side walk. His voice was almost inaudible as he corrected himself, "She was *alive* when I left."

He looked away, right into the frowning faces of Ben and Sandra, who'd undoubtedly been standing behind the bakery door all along, watching the whole scene.

Steve swiveled his head around to loosen his neck muscles and then wiped his nose on his shirt sleeve, inhaling snot deeply into his brain cavity. As if he'd suddenly thought of something, he abruptly turned around and walked away. His arms made jerky movements like someone who is talking and trying to bring a point across.

I smiled briefly at Ben and Sandra to show my gratitude for them being there, put the bag in the car, and locked the doors. It was House-of-Variety time.

Just as I was crossing the street, a blue Chevy came raging around the corner from Rembrandt Lane, tires aflame. Two giant leaps saved my butt.

Once more standing on the sidewalk, I stared after Steve Krieger. Trembling with indignation, I yelled, "You bloody *Klootzak*!"

Chapter 6

I have seen nothing.

When I returned from my shopping escapade the house and barn were locked up, but Hal's truck was parked in the driveway. He must have gone off for a bike ride with the gang.

Bobby and Hal had been biker buddies for years. They spent most Sunday mornings in front of the barn, hovering around their Harleys, playing the rock 'n' roll that got our generation through the sixties and seventies. Around noon, unless a hurricane blew in, an improbable event, other Harley aficionados joined them. After showing off mysterious additions and alterations, they'd take off to do what their clothing exclaimed they were born to do.

Mab and Dooley liberally deposited snot and slobber on my jeans and shoes as they sniffed to check if I'd been unfaithful, but after they assured themselves I hadn't petted any strange dogs they happily followed me as I took the needed three trips back and forth from my car to the kitchen. It was nearly four o'clock when we brought the last bags in.

Moon crisscrossed in front of my feet, trying to tackle me while she talked in little motor noises. As I put the grocery bags on the table she looked up at me adoringly, her sapphire eyes at an impossible angle to each other. I noticed some muscle straining going on in her rear as she got ready to jump on the table and realized she wasn't adoring me but the bags. "Don't you dare!" I said sternly, and the eagerness left her eyes as she changed her body posture and innocently began to lick a front paw.

The muddy trail of boot prints had been swept up, and the remnants of the Sunday paper now lay neatly folded on the table. The coffee cups had been put in the dishwasher, the pot cleaned, and the counter wiped. I smiled. Hal the Stealth Cleaner had been at work, sneaking behind my back to ensure I wouldn't be a witness to his unmanly domestic depravity.

My visit to the House of Variety had netted me a number of items we had absolutely no use for and several of which I had no idea what they were. I'd probably add some of the latter to my birthday-gifts collection and so let others solve the puzzle of what to do with them. After the incident with Steve I had felt completely justified in expanding on the initial list. Comfort shopping.

I jammed the frozen foods in the freezer compartment and quickly slammed the door shut for fear that my haphazard stacking technique would cause an avalanche. When I opened the refrigerator door I noted that every plastic container I owned must be in there, many filled with unidentifiable fermenting obnoxia, as Hal called it.

One of the few house cleaning things he ever did openly was reorganizing the fridge. I could never tell when one of these episodes would be coming on. It was something like spontaneous combustion or epilepsy. Suddenly he'd be crouched in front of the refrigerator, door wide open, holding up one container after another and asking me silly questions. *What's this? What's that? How long has this been in here?* As if for reason of my being the female of the species this appliance was my territory and responsibility. As if he didn't actually live here, too, but was sent in by the Homeland Security Department, even though, to my knowledge, nothing had ever exploded in the fridge. So far. I usually tried to get out of the kitchen, or even out of the house, when he went on these rampages. It was easier to hear about it later, when he was ready to give me a synopsis instead of the boring blow-by-blow. Also, I was sure he could figure it out for himself, being a scientist and all. If he really got in a bind, he could always take it to his lab and analyze the stuff.

Plastic containers I carefully wrote at the top of the clean sheet of the shopping list. Handy, those magnetic pads. Oh yes, *screw* Guilt.

The phone rang, and with my mind still on screwing Guilt I picked up, clamping the receiver between my head and shoulder. My *Hello?* was answered by a click-click, followed by the quietest of silences. I tapped the receiver with the tips of my fingers, a totally useless gesture, and held it to my ear again. Nothing. I said *Hello-ho?* a few more times, then pushed the end button. I hoped this wasn't what I thought it was.

An immediate ringing almost made me drop the phone. I pushed the talk button again. "Hey, this isn't funny!"

"What?"

"Who is this?" I demanded.

"Fae? Is that you? Is something wrong?" It was Grace, Hal's sister.

"No, everything's fine. How are you?" I noticed some freshly spun spider webs on the ceiling. My little Charlottes at work again.

"Am I interrupting something? I can call back later?"

"No, that's all right. It's nothing. Did you call a minute ago?" I crouched down, pushed some containers to the back of the shelves and began stuffing more perishables in the refrigerator.

"No? I tried, but your line was busy?" A kindergarten teacher, Grace had the tendency to turn every statement into a question as if she were perpetually unsure of herself. Definitely not true. "I just called to remind you that the boys will be over this coming Friday to spend the weekend?"

Grace and her husband, Matt, had planned a ten-year anniversary trip to San Francisco, and Hal had generously offered we would take The Boys. In a rare show of trust, Grace had consented.

The boys were Hal's eight-year-old twin nephews, Jesse and Jamey, alike only in their unbridled energy and an uncanny ability to make themselves invisible at times of mischief. Shape shifters of the first order. Since they were Hal's blood, I'd made him climb up to rescue them from our roof a couple of years ago. Lucky for Hal, our last home wasn't three stories.

"Do you want us to pick them up?" I asked.

"No, Matt and I will drive them over after school?" Matt was the principal at an *alternative* high school. One of those funny euphemism Americans are prone to invent, this one with the unintentional double-entendre of it being more an alternative to juvenile hall or a mental institution than to a regular high school. I'd always had difficulty picturing mild-mannered Matt, a reincarnation of St. Jude, handling this tough job, because I had an image of him as a kid stumbling around with a giant, daily refreshed, kick-me sign pinned to his back. Maybe he had an alternative personality at school.

"Is that all right with you? About five?"

"That's fine, Grace. It will be fun to have them." Outrageous fun. I mentally ticked off a list of what I should remove, hide, lock up, anything five feet up from the floor.

"Are you sure? I know they are a handful?" That was definitely not a question. How Matt and Grace had produced Jessie and Jamey should stump the world of genetics. Matt and Grace were Good. So good, they were annoying, but Grace more so than Matt, because he didn't know he was good. Or maybe he did know but just didn't parade it around. Was just Matt. Grace, who had always been able to favorably compare herself to Hal, whose youthful Odyssey could fill an encyclopedia of psychedelia, looked down from a solid pedestal at the rest of frail humanity. Somehow goodness dissipates when people flaunt it. It's like praying on the street corners. I suspected the boys' genetic material had gone sideways but hoped they wouldn't go on their uncle's perilous journey.

"It'll be great! I think Hal's planning to take them to the zoo," I sort of lied. He would after I told him. There actually was a little, year-round zoo off the road to Modesto with a few shivering monkeys, a molting lion, and some other unhappy animals. "We'll have a wonderful time! Don't worry!"

"We could make it another weekend?"

I'd forgotten that my reassurances, when stated in the negative, always caused Grace intense discomfort. Like a two-year-old, she'd pick up the last words only. That's how *Don't worry* became *Worry!*

"See you Friday!" I said with finality, once more focusing on the spider-webbed ceiling. After a significant sigh Grace capitulated by thanking me and that ended our conversation.

Zoo!!! I wrote under *Plastic containers* on the shopping pad. Hal and I should have a serious brainstorming session to think up a few more things to do, or forty-eight hours could turn into an eternity. *Brainstorm!!!* I wrote under *Zoo!!!*

I looked at the phone. I should call Gwen to set up a time to meet. Bring her up to date on the latest developments. Lani.

I dug around in my purse for her business card and dialed her home number. She picked up on the third ring.

"I found her," I said by way of introduction.

"Oh, Fae, I'm so sorry!" The rest of what she said was lost because Mab and Dooley began to bark loudly, and then I heard the abrupt braking of a truck in our drive way.

"Someone's here," I yelled in the phone. "Can I call you back later?" I couldn't hear her answer over the canine pandemonium.

As I placed the receiver back on its cradle, I peered out the window. The glare of the low sun bounced off the glass, blocking my view, but an icky feeling came over me, a sensation of having been dunked in some sticky substance. As soon as I opened the door the dogs stormed out. I stepped out on the back porch and raised my hand to shield my eyes from the sun.

It was Steve. Sitting in his Chevy. He'd parked under the beech trees with the front wheels on our lawn, leaving deep ruts behind the absurdly oversized tires. He'd rolled down his window and was staring at me with what I supposed was his darkest look.

Dooley trotted ahead of me and stopped a little away from the truck, alternately barking and growling, ears and tail in the air, hair around his neck and back standing up. Then he strutted over to the truck, aggressively lifted his leg and peed on the left rear tire. Mab began to circle the vehicle, doing a sort of bunny hop while making whining sounds. Dooley returned from his mission and planted himself beside me. He raised his big head and looked up at me, waiting for further instructions. My every unspoken wish was his command. "Good boy," I whispered.

"Steve!" I called out as if I'd been expecting him and, my hand on Dooley's bristling back, I stepped off the porch.

We'd covered half the distance between the house and Steve's truck, enough in my opinion, when Steve snarled, "Who the hell do you think you are?" He glanced at Dooley and raised his window a couple of inches.

Hadn't he asked that same question earlier, in town? I stretched my mouth into a wide imitation smile until I thought my face would split in half.

"Who the hell do you think you are?" he yelled again after rearranging his face into an even more appalling composition as if he were posing for a Hallowe'en mask. He was clearly not taken in by my phony friendliness, but at least he stayed in his truck, safely behind the closed door.

Was he actually expecting an answer? I knew the answer. Kind of. The smiling was making my ears twitch so I replaced it with my how-dumb-can-you-be? look, which was slightly more relaxing to my facial muscles.

Taking comfort in feeling Dooley's low growl under my hand, I waited for Steve's next move. But he just sat there gaping at me as if he had actually figured out the answer to his question.

An enormous rumbling sound suddenly distracted both of us from our staring contest. Hal turned the corner of the driveway on his Harley, followed by Bobby and the rest of the gang in full, black leathers. I looked back at Steve and noticed with pleasure that he appeared to have gone into mild shock.

Hal parked his bike in front of the barn, next to his project barbecue. The other riders lined up neatly beside him. After taking off their helmets, shaking their hair loose, and sticking their fingers in their ears to adjust their eardrums, Hal and Bobby walked over to me, swaggering more than usual.

"Is there a problem?" Hal asked. He looked over Steve and his truck as if they were one and the same object.

His face twisted in a snarling mess, Steve turned on the ignition, rolled up his window half-way, and backed up his truck a few feet. Then he shifted gears and drove off, yelling something rather nasty that ended in "yourself."

Hal traced the edge of one of the ruts with his boot, shook his head and looked at me.

"He thinks I fingered him for Lani's murder," I said in answer to the unspoken question on his face.

Bobby looked at me sideways but said nothing. The others came clanging over and they all stared down the driveway where Steve's truck had disappeared as if they were sorry he'd left in such a hurry.

"Coffee, anyone?" I called out, and without waiting for a response I walked back into the kitchen.

"What was that drunken mink doing here?" John demanded as he came through the door. We addressed Johan van der Meer as *John*, but we usually referred to him as *The Judge*, because that's what he was. I'd never seen John in his robe, but I imagined him to be quite an impressive figure, and not just because he was awfully good-looking in a Gregory-Peck kind of way except for a slight crook in his nose. He was well over six feet tall, had a head of thick, dark brown hair that was graying beautifully at the temples, startlingly blue eyes, and a voice like the one I heard booming from heaven in my doomsday dream. He sure wouldn't need a gavel to get me to come to order!

"I don't know what he wants from me," I said nonchalantly, trying to sound as if it were no big deal. Shaking inside. Some nerve, showing up at my home after practicing his hit-and-run skills on me.

John looked at me intently. "If that weasel is bothering you, I'll have a talk with Bob." He sat down at the cherry table, took out a package of Drum tobacco and began rolling one of his own, concentrating, a deep frown causing his heavy, black eyebrows to join together.

I suspected Steve had involuntarily visited the courtroom on a few occasions—drunk *and* disorderly? as if there's any other way to be drunk—but didn't ask. I poured water in the coffee maker and measured out coffee for my customary paint-your-wagon brew.

Paul Smit, our local pharmacist, neatly wiped his boots as he came in, followed by Pete van Nuys, proud owner of the House of Variety, and Sam Verhoog, my colleague who taught French and German at Sandhill. Hal and Bobby sauntered in last. After discarding jackets and loosening buckles, belts, and whatever else held all that leather together, they were all finally sitting down around the table.

I looked up from my coffee-making and sent out my standard warning glances for them not to lean back and tip their chairs. I'd already had two chairs glued back together after one of these Sunday sessions. Sam started to lean back, as was his habit in the classroom, but then smirked at me. Apparently, hitting his head on the blackboard once or twice had improved his thinking skills. He was the latest and youngest addition to the Sandhill staff, and he was popular, especially with the female students, the cause being a toss-up between his tall-blond looks, his easy-listening teaching style, or the fact that he rode his bike to work, always an attractant for the impressionable.

The coffeemaker began to sputter and I quickly stuck the pot under the filter, which I'd forgotten to do because it was difficult to concentrate on anything with these guys around. Even with them sitting down I felt dwarfed by these men. And ... flustered. So much testosterone.

I gazed at the coffeepot. Drip-drip-drip. How interesting.

When I looked up there were still six of them, pretending to fit in those cherry chairs, pretending they hadn't been staring at me. All smiling at me in a way that made me feel sorry for myself. I knew that they all knew about my finding Lani.

Seven can play this game! I pretended to be fascinated by the filling coffeepot again, pretending to be a good *huisvrouw*.

They had nothing on me. Perched on the bedroom balcony, I'd watched them a few times as they were adjusting and polishing their machines. I once witnessed Bob and Hal talk for half an hour about one stupid bolt on the back of Hal's bike. At least, I think that's what they were talking about, because they kept staring at it as if they were gazing into the face of the Virgin Mary. My idea of the art of car maintenance was to hurriedly spray the dust off after making sure the garden hose was on the jet setting. I couldn't wrap my mind around why they were so obsessive-compulsive about such a dangerous mode of transportation. Maybe that was just it. *Thunder and lightning.* Was I a jealous wife? To be so adored. It would probably get on my nerves. *Philophobia?* Fear of love.

No one spoke as the Judge's tobacco was passed around. Even Paul rolled a meticulously shaped cigarette. He didn't smoke, of course, being a pharmacist, but he liked to partake in the ritual. Hal stoically lit one of his own ready-mades and passed the bag directly to Pete. Pete also didn't smoke but rolled them anyway, seemingly only so he could use his perpendicularly grown ears as handy cigarette holders. I kept meaning to ask him what he'd done with all the cigarettes I'd seen him roll and stick behind those ears.

I put out creamer, sugar, and milk (for show only, because none of these guys used any of this sissy stuff), and some large mugs and spoons. As I poured the coffee, Hal opened the cookie tin, checked the contents, apparently deemed the coconut wreaths and windmill cookies manly enough, and after taking a handful handed the tin to Bobby. Hal was definitely not Dutch or he would have known one takes only one cookie at a time and never more than two per session, one for each cup. Bobby took Hal's lead and also grabbed a handful. His un-Americanized mother, Janny, would have been appalled, made him put them back, after slapping his hand.

I emptied the pot into the last mug and wrote *cookies* on the shopping list in very big capital letters. When I turned around, Hal was squinting at the pad, then he grinned and stuck another whole cookie in his mouth, chomping away. I made an oink-oink sound. Now both Hal and Bobby were grinning. Shaming, a national Dutch pastime, wasn't working. Dutch Fae was fighting a losing battle.

John turned to Bobby. "Bob, do me a favor and visit that affront to society. Let Krieger know he'll have his ass in a sling if he doesn't quit doing what he's doing." John took a deep drag off his cigarette to emphasize what he'd just said, then added, not quite under his breath, "Little prick!" and shrugged at me by way of apology for not finding more appropriate synonyms. The English teacher couldn't think of any either, so I shrugged back. No big deal, just don't eat all my cookies.

"Consider it done," Bobby answered with a barely perceptible sideways glance at John.

My personal Dirty Half Dozen. Robin of Locksley. Sir Wilfred of Ivanhoe. The Cartwrights. Zorro. Ben Turpin. All my childhood heroes in my kitchen.

Hal reached down, grabbed something out of one of the bags I'd shoved under the table and held it up high.

"Groovy!" said Pete, probably unaware his wife had just sold me the thing.

"Cool!" said John.

"Far out, Man!" said Paul.

Instant sixties. Just add some tie-dye and a few peace signs. Whenever they had been out riding these guys would all begin to talk in clichés, and really horribly dated stuff would come out of their mouths, even out of the mouths of Bobby and Sam, who'd been mere babes in the sixties.

I now wondered if this was a phenomenon similar to gang language or related to my mother's Speaking in Tongues. Upon being Born Again, my mother had been duly Filled with the Holy Spirit and as proof hereof she had received the Gift of Speaking in Tongues. Since Speaking in Tongues was the main outward sign (and the only I ever detected) that one had been Filled with the Spirit, it was a much-coveted gift, the absence of which being an indication that the Saving had not truly taken hold and was therefore doubtful or at least incomplete.

To us, the Van Dalen kids, Speaking in Tongues sounded pretty much like a recitation of the main line of Little Richard's *Tutti-frutti* interspersed with other perplexing words liberally peppered with the harsh Dutch G, which my mother, being American, substituted with a choking sound that begged for the Heimlich maneuver. Always to our consternation and intense discomfort, my mother practiced her Speaking in Tongues in a variety of public settings outside church. She was convinced that what she was saying, though not understood by her ignorant Dutch audience at the grocery store, or by herself for that matter, would some day be understood by a passerby visiting from some far-away country in Africa. Since what would happen next wasn't quite clear and since Africans were few and far in between in the Netherlands, the Gift of Speaking in Tongues seemed not one of the most practical gifts. And, none of us really enjoyed going shopping with Mom.

"What's this supposed to be?" Hal asked, lifting his eyebrows.

I wasn't sure. It was obviously artistic. It was a ceramic pot of some kind but open at both top and bottom, and with long, yawning faces on three sides that had holes in the eyes, nose, and mouth. It was probably a candle holder, but I refused to say so. If Hal was going to put me on the spot ...

I raised my eyebrows even higher than he had his. "It's what you wrote on our shopping list."

A flicker of a frown crossed his face. Then he shook his head and grinned. "I'd better clean up my handwriting," he said as he stuffed the pot back in the bag.

The smokers were all puffing on their cigarettes. I opened the window over the sink and looked out. It was nearly dark now and the barn light had come on.

Next to the row of bikes stood a woman. She was too far away to see her face but close enough to see she wasn't dressed for riding a motorcycle. Not in that red, horrendous muumuu.

I squeezed my eyes shut, made a wish, then opened my right eye. She was still there. Just in case, I squeezed my eyes shut again, then opened my left eye. And I screamed.

"Hey! It's OK," Hal said, pulling me to him with his arm around my waist. "I didn't mean to sneak up on you."

I was about to call him a big, fat liar because he loved sneaking up on me, did it all the time, when my eyes were drawn to the woman again and as I was staring at her she evaporated.

I let out a deep sigh of relief. What was she thinking?

"Leave me alone!" I whispered.

"What?" Hal gave me a funny look, then peered out the window, clearly seeing nothing but the barn, the bikes, the barbecue. Even if she'd still been there, that's all he would have seen.

"You guys should eat the lasagna you made yesterday," I said to divert his attention and to get rid of the two-square-feet lasagna.

"Good idea," he said and moved toward the refrigerator.

But I was faster, wormed past him and strategically blocked his path. God forbid he should start digging around in there, hold up every item I'd stacked on top of the lasagna earlier. We'd never get to eat.

After some major rearranging of the second shelf, I handed him the glass baking dish and sat down at the table. It was *his* lasagna, after all.

While Hal cut and heated up big chunks of lasagna, the smokers extinguished their cigarettes. I transported the ashtray outside and put it on the porch railing. On my way back in, I cracked the window near the back door to let the cross breeze blow the residual stink out. I glanced at the barn. Nothing. Then I sat down again between John and Bobby, and waited for my piece of the pie.

Except for a little bantering about needing forks and my handing them both forks *and* knives, we were quiet while we ate, their minds on food and food alone, mine on how to pry information out of Bobby about what they'd found out so far concerning Lani, without drawing everyone's attention.

I played with a piece of pasta while trying to think of a good opening line. On rare occasions I wouldn't mind being a man for a few minutes, an hour tops if I need to move heavy objects. I was sure none of the men in my kitchen would have had any problems coming up with an opening line. (Hal's had been "May I buy you another drink?" Nothing original, but I know why I fell for it, and it wasn't the proper *may*. Straight from the Handbook for Highly Effective Alcoholics and vastly underrated by non-alcoholics, this silver line has been most prolific in germinating countless booze-propelled relationships whose eventual and inevitable bitter breakups lined the pockets of those in the way of Shakespeare's Utopia.)

I finally thought of a pretty good line, casual enough for a by-the-way inquiry, nothing to make them all drop their forks. But before I knew it they'd all hogged down their food, including seconds, and my opportunity had passed as the general conversation was started up again with compliments to the cook, and Hal collected the plates to deposit them in the sink and began making another pot of coffee.

I put my unfinished portion on the counter so as not to hold up a new round of compulsory after-dinner Drum rolling and went out to retrieve the ashtray.

"When's school starting again?" Pete asked as he carefully distributed tobacco on a paper for another never-to-be-smoked ear ornament.

"Two weeks from Tuesday." *Two weeks, one day, fourteen hours, to be precise.* I was sure my face showed the lack of enthusiasm I felt. Burn-out. And my manuscript boxed up again until the summer. I looked over at Sam. He didn't seem too distraught over having to begin school again. He wasn't trying to write a book.

"What are you teaching this coming semester, Fae?" The Judge's voice was so filled with interest, I was tempted to inquire if he planned to enroll.

"Well, Shakespeare, of course. And a class on the development of drama. Three courses in all." I wiped some imaginary spots off the counter and kept rubbing long after they were gone.

"I read some Shakespeare in college," Paul said. "That language! Give me Latin anytime. Everything by the rules."

I wondered how *he* would have done with a mother who spoke in tongues.

"So, you'll be pretty busy these coming weeks," Bobby noted, unable to completely keep satisfaction out of his voice.

I gave him the most innocent look I was capable of producing, knowing it would have the opposite effect on him who was professionally trained to be suspicious. Indeed, a shadow of doubt crossed his face, he bit his lip, and then I'd swear I heard him mumble, "God, help me," or some common prayer to that extent. John grinned and quickly had to grab his cigarette before it fell from of his mouth. The others suddenly seemed mighty interested in the pattern of my table cloth. *Had Hal told them about my vision?*

I sat down between Bobby and John again, a sweet smile on my face. This was, after all, just a conspiracy to lighten up the conversation and avoid the Lani-is-dead-and-you-found-her issue, and it worked like the cherry scent in an outhouse. That got me to thinking.

"Why cherry?" I asked.

They looked at me, uncomprehending.

"Why do they use cherry scent in those outhouses?"

Now they looked at each other, still uncomprehending, but checking if they weren't the only ones at sea.

"I mean, is there some sort of agreement between the manufacturers of those portable outhouses to use only cherry?" I wasn't sure why this subject suddenly fascinated me. Perhaps it was the apologetic smirk on Hal's face as he turned to look from one buddy to another.

"Why not ... banana?" I asked.

"Apple pie?" Sam decided to play along.

"There's apple pie for dessert?" asked Pete, who must not have been paying attention as he'd been staring at his reflection in the window, turning his head to see how he looked with two cigarettes lodged behind his ears.

"You know, they now make candles that smell like pies," Hal said, obviously relaxing now we had veered off my initial subject.

"Yes, instead of having a double serving of pie you can just burn the candle at both ends. Well, think about it. Outhouses. Why cherry?" Having given them their assignment, I got up. "I need to go make a phone call."

Leaving the Merry Men, I went upstairs to my office and called Gwen.

After I'd told her the whole story about finding Lani, she was quiet for a while, then said, "I wonder if ... " and stopped.

"What?" I asked, anxiously.

"Oh, I just had a feeling. Maybe it's nothing. Never mind."

But I *did* mind. "I had a dream about Lani last night. She was beach combing." I described the details of my dream. "I felt that she was connecting with me, knew I was watching her. As if she were showing me something, yet withholding the information." Then it came to me. "She was playing a game, presenting me with a puzzle."

"That's ... hum ... different," Gwen said. "Strange."

"And then I saw her standing behind my house earlier this evening. She was wearing the same red muumuu as in my dream."

"A red muumuu?" Gwen sounded as if she were gaping on the other end of the phone.

"Yes, does that have any special meaning?"

"What? The red muumuu? Good grief!" Gwen exclaimed. "No, just that she's a bad dresser."

We were silent for a few moments. Somehow the muumuu seemed more shocking to the both of us than the fact that I'd seen her. There's no excuse for bad taste.

"I've also been getting phone calls. Dead calls."

"Ah, you know about that. Electrical interference. Seems a little soon for that." Gwen said. "Were you very close to her?"

I squirmed in my seat. "I guess you could put it that way."

"Why am I suddenly thinking about cherries?" Gwen asked. "I'm smelling cherries."

"Well, I've got six men downstairs in my kitchen, my husband and his friends, and they were all pretending nothing had happened." I explained the stream of consciousness that had led me to the outhouse.

"I don't believe that's why I was smelling cherries," Gwen said, laughing. "I'll have to meditate on that."

We discussed the logistics of getting together the coming week, but two of her people had just called her saying they were down with the flu and I still had quite a bit of work to do before college started, so we decided to put our meeting off until the following week.

"But if anything happens or you need to talk, Fae, just call me. Anytime. You have my work number."

I thanked her. It felt good to have some backup. Being psychic, intuitive, or whatever the *mot du jour* was, had been a lonely existence in a way. Talking to Gwen was like coming out of the closet.

After hanging up, I stared at the stacks of papers on my desk that constituted my novel, a mystery set in Amsterdam, and my mood immediately plunged from gratitude to bad attitude until I was feeling intensely sorry for myself. My intention had been to dedicate this winter break entirely to editing my novel, but it was going much more slowly than I'd expected, because some of what had seemed profound or funny when I'd started writing the story nearly eight years ago now appeared infantile. Or just plain stupid, in a few places. I'd been doing a lot of eye rolling and rewriting, and the editing required much more concentrated effort than the original creation, which seemed to flow through me. Now I'd have to pack it in again. *Woe is me.*

But I pushed the stacks to the back of the desk, because packing it in seemed too drastic, too abrupt a transition. Perhaps I would have a block of time, here and there. Although, my experience had been that these blocks of time evaporated almost as soon as they materialized. I had done absolutely nothing for school since the eight-week winter break had begun, and constructing the outline and lecture notes for my Shakespeare course alone might take me a whole week. My great comfort was that I was teaching Shakespeare, so once I got going the winter of my discontent would turn glorious summer.

I grabbed a large pad, leaned back in my chair as far as I could, put my feet on the desk, and began to doodle on the clean sheet. First, I needed to decide what theme to build my lectures around and then which plays to incorporate.

Murder, my hand wrote before I knew it.

Murder? I looked at the word with surprised satisfaction. *Hamlet. King Lear. Macbeth. Othello. Richard III. Titus Andronicus.* Stabbings, smotherings, poisonings, hangings, drownings. Jealousy, loyalty, lust, power, revenge.

Across the top, next to *Murder*, I wrote *Method* and *Motive*. I was beginning to feel inspired. I tossed the pad on my desk, put my feet back on the floor, and dragged my *Complete Works of Shakespeare* off the shelf over my desk. Leafing through the book, jotting down notes, I was soon lost in one of my favorite worlds. I vaguely heard the kitchen door open and close several times and the bikes roaring off, one by one.

"Fae?"

"Yes?" I stopped writing in mid-sentence. Hal stood on the stairs, staring at me with a quizzical expression on his face.

"Did you just get up here?" He looked down the stairs, then back at me.

"I've been up here for a while. Why?"

"The TV is on." He frowned and glanced down the stairs again.

"Yes?" I could hear a voice droning.

"You didn't turn it on? I thought you were in the living room." He took a step down. All I could see now through the banister was his head with his hair still sticking up in all directions from the bike ride.

"Been up here for about half an hour. Maybe it's a short," I offered lightheartedly.

"Yeah, maybe." But the frown didn't leave his face.

For a few seconds, our eyes locked. Then we both looked away, as if we were ashamed of what we were thinking.

Shorts don't turn televisions on, people do.

Chapter 7

Angels and ministers of grace defend us!

Early Monday, I awoke from a night of many dreams, none of which I could clearly remember, to the rhythmic sound of rain sweeping against the window. I pulled the quilt up to my chin and rolled back and forth until my body was wrapped in a cozy, tight cocoon.

Hal was already downstairs noisily involved in his morning rituals. He got up hours before he had to be at work. He claimed he needed all that time to wake up, but it seemed if he'd sleep longer, he wouldn't need so much time to wake up. The key part of his routine was to watch the morning news several times in a row, so he could be sufficiently depressed by the time he had to leave. The artificial intonation of some newscaster's voice sounded from the living room.

Half-heartedly, I un-cocooned myself and got up. In the bathroom, I splashed some icy cold water on my face, brushed my teeth, and drew my fingers through my hair. Pulling on my royal blue robe, I stumbled downstairs.

In the hall, Mab welcomed me with her little happy dance, like a Lipizzaner horse, and Dooley playfully pushed me around with his big head. The greasy odor of reheated pizza drifted toward me as I entered the kitchen. The original version dated back to last Wednesday. Tuesday? Hal ate strange, nauseous things for breakfast.

I poured myself a cup of real coffee. A slice of shriveled-up pizza lay on a plate next to the coffee maker, little puddles of coagulated fat on the pepperoni. I quickly covered it with a paper towel to get it out of my sight. After filling Hal's thermos with the rest of the regular, I put together a pot of decaf.

"Hey, what did you do with that other slice of pizza?" Hal was talking with his mouth full.

"It looked dead, so I gave it the last rites and buried it." I took a slurp of my hot coffee and burned my mouth.

"It's kind of old. It doesn't taste that good anymore." He picked up the paper towel and wistfully eyed the dried-up wedge. "Actually," he went on, "it didn't taste that good to begin with. It was undercooked."

"Why are you eating it then?"

"Well, you can't just throw it out!"

"You could feed it to the dogs," I ventured.

"Too much salt in it." He placed the slice in the microwave and pushed the buttons.

I picked up the local section of the newspaper and went into the living room to hear if the weatherman made more sense than my husband. The weatherman predicted it would rain today, then he went on to explain a graphic representation of several decades of rainfall showing we'd had more than our share this winter. Above *normal*, he stubbornly kept saying. We'd had either droughts or floods since I'd moved back to California, so I wasn't sure what *normal* had to do with the weather and wasn't worried. Rainy days made me feel more at home than anything. Hal might still have his floating porch ferry.

I changed the channel. Some demonically possessed woman was singing as she pushed around one of those vacuum cleaners with a view. Who'd thought that up? Some guy who never vacuumed, no doubt. Why would you want to look at the crap sucked out of a carpet? How disgusting. I flipped to the next channel, an antiques show. A rather distinguished-looking gentleman with an unashamedly openly covetous look in his eyes was stroking a small urn. *Get a room.* The man next to him looked bug-eyed, as if he'd just downed a quart of Hal's coffee. "I worked in Peru for 25 years and stole this from a sacred burial site," I could hear him say, even though I'd just muted the sound.

I turned my attention to the paper and began to skim the regional news. There was a two-paragraph report about the discovery of a woman's body on Blackberry Road. The cause of death was listed as "unknown," and her name was withheld pending notification of family. As if everybody and his dog in Londen and surrounding area wouldn't know by now who she was. *Had been.*

Hal came in and sat next to me. He draped his arm around my shoulders and nuzzled my ear. "What are you planning to do today, Babe?" he whispered in what would have been his sexiest voice were it not for the pizza breath.

"I'm going to work on my Shakespeare outline," I whispered back. "And, right now, I'm planning to get myself another cup of coffee. You want one?"

"I could go for one more cup." He bit my ear. I wasn't sure what he was playing at, because he'd have to leave before anything very exciting could develop.

In the kitchen, I filled Hal's cup from the thermos with the real drug, straight and sooty. As I picked up the coffee pot with my decaffeinated version, the copper lamp over the table flickered ever so gently behind me. I might not have noticed had it not been for the chill that ran down my spine like a creepy rodent.

Suddenly, all hell broke loose.

The microwave came on with a piercing sound, the toaster began to glow, and the mixer on the other side of the drain board began to mix air and dance toward the edge of the counter.

I caught the waltzing mixer just before it plunged to its certain death. Immediately, the coffee pot in my hand exploded, covering the front of my bathrobe with a mosaic of glass and steaming hot brew.

"Holy shit!" I shouted. I quickly pulled the garment away from my body, opened the cold water tap, and wet the dishrag to dab at my robe.

Mab and Dooley bolted across the kitchen and tried to escape through the closed backdoor. I hurried over to let them out and ran back to the counter.

"Hal!" I called at the top of my lungs, pushing the appliances back against the wall. "Hal!"

Hal halted in the doorway to survey the situation. Only, he didn't seem to realize we had a "situation."

"Are you making breakfast?" he asked, incredulous.

I tossed him an exasperated look. He frowned at the mixer, which was dancing toward the edge of the counter once more, and finally something connected in his brain. He lunged toward the ballerina appliance and pulled the plug. At once, the microwave and toaster shut off, too.

But now the lamp over the table flickered several times again and then, with unexpected violence, its bulbs exploded. Hal took a leap to shelter me from the flying glass.

The next moment, the kitchen was filled with a hollow silence.

We stood holding on to each other, Hal rubbing my back. When it seemed all was to remain quiet, he placed his hand under my chin and lifted my head. "Are you all right?" he asked, almost squeezing the breath out of me.

"I think so." I looked around in amazement at the mess of coffee and glass, and caught a glimpse of Bluebelle calmly disappearing through the closed door to the hall way.

Hal let go of me and went over to the table to check out the lamp. As he reached for it, the copper shade began to swing erratically. Behind me the hot water tap abruptly turned itself on, full blast.

Hal cast me an accusatory look, as if somehow I were orchestrating these tricks.

I wasn't, of course, but I knew who was. And I was determined to stop her.

It was casting-out-demons time!

Casting out Demons was done by shouting at the top of one's lungs at the possessed (nearly all Gifts of the Spirit I knew of required some form of shouting and thus a large lung capacity). Since the Devil was lurking everywhere, waiting to trip us up (but then, God was always testing us, too, which was a bit confusing), his busy demons were a constant concern in our household. This became especially so after Sister Alkema moved in with us during one of my father's prolonged absences.

Sister Alkema came to us from Switzerland by way of Africa, or perhaps India, where she'd been a missionary, which made her a VIP for the Lord in my mother's eyes. My father, who met her a few times before he disappeared once again and she moved in, was the only one unimpressed: be it behind her back, he unceremoniously called her *Horse Face* (we quickly figured out this was not some honorary American Indian name).

What I remember most about Sister Alkema was that she knew everything and thus was never wrong, that she walked and talked with God, and that at some point during her stay with us in Amsterdam she became convinced I was possessed by demons. I forget what I'd done this time that caused her to come to this conclusion. Maybe I'd told her something I wasn't supposed to know. Foaming at the mouth, she stood over me, hollering and waving her arms. She had a long face and very large yellow teeth, and in her ecstasy of casting out the devils she indeed looked like an insane horse about to trample me. My mother, standing behind her, for once wore a highly skeptical expression on her face. Sister Alkema mustn't have been too successful in her efforts, because Casting out Demons became a routine at the Van Dalen residence. For months on end, this woman was a complete terror in our home, until my father finally returned and cast her out.

Now, it was time to put my demon know-how to work. Not that I thought Lani had become one, but she sure behaved like it. "Stop!" I yelled. "Stop this immediately!" I screamed. "Enough! Cut this out!" I was furious and not going to take it anymore.

The lamp quit swaying and the tap turned itself off.

"Who *are* you yelling at?" Hal asked, a deep frown on his face.

"Who cares? It worked, didn't it?" I was still in the hollering mode. Hal took a step back as if he'd been hit by a blast of his own pizza breath.

After a moment's hesitation, I explained more quietly, "At Lani, of course. It's Lani. Don't you see? She must be unhappy, or stuck in limbo, or something." This was a shocking statement for a Protestant to make. Only Catholics had a limbo (or they used to when I was growing up, anyway), a sort of second-chance heaven/hell, which seemed a lot more gracious than the heaven-or-hell-only choice us Protestants were stuck with. But then, I wasn't sure what Lani had been. "She's the one doing all this." I waved my arms around.

Hal slowly nodded in agreement. For an instant I thought my words had made sense to him, but then he lifted one side of his face in disbelief and snickered. "Well, that sure explains everything."

"Don't make fun of me. You saw what happened!"

"I'm not making fun of you! I just think she's dead, that's all!" He shrugged. "Dead and gone."

I rolled my eyes but decided not to debate him any further, knowing he would pooh-pooh any paranormal event and explain it with his precious science rather than accept that the infinite can't be understood through the finite. Hal prided himself on the objectivity of the scientific method, which is largely a delusion, a crock, since no human observation can be truly objective. But if anyone said *UFO* or *alien*, he'd suspend all disbelief. Yes, Harold *Roswell* Nelson had a gaping hole in his logic armor. (That was his real middle name.)

We cleaned up the mess in silence, not being on speaking terms until I said so. When we finished it was half an hour past the time he usually left for work. He hurried to get his coat and briefcase.

"Drive carefully," I said, as I always did.

"I will." His standard answer. Holding me a little longer than usual, he asked, "Will you be OK?"

"I'll be fine," I assured him with newfound resolve, squirming out of his loving arms. I had, after all, just successfully performed my very first exorcism. Sister Alkema would have been proud of me.

"I'll call you from work." He always called me from work when I was home.

I nodded. We kissed goodbye.

The rain had stopped, but the sun was still hidden behind a solid, gray layer of clouds that covered the entire sky. The air was humid and heavy.

From the back porch, I watched Hal drive off, all at once feeling very lonely despite the dogs and cats around me. Mab found a dry spot and lay down in the driveway, mournfully gazing after Hal's truck.

I put some food out for the dogs, hoping Mab would break her vigil before Dooley ate all of it, and went back into the house, ushering the kitties in with me.

Everything in the kitchen seemed to have returned to normal. I sat down, folded my arms on the table and rested my head on them, closing my eyes. These blues weren't coming from the gray sky outside or from the silent phone calls or even from my *mano a mano* with the appliances. It wasn't Hal the Unbeliever either.

Guilt and Anger were warring to get the upper hand. Guilt droned on about how I'd had only one short crying spell—after Bobby left Saturday night, in the bathroom when I was getting ready for bed—and that wasn't enough. How I'd pushed all thoughts of Lani deliberately aside. Gone shopping. How I'd told myself it would be better to wait for the medical examiner's report to find out what had happened, but I should have cried more or longer or harder. I was feeling too little empathy, was irrationally irritated with Lani. As if she'd died purely to annoy me.

As always, Anger's fiery rebuttal provided me with a solid alibi. Someone as self-centered as Lani shouldn't be able to make me feel so guilty and cold hearted. She'd worn me down, and now I simply couldn't find more grief and sorrow. If she'd just quit the booze, she'd be alive and well today, and I wouldn't have had to dig around inside myself for the required feelings of compassion. Besides, she hadn't really left. She was still bugging me, playing head games, showing up in my dreams, at my house.

Guilt and Anger were having the time of my life when the shrill sound of the phone almost made me fall off the chair. For a moment I wondered if I should pick it up or not. This would be about the right time for another one of those silent messages. With a martyr's sigh, I picked up anyway.

"Fae?"

I tried to recognize the man's voice from this one word and didn't answer immediately. Maybe it was that dorky Steve, still wanting to know who the hell I thought I was.

Finally, I responded, "Yes?"

"This is Jason." His tone indicated that his name should mean something to me. It didn't. "Who is Jason?" I thought.

"Lani's son," he answered.

Had I spoken out loud? To cover up my embarrassment, I began to talk rapidly. "Jason! I'm sorry about your mother. How are you doing? Where are you calling from?"

"I'm at the house. They called me Saturday night. I drove down from Sacramento yesterday." His voice was deep and melodious, but I suddenly got a sense of him speaking from a great distance instead of from his mother's home, nearly next door.

I'd never met Jason or either of his two sisters. Each of them had a different father. Three marriages, three children. Jason, the youngest, was the fruit of Lani's union with Willem de Weder, whom I had met once when we were in the process of buying the house from her. Willem was a short man in his mid sixties with a substantial beer belly and baggy eyes. Though he seemed rather nice, Lani would complain every so often that he was stalking her in between his relationships with other women, when he had time to obsess about his ex-wife again. But as soon as I'd press for details or ask why she didn't call the police, she'd invariably change the subject.

"Fae, could I come over to talk?"

Jason's request took me by surprise. "Well, sure, Jason! Do you want to come over now?" I then realized I wasn't dressed yet, but before I could ask for some time, he said, "How about in an hour? Would that work?" Consideration in his voice.

Again, I had the feeling I'd spoken out loud, or maybe he could see me sitting here in my damp robe. Pulling the collar uncomfortably tight around my neck, I answered, "That's fine, Jason. See you in an hour."

I wondered what he wanted to talk about.

Upstairs, I took a hot shower, followed by a cold blast, shock therapy to wash away the blues and rewire the brain. Singing along with Aerosmith's "Walk This Way," I put on my purple, crinkle-velvet skirt and the matching, deeply V-necked sweater, turned around in front of the mirror and then sat down at my dressing table.

It took a while to blow dry my hair, because I followed an impulse to try out an alternative hair style, something I do only when I'm in a hurry. The little gray pathways at my roots made me give up, and I had to wet my hair all over again with a spray bottle. Soon those pathways would become avenues. I discarded the thought of experimenting with my eye shadow as quickly as I had it, put on the denim-blue, a perfect match, and then brushed my lashes with several layers of mascara. "Foxy Lady," Jimi Hendrix shouted, right on time.

I was just about done when the doorbell rang. I took one last glance in the mirror to make sure the back of my skirt wasn't stuck in my panty hose before I went downstairs and opened the door.

To my surprise, Jason de Weder looked like an angel.

Chapter 8

Marry, this is miching mallecho; it means mischief.

My mouth dropped open, and I hung on to the doorknob, gaping like an idiot. Outlined by the dark sky stood the most gorgeous man I'd seen in a long time.

Jason was about six feet tall. His hair—of the platinum blond his mother had once so desperately tried to achieve—was loosely pulled back in a short pony tail, a few strands falling over his high forehead. His face was flawless: a straight and proportionally perfect nose, a man's mouth with a slightly curving upper lip, and a strong, well-shaped chin.

But the most remarkable features of that face were the eyes. When I was child, I'd seen such eyes painted in pictures of a Eurocentric Jesus knocking at the door of my sinful heart. Bright blue, intelligent, and understanding eyes, set off by dark lashes and slightly arching eyebrows.

I finally stopped gawking at him and opened the door wider.

"Hello! I'm Jason," he said and smiled at me.

"Fae," I said, thought for a moment, came to the conclusion that this was indeed my name, and then repeated, "Fae."

Feeling rather foolish, I moved aside and with a slight wave of my hand gestured for him to enter. He stepped past me into the hallway and halted at the door leading to the dining area. After telling Mab and Dooley to go to the back again, I closed the front door and followed Jason as he walked through the dining area, up the two steps to the living room.

He looked around. "You've switched the living room to the back," he said approvingly. "Aunt Claire often talked of changing things around but never did. And I noticed you've added some color to the woodwork outside."

"Periwinkle," I supplied.

"Yes. It was one of my aunt's favorite colors." He gazed at me with those eyes.

I looked away. Well, well, I'd been finishing aunt Claire's projects, so it seemed.

"Quite a conversation piece, isn't it?" he next remarked, amusement in his voice.

When I glanced at him, his face was lit up with a conspiratorial smile. I followed his eyes to my magic basket.

This stranger knew me too well. Flustered, I asked him to take a seat and offered to get some coffee.

Like most of my guests, he chose the love seat. His eyes swept over the rest of the room, out the French doors, and as they came to rest on the spectacle of the blooming orchard outside, the humorous sparkles in them softened to a quiet awe. But when he looked back at me and noticed I'd been observing him his eyes became suddenly veiled, as if part of him left the room.

Feeling uncomfortably naked, metaphorically speaking, I was glad to escape to the kitchen for a moment, away from this man who saw far too much for my taste. Although I found this level of perfection of the human form somewhat disturbing, a left-over sentiment stemming from frequent warnings that the Devil comes in the guise of an angel of light, my artist's heart was captivated.

It also seemed I was having my very first hot flash, if that's what it was, or else, my head was on fire. The palms of my hands were moist. I wiped them off on my skirt before pouring coffee from the thermos into a couple of mugs. That reminded me. *Coffee pot*, I wrote on the shopping list. I placed the mugs, creamer, and sugar on my red-lacquered serving tray and sidled through the swinging door back into the living room.

"Do you mind if I smoke?" Jason asked as I put the tray down on the coffee table.

"Not at all." Strangely jubilant to find he had at least one vice, I immediately wondered what else I could discover to be wrong with him that would erase the stigma of being too beautiful.

I handed him the ship-shaped, silver table lighter and moved the Delft blue ashtray to a central position on the table. Then I sat down on the far end of the large couch, making the orchard spectacle my background. Almost instantly after he lit his cigarette the room filled with heavy, pungent smoke.

"Lani told me a lot about you." He looked right past me at the large palm that stood in the corner, next to the French doors.

Dutch Fae raised her eyebrows. Coming from a cultural background that still distinguishes between elders and peers, with a language that still distinguishes between the familiar and polite address, my disapproval of his referring to his mother by her first name was a given. "She's your mother. Show some respect, " I almost said, before I remembered how little respect I'd been able to muster up for Lani and how seldom she'd spoken of her children. In fact, she had talked about them so rarely, it almost seemed as if she were in denial of having children.

But it was more than just his first-name use that was making me feel uncomfortable. I sensed he had made this statement to negate some of the intuitiveness he had displayed so deliberately earlier. Suddenly, I was convinced Jason was playing a subtle hide-and-go-seek game. But why?

"She did?" It wasn't a genuine question, but I did feel like asking, "When was that?"

Almost imperceptibly, he glanced at my face to check the sincerity of my surprise. He must have seen my skepticism, because he looked away again quickly, this time at the rug covering the oak floor. His eyes slowly followed the colorful Middle Eastern design until they landed on my shoes. Then he seemed to be contemplating my high-heeled pumps. Deep purple.

A small roll of ash fell off the tip of his cigarette and landed on his jeans. I scraped my throat and looked at the unused ashtray. He took the hint and tapped his cigarette over it.

"She told me you were very good friends, and … " His voice trailed off from the unfinished sentence. So I could fill him in on the subject?

Not that *good!* Guilt whispered. Waiting for a real question, I began swinging my crossed leg while admiring the intricate cable pattern of his hand-knit, crème sweater.

"I didn't see her very much after I moved up to Sacramento. Work is taking up most of my time." He sighed and stared at the glowing tip of his cigarette.

I was wondering when he would come around to asking what had happened to his mother. How much did he already know from the police?

"The only thing they told me was that … she was found outside her home." Again, he seemed to have tuned into what was on my mind.

And again, I didn't fill in the blanks he was leaving. Was that really the only thing they had told him?

Then, for the first time since he'd sat down he looked straight at me and finally asked, "Do you know what happened to her?"

"No." I said it quietly. I wasn't about to tell him I was sure she was murdered because I'd had a vision. Uneasy, I reached for my pack of cigarettes on the table.

Jason looked at my hands as I shook the pack, took a cigarette, and fumbled with it before placing it between my lips. He got up, reached for the lighter and flicked the flame in front of me. I bent slightly forward.

He said, "You'd better turn that around."

I wasn't sure what he meant. With his index finger he indicated my cigarette. I took it out of my mouth and looked at it, then put it back, filter end between my lips. He lit my cigarette. His face close to mine.

I took a plunge into those wonderful eyes. "Thank you," I said.

He sat back on the love seat. "Do you know who found her?"

"*I* did."

"*You* found her?"

"I *did*."

"How did you come to find her?" His face was blank and his voice reflected only a clinical curiosity.

Lani, she, her? He's talking about his mother! His dead *mother.* His choice of words was getting on my nerves, and by now I found this whole conversation quite bizarre altogether, since most of it seemed to be taking place without words. It seemed Jason and I could conduct a completely non-verbal dialogue.

Maybe the police had already informed him of this, but I simply couldn't bring myself to tell him I had found Lani, smelling like a distillery, face-down in a muddy ditch. No matter how calm and collected he appeared and how coldly he referred to her, he was still her son.

"I had a flat tire at the walnut orchard. I found your mother by accident."

He showed no emotion, but for a few moments he seemed in deep thought.

"Did she ever talk about me?" His voice now had taken on a strangled quality, belying the look of detachment on his face.

I suddenly felt intensely sorry for him. Lani had simply been too involved with her man-and-hair troubles to be bothered with the fact that she had kids.

"She mentioned that you work in your father's import-export business. That you're a lawyer," I said carefully. Other than that Jason was her youngest son by Willem de Weder and didn't look one bit like his father, a fact I could now wholeheartedly attest to, Lani hadn't said much else about him. I felt strangely embarrassed I couldn't tell him that his mother had said to me she was proud of him, had loved him, and I wished Honesty would allow me to do some creative embellishing.

"That's not totally true. I only went to law school for one year. It wasn't for me. When I quit, my father offered me a job in his company. He now has all but retired and basically lets me run the business." He finally stubbed out his cigarette. I noticed the tobacco stains on his fingers.

"She was dif-fer-ent." He said, pronouncing all three syllables. He searched my face. "You know what I mean." The last sentence was a statement, not a question.

I automatically nodded, neutrally, but I had a feeling that, actually, I did not know what he meant with *different*.

A sense of relief seemed to have come over him. A change had taken place. I didn't know what it was I had said or done to bring this change about, yet I knew I had something to do with it.

Jason glanced at his watch, a signal this was to be the end of our conversation, for he got up abruptly and announced that he had to leave.

On the way out, I asked who would be planning his mother's funeral.

"My sisters are coming down this morning. I guess we'll make the arrangements together. We'll have to wait until her body is released."

"Are you staying at the house?" I opened the front door for him. "In case I find out anything else," I quickly added as an explanation for what he might consider undue curiosity.

"Yes, we may as well. There's no reason why we shouldn't." He didn't seem so sure.

After a final exchange of the usual parting advice to take care, he turned and walked over to a silver Jaguar, which in my earlier consternation I had failed to notice. I called the Mab-and-Dooley escort service off, then closed the door and walked back into the living room and looked around.

Jason's presence lingered. I felt unsettled and couldn't quite figure out why. What had happened, exactly? I had a sense of having been interrogated, evaluated, that I had given him something and didn't know what it was.

I cleaned up the coffee table and carried everything into the kitchen. As I emptied the ashtray, I noticed the name *Gauloise* printed on the butt of Jason's cigarette. How incongruent for someone with his angelic looks to smoke such a strong brand, to smoke at all. How often would he have to have his teeth cleaned to keep them so white? I wondered if he had any cavities at all. Soon, my mind was off in all directions.

When I regained consciousness, I was thinking about my Shakespeare course and had no idea how I'd arrived there even after I played my little game of back-tracking: going from one thought to the one before, tracing how I had come to think about a particular subject. My little sanity check, *little* being the adjective modifying *sanity*.

Moon was begging to be fed. I filled one side of the double bowl to the rim with fresh water and the other with mature kitty food, all the while making sure not to fall on my face, because she kept trying to tackle me. Mellow, upon hearing the clattering crunchies, burst through the swinging door, slid over the tile to the bowl, and after pushing Moon out of the way began to pig out. Moon just rolled over on her side and watched him eat.

I was just about to go upstairs to get back to work when Jason called for the second time that morning.

"Someone's ransacked the house, Fae!" he said without much of an introduction. "The whole downstairs is a mess! He went through everything!"

"Who's *he*?"

"It must have been the guy who almost rammed me when I drove up. He was in a blue truck. Do you know who that could be?"

I knew a few people who owned a blue truck, such as Hal, but the person who came to mind first was, of course, Steve.

"Steve Krieger." I said.

"Who is *he*?"

"Steve is ... was ... your mother's ... uh ... boyfriend." I hated using that word for someone over thirty, it sounded so terribly juvenile. However, *paramour* or *lover* both sounded like debauched characters in a Flaubert novel, *partner* too business- or cowboy-like, and *significant other* too clinical or as if a noun were missing. Other *what*? Besides, all were totally inappropriate in Steve's case. *Steve the Significant!* Significant Suspect, perhaps.

"Her *boy*friend?" It sounded as if he had to swallow very hard before he could say the word.

I thought maybe he hadn't understood, so I ran down the list of rejected synonyms.

He interrupted me. "I know what a *boyfriend* is, Fae! I just had no idea my mother was involved with someone."

I noticed this was the first time he had acknowledged Lani was his mother, except when he introduced himself to me over the phone as her son. "Well, she was *involved* with Steve." I liked that word. *Involved.* Just the word I had been looking for. Now I only had to find an appropriate noun to match.

"What do you think he wanted?"

"I couldn't say, Jason, but if I were you, I'd call the cops."

"The *police*, you mean?"

Was he correcting my English? "The cause of your mother's death hasn't been determined yet. They're still investigating and ought to be told that Steve Krieger broke into the house."

"Are you saying she was murdered? He's a suspect?" Jason sounded genuine, but I wasn't sure if it was surprise I was hearing in his voice. *A little too eager?*

"What I'm saying is that he might become a suspect if it turns out your mother's death wasn't an accident." I would have thought that the cops/police at least would have told him something about the circumstances.

For a few seconds it was quiet on the other end. I waited for him to speak again.

"Fae, would you do me a favor and come over? He may have taken something, and I would have no idea. I can't imagine what he was looking for."

I told him to give me half an hour and hung up.

It would only take me five minutes to drive to Lani's house. Why did I tell him *half an hour*? The word *breakfast* suddenly sounded in my head. That must be it: I had told him *half an hour* because my subconscious was telling me I needed to eat breakfast first.

I prepared a large bowl of Brinta, the simple Dutch cereal of ground wheat flakes I was raised on—no additives or preservatives. I poured rice milk and sprinkled two heaping spoonfuls of sugar over the flakes, musing that obsessions should rightfully be reserved for wicked things, not for good habits such as eating healthy.

After finishing, I sat at the kitchen table and smoked a cigarette, dawdling to postpone the inevitable trip to Lani's house. I was tempted to phone Jason back and explain that my coming over would be of no use to him. I hadn't been to visit her for some time, so if Steve did take something, I probably wouldn't be able to tell.

Although this was a better excuse than my subconscious's cold-cereal cue I'd cooked up earlier, the real reason for my reluctance was that the prospect of entering Lani's home made me feel rather edgy, because I was afraid it would open the door even wider to her unwelcome visitations.

It could be my imagination, but I suspected she was behind the dead phone calls. These calls had happened a number of times before, always when family members or friends had died. After a week, the phone would start ringing every day at the same time, but when I'd pick up, no matter after how many rings, there would be nobody there. The caller ID would say *unknown caller*. Always a disconnect when the answering machine kicked in. Twice, the phone company put a tracer on, but the day the tracers went into effect the calls abruptly stopped. Maybe it was a coincidence that this happened each time someone died. Maybe this was a whole series of coincidences I was weaving into a significant pattern. Maybe it was market research. I had no real evidence other than a solid pattern stretching over two decades.

If it was not my imagination, Lani hadn't waited a week.

After calling myself a wimp, I put on my raincoat and black rubber boots, and got into the car. A fine rain drizzled down on my way over to Lani's house. I parked in front of the detached double garage and began to walk up to the red-and-yellow brick house. A large, two-story structure with many tall, narrow windows, it was reminiscent of an Amsterdam canal house. The path to the front door was covered with slippery moss.

I looked up at the house. A slight movement drew my attention to a small window in the center of the second floor. As I tried to blink the rain out of my eyes, I felt my mascara begin to run into the raccoon look.

In front of the lacy curtains covering the window stood a quiet figure.

It was Lani, looking down on me.

Then, she had the gall to wave at me.

Chapter 9

But break, my heart, for I must hold my tongue!

As I was sending an urgent mental message to Lani to quit pestering me, Jason opened the front door.

"Thanks for coming, Fae. The sheriff's already here." He turned to introduce me to Bobby who had appeared behind him in the hallway.

"Fae and I know each other." Bobby, who was not the sheriff, nodded at me in greeting. The paw prints had been removed from his trench coat. He must have parked his car behind the house.

The large living-annex-dining room was indeed in shambles. At its best, Lani had kept this room looking as if it were perpetually in redecoration mode. Ochre, crushed velvet curtains, drawn almost to a close, allowed only a few slivers of daylight to enter the room. The walls, covered with sickish-looking alabaster paper printed in an English ivy pattern, were hung with clustered arrangements of oil paintings depicting pastoral scenes under depressingly looming skies. In the dining area, variations on the theme of Van Gogh's malnourished potato eaters ironically stared out of ornate, golden frames.

A set of drab sage, overstuffed chairs and a long couch—all very Victorian, complete with skirts to cover the offensively naked legs—formed a sitting area on a large Persian rug, the only thing of beauty. An assortment of small tables, covered with fringed tablecloths, were lined up against the walls to exhibit a great variety of old and antique plates, statues, and vases, which Lani had bought at auctions and from personal ads. Unashamedly, she'd passed them off as family heirlooms. In a way, they were, of course—just not her family's.

The somber atmosphere gave me the feeling of having taken a depressing step back into the nineteenth century, the time of whalebone corsets, before women had the right to vote.

Now, tables were knocked over, the rug was pulled up on one side, paintings hung askew, and the floor was strewn with the knickknacks that once had made up Lani's little shrines to a heritage she couldn't honestly claim. I didn't remember ever having seen half the stuff during my prior visits and surmised that she must have expanded her collection.

In the far corner of the front room lay the large, copper cage that was home to Lani's Congo African Grey parrot, her only pet. I'd never known birds could be so smart. When I had taught him his French vocabulary, he had learned fast and rolled his *r*'s like a native speaker. But he could also be quite ornery, shrieking when he wasn't pleased about something or not getting enough attention. Now, he was quiet. He sat in the opened cage, looking a little dazed, his head turned at an impossible angle as if he were trying to see matters from a different perspective. The tray of his cage had been pulled out and lay nearby on the couch.

I looked at Jason, who was standing in the doorway behind me, running his fingers through his hair in exasperation.

"For Pete's sake, what happened to this room?" he exclaimed.

I surveyed Steve's handiwork again. "Didn't you say Steve Krieger did this?" His question confused me.

"I know. But what I mean is, what did *she* do to it? Where did she get all this junk?" He let his eyes sail around, then waved his arm through the air. "The last time I saw this room it was decorated in a light Scandinavian style with beige and white rugs all over the place and Dutch Piet Mondriaan prints on the walls. And where did she get that horrid bird? It just screams all day long and won't shut up unless you cover the cage." He glared disdainfully at the animal, shook his head, then walked over, slammed the door shut, and threw the large black cloth that was lying nearby over the cage. "Little twerp!"

"Hey! Hey! *Merde!*" the horrid bird screamed.

"That's Solo. He came with a few of the paintings." I silently calculated that Jason must not have visited his mother for at least a year, because for as long as I'd known Lani this room had been going in a distinctly Victorian direction. I'd never seen anything even slightly Scandinavian here, except for her hair.

"Fae, do you have any idea what Krieger could have been looking for?" Bobby asked, his eyes still on the pad as he finished writing what I guessed was a descriptive narrative of the scene.

"Shoot, Bobby, I have no idea. Money? Jewels? His drugs? Her will?"

"Her will?" Bobby and Jason said in make-a-wish unison.

"She had a will?" Bobby's question was directed at me, but I noticed that he was watching Jason out of the corner of his eye. The latter, who appeared to be totally unaware that he was under observation, sank down in one of the chairs and lit a cigarette. A deep frown creased his perfect forehead when he looked up at me.

Why wouldn't Lani have a will? I thought. "I'm not sure, but I believe so. She had a lawyer in Modesto. She must have had one drawn up, because a few months ago she mentioned wanting to make some changes. *Adjustments*, she said."

Actually, Lani had made this remark during one of my last visits to her home, following my insincere show of admiration for one of her newly acquired paintings, a scene with a young shepherd molesting an even younger shepherdess while a bunch of bored sheep looked on. The boy was dipping his hand inside the girl's loosened bodice, fondling her breasts with a saintly look on his face as she gazed up at him in stupid adoration. I spotted the painting, hanging sideways, over the couch between the two front windows.

"I hope she didn't leave me that bird. I'll have it put to sleep," Jason said between his teeth.

That should quiet it down.

"Well, I'll check on this and let you know what we find out, Mr. De Weder." Bobby stuck his pen in his chest pocket and closed his note pad. He needed to comb his hair.

Jason got up and extended his hand to Bobby. "Thank you for coming over so quickly, Sheriff Van Zand. I appreciate your help."

Bobby handed him one of his cards. Jason looked at it. "*Detective* Van Zand," he corrected himself.

"Since Mr. Krieger was a frequent visitor, his fingerprints are likely to be all over. There is no sign of a break-in, so I suspect he has a key. We might be able to fix that."

Bobby's demeanor was so much more serious from his relaxed Sunday-biker look, I was surprised to see a smile on his face when he turned to me and said goodbye.

As Bobby was about to step out into the hallway to leave, a salvo of gunshots disrupted the quiet outside. At least, that's what it sounded like to me. But neither of the men seemed to be alarmed, and when I heard a car door slam, I realized why. The front door opened and shut with a bang, followed by heavy footsteps and the scraping of heels on the stone tile.

"Jase! Jason? Jase, are you here?!" a husky but distinctly feminine voice called out.

A moment later, the door swung open wide and a giant apparition completely filled the doorway. Arms outstretched, she floated over to Jason and began to hug him and slap him hard on his back. This woman was enormous, in all three dimensions. I thought she was going to crush and pummel him to death. But Jason calmly stood his own, hugged her back, and got in a few whacks of his own.

"How're you doing, Babe?" she asked while she hugged him one last time.

"I'm great! Fine." He gently smiled at her.

Not the answer I had expected him to give in view of his mother's so very recent demise.

Before I knew what was happening, the woman had turned around, arms outstretched again, and two giant leaps later she'd planted herself in front of me.

Cautious, I took a step back. I feared she was about to lift me off the floor, unrestrainedly hugging and slapping *me* on *my* back, and then hold me at arm's length like her favorite childhood rag doll. I tried to make myself as tall as possible. Standing on my toes, I gave Bobby a desperate look. But he did nothing to prevent the anticipated assault and just backed into the doorway, staring at the woman in disbelief.

I wasn't sure I'd survive and squeezed my eyes shut.

"You must be aunt Fae!" she said.

My eyes flew open. *Parblue! Aunt Fae?* I had no idea when we had become thusly related but was so happy I was still standing on my own two feet that I smiled benignly. "Just call me *Fae*." After all, I wasn't that much older than she.

"*Fae*, it is," she said, politely holding out her hand, which I shook with deep feelings of relief and gratitude. Now that the danger had passed, I glanced over at Jason and then looked back at her again, amazed that these two had any genetic material in common.

Upon closer examination, Margaret Peterson—or Sasha, as I later learned she was known to apparently everyone but Lani—wasn't quite as Sasquatchian as she seemed at first. Enormous platform shoes and a thick pony tail standing upright on top of her head easily added at least a foot to her height, and a wide India-cotton skirt, tie-dyed in all colors of the rainbow and gathered at the waist, added extra volume to her ample hips.

Sasha Peterson was quite a vision. Her skirt was topped by a tight-fitting, low-cut, black T-shirt that put her big, round breasts on exhibit. A red, fringed shawl was draped around her shoulders. Her hair was dyed jet black and shaved on the bottom to a third of the way up her skull. Her large, almond-shaped eyes were of an unnatural green that could only come from Hallowe'en-issue contact lenses. Along the edges of each ear she wore about a dozen pierced earrings, two more had been inserted into the left nostril of her nose, and one was dangling from her right eyebrow.

I blinked a few times, but as I was taking it all in, I realized her clothing showed taste, an artistic flair for composition. I was sure she spent as much or more time than I did getting dressed, matching things.

Jason introduced his sister to Bobby, whose professional training had apparently helped him recover from the shock. *Country boy meets city girl?* He told Jason he'd be in touch, not to worry about walking him out, then nodded at Sasha and me and left.

Sasha walked over to the couch and began padding it with both hands like a cat preparing a space to lie down. She then turned around and dropped her colorful rear, kicked off her platform shoes, and spread her long legs in a highly unladylike manner. Leaning her head back and looking up at the ceiling, she let out a loud "Ah!" She then straightened herself somewhat and slapped the pillow next to her in an invitation to Jason.

He laughed as if she were terribly amusing. "Do you want me to get your bags out of your car?" In answer, she rummaged through her black velvet, drawstring purse and tossed him her keys.

"Thanks, Bro. I'm bushed!" she yelled after him. Exaggeratedly, she sagged down even deeper than before until she had practically slid to the floor. It wasn't until then that she looked around, noticed the mess, and frowned. "Guess my mother must have been decorating again."

"The house was broken into," I said.

"Oh," was all she said, and she stared across the room.

Since she didn't ask for more information, I didn't volunteer any, figuring Jason could tell her what had happened.

Despite a total lack of resemblance and an obvious difference in life style, I sensed there was great love between these two, a closeness likely born out of their less-than-perfect childhood.

At our very first meeting, and afterwards in numerous installments, Lani had told me the sad saga of her marital history in the frank and careless manner Americans discuss such matters, which after all these years still surprised me. In the Netherlands, the Calvinistic outlook of course was that marriage was a holy institution, no matter how many unholy things went on behind closed doors or how much the partners grew to despise each other. Divorce was only whispered about and then only behind the divorced person's back. One did not marry a divorced person, because in the eyes of God there was no such thing as *divorce*. On the whole, they stopped just short of requiring divorcés to wear a scarlet *D*.

But in the Land of the Free Lani wasn't burdened with such constraints, and she enthusiastically discussed each failed union with her absurd brand of humor.

According to Lani, her first husband, Terry Le Coeur, suddenly disappeared one month before the birth of her eldest daughter, Alicia. When he was repeatedly spotted in Las Vegas, Lani divorced him and soon married Sasha's father, Jack Peterson. When Sasha was three, Jack slammed his truck into an old oak tree, his sole companion a half-finished bottle of whiskey bearing the same first name.

Two years later, Lani tied the knot with Willem de Weder, alcoholic number three—these strange and incomprehensible relationships often manifest themselves in clusters—and Jason was born a month after the wedding. Their divorce, after ten years, did not end the tempestuous relationship. Within five years they were remarried, staying together off and on for another turbulent decade, followed by a second divorce. (Lani had referred to Willem de Weder as "my third-slash-fourth husband.")

I had heard the bits and pieces of this story so often that it had almost given me hives, so I couldn't help wondering how the Le Coeur-Peterson-De Weder children had been affected by Lani's chaotic conjugal history.

Jason came in carrying a beaten leather suitcase covered with peeling stickers and strapped shut with two equally worn leather belts. He was followed by a picture-perfect woman in her late thirties.

"Look who I found wandering on the premises!" he exclaimed.

"I only just arrived," the woman snapped, apparently both as explanation and general greeting. She immediately noticed the condition the room was in. "What happened here?"

"We had a break-in," Jason said. "We think it was the guy Mother was... involved with." There it was again. *Involved.* Rolled up. He couldn't bring himself either to use the *boyfriend* word. "I'll tell you later." He cleared part of the floor with his foot and put Sasha's baggage down.

The woman regarded Sasha's crummy suitcase with distaste and then noticed me. "I don't believe we've met," she said, tilting her head backward as she held out a slender ivory hand, nails carefully manicured and polished a soft burnt orange. "Alicia Howard."

I know *we haven't met.* Reluctantly, I shook her beautiful hand with my I-hate-garden-gloves paw. "Fae Nelson."

Alicia Howard, née Le Coeur, was about five eight, slender, and dressed in a forest green, heavy silk suit she'd spent a mint on. Her copper-colored, wavy hair was cut to shoulder length and brushed back from her forehead. I felt a slight shock when I found Lani's light-blue eyes looking out of Alicia's unfamiliar face.

"Fae lives next door. She was a friend of Mother's." Jason seemed embarrassed by his sister's brusque manners.

Evidently, this disclosure was not a recommendation, because Number One Daughter quickly let go of my hand. Immediately, her cool eyes dropped from my face to my black rubber boots, and then she turned her back on me to face Jason and Sasha.

I knew I'd fallen from grace before ever ascending and stared at my socially unacceptable hand, turning it over several times. I glanced at Sasha and found she was monitoring my reaction to her older sister, an undisguised smirk plastered on her face. She gave me a conspiratory wink, pushed herself to an upright position, and announced, "I think I'll go *freshen up*," in an intonation and with a face as if this expression should cause massive eruptions of merriment. But when nobody reacted, she just left the room.

"Fae found Mother," Jason said animatedly. He could have been talking about my prowess as a gardener (or perhaps not, since I'm rather a hit-and-miss adventurer in that area).

If this bit of information was meant to endear me to Alicia, it didn't work. She looked over her shoulder at me as if I'd committed a *faux pas terrible* by stumbling upon her mother in her dead condition.

Automatically, I grimaced at her apologetically.

"Really?" was all she said as she turned back to Jason. "Darling, would you please get my luggage out of the car and take it upstairs to my room?"

Whatever manners Lani and consorts had taught little Alicia, Mrs. Howard had apparently plumb forgotten all of them. This gal was rude. I was glad when she left the room right behind Jason.

For a few minutes, I stood alone in the middle of the room looking around at all the dislocated Victoriana. I heard Jason return and go upstairs. The downstairs toilet flushed. I too should *freshen up*. I crossed the hall and climbed up the winding stairs to the second floor. I paused briefly before entering the bathroom. This was where Lani had been standing in front of the window when I'd walked up to the house. I wondered what would be behind the door.

But there was nothing if I didn't count the strong, sweet cherry scent coming from a sticky-looking air freshener shaped like a white plastic sea shell. I fanned the air in front of my face, opened the medicine cabinet, and moved some bottles over to make space for the smelly object. Then I cracked the window, washed my hands, and styled my hair with my wet fingers.

As I opened the bathroom door to go back downstairs, I heard Alicia hiss. "What is she doing here?" Then she said something else in an angry whisper.

"I asked her to come over, because I thought she might be able to tell if anything were missing. But I don't think even Mother would be able to tell." Jason's calm voice. "She's a friend."

"Well, she isn't *my* friend! Mother always hung out with weirdoes. Who knows what kind of whacko she is."

"Fae is a respectable college teacher. She's not only much better educated than you are, Sis, she has far better manners! I suggest you keep your airs in Idaho!" He was no longer whispering.

"For all we know, she could have just killed Mother." Alicia's venom was like that of a baby rattler: fast flowing and unrestrainedly released.

"*For all we know?* What makes you think Mother was murdered? We know no such thing."

"Sixty-year-olds don't just keel over."

She had a point there. *Sixty, huh?*

"Just mind your manners," Jason cautioned his sister in an emphatic staccato. "By the way: Mother was sixty-four!"

Sixty-four, huh?

I smiled. He certainly didn't sound like the youngest child. I was so pleased with the way he had turned out, I forgot I had nothing to do with it.

Jason walked past the half-opened bathroom door I was hiding behind and went downstairs.

It would have been too embarrassing to exit right then, so I waited for about thirty seconds before stepping out on the landing. The door to Alicia's room stood wide open. Darn! I tried to sneak by, but she saw me and called out. "Fae?"

Caught, I turned and falsely smiled at her. Anger murmured in my ears to hit her with my best shot. Kindness whispered to cool it: the woman had just lost her mother. *Lost?* Spite commented. *Lost? Not really, we all know where Lani is.*

I stepped into the room and leaned against a tall chest of drawers. It was a large room with white gauze curtains in the windows and white lacquered furniture. Alicia was in the middle of unpacking one of two brand new, tan leather suitcases placed on the large bed. Carefully arranging a taupe woolen dress on a satin-covered hanger, she smiled back at me. Then she blinked her eyes against the onset of tears I saw no sign of.

"I hope you don't think I've been rude. It's been so hard!"

Maybe Jason's short and to-the-point sermon had had some effect, although this didn't sound like an apology to me.

Almost as if she were unaware of my presence, Alicia rattled on as she continued to unpack. To avoid having to show too much sympathy, I just kept my eyes on her suitcase.

Two years ago, her husband had given up a lucrative partnership in a prestigious San Francisco law firm to drag his poor wife and two young daughters to a large farm in Idaho. While the kids didn't know any better, Alicia dearly missed the posh parties and high-profile friends. As if that wasn't bad enough, hubby Charles now insisted on being called *Chuck*, had developed an unnatural taste for anything that could be barbecued, and constantly smelled of cow manure.

Chuck sounded fine to me, except maybe for the cow dung. Listening to Alicia's babbling with half an ear, I wondered why she was telling me about her little miseries and pondered why she hadn't said a word about her mother. Her upsets had nothing to do with the woman in the county hospital morgue.

As I leaned further backward, behind me on the chest something began to wobble, and I quickly turned to check. A brass standing lamp in the shape of a flower was dangerously close to losing its struggle with gravity. I grabbed it just in time and moved it toward the center. My eyes fell on a plane ticket.

It was a two-way ticket from Western. I was about to turn away when I noticed the departure date from Boise: *January 27*.

Thursday. Two days before I had found Lani.

"I come here as often as I can," Alicia continued her lamentation.

Why hadn't I ever met her on these frequent visits? Why hadn't Lani ever mentioned that her daughter had come to stay?

"It's so far, you know!"

Sure is! It took you five days to get here.

Where had she been hanging out?

Chapter 10

Larded with sweet flowers.

Shaking her head and still muttering about the indignities she was forced to suffer in Idaho, Alicia opened her second suitcase. For a moment she stared at its contents. Then she wrinkled her pretty, little nose as if she'd unexpectedly come upon a decomposing fish and quickly dropped the lid.

But not before I had seen why. While in her first suitcase everything had been carefully folded and arranged, these clothes looked as if they'd been packed by Mab and Dooley. Someone had been in a terrible hurry.

"Let's do something about lunch," Alicia said, a little too brightly. "I can finish this later." She swept past me out into the hall way, casting an inviting look over her shoulder.

Had I made a sudden friend! I could hop, skip, and jump for joy.

I followed her down the stairs into the living room where Jason and Sasha were straightening up. It looked as if they could use some help, so I walked over to Solo, removed the black cloth, and picked up his cage by the large ring at the top. Careful not to allow any of my digits to stick through the bars, I slid the tray back into the bottom. My efforts were rewarded with a barrage of maledictions.

"*Fou! Bête! Crétin!*" he screamed. I was about to tell the "little twerp" to shut up, when he said demurely, "Oh-la-la, pardon my French!"

"Whoever taught that bird how to speak!" Alicia said, dramatically holding the back of her hand up to her forehead and casting her eyes ceilingward.

O, God, if she only knew! I was getting a cookie of my own dough, as they say in Holland. Although, I could have sworn I never taught him any swear words, just *vous êtes très belle, je t'aime, bonjour,* and mush like that.

"What about lunch, guys?" Alicia asked in her take-charge manner.

"Yeah, what about it? Is there anything in the kitchen?" Sasha asked while giving a last little nudge to a painting.

"I can check but I doubt it." Big Sister hesitated before adding, "Knowing Mother."

She was right. Though I had eaten right before coming over, I helped her scout out the kitchen, but all we found in the refrigerator were a few cans of generic-brand beer and some molded cheeses that weren't meant to be moldy and that would truly have interested Hal. There were a lot of frozen entrées in the freezer compartment and canned goods stacked in the pantry, but none we could combine and rightfully call lunch.

"You could come over to my house." I said it sweetly but let just enough doubt seep into my voice so that to my relief Alicia immediately declined the invitation, thanking me for my thoughtfulness. She couldn't help glancing at my boots again while she did this.

With effort, I kept a smile off my face. Those dorky boots were good for something.

"I think I'll go into town and get some supplies. We'll be here for a while anyway." She didn't sound too happy about that prospect.

I looked at my watch. It was close to one o'clock. Time to go home and work on my syllabus. I took my leave and drove off thinking about dirty laundry and how none of her three children seemed to be grieving much over Lani's death. What a sad family.

After unsuccessfully having tried to circumvent the Mab and Dooley Welcoming Committee, I took off my infamous boots and shook out my raincoat, two Dooley-sized paw prints in mud on the front. *Off! Off!* didn't seem to ring a bell with him. The rain had been coming down in buckets again on the way home. I took a few towels from the stack we kept on the porch and rubbed the dogs down. Then we all went into the kitchen.

The light of the answering machine was blinking. Pantyhose-footed, I walked over to the cherry phone stand and pushed the play button.

"Hi, dahling! Just wanted to ... uh ... talk. Give me a ... uh ... call. If you can." The sound of Lani's slurred voice turned my skin icy as if a gust of freezing wind had blown in. I was so spooked that I couldn't pay attention to the second message and had to push *play* again, which meant listening to a rerun of Lani's request.

The second message was from my friend Kate O'Farrell, who asked if we could have lunch the next day.

I was still half in shock and trying to figure out how Lani's voice could be on my answering machine, when I noticed that the digits on the microwave indicated that it was now 88:88 o'clock. I knew that couldn't be true. A quick glance at the coffee maker brought further relief. It flashed 12:00, signaling that it needed to be reset for the second time that day.

Bless my heart! The power had been off. Lani must have called Saturday evening—before she had died, not after. Hal had probably listened to her message, saved it, and then forgotten to tell me about it. The machine's power-outage feature had rescued her message as newly incoming. And Kate must have called when I had been out, after power had been restored.

I was so happy with this unsupernatural solution to the mystery that I almost danced around the kitchen, but instead I decided to give Kate a quick ring to let her know we were Two for Tuesday.

An hour later, I detached my ear from the phone. I'd given her a complete rundown of the events of the last three days. We agreed to meet about noon at Full of Beans to go over the details more thoroughly.

Kate, my best friend and confidante, was pretty much a straight arrow, which also accounted for my not always being happy with her. We had met in Berkeley, lost touch for a while, and then hooked back up when I first got sober. By then, she was already a few years old, as we say, and she became my temporary sponsor. That was more than fifteen years ago, and she was still my temporary sponsor. Kate made large charitable contributions to the University of Life-long Learning, at which I was receiving the most significant educational experience ever. "How to live life on life's terms," she called it. She often talked like that and about herself in the third person. "Kate needs to focus on Kate." A bit peculiar, but whatever situation I'd found myself in, she had gone before me. I was never alone, and for this I could be nothing but grateful.

Eyeing the rebellious appliances with suspicion, I opened the door of my faithful fridge, the only one not to have taken part in the uprising, and grabbed a bag of bagels. I sliced one and plopped it in the toaster. It did its job and spit out the two halves without any funny business. Just a little burnt. Under the watchful eyes of two street-urchins, I loaded both pieces with cream cheese and blackberry jam, and sat down for lunch. If we taught these dogs anything, we taught them how to beg properly. I saved the last morsel and dividing it between them for reinforcement. They looked up at me for more, as usual making me feel unbelievably stingy.

I spent the next hours leafing through my notes and thinking up clever questions to ask on quizzes, taking a short break mid-afternoon when Hal called as promised. I brewed a small pot of Earl Grey while we talked. He said he'd be home a little later than usual. We ended our brief conversation by reaffirming our eternal love for each other: river deep, mountain high, back-porch-ferry wide.

Sipping my tea, I went back to my office, Dooley following me every step of the way. He draped his large body over the easy chair and soon was sound asleep again. Mab hadn't budged, but her eyes followed me as I sat back down at my desk, where Mellow was lying stretched out, fancying himself to be a fluffy paperweight. I had to cure him of his delusion before I was able to get back to work.

At five o'clock, I closed my books, sorted the paperwork I had generated, and went down to the kitchen to figure out what we'd have for dinner. The animal kingdom migrated with me.

Hal and I didn't often get a chance to eat together, because I taught night classes. This cold day, I decided, called for an old-fashioned Dutch *hutspot*, which is nothing exotic, but simply equal amounts of potatoes and carrots with some onions cooked in the same pot, drained, and then mashed together. I defrosted a cut of beef, seared it, added some tomato and onion, and then left it to simmer. Next, I hauled potatoes and carrots out of the cellar and began the tedious job of peeling, scraping, and pitting.

Mind-numbing chores like these are conducive to deep thinking, and presently I was indeed in deep thought. Going over what had happened that day, my thoughts drifted to Lani and then on to some of her better qualities.

I had all but forgotten about those. She had actually been funny and entertaining, often generous and usually kind to me—in her own way. I would miss her—in my own way. I cried freely while chopping the onions.

I put the pan on the stove to be lit as soon as Hal came home and went into the living room. My cheeks still wet, I sat down and leaned back, pulling my feet up on the couch. In my mind, I saw Lani's face, her light blue eyes smiling. I whispered a blessing for her and sniffed.

Alarmed, I sat upright and sniffed the air again. A strong, flowery scent surrounded me. I looked around the room to find the source, but there was nothing that could produce that wonderful smell. It was the unmistakable fragrance of roses.

Lani's favorite flowers.

Chapter 11

**And let me speak to the yet unknowing world
how these things came about.**

"They call that *spiritual flowers*," Gwen said to me. "You must have been thinking about her."

"I'd just said a little prayer for her," I admitted reluctantly.

Gwendolyn had called to find out how I was doing, and she had caught me just on my way out to meet Kate for lunch.

"Spiritual flowers are like a thank-you note. Spirits often communicate through electrical objects like the phone, but sometimes they communicate with fragrances," Gwen explained. "That's really nice of her!"

I *really* didn't think so at all and broke out in a tirade about the kitchen insurgency that had not been so *neat*. "Why is she doing this?" I asked.

"Well, you know what you get when you sober up a drunken horse thief, don't you?"

"Sure! A sober horse thief," I answered. That was an old one. Ha-ha.

"It's pretty much the same with people going to the other side. They don't change instantaneously. They don't turn into angels. Lani's basically the same person she was when she was here."

"And the good news is?"

"The good news?" Gwen cleared her throat but didn't immediately say anything.

It seemed that if she had to think about what the good news was, it must either not be that good or she was making something up.

"The good news is that you do have some control. She has easy access to you, because you're like a radio tuned in to just the right frequency. She has something to tell you, else she wouldn't be doing this. Now, the more uptight you are, be it angry, upset, fearful, the more energy goes into this situation. So, go with the flow, just relax!" Gwen said lightly.

I was just about to point out that it was difficult to relax with suicide-bomber light bulbs bursting all around me, when she said, "Oh, I'd better let you go. You'll be late meeting Kate."

Before I knew it, she had hung up. Next time I'd see her, I'd have a good talk with Gwen. She hadn't been as forthcoming as I'd expected her to be, and I needed to learn more about what was going on.

"You look like a veritable fairy queen," went Kate's greeting. She took off her floppy navy hat with a giant peachy flower and shook her head to loosen her curls. The plum-colored pant suit looked gorgeous on her. She tossed her coat over a chair and gave me a little bear hug. One of her most endearing attributes was that she was shorter than me. It was only an inch, but still.

"I wish you'd stop saying that!" I sighed but smiled at her. It was typical of Kate never to forget anything I told her. As it does in English, *Fae* means *fairy queen* in Dutch. (It's spelled *Fee* but pronounced the same as in English.) Only, in the Netherlands it's not considered to be a proper first name, just a rather sugary fairy tale character. It would be the equivalent of being called something like Tinkerbell in America. The teasing had been *ad nauseam*.

As we sat down across from each other, Kate looked at me with the usual mischief glittering in her chocolate eyes. With her unruly, bright auburn hair and light, freckled skin, she could be a poster child for Eire. But Kate was not a child. She had just turned forty-two and was very proud this, as she should be, because for many years the odds were against her living long enough to reach the age of thirty.

I had arrived a few minutes earlier at Full of Beans, and Phil, I-am-your-waiter-Phil, had already poured me a large mug of strong decaf while I waited for Kate to show up.

"So, tell me how you are," she commanded and to Phil, "I'll have an espresso, please, a triple." Quite fearless, this little woman.

I put my cup down. Talking to Kate was like going to confession. Not that I'd ever been, but I was pretty sure she had. Long ago. Being *Katherine Mary*, she had to. Kate was quite adept at getting you to lay bare your soul, squeal on yourself. When she asked, "How are you?" she actually wanted to know the answer. Otherwise, she'd pry your little heart open. Kate didn't much believe in pussyfooting around, maybe because she didn't have a lousy childhood to blame her old behavior on.

"Fine!" I said, my face too straight to convey true honesty.

For a few seconds she stared at me intently, then a cluster of crinkles appeared around her eyes and she burst out in exuberant laughter.

I gave her a wicked, little smile.

"You're not *fine!*" She drew the four-letter word out in a nanny-nanny-boo-boo manner. "Fae, there's no way! What have you been thinking?" Now she was beginning to sound like Jack Nicholson in *The Shining*.

"Oh, I don't know!" I looked at her hair. Good cut.

"Are you feeling guilty?" Elevated eyebrows above wide-open eyes produced a sardonic look.

"No! ... Yes! ... I don't know!" Unless it had been done beforehand, it could sometimes be difficult to make up my mind.

"Fae-hey! You think Lani's death is your fault?" Now her voice was soft and deceptively gentle. She was going in for the kill.

"I don't really think that ... Yes, I do. I can't help feeling that way. Somehow, I can't get my head and my heart to stay together on this. Irreconcilable differences."

"Let it go, Fae! Lani's death had little or nothing to do with you. You're not that powerful. If you were, she'd be sober and alive today, wouldn't she?"

Phil came over, and we each ordered a sandwich. Kate went for the turkey with everything on it and extra mayonnaise, and I asked for my usual tuna on dark rye. I'd never tasted any of the other sandwiches at Full of Beans, which meant I ate a lot of tuna.

When Phil was out of hearing range, I said, "I do feel guilty. If only I'd been nicer or had dragged her to the meeting that night, she'd still be alive."

"We don't *drag* people to meetings, remember?" She was right, of course.

I remembered, too, how long it had taken me to finally quit. Actually, quitting hadn't been such a problem. I had done *that* practically every morning for the last eight long years of my drinking. Again and again. Especially when my hangovers became so bad they seemed like out-of-body experiences, and I thought I was dying. Full of fear, I'd pray my drunkard's prayer, pleading with God, promising I'd never drink again. This promise, I could never keep, because at about four o'clock in the afternoon, as I began to feel a little better, something would happen in my brain, in my memory bank. I had a real talking head: *It wasn't so bad. I can handle it. This time, it will be different. Just a couple of drinks will make me feel better.* And off I'd go on the merry-go-round of drinking, hangover, remorse, and denial all over again.

Knowing all this, it was clear I hadn't been in charge of Lani's behavior. "There is something I should or could have done!" I said stubbornly, acting as my own prosecutor going for a guilty verdict.

"OK! Like what? You want to go down the list?"

I didn't have a list. Damn it! I just wanted to be responsible. But at the same time I was aware that if Kate should suddenly turn around and say, "Yes, Fae, you are guilty. It's all your fault that Lani's dead!" I would vehemently deny any responsibility and probably tell her to take a hike.

I needed to hear her say the things she was saying, so I continued to play the Devil's advocate, and Kate continued to reason with me, mostly in the one-liners I knew so well. In sponsor mode, she reminded me of an educated and slightly more tactful version of Rita. If I'd ever told Kate this, she'd probably have a fit.

"Well?" Kate the School Teacher finally asked as if she were talking to a six-year-old.

"Well *what*, Kate? I can't help how I feel right now. You always say it's important to acknowledge our feelings. Should I ignore them now?" I was snapping at my best friend.

She ignored my snottiness and calmly went on, "There's a difference between feeling a certain way and wallowing in those feelings, especially if they don't make sense or are based on a lie you've told yourself. Your thinking precedes your feelings. Check your thinking and your feelings will change."

God, she knows everything! This Queen of Clichés! I stared out the window. She reminded me of a psychiatrist I'd gone to see when I was really depressed, coincidentally close the zenith of my drinking career.

The first thing he had asked me was if I drank or used drugs. Figuring it was none of his business, I told him I did neither, a half-truth slash blatant lie. By that time, I had long ago abandoned the niceties of French wines and four-ounce crystal stemware, and since I'd never even liked the taste of wine, just drank for the sake of getting drunk, I'd decided I might as well buy something cheap to slurp out of my sixteen-ounce tumblers. I had come to see a psychiatrist because I was depressed, not because I drank half a gallon of wine every day.

As if he hadn't heard me, this Healer of the Mind went right on and asked if I had ever suffered from black-outs. I answered that if I ever had, I couldn't remember. In fact, I had no idea that the times when I'd suddenly come to and couldn't remember what I'd done, where I'd been, with whom I'd been—or was still with—were called *black-outs*.

Next, he asked me if I'd ever heard of ant abuse. Why was he suddenly talking about ants? I was thoroughly convinced he needed to have his own head examined and stated so. When he calmly told me that part of his education had been to go through analysis, this made me even more depressed. If it had done so little for him, how could it help me? I never went back. But his persistent questions nagged me the rest of my drinking days.

Phil placed our food in front of us. I'd lost my appetite but took a bite out of my sandwich anyway. It was tuna, so I kept eating.

"How is your book coming along?" Kate asked.

"My novel?" Kate was one of the few people who knew about my novel. Was I still mad at her? I had to change gears. "I did get some editing done during this break, but my job is interfering again."

"Why don't you take a sabbatical of a semester so you can concentrate and get it finished?" She suggested.

"We can't afford it. Maybe next year." Not being able to write bothered me more than I cared to admit.

"Where there is a will, there is a way."

"And where there is Kate, there is a cliché," I rhymed, almost blowing coffee out of my nose because I thought I was so funny.

Kate looked at me with a wide grin on her face. "Touché, but I like clichés. They're not clichés for nothing."

"I know, I know, ancient wisdom."

Kate swallowed an enormous chunk of her sandwich. "There's something I feel I need to tell you."

"You *feel* you need to tell me?" I opened my eyes wide.

She dismissed my childish sarcasm with a wave of her hand. "I might get in trouble with the board if they ever find out I talked about this, so the least you can do is show some appreciation." Kate was the director of a school that was part of a private group home for severely emotionally disturbed teenagers.

"I appreciate. Tell me!"

"You know Lani volunteered at our school, every so often."

"I'm aware of that," I said, although I wouldn't exactly have called Lani showing up, quite plastered, to interfere with the counselors and teachers *volunteering*.

"What I didn't tell you was that after the staff complained about Lani, they insisted I get rid of her, because she went from bad to worse and was causing major problems. So, I told her she was desperately needed in the office because the filing was backlogged. After a couple of hours of practicing her ABCs, she suddenly remembered an appointment, and we never saw her again."

I should have consulted Kate when Lani was bugging me, instead of trying to wing it on my own, I thought and then immediately felt ashamed of thinking it. "What major problems are you talking about?"

"She and one of our boys repeatedly got into confrontations, the last time because she wouldn't allow him to sharpen his pencil, which was none of her business and therefore not up to her to decide. It was nothing but a power play, but to him, it was a major deal. You see, he hates older women with hair dyed that Marilyn Monroe kind of blond."

"You can't be serious!"

She could and she was. "They remind him of his mother who was the main abuser at home. The day Lani showed up with her hair that color was when the more serious trouble began. Somehow she knew how to push his buttons, and he's got more than a corporate telephone. It built up until that pencil incident. Lani was very provoking and belittled him in front of his group."

"I can't imagine Lani behaving that way. She could be a pain and self-absorbed, but to deliberately hurt another human being? It simply doesn't sound like her."

Kate looked at her hands and was quiet for a moment. Then she went on, "He threw his pencil at her, then his desk, and he had to be restrained because he was about to attack her. He's over six feet tall and strong as an ox. We had to keep him in position and called 911. They hauled him off, and he spent several days at the hospital for evaluation."

I knew that *in position* meant face down with people sitting on arms and legs for as long as it took for a violent outburst to blow over. This was allowed if needed either for the protection of others or the student self. Most kids at Kate's school had suffered severe abuse, and explosive behavior was common among them, but more often they turned their pain and rage on themselves.

"It seems to me that having angry outbursts is a lot healthier than practicing self-mutilation or being suicidal."

Kate nodded in agreement. "This boy can become very violent, but after they evaluated him he was returned to us. They didn't consider him dangerous, because his behavior could be modified by upping his medication. We got him back because of the Least Restrictive Environment law."

Basically, this law requires that children with disabilities are educated in the least restrictive setting they can function in. If they can learn in a regular classroom, they are not to be placed in a special classroom. For Kate's kids, the group home was the least restrictive environment. A step up would be a closed institution.

"He came back all drugged up, like a zombie. But we discovered he's been palming his medication since his return."

"And?" I was waiting for the clincher.

"And ... he disappeared."

"What do you mean, 'he disappeared?'"

"He took off Friday, and we haven't seen him since. The board wants to keep it quiet. We had to report him to the sheriff's department as being AWOL, of course. But they don't want anyone else to know."

"What are they so worried about?" This wasn't the first time a kid had just walked off. There were no fences to keep the kids in; the group home was not a prison, although they were supposed to be under twenty-four-hour surveillance.

"There have been complaints. Some valid, I suppose. The fact is, the neighbors don't want a school with kids like these near them. They figure if they make enough of a ruckus, our license will be pulled or we'll have to move elsewhere." She frowned.

"So you'd have different neighbors?" I wasn't sure I'd want to live right next door to her group home either, and I had worked with kids like these.

"This case would give them some powerful ammunition." A pained look appeared on Kate's face. "But why I'm telling you all this is because I'm worried that this boy may have killed Lani."

"Well!" I said, not knowing what else to say.

We sat quietly staring at our plates for a while. Neither of us had taken a bite of our food since Kate had begun to share her secret, and a concerned Phil came over to our table to ask if the sandwiches were to our satisfaction. We reassured him by each taking a big bite to demonstrate how good they were and asked for more coffee, which he promptly brought.

"Have they determined yet how she died?" Kate stirred an inordinate amount of sugar in her coffee. I wondered how she stayed so slender. She ate like a pig, too. I mean, she ate a lot; she had good table manners—American style.

I watched her stir her coffee. "No, not that I know. They're doing an autopsy. Or, they did one yesterday, I think."

"Could she have fallen and drowned in that ditch?" Kate asked with hope in her voice.

"I doubt it. There was no water in that ditch to speak of, just mud. Besides, she had some large bruises, Bobby said." Not to mention the vision I'd told her about.

"Bobby's handling it?" Her eyes sparkled as she mentioned his name.

Kate liked Bobby, and Bobby liked Kate. They were very cute when they were in a room together, blushing like two awkward teenagers *sans* pimples.

She suddenly looked embarrassed, as if she'd become aware of the impropriety of showing her lovey-dovey feelings for Bobby while discussing Lani's death, and looked at the remnants of the sandwich on her plate—to still her beating heart. No, to take yet another big bite.

"Yes, your Detective Van Zand took the report and he's leading the investigation," I said and then asked, "Are you two still seeing each other?" as if I didn't know.

"What do you mean? We've been dating for five months!"

"Only five months?"

"Five months and five days," she said. "So what do you think?"

"I think you ought to wait at least ten years before you get married, like Hal and I did."

"I mean about how Lani got killed!" She didn't need my advice. She wasn't going to follow it anyway. It was more blessed to give than to receive advice.

"I have no idea. Well, I do have a few ideas, and you just gave me one more, but I'd rather not spout them, because they're probably all wrong." Modesty was usually the quiet member of the committee.

"Nah, come on!" Kate said.

And I spouted.

Chapter 12

**When sorrows come, they come not single spies,
but in battalions.**

Lunch with Kate stretched out until after two o'clock, because we visited the House of Variety, where I was very good, only buying a new coffee pot, and Kate was very bad, and then we went to Ben's Warme Bakkerij, where we both were bad. We sat on the bench in front of the library, each with an enormous chocolate croissant. The sun came out and shone on our faces.

"I think you're right ... Steve Krieger looks pretty good as a candidate." She made it sound as if she were going to vote him into higher office. "But then Alicia ... with that plane ticket ... I like that one, too."

I took a bite out of my crispy croissant, moaned in ecstasy, and with a full mouth said, "Jason lives in Sacramento and Sasha in Berkeley, both near enough to have dropped by. And what about Willem? What if he got mad about her seeing Steve?"

"Basically, it sounds as if anyone of them could have done it. What did Jason want to find out from you, for example? What is he hiding?" Kate nodded her head in agreement with herself. "What you need is a good, old-fashioned motive!"

Just knowing her was motive enough for me. I wasn't sure if it was Guilt or Spite talking in my head. "Or a butler. I guess nowadays that would be one of those newfangled personal-organizer people who clean your closets," I surmised. "*The personal organizer did it* doesn't quite have the same ring to it."

"Then, of course, it may have been a crime of passion, in which case there will be no motive," Kate said as if I hadn't spoken. "Now that would make it much harder to pin down who was responsible." She seemed quite relieved that her runaway was not the prime suspect after all.

A young woman I didn't recognize walked by pushing a light blue perambulator. Kate couldn't contain herself. "Oh!" she cooed. The woman stopped and allowed Kate a peek in the baby carriage.

"Oh!" Kate cooed again, though when she turned back to me I knew something was dreadfully wrong, and I thought maybe her last Oh! hadn't been a coo at all. Perhaps a dirty diaper. I rarely make a fuss over babies, puppies—yes, but from the look on Kate's face, I just had to see this baby.

When I did, I almost spit my piece of croissant out. This child was without a doubt the ugliest I'd ever seen. It had close-set eyes, a large mouth that slashed its face in half, and ears that stuck out perpendicular to its head. All around its forehead, nose, and mouth were deep grooves so that it looked like a miniature of a very old man.

I pulled my head back. I was speechless. I couldn't figure it out. The mother was pretty good looking. Whom—or *what*—had she mated with?

The proud mother smiled at us expectantly, waiting for our comments. She didn't know.

"Hmm," Kate said, trying to compose herself, "How old is he?"

"Eight months and twelve days," the woman answered. She then gave us his stats as to time of birth, birth weight, and how much overdue he was.

Kate and I nodded our heads at each detail the woman disclosed as if that was about what we expected from as strapping a boy as that. Then Kate looked up at the sky and said, "Nice day!"

"Yes, it is," the mother agreed, gazing at her baby. She rocked the perambulator. "I'd better be going. It's time for his feeding." And she walked on.

We were silent for the longest time. We didn't dare look at each other for fear of showing our reaction to the baby, which could be anything from horror to hysterical laughter. With a guilty look on our faces we finished the croissants.

After a while, Kate looked at her watch, "Oops! Got an appointment with some parents at three!" She gave me another one of her little bear hugs. "Be good now!" She wiped something off the corner of my mouth. I thought she was going to pinch my cheek. "And don't forget to go to a meeting!"

"Yes, Mother Katherine Mary!" I hugged her back. The Kate and Fae Detective Agency had dissolved for the time being.

When I got home I took Mab and Dooley for a walk through the orchard to the creek. Every so often, I had to touch some of the almond blossoms. It seemed impossible that such fluorescent, tender flowers could grow out of that dead-looking, gnarly wood. Dooley sauntered behind me, stopping at every other tree until I was sure he was peeing on empty. Mab ran around sticking her nose in every rabbit hole she could find, hoping one of the residents would jump out. She wasn't fast enough to ever catch a rabbit, and I'd have no idea what to do if she'd accidentally get a hold of one. Yell, "Let go!" I supposed.

After going around twice in a circle, along the creek, back into the orchard, and back to the creek again, we went home. I settled myself in the study with a cup of tea, determined to get to work, but I had barely opened my *Shakespeare* when the phone rang.

It was Rita. "Fae? I need to talk! Can I come over?"

I didn't ask her why. She was crying, which meant something must be very much amiss, because Rita wasn't the crying type. I told her to come over right away.

She lived on the other side of Londen on Wilhelmina Road, but less than thirty minutes later I heard her car drive up. I opened the door before she could ring the bell.

Rita fell into my arms, sobbing. I held her until she was able to speak.

"She's in the hospital, Fae! She was raped! Sarah was beaten and raped!" Her voice raw, her chest heaving.

I had to climb out of a deep ravine of fear before I could finally ask, "Is she alive?"

Rita nodded. "Barely. She was in intensive care." Then she pulled away from me, and turning around and around, arms waving, hands fisted, she hollered out her pain and anger. I covered my mouth with my hand and backed into the stair railing, not knowing what to do, too overwhelmed by Rita's grief to feel my own.

Suddenly, she stood still and collapsed. Sitting on the floor, she rocked back and forth, now crying quietly. I let her sit for a while before putting my arms around her waist and pulling her up. Steadying her every step of the way, I guided her into the living room and then gently pushed her down on the couch. I handed her the box of tissues from the side table. Speaking from some great void, I asked her what had happened.

Clutching a large wad of tissues, Rita talked haltingly. "Sarah gone to Sandhill. To register for her classes. It was yesterday afternoon. Late."

"It happened at the college?" There had never been any crime like this at Sandhill in all its history.

"Yeah, in the parking lot, after she got registered. She had to wait in line the longest time. When she gone back to her car it was dark. Them lights there are no good. She was the last one there, seemed. All alone." Rita tore at the tissues and dabbed her eyes again, but she composed herself enough to continue. "She put the key in the lock and then a hand, I mean, she felt a hand on her shoulder, and when she turned around, she got smacked in the face really hard. She tried kicking the guy, like I told her to, but she was hurt too bad and he kept hitting her with his fists on the head and all over and he grabbed her hair and pulled her down backwards and ... " She couldn't go on.

I put my arms around her again and rubbed her back. She leaned against me, shaking uncontrollably.

All of a sudden, she lifted her head, abruptly pushed me away, and sat up straight. "I'm gonna kill that fucking bastard!" she screamed as she shredded the tissues and threw them on the floor. "I'm gonna fucking kill him!"

A rage like an alien creature boiled up inside of me. "She knows who it was? Has he been arrested?" I asked, containing my anger for Rita's sake.

"No, she didn't recognize him. He hit her hard first thing. She couldn't see nothing but stars. Just got to scratch him on his face, she thinks." The murderous look came back into her eyes.

"What hospital is Sarah in?"

"Memorial in Modesto." Rita rocked back and forth again. More lines grooved her face than last Saturday, just a few days ago, and her eyes behind the bottle-bottom glasses were red and swollen. "I need to go. Told her I be back in a couple hours. Mike's there now. He don't know what to do. You know him."

"I'll follow you. Let me get my coat." I wanted to see Sarah but also felt that I needed to stay near Rita, in case she got some crazy idea in her head.

An hour later, I parked my Saturn in the maze-like parking lot of the hospital. As soon as we entered through the automated glass sliding doors into the reception hall, a deep sorrow washed over me. Ever since my mother had died a slow death I had avoided hospitals, because I no longer associated them with restoration and healing but with helpless suffering.

We walked through the long halls, made a left, then a right. The walls were painted soft peach and mint green. Pastels. I glanced at the art work, all in pastel colors like the walls. Softening reality. Fear of color. *Something-phobia.*

As Rita walked over to Sarah, I stood still just inside the room, near the door. The reassuring smile I had plastered on my face in the hallway froze into an uncomfortable mask.

Mike was sitting next to the bed, his back bent, his head hanging on his chest, both his large rough hands cupped around one of Sarah's. Her other small hand plucked aimlessly at the soft-pink thermal blanket that covered her body.

Her head was propped up against a crisp white pillow. I looked at Sarah and saw a face I did not recognize. Suddenly, it felt strangely still inside my chest as if my heart had stopped beating.

My first instinct was to look away. Sarah's beautiful hazel eyes were black and swollen nearly shut. Her pretty mouth looked grotesque. A deep gash, pulled together with large stitches, split her upper lip, which was puffed up so badly that it almost touched her bandaged, broken nose. On the right side of her scalp, near her forehead, a large tuft of hair had been pulled out, leaving a bloody wound. A glossy, transparent coating had been put on the gap. Her neck and arms were covered with large, dark bruises that ran together in a wild pattern of colors, and everywhere on her skin were bloody red scrapes and cuts.

Out of the corners of her eyes, Rita cast me a warning glance that said, "Don't let her know."

I bit down hard on my lower lip. I wanted to fall down on my knees and weep.

Mike didn't seem to notice us. His eyes were blank as if he had suspended all feeling and thought. Rita went over to him and nudged him on the shoulder. He got up and walked out into the hallway, looking down at his feet.

I went over to the bed, sat down in the chair Mike had just vacated, and softly patted the hand that was now laying by Sarah's side. She winced and pulled it away, carefully placing it next to the other on the blanket.

I didn't know what to say or do that would bring her comfort, so I whispered, "I love you, Sarah."

Her face contorted into a slight, painful smile. Through her mangled lips she whispered, barely audible, "I know."

"You need anything, Honey? You want Mommy to get you something?" Rita smoothed the blanket over Sarah's feet and then checked the water carafe on the nightstand. She took it into the bathroom in the corner and filled it with fresh water. She rearranged the cups and tissues on the night stand.

I sat quietly, staring at my hands, concentrating very hard so as not to burst out sobbing.

A young nurse came in, smiling, her blond hair pulled back tightly. I thought she should smile a little less. She looked manic. She was carrying a vase with flowers, mixed lilies and asters, yellows and oranges. She placed the vase in the alcove below the small TV that was bolted with a heavy bracket high-up to the wall. She turned the bouquet a couple of times and said, "There!" as if it really mattered.

"And how are *we* today?" she asked, using her profession's *pluralis majestatis*. Still, that infernal smile on her face.

I didn't know about her, but it should have been pretty clear how we were doing, especially Sarah. We ignored her stupid question, only Rita gave her a nasty look when she walked out.

"Your jacket, Fae," Sarah suddenly mumbled. She tried to turn her head my way.

I bent over her and asked, "What about the jacket, Sweetheart?"

"It's all torn." Large tears rolled down from the corners of her eyes.

"Don't worry about it, Sarah." I was about to add that I'd give her another one from my collection, because I couldn't believe she was worried about a dumb jacket after what had happened to her, but then it hit me: she'd been wearing the turquoise jacket when she was attacked.

Bile shot up into my throat.

"I'm going to go talk to your dad, Sweetie," I said, swallowing hard.

Sarah didn't respond. Rita sat down in the chair and began to fuss with the blanket.

Silently, I left the room. My head was swooning. I wanted to throw up.

Mike was sitting on a narrow bench against the wall outside the room. He was leaning forward with his elbows on his knees and staring at the empty wall across from him. He looked up when I placed my hand on his shoulder. His weathered cheeks were wet.

"What they do to my little girl? What they do?" He grabbed my hand and held on to it tightly. "Why'd anyone want to hurt her like that? What she ever done to anyone, Fae?"

"Nothing, Mike. Nothing." I slowly shook my head. I didn't understand much of anything anymore. I just stood there, thinking, trying to find a foothold, a glimmer of the hope and faith that seemed so abundant when things were going well. I wanted to turn toward the light, but all I saw was an incomprehensible darkness.

How could I see into that very darkness where evil lives? Identify what I didn't recognize? And between the darkness and the light, I knew there to be a vast shadowland where good and evil ran together. Good people commit evil acts. By choice or conviction or compulsion. Or by accident. What had I done to Sarah? Why hadn't that jacket burned in my hands, lit up in flames as a warning? Where had my intuitive gift been that had saved me from the sailing sheets of plywood on the freeway just a couple of weeks ago?

"Fae, will she be all right?" Mike looked up at me helplessly, not letting go of my hand but pulling on it, begging me.

However much I ached to comfort Mike, I just didn't know the answer. I knew she would never be the same again. Never.

"I hope so," I said and sat down next to him. With our arms around each other, we cried together.

Chapter 13

**For murder, though it have no tongue,
will speak with most miraculous organ.**

After a while, Mike dried his eyes with the balls of his hands and went back into Sarah's room. I walked down the hallway and found a phone in an alcove from which I called Kate. When I told her what had happened, Kate first anxiously asked the same questions I did—Was Sarah alive? Had her attacker been arrested? She was quiet for a while after my answer and then asked the same question Mike did—Would Sarah be all right?

"I'm not sure, Kate. She's badly hurt." I blinked to stop the tears that were welling up again but it didn't work, and I looked for a tissue in my purse but couldn't find one, so I wiped my eyes with the back of my hand. "But I know who did this to her. Sarah was wearing my turquoise jacket. I gave it to her. I wore that jacket when Lani brought Steve Krieger over to my house. That's when Lani told him I teach at Sandhill. It was Krieger. I'm sure of it, and it was my fault, Kate."

"What?" Kate yelled in the phone.

I could tell by the way she shouted the word that she wasn't in need of repetition. "He was coming after me."

"Wait, wait, wait!"

I waited.

This must have taken Kate by surprise, because she didn't say anything.

"Well, what am I waiting for?" I finally asked.

"First of all, you know no such thing." Kate said with determination. "Secondly, did you give Sarah your jacket for that purpose?"

What a ridiculous question! "Of course not!"

"Well, then ... " Kate said.

"Well, then ... *what*?" I snapped.

"Well, then ... " Kate sighed. "Hold off on the crucifixion."

What a crude thing for a nice Catholic girl to say. Maybe Kate isn't so nice. "Thank you!" I barked and hung up. *I'll get another sponsor. Another friend.*

I took a homicidal Rita to a women's meeting, because she asked me to. I'm not sure if she heard anything, but she seemed calmer when I dropped her back off at the hospital around nine thirty, though she glared at me when I asked her, in the nurse's way, if she'd be all right.

As I drove off, Kate was entering the hospital. I waved at her. After all, I'd just gone to the same meeting that had worked for Rita. On my way back home, my driving speed varied as sorrow, anger, guilt, disbelieve, and powerlessness ran through my head in a continuous procession.

When I got home, Sasha's lime-green-and-yellow Volkswagen bus was standing in our driveway, somewhat perpendicular to how people normally parked. I squeezed by and left my car in front of the barn.

Hal was entertaining Sasha in the kitchen. They both greeted me with unexpected enthusiasm. The ash tray was overflowing with cigarette butts, and I could see by Hal's face who had done most of the entertaining. Not him. He was wearing his long-suffering look.

As I carefully emptied the ash tray, I relieved him of his duties as a host by asking him if he'd please check out my car, with which nothing was wrong, except that it could use a quart of oil and still needed new tires. Hal almost ran out of the kitchen.

I excused myself to Sasha and went out on the porch, calling after him. I told him about Sarah. He put his arms around me, and we stood close together for a few minutes, holding on to each other.

"I'd better see what Sasha wants," I said, reluctantly breaking away from Hal's comforting embrace.

"How have you been?" I sat down at the table opposite of Sasha.

She put her elbows on the table, which took a few tries, leaned her head on her hands, and gazed at me with a vacant look. Then she pulled the corners of her mouth up, creating a smile that took a while to reach her unfocussed eyes. They were blue tonight, her pupils large and black. Sasha was a little bit high.

"Would you like something to eat?" I asked.

"Oh, I don't know," she said and let out a deep sigh.

I wasn't sure which question she'd just answered, how she was doing or if she wanted something to eat.

"I'll make coffee," I decided out loud and got up. Could you be wide awake and high, like a wide-awake drunk? I wasn't sure, would have to ask Hal sometime, him being more experienced in the area of sex, drugs, and rock 'n roll.

"Oh, Fae, I miss my mother. And I feel so guilty." Behind my back Sasha sighed again.

I almost dropped the coffee grinder as I turned around to look at her. I was about to ask her why she was feeling guilty, but she'd covered her face with both hands and seemed to have suddenly fallen asleep.

I unpacked my new coffee decanter, finished the setup, and checked the contents of the cookie tin on the table. There was none. The guys had eaten every crumb Sunday. It looked as if someone had licked it clean. I rummaged around in my cupboards and found the large tin with chunky oatmeal cookies Janny van Zand had given me at my last visit. I took one and placed the open container in front of Sasha.

She opened her eyes and stared at the cookies as if they were worms. Then finally she seemed to realize what they were and grabbed one with each hand. She looked at them in turn, bit a chunk off each, carefully placed them in front of her on the table, patted them as if they were minuscule pets, and, still chewing, lit a cigarette.

I had trouble not making a face at her for simultaneously eating and smoking.

"I just had to get away from Ali, you know. She drives me crazy!" Sasha went back to the cookies, leaving her cigarette to burn in the ash tray. The bluish smoke rose up and twirled around my copper lamp. "She's organizing the funeral, you know. For Thursday, the day after tomorrow."

She picked up her cigarette and tried to inhale smoke and swallow a piece of cookie at the same time, which resulted in the emission of some serious choking sounds. She then began to cough loudly, gulping for air. I went over to her and smacked her none too gently on the back. This didn't help her at all, because she began to cough even harder. She slapped herself on the chest in a *mea culpa* manner.

"Did they call from the coroner's office then?" I handed her a glass of water, which she emptied in one swig. It seemed to give her the relief she needed.

"They called this afternoon. Jason talked to them. He said he would call you?"

I shrugged to indicate that he hadn't called yet.

"Well, anyway. Ali decided it was her duty to organize the whole bit, you know. She's been on the phone all day, making calls to anyone she can think of, and she does nothing but order us around. Do this, do that, do what's in between. She's gone looneybitch! She acts like it's a damned wedding, or something. Mother's dead! Party time!"

I placed a mug of coffee in front of her. "You can stay here in the guest room, if you like," I offered.

"I'll be OK. I can't really blame her. The way mother treated her, you know."

I raised my eyebrows. I *didn't* know.

"Mom always put her down. No matter how hard Ali tried to please her, it was never enough, you know." Sasha took a large gulp of her hot coffee. Too large, apparently, because she began to wave her hand in front of her open mouth to cool it off. "Ali would come home with all As and one B, usually for math, and all she'd hear about was the B. She could never do anything right, you know. Mother would make her so nervous with her constant criticism that she'd become an absolute klutz. Ali, I mean, not Mom. That only made matters worse, of course. And now Ali is a bless-ed compulsive perfectionist." Sasha closed her eyes slowly, squeezed them tightly, and then opened them wide, trying to focus on my face. "Or is that a tautology?"

"I think so," I said. Now, this sounded like the Lani Kate had described, the one I had the pleasure of not knowing. I wondered why Alicia had still kept a room in Lani's house and why she supposedly had visited so often if her mother had been so terrible to her.

"I know mother just couldn't help herself. She mostly ignored me. Just handed me an allowance when I was five. I had no idea what to do with money, you know. It was so funny." She giggled.

I guessed it was.

"And Jason, he couldn't do wrong. He was mother's angel, her darling!" Just as I decided she sounded bitter, she added, "It's a miracle how he turned out despite her constant hovering. Jason's great. He was always very uncomfortable on that pedestal she built for him." She hesitated. "I'm not sure what made him more uneasy, when she was spoiling him, or when she turned against him." A sad smile appeared on her face.

Before I could ask what she meant, the phone rang.

Speaking of the angel, it was Jason.

"Fae, is Sasha there?" he asked after introducing himself and briefly inquiring after the general state of my health. (*Fine.*)

"She is. Would you like to talk to her?"

"No, that's OK. I just wanted to make sure she's all right." He sounded relieved. "The funeral is going to be Thursday."

"Yes, Sasha just told me."

"We're having the service at the Reformed Church in Londen. Alicia is handling all that." He made a puffing sound into the phone.

"What did the coroner's report say?" I asked.

"Well, they're calling it an accidental death. She had a very high blood-alcohol level. They found several empty whiskey bottles in the trash."

"What about the bruises?"

"They said that most of them were probably caused by her bumping into trees while she was intoxicated. There's also an indication she was grabbed by an arm, but those are minor bruises."

I noticed again how detached he seemed. "So, they're saying she died from alcohol poisoning?" I couldn't keep my surprise out of my voice. It wasn't that I'd never heard of this before, it was that it sounded all wrong: Lani had been a pretty healthy woman with a high alcohol tolerance.

"It wasn't just alcohol they found," Jason explained. "Apparently, she also took a load of Boozabuse. That Detective Van Zand came over yesterday afternoon and checked around to verify some of the findings. There was a bottle of Boozabuse in her medicine cabinet."

"Really?" I said.

"She must have gotten sick and decided to take a walk to get some fresh air. She would have been pretty disoriented. At some point, she passed out and fell where you found her. Asphyxia. The mud." His voice trailed off. I heard muffled sniffing noises.

I was silent for a moment, then asked if there were anything I could do to help. He said he would check with Alicia and have her call me.

Sasha and I sat at the table and talked for a while longer. After finishing her second cup of coffee, she shook her head and stretched herself. "I think I'll go home, Fae. Thanks for the coffee and the cookies." She smiled, came over to where I was sitting, and hugged me. Quite subdued but her mind seemed to have cleared. "You ought to come visit me in Berkeley sometime. I could show you around, you know. We could do something together."

"U.C. Berkeley is my alma mater. As a matter of fact, I need to go to Berkeley next week to get some books, so I'd like to take you up on your offer." I put a jacket on and walked her out to her van. It sputtered loudly as she started it. She opened the window and waved as she drove off. I watched the small tail lights disappear into the night.

Hal was in his barn sanctuary, sitting on his memento barstool, sipping a coke, the dogs at his feet.

"She gone?" he asked with a grimace. Hal didn't like being around practicing drunks or users. They made him uncomfortable, because the memories of his own struggles were still fresh. I walked up to him, and he put his free arm around me.

"She just needed to talk," I said, stealing a sip of his coke.

"I know. I thought she was never going to shut up. It was like having Lani back. In slow motion." Immediately, a guilty look appeared on his face. "I didn't mean it that way."

"Yes, you did!" I said, messing with his hair.

He smoothed it back out.

"Jason also called a little while ago." I frowned.

"Oh? What did *he* have to say?" Hal got up and turned off the lights. We walked toward the house together.

"The coroner listed Lani's death as accidental. She'd taken Boozabuse and must have drunk quite a bit of alcohol on top of that."

Hal opened the kitchen door and we went in, followed by Mab and Dooley.

"That sounds like Lani, all right," he said, shaking his head.

"No, Hal, that's what bothers me." I took my jacket off. "That does *not* sound like Lani! Not at all!" We sat down at the kitchen table.

Hal's face was filled with curiosity. "What do you mean?"

"Some months ago, Lani had a prescription for Boozabuse filled. She told me her therapist wanted her to take it."

"Well, doesn't that prove she was?" Hal asked.

"No. She laughed when she showed the bottle to me. Kind of rubbing it in to me, I guess. She shook it and said it would look great with the rest of her collection. Hal, I don't believe she had any intention of taking that stuff!"

"How do you know that for sure?"

"Because she didn't *want* to quit drinking, and she actually said she wasn't going to kill herself by taking it."

"Maybe she changed her mind?"

I was aware of his *double entendre*, but let it pass. "There is something else I just thought about. Jason said they found the Boozabuse in her bathroom. I was in her bathroom, upstairs, yesterday morning. I put something in her medicine cabinet. There were a lot of brand name over-the-counter tubes and bottles. First-aid and beauty type of stuff. I did not see any prescription bottles. The Boozabuse was not in her medicine cabinet when I looked in it. Besides, she kept all her medications and vitamins in the kitchen cabinet over the stove, with the spices."

"How do you know all this?" Hal asked.

"I noticed it when I helped Alicia look for food, for lunch."

"You're saying someone fed her the stuff unbeknownst to her?"

"Unbeknownst!"

Chapter 14

It is a damned ghost we have seen.

I called Rita early Wednesday morning to check how Sarah was doing. She said Sarah was still in a lot of pain. Rita's own agony was now completely replaced by an all-consuming rage. She gave some very graphic descriptions of what she wanted to do to the rapist, with Mike's voice sounding in the background, repeating the last few words of each sentence like a one-man chorus.

They planned to go the Sheriff's Department to find out if the perpetrator had been caught yet. Mostly, I listened and gave support for her less violent ideas, but I was more than a little worried about her and Mike when I hung up, so I called her back right away and asked if she wanted me to come along with them.

"You don't trust me?" she asked. "Fae, I won't do nothing stupid. I'm not gonna let anybody fuck ... uh ... screw up what I worked so hard for all them years." Her voice became softer. "I'm angry, OK? But I'm thinking Sarah needs me more than ever. She's had me sober all her life. Don't you worry."

Worry more! Fear whispered. She was right: I didn't trust her. I wouldn't trust myself either if I were in her shoes. "Call me when you get home," I ordered.

I sat down to read the paper. Lani's obituary was in the local section. "Died at home of natural causes," it said right after her name and age. Black on white. It had been a long time since I'd believed everything that appeared in print, but what had happened to the coroner's *accidental death*?

Alicia must have written the text. *Natural causes*, that sounded peaceful. I guessed she was right. Lani *was* found on her own property, and for an alcoholic there really is no *un*natural way to die. Anything goes: car crashes, choking, cirrhosis, drowning, falling, heart failure, murder, suicide. All are quite natural results of alcoholism.

I skimmed through the rest of the local section. Nothing about Sarah. Maybe there was something in yesterday's paper, but I didn't want to read about Sarah anyway. Words were too limiting to describe what had been done to her. I tossed the paper back on the kitchen table.

It was dark outside, a steady rain poured down from black clouds. After I fed Mab and Dooley, who looked like they'd recently visited every mud puddle around the house so that I left them on the porch, I went upstairs to work.

I had just clicked on my class-notes file, when suddenly the electricity went out and the whole house was engulfed in an almost Egyptian darkness. With presence of mind, I grabbed the flashlight out of my top desk drawer and walked downstairs to the library to call the power company from the only corded phone in the house. My dismay reached the cranky level when, instead of a real person I could vindictively hold hostage on the line for a while, a machine answered announcing it already knew about the power outage.

Since there was nothing left to do but wait, anywhere between five minutes and twenty-five hours, I decided to drive down the road and visit Janny van Zand.

The weather was quickly going from bad to worse, strong gusts of wind slamming into my car and a curtain of rain obscuring all but the next twenty feet of road. My car floated along like a boat. Essentially, I was driving on water.

From a side road, a man driving a new sedan suddenly pulled up in front of me, going about fifteen miles an hour. I slowed down until I could no longer read the "If it ain't Dutch, it ain't much!" bumper sticker.

The unpaved road to the Van Zand house was badly eroded by the recent rains, and I had to reduce my speed even more to meander safely around craterlike holes and newly erupted boulders. Under a stand of enormous live oak trees, the cows were gathered in small groups, rears in the wind, heads together as if in a stupid conspiracy.

My raincoat was drenched by the time I reached Janny's door. So much for the spray-on waterproofing. Seeing her at the stove, I went straight in without waiting for her invitation to *kom binnen!*

Janny's kitchen looked as if it had been brought over from the Old Country. Delft blue tile, depicting various rural scenes, were carefully cemented over the stove and kitchen sink. Gleaming copper pots and pans hung from racks attached to the ceiling. Large, antique wooden cookie boards, carved into shapes of women and men wearing traditional Dutch clothing, decorated the walls.

Today, however, something was off in Janny's orderly kitchen. As soon as I stepped in, I almost collided with a giant fish tank.

"Ah!" I exclaimed. "What's *this*?"

"Feng Shui," Janny explained happily.

Glaring at the slimy, unappetizing fish, I carefully walked around the tank to the enormous kitchen table. *Feng Shui*? I'd have to take note of how much great good fortune entered the Van Zand household from having guests bump into fish tanks.

Janny was stirring a pot and hadn't looked up when I entered. "How are you doing?" she asked and, as an afterthought, finally took a peek at me over her reading glasses to find out for herself.

Apparently, I wasn't doing too badly, because she immediately turned her attention to a small book sitting on a metal fold-out stand on the counter, her head tilted backward so she could see through the glasses that were precariously balanced on the tip of her nose.

Tall and stately, one could see how Janny faced life by the way she carried herself. Her short silver hair, curled loosely around her head, combined with her dark eyebrows intensified the blue of her eyes. She was in her mid-sixties, and with her classic features, she looked like a gracefully aging movie star. At first, her manner seemed a little forbidding, even gruff, but this was merely the businesslike demeanor of a woman used to running a large household of nine children and a sizable dairy farm, to boot.

"What are you making?" I asked.

"This is a bread pudding. I found it in here. My sister sent me this reprint of an old cookbook from 1761."

"How nice," I said.

"Not at all," Janny exclaimed. "My sister was always criticizing my cooking. It's been sitting on my shelf for about twenty years. It's a little difficult to read, that old print, and the language, as you know, has changed quite a bit. Twelve eggs for this. Some very strange things in this book. Why anyone would go through so much trouble to eat something as small as a pigeon is beyond me." She almost lost her glasses as she shook her head. She pushed them a little further up on the bridge of her nose, looked over them again at me and gestured at the old-fashioned, non-electric percolator standing on a crystal tea light.

"You have to excuse me. My hands are sticky. Pour yourself some coffee. Come on, go ahead. Don't be shy." She added several handfuls of raisins to the mixture in the pan. "Good thing we cook with gas. The electricity is out."

"I know." I poured myself a mug of coffee and sat back down at the table, staring down at the blue teapots embroidered on the tablecloth.

Janny looked at me over her glasses again, a longer look. "You're very quiet today. Anything wrong, Fae?" This time, she didn't turn away until I spoke.

"It's Rita's daughter, Sarah. She's in the hospital."

"What happened? She sick, poor girl?" Wiping her hands on her apron, Janny walked over to me.

I told her the awful story. "Sarah was so badly beaten, she looked so broken. What makes some people want to destroy someone else like that?" I wiped my tears away.

"Evil," Janny said somberly. "It lurks in dark corners and waits to find a willing vehicle to do its work."

Surprised, I looked up at her. "That's like saying, 'the Devil made me do it,'" I protested, even though I had thought pretty much the same thing at the hospital. "You think that man is not responsible for what he did?"

"No, I'm saying that people choose evil over good." She hesitated, walked back to the stove. "Are you keeping an eye on Rita?"

"Two eyes," I answered. Rita's pre-sobriety behavior was legendary in the area. They must have held a parade down Steen Street when she sobered up.

Janny carefully watched her bread pudding. The cozy smell of nutmeg and cinnamon mixed with the lighter scent of lemon transported me back in time, to the safety of my grandmother's kitchen. My Oma, preparing dinner, glasses fogged up, wiping a strand of silver hair from her forehead, her apron tied around her ample waist. Everything had a place inside and outside that kitchen. There was a reason for everything being as it was, so the world and its people were, if not good, at least comprehensible. Or so I believed.

"That's something else, about Lani, *niet*?" Janny suddenly said. "Tell me what happened to her? Bobby never talks to me about his work." She gave a few more powerful swirls with her wooden spoon and then turned the burner off. From a silver bin, she took a few almond-filled pastries, placed them on a crystal plate, and pushed the plate in my direction—a bribe.

I waited until she got herself some coffee and was sitting down at the table, but then I wasn't sure where to start my tale, so I took one of the pastries off the plate and began to nibble at it.

Janny drummed her fingers on the table. "Well?"

I took a second bite. This was a serious subject, after all.

She stopped her drumming and looked around as if she were losing interest and looking for something better to do.

I'd always suspected she had even less patience than I did, so I'd often given in to the temptation to try that little patience, but since character defects are much more apparent in others—it's easier to look outward than inward—my more-or-less assessments in this area were likely to be highly skewed. However, I wasn't playing games, this time, but debating if I should begin at the beginning, with my vision. I wasn't sure how she'd react to that. In all the years we'd known each other, I'd never talked about my psychic experiences, we'd never discussed our beliefs, though I knew she was a member in good standing of the Dutch Reformed Church on Wilhelmina Road. She must have her own ideas on the afterlife, and it wasn't my place to cause her to question her beliefs with talk of visions and apparitions and scents from the other side.

Leaving out all the ghostly stuff, I told Janny what had happened from Saturday night on. About finding Lani, about Steve's harassing behavior, about my visit with Lani's three children, and about the coroner's stupid conclusions, of course.

"So, someone stashed that drug in her medicine cabinet after slipping her enough to kill her." Her use of American slang sounded funny in her heavy Dutch accent. "One of her kids must have done the deed, *niet*?" She frowned as she sipped her coffee.

"I remember when Lani showed that bottle to me, and it was one of those large, dark-brown prescription bottles. I would have noticed if it had been in that cabinet, because almost everything in there was white or pink. But anyone could have left it elsewhere in the house, and then it was put in the medicine cabinet after I left." I finished my pastry, immediately thinking about seconds.

"If someone else put that bottle in there later, why didn't that person say anything about finding it?"

"Maybe *where* it was found hasn't been brought up as an issue of importance. The report just came out. Maybe someone *did* say something by now."

"You'll want to tell Bobby about this. It is a little strange, *niet?*" She picked her glasses up from the table and began cleaning them with a corner of her apron. "If there's any hanky-panky, I'm sure he would want to investigate."

"Something isn't right. She was definitely not suicidal when she drank. Although, that may be a contradiction. Then there's her children's behavior and the way they talk about her. And also what Kate told me." I related Kate's story about Lani's misadventures at the school without mentioning the disappearance of the student. "I feel as if every person is talking about a different Lani. She never behaved that way around me. She was usually generous and funny ... somewhat insecure ... rather self-centered ... really, a pain in the ass." Guilt stopped me here for a few seconds. "But certainly not mean or spiteful," I finished my evaluation as Mirth snickered, *Unlike you!*

"Well, as they say, who sows wind shall harvest storm." Janny shook her head. "She was a strange bird! She bought her eggs here, you know. Came over, last Friday. No, it must have been Thursday. Had her hair tied with ribbons into pigtails, looked like what's-her-name? Elly May Clampett from *The Beverly Hillbillies*. No string in her jeans and a lot older, of course, but I swear she even talked with that accent. 'Hi, y'all,' she said, although I was by myself.

"I just kept looking at her, but she didn't notice. She went on and on about some guy or other. Must have been that Steve Krieger you just told me about. I couldn't tie a rope to it!" Janny often literally translated Dutch sayings, this one meaning that she couldn't make any sense out of it. "She was complaining about him, so I finally asked, 'Why don't you dump the bum?' She looked at me as if I was crazy. Then she practically ran out of the hen house, jumped in her car, and drove off like the devil was at her heels. She didn't take her eggs." Janny paused to take a pastry of the plate. "I dropped them off the next morning. She seemed very surprised to see me. Wore this nice, cream-colored dress, a lot of lace around the collar and the cuffs. Hair up. High heels." With her free hand, she indicated about three inches between thumb and index finger. "In that mud! She said her eldest daughter would be visiting the next day. Insisted I come into her parlor, as she called it, for coffee and home-made cake.

"She served the coffee in antique bone china and the cake on matching plates. Gold Rose by Shelley. I recently saw some of those cups for sale. They were over a hundred dollars a piece. Drinking from that cup made me very nervous. But the cake wasn't homemade. The Van der Kamp box was right on the kitchen counter when I walked by. Anyway, I felt like the queen of England." Janny made a face like the queen of England was supposed to look, her mouth puckered forward, eyes half closed, eyebrows raised. Someone eating lemons.

I'd seen Lani in designer suits, dresses, velvet sweats, even in jeans and shirts—looking nothing like Elly May, but I'd certainly never seen her in anything lacy. Besides, she used to serve me coffee in her kitchen in mugs that said lame things such as "Bottoms Up" or "Good Morning" in ten languages. On top of all that, she once told me eggs made her break out.

I was really confused now.

It got worse when I tried to imagine Lani baking a cake. Not that she had, according to Janny. But why was she buying all those eggs? Maybe Steve ate eggs. There definitely weren't any in her refrigerator when Alicia and I looked. So, maybe Steve ate a lot of eggs. And had Alicia visited her mother on Saturday? She sure hadn't said anything about this. Hadn't she, in fact, snapped she'd only just arrived when Jason walked in with her? And Lani never mentioned it either when she came over. Or, maybe she had when I was ... not paying attention.

"You know ... " Janny suddenly looked embarrassed, a faint blush coloring her cheeks. "I don't know how to say this. You'll probably think I'm crazy, but it's almost as if Lani's here. Right here, in this kitchen. I felt it as soon as you walked in." She slapped her forehead. "Oh, I don't believe I actually said that!"

Neither did I.

I gaped at her, almost depositing a mouthful of my second-helping pastry onto her cute, teapot tablecloth. Spooked, I quickly swallowed and looked around the kitchen. I saw nothing.

Softly, almost breathlessly, Janny asked, "Do you believe in ghosts?"

Outside, lightning lit up the sky and a few seconds later a loud thunderclap shook the earth, rattling the windows. Over the sound of the wind, I heard a shrieking noise and then a gate slamming shut. The rain splashed down with renewed force.

As Janny poured us both another cup of coffee, I began to tell her all that I had left out before.

Chapter 15

And then it started like a guilty thing
upon a fearful summons.

Janny listened intently, almost continuously nodding her head, so that I began to feel slightly dizzy after a while and had to look away from her. We barely noticed it when the electricity came back on, the thunder passed into the distance. When I was finished with my story, Janny got up silently and turned the light on over the stove. It was still dark outside. Frowning, she ladled the bread pudding into a white, ceramic cooling dish.

"I haven't told anyone this, Fae, but I've been seeing things, too. The other day, I saw Lani in the hen house. Sunday, it was, the day after she died, but I didn't know yet that she was dead. I walked in and there she was, bending over, gathering eggs, it looked like. I was a bit surprised, because I'd already taken those eggs to her on Friday. I said, 'Lani?' But she didn't answer. She walked right past me out the door without looking my way. I stepped aside and could hear her dress rustle as she went by." Janny's frown got deeper. "I knew something was off when she walked right through the door. I mean, she never opened it. But I thought maybe my eyes were getting worse. Later that evening, Bobby dropped by and told me. I didn't know what to think."

I knew what *I* was thinking. "I'm not being singled out by Lani," I was thinking. Maybe Gwen had been wrong, and Lani wanted nothing from me. Maybe she'd just been making the rounds—showing off her new-and-improved celestial body. Or something. So much more to talk about when I finally got to corner Gwen.

Feeling a whole new kind of kinship with Janny, I smiled at her, but the relief I expected to come flooding through didn't arrive. I could almost hear Lani's voice, saying, "Keep dreaming, Dahling."

Janny took the pan to the sink and filled it with water to let it soak. "It's only the second time this has happened to me. The first time was when my father died, ten years ago," Janny went on. "My sister didn't bother to tell me he'd been ill for a while. She said later that she didn't want to alarm me. Alarm!" She let out a disparaging puff. "Anyway, I was reading in bed one night. Bert was asleep already, snoring. Suddenly, I looked up and there was my father, standing at the foot of the bed, smiling at me. Beaming, he looked so happy. I was really glad to see him. Then he turned around and walked out." Janny's eyes were wet. "It finally hit me that he was in Holland and couldn't be standing in my bedroom.

"I tried to tell myself that I'd been dreaming, but it wasn't a dream. I was wide awake. I went downstairs to the kitchen to heat up some milk. I was sitting there, drinking my milk, when the phone rang. It was my sister. She said our Papa had just died. I told her I already knew, that he had come to say 'goodbye.' My sister began to cry. I think she was a little jealous." She chuckled as she sat down at the table again. "Silly. You'd think she would have been happy Papa had come to let us know he was all right, *niet*?"

Maybe that's all it was with Lani. She was just coming around to let me know she was doing all right. No, that didn't sound true either.

"But this, with Lani. I don't like this very much, Fae," Janny sighed. "I like to hear a ghost story, just like anyone, for fun. But this is real, and it doesn't feel right somehow." She hesitated. "Why would Lani come to me? I didn't know her all that well. I sold her cheese and eggs, for Pete's sake!"

"I'm not sure what's going on." Truer words had never passed my lips.

"Why *me*?" she asked belligerently. "Doesn't make a lot of sense, *niet*? And why *you*, for that matter? Well, maybe that *does* make sense, because she wouldn't stop bugging you when she was alive either."

I wished she hadn't said that. "Maybe it's just because we are able to see her. Gwen says I am somehow accessible to her. I guess you are, too." I needed Janny's company in this.

"Who's Gwen?" Janny asked wearily.

I told her about Gwen Blackwaters.

"So, she's some kind of psychic then, *niet*?"

"Yes. She calls herself a 'sensitive.' She says all human beings have these abilities, but some of us are just more tuned in to them than others." I paused for a moment, thinking about Gwen's analogy of playing Chopin to perfection. "Most people have only a mild ability and call it intuition. Then, you have people like Gwen."

"That must be really awful!" Janny exclaimed. "I'm already running around like a chicken without its head. I can't imagine how that would feel."

"I don't think Gwen feels about it that way. It's just part of her reality. I'm trying to learn more about it, how to use it. If our brains work differently, allowing us to travel through time, space, and different dimensions, maybe dying is nothing more than moving on to a different dimension. If all matter is energy, then maybe we're just changing to a different level of vibration, and those who are psychic have access to this dimension, can tune in to that vibration."

"It's not that I don't believe you. It's just that, well, I guess I don't want it to be that way. It's all too complicated. Dimensions and vibrations and energy. It's so scientific." She swept some pastry flakes together on the table. "When I was a child they told me that when you die, you go to heaven, and that was it. Simple." Janny laughed. "That was easier to believe when I was little. Now, I go to church and sing and listen to the sermons, but I wish I could put it all together, so it would make sense. Things do have to make sense, *niet*?"

"I guess that's what I want most also. Put together my experiences and find out what rules we're living under, what is real, and what rules people have just made up over the ages for one reason or another." I got up and took my raincoat off the rack. It was still heavy with water.

"You want to borrow a poncho? I have a plastic one."

"Don't you need it?"

"No, I have several. I buy one each time I go to Holland. Keep forgetting how much it rains there." She handed me a lilac poncho with a large hood. "Just bring it back whenever."

I slipped my head in and pulled it over my shoulders.

"Double, double toil and trouble!" She pulled the back of the poncho over my rear end. Then she took a paper bag out of a drawer, stuffed a few pastries in it, and handed it to me. "Here!" she said.

As I walked back over to the table to get my purse, a car drove up outside. Janny glanced out the window. "Ah, there is Bobby now. You can talk to him!"

I was standing behind the fish tank when Bobby entered. He looked through the water at me. "Mom?" But then he saw Janny. "Mom!"

I felt the blood drain from my face. My stomach began to churn. *Sarah.*

Bobby had barely gotten through the door when Janny accosted him. "Fae needs to talk to you. She thinks Lani was murdered. You sit down and listen to her. You want some coffee?" He said he did and sat down.

After wiping his hand over his face as if to wake himself up, Bobby looked at me with a tired expression. "What's that, Fae? Do you have some new information?" he asked, over-enunciating each word.

I decided to ignore his attitude. "Well, something doesn't make sense," I said carefully.

"Oh?" Bobby raised his eyebrows. Someone should tell him his face would stay that way forever if the clock struck twelve.

"Do you want to hear what she has to say, or do you want to keep interrupting?" Janny put the mug in front of him a little too firmly, and part of the coffee spilled over on the tablecloth.

"I'm sorry! I was up half the night. OK, spill the beans, Fae. What is it?"

Spill the beans? Had he actually said "spill the beans?" What was next? *Just the facts, Ma'am?* Oh, well, anyway. I sat down across from him.

Now that I finally had his undivided attention, I told him about the Boozabuse. My story suddenly sounded rambling and disconnected, even to me.

When I was finished, Bobby stared at me for a few seconds, his hand in his hair as if he were holding a hat down in a hard wind. "And that's it?" he said, looking from me to his mother and back to me again.

"What do you mean 'That's it?'" Janny scolded. "Doesn't this tell you that someone else must have slipped her the stuff? Don't you see that someone pinched the cat in the dark?" She shook her head, amazed at her son's stupidity.

He didn't even wince at his mother's saying but translated it easily. "That someone got away with something? Not really! It tells me that someone picked up around the house, and about time, too. It's simple. She had a prescription filled a few months ago. We've checked. She used half the bottle."

"Half the bottle?" I exclaimed.

"Yes, we counted the pills. Half the prescription was used up. Why?" Bobby yawned, covering his mouth with his hand.

"Bobby, she never quit drinking. She drank like a fish. Why would she take those pills? That makes you extremely ill. She knew that! And if she did this on purpose, why did she go for a walk in the orchard? Why didn't she go to bed?"

"Who knows?" Bobby raised his eyebrows. "Lani did a lot of things that never made sense to normal people." He opened his mouth again as if he were going to say something else, but then he inhaled sharply, closed his mouth, and looked away.

I could tell Bobby had made up his mind to ignore what I had just told him, so I got up to leave. I huffed and puffed.

"OK, OK! I'll look into it," he grumbled as if he were doing me a favor. "You may have something there," he added reluctantly, and to Janny, "Do you have a sandwich with this coffee, Mom? I'm starved!"

"I would be too if my refrigerator was as empty as yours. Not that she should make your sandwiches, but why don't you and Kate get married?"

"Mom? We've only been dating for a couple of months!"

"Five months," I muttered as I opened the door, "and six days!"

I was still in a dark mood when I entered my kitchen. There was a message from Hal on the answering machine.

"Hey, Babe? You want to go out for dinner and a movie tonight? Why don't you call Kate? See if she and Bobby want to join us. Love ya!"

I called Kate at work. She said she'd get a hold of Bobby and call me back. Good, I thought, I don't want to talk to him for a while. I told her I'd talked to him at Janny's, but I didn't tell her about his lousy attitude and how he truly believed they'd only been dating two months.

I went upstairs to start the work I'd meant to be finished with that morning. I had made a list of plays to discuss and had luckily found my old notes on some of them, so I'd been able to go ahead and was almost done typing the class outline. All I'd need to do then was flesh out my rescued notes and write some fresh material for the plays I didn't have anything on.

It was nearly noon when I turned on the computer. After sitting through the usual rigmarole of being informed that the computer had not been properly shut off, I opened my Shakespeare class-outline document and stared at the screen in disbelief.

Except for the title, the first page was completely blank. And there was no longer a second or third page. Even a blackout would only have erased the last unsaved additions on page three, not the whole freaking document but the title. And wasn't this thing supposed to have a salvage feature in case of a power failure? I seemed to remember that it usually offered me the last saved version of whatever document I'd been working on when the juice was cut off.

I checked in a number of folders but found nothing remotely resembling my Shakespeare outline. All I had was a title. Disgusted, I pulled the manila folder to get the hardcopy, but it only contained the first page. I spent the rest of the afternoon in an absolutely foul temper, reconstructing and retyping my notes.

Hal came home before five o'clock in an annoying top-o'-the-morning mood. He sang several songs in the shower. "And if you're downright disgusted, and life ain't worth a dime, get a girl with far-away eyes." When he came out, dripping wet, he took me in his arms and made me dance a few steps around the bedroom. "Please allow me to introduce myself, I'm a man of wealth and taste ... "

I was just getting some sympathy for my Devil, when Kate's call interrupted our little party. She and Bobby would be joining us at the restaurant at about six thirty. And, by the way, what restaurant were they supposed to be joining us at?

I asked Hal. He said I should decide, as long he got to eat food, he didn't care. I didn't either, so I told Kate to choose. She wondered what Bobby would like. *Who cares what Bobby likes?* I was still a bit miffed at him. Ah! We had it: The Hungry Hungarian! Soft candle-light, twirling happy-sad violin music, and brightly embroidered costumes. A little romance for the lovers.

I told Hal of our choice. "No Hard Rock Café?" he said.

I slapped him with his towel. He grabbed it away from me and chased me down the stairs. Butt naked.

✻✻✻

Kate and Bobby were standing in front of the restaurant when we arrived, sharing an umbrella. Kate in love, animated, eyes sparkling. Bobby looking somewhat sheepish. The same way Hal had looked when we went on our first few dates, if one could call those drunken escapades *dates*.

The men took our coats and handed them to the nice hatcheck lady who was dressed in traditional costume, except that her very large bosom was exposed a bit more than was traditional. Quite a bit more, especially when she bent over to give Hal the tickets. He and Bobby looked confused, disoriented even. I thought they'd need a guide dog to find their way through the restaurant.

"What pretty eyes that girl has," Kate remarked, giving me a knowing glance, as we walked toward a comfortable booth. Hal and Bobby gave each other a blank look. They hadn't noticed the hatcheck lady's eyes. I bit my lip, thinking how funny men were when it came to mammary glands.

We argued amiably about what was good on the menu as if we all had to choose the same item. With relief, we finally figured out we could each make our own choice and did so, our waitress patiently waiting with a smile on her face. Within twenty minutes, she sashayed over to us, carrying large platters stacked with steaming food.

As the waitress placed the platters on our table, I felt a post-war-European guilt trip coming on. Due to the famine of what the Dutch called the Hunger Winter of 1944, we were taught to waste not, want not. We never put more on our plate than we could eat, and we always ate everything on our plate. American restaurants, with all those piles of food, were still giving me culture shock. I'd feel guilty if I finished it, and I'd feel guilty if I left some.

Squirming in my seat, I tried to get my breathing under control by looking around the restaurant, away from the mountains of food, at the booths on the opposite wall.

In one of them sat a tall man classically dressed in a blue blazer and gray flannel pants. He was fully engrossed in reading the menu. Across from him sat Jason.

I wanted to wave to get Jason's attention, but just then Hal moved forward and blocked my view.

All I could see were two male hands on the table, touching.

"Isn't that Jason across from us?" Bobby asked, gesturing with his fork.

"Huh?" I looked the wrong way.

"There, right across from us! With that guy. I think I know him, too. He's a lawyer. Dean Cooper, that's his name." Bobby kept waving his fork.

Kate had her work cut out for her. "Jason?" she asked.

"Lani's son. Remember?" I kicked her under the table. "Let's order dessert!"

"Good idea!" Kate went along, because I kicked her again.

"Why?" Bobby wanted to know. "We've barely started dinner. Will they run out?"

If he didn't stop waving his fork around, he'd poke someone's eye out. I'd tell on him next time I'd see Janny, if Kate wasn't going to do something about it.

I kicked Kate again. She didn't react.

"He doesn't look too distraught," Hal remarked.

"You wouldn't either if you had a mother like Lani!" Bobby retorted.

"Bobby!" Kate gave him a scolding look.

Yes, get to work Kate! "Has anyone heard the weather forecast?" I put an enormous forkful of goulash in my mouth. I had to clean my plate.

All three of my companions stared at me for a moment and then said in unison, "Rain!"

On our way over to the theater, Hal asked, "So, what was that all about?"

"What do you mean?"

"You kept kicking Kate under the table. Actually, you missed once and kicked me."

"Oh? Did I hurt you?"

"Let's say it felt good when you stopped. Was it about Jason's boyfriend?" He smiled and looked at me.

"I just didn't want to embarrass him," I said, looking away, out of the window.

"How do you know he would be embarrassed?"

"Maybe that isn't the right word. I have a feeling he doesn't want people here to know. I'm not sure why." I shrugged.

We went to the Play it Again Theater on Tokay Boulevard. It had recently been restored to its old glory with burgundy velvet-covered seats that allowed you to lean back without landing on a neighbor's lap, a giant, crystal chandelier suspended from an elaborately sculpted ceiling, and walls painted with enormous portraits of movie greats such as Harlow, Gable, and Hayworth. Ushers dressed in royal-blue organ-monkey suits led us to our seat and wished us a pleasant evening.

Kate and I spent some time in the ladies' room, checking out women's fashions and signaling each other our Mr. Blackwells with meaningful glances in the ornate mirrors.

About three-quarters through the movie, I realized I'd seen the film before. But, I didn't remember the ending until it came, and on the way home, I'd already forgotten the title, so I could probably go see the movie again in a couple of years. There are some distinct benefits in having been a drunk. Once you're sober, that is.

The phone was ringing when we walked into the kitchen. Hal picked up, listened for a moment, said "Uh-huh," then held the phone out to me.

It was Rita. "I know it's late, but I promised to call you and you weren't home earlier, but something happened so I thought I better call you," she said, all in one breath.

"Did you go to the Sheriff's Department?" I asked.

"Yeah. It was real bad." She paused. I could hear her drag on her cigar and exhale. "They tole us they didn't have any leads yet. Didn't know who done it. They're gathering evidence, they said. So Mike said they weren't doing their job and they said they're doing their best and Mike start yelling and screaming they don't care and they tole him to calm down but he wouldn't he was so mad." She took a deep breath. "Two cops came up and started to make him sit down and then Mike got really mad and punched one in the nose and they grabbed him and he began crying so they let him go 'cause he cried so hard."

"Oh, shit!" I said.

Hal gave me an alarmed look. "It's Mike. He's very upset," I whispered.

"He was crazy, Mike. He don't talk to me, Fae. He just sets around. Been staring all day, sees nothing. Didn't go to see Sarah all day." Rita was crying now. "I wanna kill him! I hate his guts!" She yelled.

For a moment I thought she meant Mike. "Rita!"

"I'll kill him! I wanna know who did this and kill the bastard. Oh, God, this is shit! Shit!" she loudly blew her nose and muttered, "Oh, damn shit."

"Do you want me to come over?"

"No, it's too late. I'll get Mike into bed. At least he's not drinking. That would be a bigger mess." She exhaled again. She sounded like a large valve releasing pressure. "I'll let you go," she decided suddenly.

"Why don't you come over tomorrow morning?"

"No, I'm going over to the hospital. And Lani's funeral's at two, you know." She noisily puffed on her cigar. "I got to get ready. Get something to wear."

"Well, call me if you need to talk. Or just come over, if you change your mind. I'll be home."

"Thanks, Fae. I'll be OK." She hung up abruptly.

I stared at the phone. Hal pried it out of my hand and placed it back on the stand. I looked at him, hoping he'd have something comforting to say. Something that would make sense.

He put his arm around my waist and guided me outside, to the back porch. We sat down on the steps and quietly watched the stars.

Chapter 16

Do you think I am easier to be played on than a pipe?

On the morning of Lani's funeral the sun was out, but a sharp north-western wind blew away what little warmth this brought. Enormous cumulonimbus clouds cast fast-moving shadows on the land, creating an eerie play of light and dark.

Hal was already whistling in the bathroom when I woke up. *Rule Britannia?* He walked in straightening a tie. I didn't know he owned a tie. I thought he had donated all his ties to charity when he bought his bike. He was also wearing a light blue shirt I didn't recognize.

A smile appeared on his face when he noticed my eyes were open. "You awake?"

I took this to be one of those rhetorical questions and merely groaned. Hal had a way of waking me up in the morning by making loud noises—be it by banging pots and pans around in the kitchen or, like today, by whistling—and then acting very surprised when he'd succeeded in ripping me out of the soothing arms of sleep. I glared at him, annoyed by his smile and his energetic demeanor so early in the day. I opened my mouth to say something caustic, but all that came out was a croaking sound.

"I've got some coffee ready." He leaned over and kissed my nose. He grinned. I must look funny. I grabbed his tie and pulled at it to haul myself up, but he pried my hands loose and stepped away from the bed, laughing.

"Where'd you get that tie?" I asked with one eye closed. It was one of those extremely boring ones, dark blue with burgundy, thin, diagonal stripes. Not that I'd ever seen an exciting tie.

"Found it in my closet. Bought it when Grace got married. You like it?"

He was so obviously pleased that I decided to be supportive. "It's very ... appropriate." I nodded slowly to show my approval. *Appropriate* and its opposite *inappropriate* were indispensable words when I was an elementary school teacher. They covered a lot of ground between them, though many more situations called for the use of the negative form, as in "Michael, it is *inappropriate* to call your teacher a *bitch*."

Hal looked down at his tie and smoothed out the wrinkles I'd just made.

"You think so, huh?" He walked over to my vanity desk to admire himself, a tentative look on his face. I rolled my eyes at him behind his back, and he caught my expression in the mirror.

"What's wrong? Don't you like it?"

He was sounding like Lani and her hair. "Hal, what's there to like? It's a *tie*! You're going to a funeral!"

That seemed to make sense to him, because after a moment of hesitation he began to hum and sauntered downstairs.

"Besides, it's your *only* tie!" I called after him. How could anybody have only one of any piece of clothing? Well, it was just a decorative noose.

The phone was ringing when I stepped into the shower, and when I walked into the kitchen some time later, Hal smirkingly greeted me with the message that Matchett had called.

Matchett, that was *Doctor* Hilda Matchett, Head of the English Department, Fear of the Faculty, Student Scourge, wanted me to return her call, of course. Whatever she was up to now, I was sure it would cost me.

Matchett was able to turn even our most accomplished students into seeming incompetents. She wrote more on their papers than they did, and all that red ink had the power to erode canyons in their self-esteem. I must say that her ten-page syllabi, filled with her minutely detailed demands and expectations, written in the tone of a ransom note, should tip students off. If they weren't smart enough to race for their drop forms after reading her outline, perhaps a semester of excruciating academic torture was just the illuminating learning experience they needed. Nevertheless, it was a good thing our buildings were all single story.

A little woman with the face of a rhesus monkey, her round eyes darting every which way, Matchett always looked as if she were ready to pounce. Inseparable from her probably real pearls and perfect Chanel suits, she was dressed to contradict, criticize, and control. I'd often been tempted to direct her to the netherworld, but her marital ties to the dean, Dr. Perry Matchett, who except for a fully developed beard looked like her identical twin, had prevented me from doing so out loud.

Maybe I had lost her phone number. No, Hal had written it down, just in case.

She picked up on the first ring. "Doctor Matchett!" she said like someone who knew what and who she was.

For a split second, I considered hanging up and making it a crank call, but I was sure she had a caller ID.

"This is Fae Nelson, Hilda." Screw titles. I knew she had hers printed on her return address labels. I still find it strange when people call themselves *doctor* without being able to cure a thing.

"Oh, yes, Fae. I called to let you know that I am scheduling you to teach this fall's Early Twentieth-century Writers course."

My morale plummeted to previously unknown depths. I made a face at the telephone.

"You are unequivocally the best qualified teacher for this course, since you are one of our most experienced faculty members."

Unequivocally qualified? No sense equivocating then, moreover because I hadn't been asked, I'd been informed. There was no bush for me to beat around. Her praise for my teaching talents would have been a compliment had it not been that our tiny college simply had no other faculty member in its teeny-weeny English Department who had taught more than three years, anywhere.

"I have some excellent notes you may want to look at," she said with great enthusiasm, apparently taking my astonished silence for an inability to express a deep feeling of gratitude.

I'm sure you do! She damned well knew I just wanted to teach Shakespeare and the drama course. Early-twentieth-century writers being her love, this woman simply refused to accept that there were English teachers who weren't thrilled at the prospect of poring over the novels produced during that time period. I was one of them.

I cursed. "*Gadverdamme!*"

Evidently, not as deeply under my breath as I had meant to do, for she asked with some confusion, "What did you say?"

"Jean-Claude van Damme," I said quickly.

"Well, I've never heard of him, but you can add him to the list. Although there is a required core group of writers, of course," she said.

Jean-Claude would be ecstatic to hear he'd been promoted from "Muscles from Brussels" to literary great. And I knew who was in that core group.

I truly wasn't feeling like myself when I coughed loudly into the telephone. I hoped it hurt.

"Are you all right?" As usual, she didn't wait for an answer. "I'm almost done setting up our fall schedule." *She would be, at the beginning of February.* "Well, we'll see each other next week and shall discuss this more thoroughly. Take care!" She hung up.

I mumbled at the dead phone for her to do the same, furious that I had not stood up for myself and now felt like the victim of a hit-and-run.

Hal still had a smirk on his face. He appeared to enjoy my battles with Matchett. "What did Matchett the Hatchet want, Honey?" he asked with false concern. He had met Matchett a few times at our faculty Christmas parties, but it had only taken him one encounter to assign her the nickname.

I glared at him. "She wants me to teach twentieth-century writers."

The smirk was replaced by a blank look. If it didn't concern extraterrestrial beings landing on top of Bigfoot in the Bermuda Triangle, one book was pretty much the same as the next to Hal. Unless it was Tom Clancy. "What's so terrible about that?" Honest curiosity in his voice.

"It's a horribly depressing group of writers. You need guides to get through some of those books. In fact, there *are* guides for some of those books."

"You mean you don't like their writing?"

"Not like? *Hate!*" I needed to rant a little longer. "I know she wants me to top the course off with Joyce's *Ulysses!*" I slammed my cup of coffee down. "It's a 650-page nebulous crossword puzzle. So contrived. When I took the course as a requirement for my degree, we had to count how many times Joyce used the word *blue* in one chapter, and the final chapter is one excruciatingly long run-on sentence. We spent fifteen precious hours on that last chapter and the significance of the lack of male punctuation. What's so male about punctuation? Something worn-out Freudian."

Hal was laughing at me.

"You just don't understand how traumatic that course was," I whined. "No wonder they all killed themselves."

"They did?"

"Some of them. Virginia Woolf did."

"So, you're afraid of Virginia Woolf?"

"Oh, that's so funny!"

"Can't you just tell her you don't want to do it?"

Ah, there was Hal's logic! I stared at him, incredulous.

"Well?" he queried, staring straight back at me.

I looked down at my hands. *God bless his simple mind!* I took a big gulp of my coffee to stall him. Without looking up, I muttered, "I don't know." I didn't want to admit that he might have hit on a solution. It was too simple, too easy. There had to be a glitch. "You mean, just say 'I don't want to teach the damned course?'" I finally asked, because he kept staring at me.

"Well, not quite like that. Maybe you could tell her that she is far more qualified than you are, or something to that extent." He picked up the paper, lifting it so I could no longer see his face, and perused the front page.

I knew he was snickering behind his paper. It shook slightly. "You don't need to be qualified, just crazy." But it felt as if a load was sliding off my back. Maybe there was a way out. Now, all I had to do was find the right way to just say *no*.

It didn't occur to me until I was sitting behind my desk—doing some more moping, and thinking I should talk to Kate who clearly had a way with words, judging by how she'd dealt with Lani—that there were far worse things than teaching a baleful course that could happen to me, that my problems were miniscule compared to those of others. After all, I was about to attend the funeral of one of them. How could just one little incident, one thing some person said or did, throw me in such an ego-driven state of fear? I decided to put the fall schedule out of my mind for the time being and to concentrate on this coming semester's course material. I would get to work and focus on the here and now.

For the next twenty minutes, I watched Mellow who had followed me upstairs and was standing with his front paws on the arm of my old stuffed chair, gazing out the window at some birds, bleating like a sheep at them, his pink mouth opening and closing with little jerks.

The hours dragged on as I finished the third and final page of my Shakespeare syllabus and organized the old notes I'd found. There were notes for about half the plays, so that was good, but they were only on hard copy. I didn't have to be psychic to know there was yet more typing in my future.

All along, I heard Hal puttering in the kitchen, cooking a late breakfast. Maybe cleaning out the fridge. He had taken the day off. The smell of bacon made me hungry, but I didn't want to go downstairs, because it was already difficult enough to concentrate, and several times I found myself staring at Mellow—the here and now—but thinking about Matchett—the future. That spoiled inner child of mine kept whining in the background. Just wouldn't shut up.

At noon, Hal came upstairs carrying a tray with two glasses of milk and a plate of Janny's oatmeal cookies. "Let's call this *lunch*," he said. He put the tray on my desk and shooed the sleeping Mellow out of the armchair. "So, how's your investigation going?" he asked as he sat down with his glass of milk and two enormous cookies. He grinned at the look of surprise that appeared on my face. "You thought I didn't know?"

"I told Bobby about the Boozabuse. He promised to look into it," I said, stuffing my mouth full. "And I'm not the only one who thinks something's rotten in the state of Denmark. Both Janny and Kate believe there's been some hanky-panky."

"My baby does the hanky-panky," Hal sang. There was a decidedly goofy side to Hal, but he couldn't sing worth shit.

I rolled my eyes. "I've been thinking about the behavior of her kids, how unaffected they seem. Maybe they're going a bit through the same experience I had right after my mother died. Suddenly, I was existing on a whole different level. Being—in absolute peace."

"You mean you were in a state of shock," Hal commented.

"Call it what you want, but it wasn't a feeling of being dazed and confused. On the contrary, I had a deep sense of heightened awareness. The sensation of being super aware, of being *in* total awareness. I was one with all and everyone. My separating ego was gone, suspended. When I'd look at other people, I saw their whole beings and knew we were all one, all connected. I had no feelings of judgment. There was only love. Everyone and everything existed in this love.

"On the second day, I realized this state of being wasn't to be permanent, because I was in a physical body and would return to the material level of things, the emotional and mental part of life on earth. It lasted three days."

"Couldn't it have been just chemicals running through your brain, making you feel that way?" Hal asked.

"Well, yes, but why would this have to be an either-or situation? Chemicals zapping the brain doesn't mean something spiritual isn't going on. The spiritual manifests itself on the physical plane by means of physical mechanics, according to the laws of the material world. You know what I believe?"

"What?"

"I believe that during those three days, I entered the Kingdom of God that is within—or at the very least got a preview of it."

"It sounds more like you were high on something."

I laughed. "You've been looking too much through your microscope."

"You mean my view is skewed, because I'm not seeing things the way you do?" he asked good-naturedly.

"No, we're just experiencing different things, or the same things in different ways."

We were both quiet for a few minutes, thinking our own thoughts, munching on cookies and finishing our milk. Hal took the tray downstairs.

Back in the physical world, physical Fae needed to get dressed and dove into her walk-in closet, accompanied by the nosy Mellow. I picked out a demure, navy woolen dress—dark but not black, which should rightfully be reserved for family—and an aubergine silk scarf that would match Hal's tie in appropriateness.

Thunderclouds building up in the sky prompted me to search for my blue leather boots. I finally found them at the bottom of the large heap of shoes that kept getting higher. Anyone who'd volunteer to walk a mile in my shoes would first have to figure out which shoes to choose.

I was still fiddling with the obligatory scarf, tying it this way and that, when Hal came up to get his blazer and raincoat. He went into his closet and came out wanting to know what I'd done with his hat. I thought he meant the ugly black one I'd knitted years ago, quite drunk, and which I'd pushed to the bottom of the garbage can the week before so he wouldn't be able to find it and salvage it again. I wondered why he wanted to wear a knit hat to a funeral. But he meant his tan fedora, of course, whose whereabouts I had no knowledge of.

"You must have put it somewhere," he said.

I was just about to pronounce my innocence in this particular hat matter, when the subject came flying out of the closet, touched ground, and then rolled to the center of the room to finally come to a halt near the foot of the bed.

I stared at the hat.

Hal walked over and gingerly picked it up. He looked from the hat to the closet, shook his head, and closed the closet door. Frowning, he slapped the fedora against his leg a few times to get the dust off.

In the mirror, I raised my eyebrows. "Was that a very localized indoor tornado?" I pressed my lips together to distribute the lipstick.

He looked at his watch. "Are you almost done? It's after one." As if nothing had happened.

"Yes, Dear! Just finishing my mascara and getting some earrings." I fluttered my wet eyelashes and smiled sweetly at him in the mirror.

Hal shrugged and went downstairs, still slapping his flying fedora against his leg.

I quickly cleaned off the smears of mascara below my eyes with some spit. I seemed to have this instant Karma thing. Whatever I did came back like a boomerang. Perhaps Hal was right and it would be better to ignore some of the goings-on in our house. Being ignored might make Lani go away. It was strange getting ready for her funeral when I could feel her presence all around me.

As Hal and I entered the First Dutch Reformed Church, the first loud clap of thunder drowned out the organ music.

Chapter 17

And flights of angels sing thee to thy rest!

"So glad you could come, Fae!" Alicia's eyes were shielded by the stiff black veil of an elegant pill box hat. Her copper hair was pulled back and sculpted into a severe doughnut-shaped bun at the nape of her neck. She wore a tight, long-sleeved, black dress with fluted skirt. A subtle border of lace accentuated the beauty of her long neck. Holding both my hands in hers, she leaned over to plant a silent, symbolic kiss in the air near each of my cheeks.

"So glad!" she shouted in my ear over the thunder and organ music, and then she turned to my consort. Offering him her hand as if to be kissed, she proclaimed, "This must be Hal."

Hal, not quite sure what he was expected to do with Alicia's proffered hand, held it in midair for a few moments while confirming that he indeed must be who he was. He then bent his head towards her, but Alicia refrained from air-kissing him, a favor bestowed on female guests only.

I suppressed an urge to poke him hard in the ribs.

As soon as we had stepped over the threshold, I'd become painfully aware of the open, mahogany casket at the foot of the podium. Lani was laid out surrounded by white satin, wearing the same red dress she had on in my beach dream, which startled me even more. A wreath of white roses was placed on her chest below her folded hands, and red roses were arranged around her head with the frizzy hairdo she'd come to show off less than a week ago. It all seemed quite improperly festive with all that red, and it made her look—thanks also to the expert make-up job—better dead than alive, I was sad to notice.

The three siblings were lined up at the right front pew. Blue-blazered Jason in the center with a serene smile on his face. Sasha, at the end, wearing an array of dark browns and purples of multi-layered India cotton that completely disguised her figure. She wore her hair down, covering the shaved sides of her head, and she had removed her nose and eyebrow rings as well as most of her earrings for this solemn occasion.

Jason's eyes met mine as he thanked me for my condolences, but his mind seemed to be somewhere else, outside this old brick church.

"Hi, Fae!" Sasha giggled nervously.

Alicia glanced over and gave her younger sister a reproving look. Instantly, Sasha straightened her face. Then, impulsively, she bent over and whispered in my ear, "What a circus!" Her face turned away from Alicia's piercing eyes, she winked at me repeatedly as if we were both in on the same joke.

I smiled indulgently, figuring she must be suffering from the same nervous hilarity I'd been overcome with when Bobby was questioning me.

I followed Hal around the front pews to the third row, and we sat down in the center of the long bench. I was careful not to look over at Lani's body again.

I had hoped she wouldn't be on display, a custom I'd always found distasteful and rather rude toward the deceased, since people tended to stare. It seemed an invasion of privacy after death. Strange this preoccupation with the husk of our being, of the flesh after it has failed us.

Hal sighed perceptibly as he seated himself beside me. The Verhoog sisters both turned around and gave us their twin Margaret Rutherford smiles. As we smiled back, it struck me how our funeral smiles were different from regular smiles, how they were only meant to acknowledge someone's presence and convey our sadness that we had to be there.

I'd never be able to tell Sam Verhoog's maiden aunts apart. He had told me several times in what way they were different, but I kept forgetting which feature went with which sister. Since they either spoke in unison or finished each other's sentences, Agnes and Albertina were usually addressed as a single human unit.

They had come to California with their much younger brother, Sam's father, over half a century ago, to find husbands that never materialized. Sam said they didn't look too hard, because they really preferred each other's company over anyone else's and couldn't bear to be separated even for a few hours.

"She looks very good," Agnes or Albertina said, and without missing a beat the other half added, "doesn't she?" Two pair of kind, gray eyes looked at me, waiting for an answer.

It took me a moment to realize they meant Lani. Hal devoutly bent his head as if in prayer, his hands turning his hat around in his lap. My dilemma about what to say in response was solved when the sister on my right continued with, "You look very good, too, Fae," which caused Hal to become even more devout.

"Thank you." I gently patted the hand she had laid on the back of the pew.

"She looks very life-like, doesn't she?" Miss Verhoog on my left said.

"It's the rouge, Agnes! The rouge!" What must be Albertina shook her head at Agnes's gullibility. Agnes did look a little confused. They both turned around again and gazed over at the casket. For the next hour or so, I would know who was who.

"But what did they do to her hair?" I heard Albertina disapprovingly ask her sister.

I thought to enlighten them, leaned forward, and raising my voice to be heard over the music, I shouted, "She did it herself!" Just as I opened my mouth, the organ stopped playing and since we were between thunder claps, my words could be heard loud and clear throughout the whole church.

People stared at me, including the Reverend Cecil Ravenstein who had ascended the podium and now stood behind his lectern, waiting for the mourners to be seated so he could begin the service. My face flushed to what I was sure was a deep, guilty crimson.

Hal straightened himself in his seat and, biting his lip, put his arm around me to show his moral support. I sank down deep into the pew, wanting desperately to be beamed up.

With his free hand, Hal handed me a program, printed for the occasion, just like in the opera. I began to study it as if my sanity depended on it.

I recognized the songs. I'd learned them as a child, and we'd often sung them in my grandparents' church, Oma playing the organ, trying to keep up with the fast-singing congregation, Opa out of key, especially after he'd lost his hearing. Opa always carried a roll of King peppermints that were about the size of a quarter, and he would hand us kids one at regular intervals to keep us quiet during the infernally long sermons. These were the songs about the god of my childhood.

When I finally dared look up again, our pew had filled up. I looked around and found to my surprise that the church was packed. A few people were still standing in the shadows in the back, near the heavy, oak double doors. I had no idea that so many people had known Lani, that so many even lived in and around Londen. In one row I spotted Ben and Sandra Dijkstra, Pete and Patricia van Nuys, and Paul and Ellen Smit, all representing the local merchants. Behind them, Kate was flanked by Rita and Bobby, who was sitting next his parents, Bert and Janny van Zant. In the front pew, to the left of Lani's children, nearest the casket, was Willem de Weder. His hand holding the program was shaking.

After a brief silence, the gathering spontaneously combusted into "A Mighty Fortress Is Our God." I picked up the hymnal from the rack in front of me, found the text, and sang along.

Two deacons, dressed in black, carefully lowered the lid of Lani's casket. One of them apparently got his fingers caught: he winced and shook his hand in pain.

My initial relief at the closing of the casket was immediately followed by a sudden panic. Irrational thoughts of Lani suffering from claustrophobia or suffocating or that maybe a mistake had been made and she wasn't really dead scurried through my mind.

I wondered why this seemed to happen every time I was at a funeral. Was it that the finality of death was incomprehensible? But my fears weren't all that far-fetched, because people being buried alive was not just a plot of some horror movie, considering they used to put bells on the caskets so that the not-dead-after-all persons upon awakening could pull the bell and be dug up. Maybe that's why they left a casket open, so everyone could see for themselves the person was truly dead.

But why then would they go through such lengths to make the person so "life-like," as Agnes Verhoog had just said about Lani's body? What was the point? That she wasn't dead? That she was at peace? It made it so much more difficult to remember that it wasn't Lani's essence in there but merely her mortal coil. I, of all people, should know Lani wasn't shut in that coffin. After all, she'd been hanging around my barn and pulling pranks in my kitchen.

When I woke up, I was enthusiastically singing "Abide With Me" with the rest of the congregation. Hal, on the other hand, was only mouthing the words, and when we got to "I need Thy presence every passing hour," I distinctly heard him sing "la-lala-la-la-lala-lalala." Church-lady Fae moved her hymnal in front of him and pointedly pointed at the text.

After a generic prayer, delivered in monotone, the Reverend Ravenstein gave a short sermon that clearly showed how little idea he had whom he was talking about. The only thing he got right was the French pronunciation of Lani's last name: pô ′shär. Although, Willem kept nodding his agreement between loud sobs.

I began to feel increasingly uncomfortable as Ravenstein talked Lani into his heaven. "We know that Lani loved the Lord! She is not lost!" he asserted.

Hal looked at me, his eyebrows raised. I indicated that I also had no idea where the good Reverend had gotten his information.

While Ravenstein's voice droned on, I began to look around. Getting lost again in my own thoughts, I could almost taste Opa's peppermint on my tongue. The church was a faithful copy of the ones sprinkled all over the northern part of the Netherlands. Dark-red brick with high-placed gothic windows, the only concession to worldly beauty the colorful, stained glass. But, no images in the glass. No statues or carvings. No crosses. No Jesus with his arms spread out. No angels bringing good tidings, and—certainly—no comforting Mother Mary. When the northern Europeans renounced the Catholic Church, they also renounced its show of wealth and beauty depicted in these graven images. Irate iconoclasts stormed into the Roman Catholic churches and destroyed the paintings, statues, and altars that had for centuries been the subject of dissension. There was nothing to destroy here. Austerity had found its home. *A mighty fortress is our God.*

Uncomfortable, I began to wiggle on the hard oak bench. Hal took my hand and began to stroke it absentmindedly.

" 'Yea, though I walk through the valley of the shadow of death, I will fear no evil,' " Ravenstein read. I recognized the Twenty-third Psalm.

A strange sensation like a cold blast of air all of a sudden hit me in the back of my head. I turned and glanced once more at the rear of the church. Across the center aisle, in the last pew, sat Steve Krieger. He was all by himself, wearing a green cap he hadn't bothered to remove, his eyes staring glassily ahead. On his right cheek was a bandage.

My heart skipped a beat. I had to tear my eyes away from him. I needed to talk to Bobby again, this time about Sarah.

After advising us to go in peace, the Reverend descended the podium. We stood quietly as he walked through the aisle to the doors, where he positioned himself to shake hands with the mourners.

Rita and Kate were busily talking to each other while they walked out. Janny, right behind them, dangerously waved a large, black umbrella in an apparent attempt to get a point across to Bobby, but in the process almost impaling several people, who quickly shied away from her.

Hal and I were some of the last to leave. We had just shaken hands with the Reverend Ravenstein and were standing on the threshold when suddenly there was quite a commotion in front of the church. Someone was shouting.

"How dare you show up after breaking into the house!" Alicia's voice had risen to an ear-piercing screech.

"Get out of my way!" Steve unceremoniously pushed her aside.

Alicia lost her balance and fell against her brother, who steadied her. Jason gave Steve an icy look and said, "I think you had better leave!"

"Why? What are *you* going to do about it?" With these words Steve slithered over to his truck, which he'd left in front of the church in the no-parking zone. I noticed it had a few more dents in it than last Sunday. He got in, slammed the door, and revved up the engine.

As he drove off, he rolled down the window and yelled, "You *fag! Fag!*"

Behind me, I heard Willem de Weder loudly gasp for air.

Chapter 18

One fair daughter and no more.

The brief grave-side ceremony consisted mostly of the tossing of roses handed to all from a large, beribboned twig basket by the seemingly dentureless man who had earlier served as a deacon, the one who didn't get his hand caught.

After the man handed her the allotted flower, Sasha grabbed herself another handful and dropped them one by one on the casket. Her cheeks were wet.

Standing next to her, the grieving Willem said, "Sweets to the sweet."

Through her tears, Sasha cast her stepfather a glaring look and turned around so quickly that she lost her balance and almost fell backwards into her mother's final resting place.

I dropped my flower and whispered, "Go with God," as I sincerely hoped she would.

Hal and I got back into our car, and in silence we followed the line of black limousines to Lani's house, where a gathering was to be held to feed the living.

A serious-looking young woman dressed in *Upstairs, Downstairs* fashion—the downstairs part of it—begged us for our coats and umbrellas as we entered. As if we were in some enormous mansion and could get lost, she then directed us to the living room, where we found Alicia waiting.

The large sliding doors that separated the Victorian living room and dining room were open. A long table covered with white lace was placed against the far wall. A large, gold-rimmed, white soup tureen, stacks of matching china, and fanned-out silverware and napkins started the table on the right.

I noticed a distinctly French theme in the sliced baguettes, large chunks of paté, wedges of Boursin and Camembert, and the less classy La Vache Qui Rît, whose goofy cow faces smirked out at us from their wrappers. Toastettes surrounded some lone pieces of Gouda and

Edam in deference to the Netherlanders. In the center of the table stood an enormous bouquet of deep-red roses. On the far left end were several steel dispensers, small brass plaques hanging from the spouts, indicating the contents. Next to that, clusters of uncorked French wines and gleaming crystal stemware.

Alicia, standing next to me near the doorway, flipped the little veil up over the top of her hat and looked at me expectantly.

Was I supposed to say something? It was a *funeral*, for heaven's sake! Oh, well. "It's very nice," I remarked with measured admiration.

Frowning at me as if she'd expected me to make a more thorough compliment, she said in a defensive tone, "Mother was French, you know."

I stared back at her. I knew not all people around these parts could boast of a Dutch heritage and that Lani was something else altogether. But *French*? She'd told me once she was Irish. And when I'd been unable to reconcile that with her French maiden name, Pochard, she'd explained that she'd been adopted by Pierre and Jeanne Pochard, who had taken her from a New York orphanage, at the age of five, and had subsequently moved their little family to California.

My confusion must have shown on my face, because Alicia went on, "They spoke French at home when she grew up." She looked away and peeled off her tight black gloves, gesturing to the guests to please be seated at the small, elegant, round tables that were placed around the room. Except for the large couch, the overstuffed furniture had been removed.

Lani's French connection finally cleared one thing up for me: Solo's foul language. I looked over at his cage. It was covered with the black cloth to keep his mouth shut.

About twenty guests, mostly close neighbors, had joined us to partake in the late lunch or early supper. Hal picked the table in the center, and we sat down with Kate and Bobby. Willem, his eyes red, asked if he could join us. When everyone was seated, Sasha blew in with faraway eyes and a lost smile hovering around her lips.

The Reverend Ravenstein stood with a mournful look on his face and asked for the Great Spirit, whom he chose to call *Lord*, to bless the food. His blessing reminded me somewhat of the lengthy prayers I used to say when I was still drinking and never quite sure if I'd made myself completely clear and would rephrase my urgent requests, just in case. The god of my understanding was either hard of hearing or not so terribly bright. He may also have suffered from attention deficit disorder, thus needing frequent reminders.

Behind Cecil loomed the oil painting of the petting couple. Before he sat down, he looked with a pained expression over his shoulder at the painting as if its presence had possibly nullified his prayer.

Willem loudly blew his red nose in an enormous, white handkerchief. Alicia, who was seated at the table next to ours, looked over with obvious disapproval. I, too, hoped he would bag that rag while we were eating.

As the tables took turns helping themselves to the French onion soup and multitudinous cheeses, I was surprised to discover that Hal and Willem knew each other. I knew they hadn't met that time Willem had been present when I was negotiating the purchase of our home with Lani. It soon became clear that he must have hit some of the local meetings when he was in the neighborhood. *Stalking Lani?* Her stories really made no sense any longer, if they ever had.

"I tell you, that boy of mine. Who would have ever thought? What did I do wrong?" Willem whispered to Hal. "I haven't had a drink in over a year. Three-hundred-seventy-eight days, to be exact. But I sure could use a belt of whiskey right now!"

I wasn't sure what his going out and drinking was meant to accomplish, but he looked about ready to cry, and I was afraid he would take that dreadful handkerchief out of his pocket again. But he didn't do either.

"That should straighten Jason out," Hal whispered back, a deadpan look on his face.

Willem glared at him for an angry moment, but then a reluctant smile appeared on his face. "You're right! I'm not making any sense." He wiped his hand along his forehead.

When it was our turn, we dished up our food and quietly sat down again to eat. Very little conversation was going on, except at Sasha's table, from which muffled laughter came now and again.

After a while, Willem broke the silence. "I guess I've known all along. I just couldn't admit it. My son ... " He glanced over at Jason who was sitting next to Ravenstein. Jason raised his head. Father and son locked their curious eyes on one another.

"Well, this is all very French, isn't it?" Kate said just to make light conversation. She genteelly dabbed at her mouth with her linen napkin.

"Gouda isn't French!" I said, figuring she meant the food.

Kate wrinkled her nose and sent a tortured look my way, because I'd assaulted her delicate ears by pronouncing *Gouda* with the harsh Dutch *g*, which probably sounded to her as if I were in bad need of a spittoon or Willem's handkerchief.

Our attempt at discourse was herewith aborted, and we would have continued to eat in utter silence had it not been that Sasha decided to play one of Lani's old Edith Piaf records. "La Vie en Rose" suddenly blasted through the room.

In an undisguised huff, Alicia immediately took hold of the situation and turned the volume down to a level at which conversation would once more be possible.

We still didn't talk much in our little group.

In due time, the tables were cleared by the role-model maid and a red-haired youth who seemed to have materialized out of nowhere. A tall, dark man in his early forties, dressed in tails, quietly oversaw their efforts from the doorway. Kate recognized him as Mark Brandenburgh, an old high school classmate of hers who now owned a catering business that operated out of Modesto. She finger waved at him. He nodded back politely.

People began to move around and change places while the coffee and *petit gâteaux*—which to my barely disguised merriment Alicia pronounced "pay-teat gay-toes"—were served.

One of the Verhoog twins came to our table and hesitantly offered her condolences to Willem. She said, "I'm not quite sure if this is appropriate," then added in a whisper, "you being an ex-husband, and all."

Willem assured her that he appreciated her kindness. "Thank you, Agnes."

I wanted to ask him by what trick he could tell the twins apart, but then the other sister came over and said, "Maybe we should go now, Albertina. We may just get home before the next storm!" They proceeded to go around the room taking their leave of everyone.

Kate and Bobby left our table to join Janny and Bert. Hal and Willem moved to one of the tables on the side and began a man-to-man talk.

I was sitting all by myself, enjoying the last bites of my "pay-teat gay-toe," when Sasha plunked down in the chair next to mine. She was holding a glass of red wine, which she began swishing around and around rather dangerously above the white lace table cloth. "Tart stuff!" she said. "But it works!"

I knew what she meant.

She sniffed at the wine and then took a long swig that emptied the glass, making a sour face as she swallowed. She stumbled over to the long table and refilled her glass.

"So, wadda-ya-think?" she asked as she sat down again and now rather demurely began sipping her wine.

I thought she must have started sometime before the church service, but she probably didn't mean that. "*Très chic*," I said, rolling the *r* exaggeratedly.

Sasha grinned. "I picked Mother's dress, you know. Ali actually let me do that one thing, you know. Of course, then she was furious about the choice I made. Like they'd care in the hereafter, or whatever, what she'd be wearing. Knock, knock! Can't come in, dress code enforced at all times. No shirt, no shoes, red dress, no service!" She was slurring a bit. Feeling no pain or perhaps too much. "Of course, I had no idea they'd show her off. Ali insisted on that."

A large blob of whipped cream fell off my fork and landed on my dress. I fumbled with my napkin but then decided I'd better wash it off with some hot water in the kitchen. I excused myself to Sasha.

When I opened the kitchen door, Alicia was standing next to Mark Brandenburgh near the sink. Just as I was about to make my presence known, I noticed a hand gently kneading her beautiful behind. Then, they turned to face each other, and both of Mark's hands now rested on Alicia's derrière while her arms encircled his neck. As I watched them French-kiss, I heard a noise behind me.

"Naughty-naughty!" Sasha's voice called out over my shoulder. She let out a peal of laughter.

Startled, Alicia broke loose from Mark and twirled around, her pretty face an unbecoming beet red.

I stepped back, slammed the door, bolted past Sasha, and quickly ran upstairs.

Kate was right: quite a few French things were going on in this house. *Honi soit qui mal y pense!*

Hearing Sasha stumbling behind me on the stairs, I ran faster, dove into the bathroom, and locked the door behind me. I turned the hot-water tap on full blast and grabbed the towel off the rack. The whipped cream had made a long trail down the front of my dress. I dabbed at it with the wet corner of the towel.

"Fae?" Sasha's voice came from the other side of the door over the sound of the splashing water.

Damn! Maybe I could flush the toilet. Or sing something loud enough to drown her out.

"Fae-hay!"

It suddenly occurred to me that I hadn't done anything wrong. Only, I couldn't seem to stop laughing. Why had I run upstairs and locked myself in the bathroom? I turned off the tap, carefully opened the door, and peeked out.

"Fae? You OK?" Sasha was trying to get her eyes focused on me, but I could tell she was going to have a hard time accomplishing this, because she was practically cross-eyed by now.

"Sure!" I said cheerfully. "Do you need anything? I'll be right out."

"No, juss tought. Nevuh mine!" She hiccupped, turned around, and wobbled downstairs.

I shut the door again and washed my hands. By all means, *Honi soit* ... , but what *was* going on in this house? I had to think, and bathrooms had always seemed notoriously suited for that kind of activity.

Sitting on the fluffy toilet seat cover, I looked down at my dress. There was no sign of a greasy streak, the whipped cream trail had completely disappeared. Amazing this sueded material! All my clothes should be made out of it, then I'd never have to wash anything again. And all the furniture. Curtains.

This wasn't exactly the kind of thinking I'd meant to do when I sat down, so I got up, and unlocked the door.

Alicia was standing in the hall when I came out, nervously plucking at her classy dress with both hands. Though her face had returned to its normal pale hue and everything about her was in the right place, she gave a disheveled impression. "Could I speak with you?"

I'm sure you can, but the question is may *you*.

She didn't wait for my permission. "I know what this must look like. I know what you must be thinking."

We had another psychically endowed entity in our midst or a mind reader. "Oh?" was all I said. Could she possibly know that I suspected her of killing her mother?

"It's been so hard! So difficult! Oh, you couldn't possibly understand!" Her claim to uniqueness was a sure indication she was revving up to a full-blown jeremiad again. She shook her head, almost dislodging the cute, little pillbox hat, in sincere commiseration with herself.

I really didn't want to hear it and began to squirm, trying to sneak past her. Why would she bother to explain something I couldn't understand? Just as I was going to suggest we might talk some other time, that would hopefully never come, the floodgates opened. A genuine tear ran from her left eye down her left cheek. Now she would be unstoppable.

Dear me! my very own Self-pity lamented. Was it too late to escape? *One cannot walk away from a weeping woman, can one? That's only if one is a man, Stupid!* Almost imperceptibly I moved sideways with my back against the railing towards the stairs.

She stepped toward the railing and blocked my escape. "I have fought this, but I have known Mark since high school!"

I wasn't sure what this was supposed to explain, but I had a lurid picture of her mud wrestling another woman who was wearing a skimpy tank top with the word "Lust" written in gothic lettering on the front and back. "Uh, Alicia ... ?" I touched her on the shoulder. This really works well with dogs when they're about to do something you don't want them to do.

But Alicia ignored my feeble attempt to stop her. "It's been so difficult with Charles. He's not the same man I married. We're practically bankrupt. He put all his money in that farm. He doesn't understand me." She wiped her right cheek, the wrong one.

Her whimpering voice reminded me of Lani's. I really saw the resemblance now. *Poor me, pour me another drink.* Only, Alicia didn't drink as far as I knew. Her compulsions lay elsewhere. She could use a drink, though. She *should* drink.

"Why don't we go downstairs and you can have a nice glass of wine," I said smoothly.

She blinked a few times but didn't fall for it. "It's been so difficult!" Her favorite phrase. "Mother found out, and she threatened to tell Charles. I was desperate!"

Aha! She was confessing! Telling me her motive! I perked up my ears, but she just kept going on about Mark. How he did understand, how kind he was, how they had a real bond that couldn't be broken.

Mark this and Mark that. The same obsessive way Lani had jabbered on about Steve Krieger.

I kept asking myself why she was telling me this stuff. Image control? Maybe she simply couldn't stand being found out. Found not to be perfect. *Atelophobia*? Fear of imperfection?

So what? Who is perfect? Not you, Mercy whispered.

I stuck a semi-understanding look on my face and gave up on trying to change the course of my destiny.

"Mother!" she spat. "She found my plane ticket. Snooping through my suitcase. Threatened to tell Charles. I just wanted to die!" She had to take a few deep breaths before she could continue. "Not that she cared about Charles. She couldn't stand him. Just because he was my husband. No other reason. He asked her for a loan so we could keep afloat until this spring, after the new calves would have been born. He came all the way out here to talk to her. She humiliated him. Said she couldn't care less and that he was too dumb to lend money to."

Ouch! That must have hurt. Again, the Lani I had never met surfaced. I hadn't been aware that Chuck had come out here either. Had that been the last time?

"When he came back home, he just wasn't the same. That was in the fall. He wouldn't tell me what she exactly said, but he began to drink." More deep little breaths. "Beer!"

Insult to injury. So, the genteel Alicia was saddled with a beer-guzzling, barbecue-devouring flunky lawyer. I could see how this would be a problem. Irreconcilable differences. Cruel, but not unusual.

She gingerly wiped her eyes with the back of her hand, then suddenly raised her head and straightened herself as if with new determination to face life on life's terms.

Jason's head appeared at the top of the stairs. He glanced at me, then at Alicia, assessing the situation. "What's going on, Sis? Are you holding Fae hostage here?"

His older sister gave him a nasty look and snapped, "Mind your own business!"

"I'm afraid it's everyone's business now," he said airily. "Sasha's just introduced Mark to the whole congregation as her 'illegitimate brother-in-law.' It must have been too much after what happened at church with Krieger. Most people left. I believe the Verhoog sisters went home to embroider a giant *A* for you to wear. Or maybe an *H* for me."

I could tell by his smile that he'd been relieved of a burden. He was free. Was that all he'd wanted to find out when he came to visit me, if Lani had told me he was gay? Why? And, I happened to know for a fact that the Verhoog sisters had given up embroidering years ago because of their arthritis. Besides, hadn't they left before the adulteress had been exposed?

Alicia made a earnest attempt at wailing again. "Oh, no! I could just die!" But Jason gently guided his sister to the staircase, smiling over his shoulder at me. "Come on, let's face *la musique*."

I waited a little while before following them. Almost everyone was gone when I came downstairs. Ravenstein was quietly talking to Alicia in the hallway. Her chin stuck slightly more forward than it normally did, it seemed. He looked as if he couldn't get away fast enough, an openly disapproving expression on his face, or else all that cheese hadn't agreed with him.

From the living room sounded Procul Harem's "Turn a Whiter Shade of Pale." Sasha was asleep on the couch, snoring loudly. I pulled the quilt from the back of the couch and draped it over her.

Hal and I were getting ready to leave when Jason came up to us.

"I almost forgot," he said. He searched the pocket of his blazer, pulled out a business card and handed it to me. "Mother's lawyer asked if you could be present tomorrow morning at the reading of the will. It's in Modesto. At ten. He said he'd call you tonight."

I guessed she had left me that damned painting after all.

Chapter 19

Who calls me villain?

And indeed, Lani's lawyer called Thursday evening after dinner, just as Hal and I were playing Trivial Pursuit. Hal was on a winning streak—he had a better memory for trivia and, as usual, he got the easier questions—when the phone rang.

I answered the call in the kitchen but stood in the doorway to keep an eye on Hal, so he couldn't read the cards ahead of time. My brothers all cheated heavily at Monopoly, and that taught me never to trust a male opponent. Fighting dirty seemed part of their strategy.

Mr. Alston Wiley of Caspar, Wiley, and Banning introduced himself and respectfully requested that I be present the next morning at the reading of the will of the late Ms. Melanie Pochard.

Melanie?

He spoke in spurts as if he kept running out of steam, with suspenseful pauses between every three or four words. He sounded very important, and I was sure no one had ever called him *Al.* The only thing he would let on, besides the directions to his office, was that Ms. Pochard had "remembered" me. I already knew this, of course, and I'd been hoping she'd soon forget me.

Hal left very early Friday morning, before six, when it was still pitch dark. He had to catch up on some of his lab work since he'd taken Thursday off but said he'd be home early to welcome his nephews, who were to be dropped off by Grace and Matt.

After trying on three outfits, none of which seemed right for attending the reading of a will, mostly because I had no idea what someone should wear to such an occasion, I finally settled on my magenta dress with the tight short skirt and long black jacket.

I was putting the last touches on my appearance when Rita showed up, ready to clean my house from top to bottom. She sat down behind me on the bed while I brushed my hair.

"How's Sarah?" I asked.

"She's doing better. Coming home tomorrow. Still got a lot of pain. We haven't told her." She moved her unlit cigar to the corner of her mouth.

"About them not finding the guy who did this?"

"Yeah. Figured it wouldn't do her no good. No good at all." She stared out the window. "Probably make her scared. She hasn't asked about it."

I put my silver teardrop earrings in.

"You look nice," Rita said. "You always look nice."

"Thank you." I turned around.

"I wanna thank you for being so good to Sarah. For helping her, specially now. She thinks the world of you. Wants to be just like you, Fae, and that's not a bad way to be."

My smile faded. I felt like a fraud. All I could suddenly think of was that Sarah had been wearing *my* jacket when she was attacked, and that Steve Krieger was now walking around with a bandage on his ugly face. Why hadn't I known that something awful would happen to Sarah? Had I ignored some major psychic warning, because I'd been too preoccupied with my irritation with Lani? I'd have to find out about Steve Krieger, where he was when Sarah was attacked, and what was under that bandage. How would I do that? I'd have to keep all this secret from Rita. She and Mike might go after Steve. Then everything would be even more horrible.

"Fae?" Rita said. "What's wrong?"

I looked at her. "Nothing. It's nothing." *Everything. It's everything.*

"Where you going?"

"I'm going to Modesto. They've asked me to be there at the reading of Lani's will."

"That means she's left you something." She chewed on her cigar some more. There wasn't much left. Her raspy voice went on, "I wonder what?"

"Oh, I don't know. Maybe that painting I told her I liked, or Solo."

"Solo?"

"Her bird, a Congo African Grey parrot."

"Giving you the bird, huh?" her laugh ended in a coughing fit. "I better get started," she finally gasped.

I didn't mind being the butt of her joke. It was a relief Rita had reason to laugh again. She was busy telling Moon off about sitting on the kitchen table when I left.

Looking through my purse, trying to figure out what I'd forgotten this time, I got into my car. When I adjusted the rearview mirror, the reflection of a big, black, hairy face appeared. I turned around to Dooley, who was sitting happily in the backseat with a silly smile on his face. He must have snuck in and laid down when I was closing the barn door. I had to drag him out. Mud covered the velour upholstery of the driver's seat I'd already sat down on, and the rear seat was one big mess. I looked at the back of my dress. Too bad, no time for a change of clothing.

Dooley, looking injured, sagged down on the grass. I rolled down the window and promised he could come with me another time. He turned his head away, wouldn't look at me. The whole car smelled of eau de Dooley as I drove off.

The offices of Caspar Wiley and Banning (no commas, as I found out) were located in a turn-of-the-century Victorian in an old part of Modesto—as old as it gets in California, that is. The house, painted in subdued grays, was surrounded by an unnaturally green lawn and meticulously trimmed shrubs, all looking a bit like an arrangement for a toy train set.

I walked up the front steps and went through the heavy mahogany door to find myself in a large, dark-paneled, high-ceilinged reception area. Somewhere behind an enormous desk sat a petite young woman.

"May I help you, Ma'am?" she asked, shaking her blond curls out of her face. A sign on her desk said her name was Heather Baley. *One of the Heather generation.* She smiled as if she were ecstatically happy to see me, showing two rows of perfect, little, white teeth, clenched together for a cavity check.

Before I could answer, she'd placed a clipboard with a form in front of me on the counter, shaking her curls out of her face again.

"I'm here to see Mr. Wiley." I let her check out my teeth.

"Are you here in regard to the Pochard estate?"

A little lawyerette? "Yes, I am," I said. "I'm Fae Nelson."

She took the clipboard away from me. "Mr. Wiley is expecting you, Mrs. Nelson," she said, giving me a rather strange look I couldn't quite figure out. "Please, follow me."

Aerosmith's "Walk This Way" sounded in my head as Heather Baley guided me through one hallway and then another. Her wobbling gait on too high heels tempted me to do a Tyler routine behind her back, but kindness admonished me to do unto others, and besides, it was a pretty amazing feat to be able to walk on those heels and vigorously shake her head at the same time. She finally stopped and knocked on one of the large doors on our left.

As I entered, Mr. Alston Wiley rose from his desk and crossed the room to greet me. The first thing I noticed about him was that he was very short, and then that he was very fat, and then that his head shone like a helmet. Large, bushy eyebrows compensated for the lack of hair on top. After he claimed that it was a great pleasure to meet me, he sent the head-shaking, wobbling Heather to get coffee for us.

Jason and Sasha were comfortably seated on a mocha leather couch that appeared to be at least twelve feet long.

Sasha was sitting with her legs crossed, swinging the one on top as if she were kicking something away from her. She didn't look too with-it this morning, her eyes puffy and bloodshot, nervously dragging on a cigarette, trying to blow circles. She'd found yet another way to combine masses of India cotton in various layers. Black and purple, today. Lifting the hand holding her cigarette, she waved at me, but the smile she gave seemed to cause her some pain. She said nothing.

Jason got up, shook my hand, and simply said, "Hello, Fae!" He looked casual in jeans and a burgundy sweater. Relaxed. Happy.

In a high-back, tan leather chair sat Alicia, upright, her ankles contraceptively crossed, her hands folded in her lap. She wore a stunning black-and-white, polka-dot outfit, topped with a wide-brimmed, black felt hat.

"How are you, Fae?" she asked and immediately looked away at Mr. Wiley. I figured she might be not a little embarrassed about her outpouring of sisterly love and dirty little secrets.

Mr. Wiley offered me a chair, a twin of the one Alicia was sitting in. I looked uncomfortably at the many buttons before sitting down.

The bald, little lawyer seated himself behind his jumbo desk. He cleared his throat while slowly opening an over-bloated accordion file.

I wondered if he were sitting on a pillow or if he had one of those crank-up-able chairs. According to any of the natural laws I was aware of, he really should have totally disappeared behind that desk.

He took a large manila envelope from the file, cleared his throat again and looked up at us. "Yes," he said, closing his eyes and holding the envelope as if he were doing a psychic reading. "Yes. This is the last will and testament of Melanie Pochard. Your mother." He opened his eyes and looked at Jason, Alicia, and Sasha in turn. "And friend." He looked over at me.

I looked down at my shoes and chewed on my cheek.

Alicia moved impatiently to the edge of her chair. I thought she might slap the fat, little man with her pretty purse. But she just glared at him.

Jason was observing his older sister with a bemused look on his face. Sasha's eyes were closed, and she looked as if she were about to throw up.

"Yes," Mr. Wiley said once more, and he opened the envelope and took out a package of papers. We were getting closer. Slowly, he began to read the document before him.

I had forgotten how boringly repetitious and multi-syllabic legal lingo is, with its page-long Joycian run-on sentences, and lost interest somewhere right after " ... of sound and disposing mind and memory, do make, publish and declare ... "

I was thinking about what to do the rest of the day before the boys came, to avoid having to work on my class preparations, when Alicia gasped loudly.

I looked up to find four pair of eyes trained on me. Bewildered, I sat up straight. "What? What is it?" I had no idea what was going on. "Would you read that again?"

For what seemed like the longest time, nobody spoke. Then Alston Wiley looked down at the document again and read, "To my dear friend and confidante, Fae van Dalen-Nelson, I give, bequeath and devise my property at Blackberry Road: my house and all its contents and the one hundred acres of surrounding land. I also give and bequeath to Fae van Dalen-Nelson what funds have accumulated in my portfolio as handled by the firm Grayson & Grayson, currently exceeding the sum of two-hundred-and-thirty-thousand dollars, an exact accounting of which said firm shall provide."

I was stunned.

So were Lani's children.

Sasha jumped up and ran out. We could hear her gagging and throwing up in the hall on the beautiful, gold-colored carpet.

Jason's eyes were distant. He rubbed his chin, got up, and began pacing through the office.

Alicia's face first lost all color, then a deep crimson came seeping up from her neck. She stared at me, her blue eyes filled with such an icy, deep hatred, it could have served as a defense lawyer's show-and-tell to explain the concept of temporary insanity.

If she kills me now, she'll probably only get five months probation. I was extremely uncomfortable sitting so close to her.

"Well, I guess you got what you came for!" she hissed, her eyes narrowed to dark, glittering slits.

Anything I'd say would set her off even more, so I pursed my lips and mentally turned the little key.

"Alicia!" Jason called out. "This has nothing to do with Fae!"

"What do you *mean*? Nothing to *do* with Fae? She just inherited *all* of mother's money and property! *How* do you think she did that?" Alicia was a little hysterical, if one can be a little of that.

"Mother's will isn't about giving everything to Fae, it's about giving nothing to us." He shook his head. "Don't you see?" He was clearly appealing to Alicia's common sense, a misnomer in general and in her case something quite nonexistent.

"All I see is that Mother left me a fucking make-up mirror and you that stupid shepherds' painting—hint, hint—and Sasha a bunch of crappy clothes that don't fit her. Fae talked her into this. I know she did!" She turned to me again, an index finger pointed at my face. "You! You had her change her will, and then you … you killed her!" Spittle flew as she turned back to Jason. "I told you so."

I stared at her in disbelief. She *had* told him so, and now she was telling me to my face what I'd overheard her say the day Steve had ransacked the house.

For a few seconds no one spoke. Now all eyes were focused on Alicia. The meanness of her words echoed in the room.

If they only knew they are all three suspects in my book.

Sasha, coming back in from the hall carrying a paper cup, caught Alicia's tirade. She gave her sister a dark look. "Ali, you're so full of shit!" She then directed herself at me, an apologetic look on her face. "I'm sorry, Fae! We suspected Mother would maybe do something like this, you know. I often thought she'd just drag someone in off the streets and leave all her earthly goods to him. Like that Steve character, you know. I'm just glad it's you and not him."

"Mother loved us! How can you say that? And you, Jason, she loved you most of all! Always fawning over you!" Alicia's voice was shrill with anger.

"That was a long time ago." Jason looked tired. "Sasha's right. These last few years, Mother couldn't seem to stand the sight of any of us. You know how she was."

"It's not true! You don't know what you're saying!" Disgusted, Alicia picked up her purse and angrily stomped out of the office.

On my way home, I stopped at a tire shop and had them replace the whole set, including the spare. Sitting in the waiting room for more than an hour gave me time to think the situation over. As soon as I got home, I called Hal at work.

"Everything? You mean *everything?*"

"Everything, except a few minor items she left to the kids. I wasn't listening too closely, but I think she left her make-up mirror to Alicia and her clothes to Sasha."

"What for?" he asked.

"To add insult to injury, I guess." This family seemed to be doing a lot of that.

Hal was quiet.

"I can't believe a mother would behave this way. This just isn't right!"

"I'll be home about four-thirty. Let's talk about it then. OK? We'll figure something out." He sighed. "She was really a lot weirder than we thought." With that final observation, we kissed long-distance and disconnected.

I hadn't told Hal that possibly the most hurtful item was the one she'd left Jason, the painting of the petting heterosexual couple. Even Alicia had picked up on that. So, his mother and both his sisters had known. That left Willem he had been trying to keep it from. But why? Willem might not be thrilled, but he'd get over it, adjust.

When I shooed Moon off the table, it turned out he'd been lying on top of a note from Rita saying she'd gone to visit Sarah and would be back early in the afternoon.

Sarah! Sweet Sarah. I should have dropped by the hospital when I was in the city. With all that ruckus at Alston Wiley's office I'd totally forgotten that Sarah was still in the hospital. I needed to talk to Gwen about Sarah. About the jacket. I dialed Gwen's home number and left a message asking her to call me when she got back. It wasn't any kind of emergency so I didn't want to call her work.

I thought about the conversations I'd had with Gwen, and again it struck me how unfair it was that I rarely knew enough to change things. I hadn't been able to save a life yet, except my own a few times. Though, if I saw something that was to happen in the future and could change it, then what had I seen? Not the future. It couldn't be the future, if I could change events. It would fall in the realm of possibility and wouldn't be foreknowledge. You can't *know* something that *might* happen. That's just deductive reasoning or, at a lower level, guessing. That illusive common sense. Knowledge is definite. Knowledge simply *is*. Or maybe not, if I allowed Hal's parallel universes into the equation.

It might be better if I stayed in this one universe, since it was confusing enough. Where had this headache come from? I needed to get myself to a meeting for some spiritual food. I checked the listings. There was one at two o'clock higher up in the hills I could make if I hustled. I looked the address up on the map in my car and left in the middle of a glorious cloudburst.

The meeting helped. Halfway through, I began to feel less frazzled, more centered, more Fae. As we wrapped up in the usual manner, I glanced over at the door.

A woman was leaving. Brunette, frizzy hair, long red dress fluttering in the wind as she stepped out.

Had Lani finally made it to a meeting? If so, she must have found a celestial hair salon.

Chapter 20

Look, where it comes again!

"You're rich!" said Rita. "Now you can quit that job and write all the time. Finish that book of yours."

I hadn't thought about that, and I couldn't remember telling her about my book. Must have. Maybe she'd seen it on my desk or when I was pretending to be editing it when Lani had come over. I looked hard at her face to check if she was being sarcastic, but she seemed to be perfectly sincere.

I wanted to explain what the problem was but hadn't quite figured that out myself. Other than that Jason and Sasha were disappointed and Alicia had accused me of murdering Lani and wanted to kill me herself, my own conscience seemed to be the biggest problem. What Lani had done was most unnatural. Mothers take care of their young.

I looked down at my cup of coffee.

"So, why you looking like you just lost something precious?" Rita asked. "Cheer up, Kid! Your prayers been answered."

"It's just that … ," I had to say it, and it might as well be to good, old Rita. "I couldn't stand her much in the end. I just wanted her to get out of my life. I didn't want to hurt her feelings, but she drove me crazy with her stories. It was always one problem after another. Drama after drama. There were days when I dreaded picking up the phone, because I knew it would be her and she'd talk until my ears whistled. But when she'd go on one of those long drunks and wouldn't call for a while, I'd worry that she'd gotten in an accident. I even went over to her house a couple of times to see if she were OK."

"Sounds like you really earned that money, Fae," she said casually. She got up and put her cup on the kitchen counter, but then her spine suddenly stiffened. Her back was still toward me when she said, "She was a bitch!" She turned around. "A real bitch!" Anger flashed behind the thick glasses.

My eyebrows raised themselves.

"And don't you give me none of that 'we don't use that word for our sisters' crap!" She said loudly. "She weren't no sister! She got to Mike, you know."

I hadn't known. But now I did. It explained a lot.

"Long time ago, but she did. Didn't last worth shit. But she *had* to do it. Wouldn't leave him alone, pretending she needed work done around the house." Rita scraped her throat. "Only piece a work was her. And her still married to Willem. The bitch!"

"Well!" I said. What else could I say?

Did Rita ... ? But I dismissed that thought before I finished it. Rita would be very busy if she killed every woman Mike had been with. She'd raised her seven children mostly by herself, Mike only coming around when he thought it was mating season, which didn't confine itself to just his wife, as she'd told me. It wasn't until Mike had gotten sober a few years ago that they'd settled down in their uneasy partnership. But before then, he'd been a rather willing prey of seduction, if that's how she wanted to reconcile with the past. Besides, as she'd said, the incident with Lani was so long ago, and Rita didn't seem the waiting type. Or, was she? Had Lani's persistent presence at my house brought back old memories?

"You deserve that money, Fae. Take it!" She walked over to the door and stood there for a while as if trying to make up her mind. Then she said, "I better go now. Get Sarah's room tidied up for her to come home."

Yes, she'd better. I was embarrassed I'd told her about my little problems. They were so absurd compared to hers. And I didn't want to have to add her to my list of suspects. She'd suffered enough.

"Oh," she said as she opened the door, scratching her head like Detective Colombo. "You a suspect now?"

"What in the world do you mean?"

"Kate told me you talked to Bobby and he's gonna look into this Antibooze thing. What if there's something to it?" She closed the door slightly.

"Why would I be a suspect? I found her!" Immediately, I realized this was the dumbest thing I'd said in a long time.

So did Rita. She shook her head. "Fae, Fae! You're something else. You think everyone's like you."

"No, I don't!"

"Oh, Honey, I mean you think all people play by them rules you keep. They don't, you know. Good thing it's Bobby looking at it. But don't go talking about no dead dogs walking around. People don't understand them things. It scares 'em." She shook her head some more, stepped out on the porch, and closed the door behind her. Her truck farted loudly as she took off.

What was Rita talking about? No, I didn't think everyone played by the rules I myself struggled so hard to keep. Why else would I suspect about everyone of having killed Lani? The rules I learned sitting in Oma's kitchen, the same ones my mother taught me, were simple enough: don't lie, steal, or cheat, treat others the way you want to be treated, help those in need, and admit your wrongs. I didn't understand people like Steve or Lani or Alicia. Did they ever think, "Now why did I do that?" Were they ever repentant about something they'd done? Did they ever stop themselves *before* they did something hurtful? What rules *did* they live by?

And I hadn't said anything to Bobby about the ongoing psychic phenomena. I hadn't even told him about my vision. But maybe Hal had. Maybe that's why Bobby was so reluctant to listen to me. Had he known about the inheritance?

The inheritance! Now that Rita was safely out of the way, I called Kate. She'd understand.

"That's wonderful, Fae!" Kate exclaimed without hesitation.

I hemmed and hawed.

"Aren't you happy? What's the problem?"

"Nothing!" I was all alone in the world, that was the problem. I'd tell her about the mess with Matchett some other time, when she'd be more receptive to my woes.

I decided not to talk to anyone else until Hal came home and to lie down on the couch for a while. I was just getting comfortable when the phone rang. I got up and answered the call in the kitchen, but no one responded to my hello. Feeling mighty cranky, I pulled the cord of the answering machine out of the jack, almost busting the little plug, and went back into the living room. But I could still hear the phones in the library and upstairs in the bedroom and in my office when they began to ring. Finally, after about fifteen rings, it was quiet. I sighed deeply and closed my eyes. *Doesn't anyone in the hereafter ever lose a number?*

My power nap was rudely interrupted when two cats raced through the living room, upsetting several small stacks of books I had strategically placed around the couches for future reading. Mellow used my stomach as a springboard and landed on the back of the sofa. Moon sailed around the coffee table and came to a stop next to me on the carpet, flicking her tail, eyes very large and black.

They were upset about something, but I couldn't tell about what. Just as I was trying to get to the bottom of this, Mab and Dooley howled that Hal was home.

I'd read somewhere in one of those paper-guru women's magazines that the little woman should let her husband unwind and not immediately bombard him with all the trivial problems of the day. But following this seemingly sound advice would only result in Hal side-tracking me with some long story about a lost petri dish, or something. Besides, no such little woman lived at our home.

Hal said his day had been "fine," and with that out of the way, we could immediately get to Lani's ridiculous will. I poured us each a large mug of hot Formosa Oolong, and we sat down together at the kitchen table with the cookie bin in between us. The boys were being dropped off around five, so we didn't have much time to talk.

Hal and I looked into each others' eyes and we both sighed.

"What do you want to do?" he asked.

"Give it to her kids. They'll run the will through probate, then we'll find out how much the estate is actually worth. Divide it between the three of them. Alicia may sue me anyway. She's pretty mad."

"Maybe you should go see a lawyer next week and get some advice. I guess you could get a copy of the will and have someone go over it." He hesitated for a moment. "Are you sure you don't just want to keep it? I mean, she did intend for you to have it."

"I'm sure. It doesn't feel right. She only left everything to me because she was mad at her kids. Who knows, she might have changed her mind again had she lived longer."

"What was she so mad about?"

"Let's see. Alicia was having an affair. *Is*, I mean. But then Lani had plenty of those herself. Jason is gay and has worked for his father for years. Maybe she was mad about either one of those things. Sasha has a drinking problem. But then, so did she herself. I really don't know why she was so hateful to her kids. I have a feeling it's all about personalities more than anything."

After a brief pause, Hal said, "I always thought she was pretty flaky, but this is plain nasty."

"At least she was consistent by cutting off all three of them. Apparently, she treated each of them very differently as they were growing up. Jason, she used to adore. Sasha, she used to ignore. And Alicia, she used to stomp in the floor."

"Well, you can't change any of that."

"I know, but I can change what she did with the will."

"To thine own self be true." He took my hand and brought it to his mouth and gnawed on it.

Our sentinels, Mab and Dooley, began their welcome howl again.

"There's Door Matt and his Amazing Grace." Hal grinned.

"Be nice! She's your sister," I said but snorted as I tried to suppress my laughter.

We went outside to greet them and keep the dogs from mauling the boys with love.

"Aunt Fae! Aunt Fae! We brought you a present!" Jesse yelled as soon as he got out of the car, which was practically before Matt was able to park.

As soon as they'd been able to talk, I'd insisted the boys call us *aunt* and *uncle*. Hal thought it was terribly funny when they began addressing him as *uncle*. But Grace rather liked the old-country habits, and—her vote carrying veto power—Aunt Fae got her way.

Jesse was holding a large box with a big, red bow in front of him. Dooley plucked the bow off the box, then immediately dropped it, because what he really wanted was the box. Jesse lifted it up high over his head. Mab retrieved the bow and dumped it at Jamey's feet.

Trying to throw the crumpled and slobber-covered bow on top of the box, Jamey yelled, "It's just a box of chocolates!"

I clapped my hands as if delighted with surprise. "Oh, you shouldn't have!" I was serious. Except for the chocolate croissant with Kate, I'd been pretty good for over a week now keeping my chocolate habit under control. Despite everything.

Jamey climbed on Hal, who tousled his hair and then threw him over his shoulder. Jesse handed me the package with unconcealed pride. "I picked it out myself!"

"It's just a box of chocolates!" Jamey yelled again from behind Hal's back, his face already red from hanging upside down.

"Shut up!" Jesse hollered at his brother.

"Boys!" Grace feebly admonished.

I was surprised how glamorous she looked in the softly shimmering avocado silk dress she was wearing, with her straight, dark-brown hair cut in a short bob. Nothing of the kindergarten-teacher-sack-dress look about her today.

"You look fantastic, Grace!" I said, stopping myself from telling her she looked quite sexy. Grace didn't do *sexy*.

Behind her back, Matt suggestively wiggled his eyebrows at his wife and smirked at me. He had great plans, I could see. He retrieved a large weekend bag from the trunk of the car and dropped it at Hal's feet.

"There are enough clothes in here for about a week." Grace looked over at the boys, shook her head, and smiled, "Well, at least for two days."

Hal somersaulted Jamey off his shoulder and picked up the bag.

"You guys behave yourselves!" Matt warned his offspring, wagging his finger.

The boys went into an absolute laughing frenzy, seemingly losing all muscular control and goofily falling against uncle Hal.

"We will!" Hal answered. This floored the twins.

Again, I marveled at the strange effect Hal had on his nephews. I could see we were about to have one long, hilarious weekend.

The four of us waved as Matt and Grace drove off and made their getaway.

"What do we want for dinner?" Hal asked, tossing the bag in the air.

"Hot dogs! Hot dogs!" they chanted. Followed by the dogs, the three boys stumbled unto the porch and into the house.

By the time I entered the kitchen, Hal was already digging around in the refrigerator. "What did you do with the hot dogs?"

"They're in the freezer." Boys and dogs were jumping around. It was a bit too rowdy for my taste, so I opened the door and called Mab and Dooley to go back out. Mab sent me a disbelieving look, turned around, and trotted off through the swinging door into the living room. "Hey! Hey!" I shouted after her.

"You!" I pointed at Dooley. "Out!" As if I'd beaten him with a stick, he crawled under the table, or at least he thought he had, but his back end was still sticking out. "I see you!" I said, closing the door again. *Never mind, give up, Fae.*

"Come! Mab! Dooley! Come!" Jesse called out. Mab immediately came running out of the living room and Dooley left his hiding place. Both happily followed Jesse outside. Jamey let go of Hal's shirt and ran out after his brother.

Hal put his hotdogs on the counter and went into the living room to start a fire. Within five minutes, the boys came storming in again with the dogs in tow. Jamey joined Hal at the fire place. Jesse crouched beside me.

"Aunt Fae?" he asked. "Who is that?"

"Who is who?" I was on a search and rescue mission in the fridge for the relish and any other conceivable hot dog condiment. *Steak sauce?* I handed him a couple of bottles.

"That lady!" He put the bottles on the table.

"What lady?" I looked at him.

"That lady in the red dress!" He pointed toward the window over the sink.

I got up and turned around.

Under the almond trees stood a lone figure quietly looking at the house.

"That's no lady!" I said quickly, and silently I added, "Get an afterlife, Lani!"

Chapter 21

O most pernicious woman!

Even the nicest zoos always had a depressing effect on me, and the Albert Vrygeboren Animal Garden was no exception. Albert Vrygeboren, a wealthy farmer whose last name ironically means "born free," a not uncommon surname in the Netherlands, founded the zoo in the fifties. It was open only weekends, year-round, but in the winter half the cages were empty and no special events were scheduled.

Though Albert's heart surely had been in the right place, because everything possible had been done to provide accommodations that mimicked their natural environment, the animals looked forlorn in their pens. The lemurs on their small island filled with rocks and bushes didn't seem to have it so bad, but the big cats, such as the lions and tigers, were a sad sight to behold. They paced back and forth continuously, and I wondered if perhaps they'd become insane after years of incarceration. The large birds sat on the dead branches of dead trees planted inside their cages.

Jesse and Jamey noticed none of this. Grace had told them that a visit to the zoo was on our schedule, and they'd been so excited that we hadn't been able to tuck the grunting, snorting, and growling boys in until midnight.

I had hoped they would sleep in, because the zoo didn't open until eleven. But they were up at seven. This meant a slight entertainment discrepancy. Like a slothful parent, I sent them downstairs to the TV and tuned them out to fall asleep again in my warm bed. Early-rising Hal went with them to make sure they wouldn't be watching some whose-baby-is-this-anyway? talk show that would forever render them impervious to all social training.

When I came down just after eight, they were all three sitting on the couch, laughing at a plumed creature that was being killed several times in a row, then miraculously coming back to life, wildly yodeling at its enemies. A *Road Runner* knock-off. Uncle Hal and his nephews were happily eating hot dogs from paper plates.

I poured myself a cup of coffee. Breakfast had been served.

It took forever to get everybody washed and dressed and combed. I felt like the mother of ten. Remembering that my mother used to check our ears every day, perhaps because we all exhibited hearing problems, I checked out the boys' ears, pretending to know what I was looking for. They thought this was horrendously funny, insisted I check out Hal's ears, too, and were duly impressed with the power I wielded when I sent him back into the bathroom and he actually went.

Despite all this clowning around, we were still half an hour early for the zoo. The boys whiled away this time by playing catch until Hal showed them how to climb the gate. I stood by, nervously admonishing them to be careful, hoping I wouldn't have to hand the boys back to Grace with, "I'm sorry, but their necks were accidentally broken." At exactly eleven o'clock, the ticket vendor appeared and told them they had to come down, because it would be too difficult to open the gate with two boys and a grown man hanging from the bars.

The boys first wanted to see the polar bear.

"Isn't it too warm here in the summer for a polar bear?" Jamey asked.

"They bring blocks of ice for the bear in the summer," Jesse said.

I certainly hoped so. The bear seemed happy enough, floating on his back in a small, peanut-shaped pool. "Look at those cute black pads on his paws," I said.

"Those paws could kill you with one swat," Hal remarked.

"So what? They're cute!" I said weakly.

Hal snorted at me. "Cute! The biggest polar bear they've found weighed over two-thousand pounds."

"Is he always alone? Doesn't he have a wife, a girl bear?" Jesse wanted to know.

"Bears don't get married," Jamey said derisively. "They mate!"

A young mother standing near us gave Jamey a disconcerted look and took her little girl, who was about the same age as the boys, firmly by the hand and walked off to safety.

As we stood in front of the large, heated cage filled with rowdy gibbons, Hal, who had been a volunteer docent at the zoo for the past few summers, stepped into that role. "Gibbons are apes, so they have no tail. They mate for life and live in family groups. When they wake up in the morning, they scream and act scary for about half an hour to warn other gibbons to stay out of their territory. They're native to southeast Asia, but they're an endangered species because the rain forests are disappearing."

"Do they bite?" Jamey asked as he stuck his finger out to investigate.

"Yes! Hard! Keep your hands away. They're mild-mannered in the wild, but they get mean after they've been in a cage for a while."

Hal walked on with the boys. I had a difficult time tearing myself away from the gibbons cage and not because of Hal's educational speech, but because I kept seeing a whole bunch of Hilda Matchetts, climbing around in their bare butts. When I imagined them all wearing little Chanel suits and little pearl necklaces, the resemblance was simply uncanny. I thought I could practice saying, "Hell, no, I won't go teach that damned course!" in front of them. But then Hal grabbed me from behind and whispered in my ear, "They sure look like her, don't they?"

I asked innocently, "Who?"

"Matchett the Hatchet, who else?" he said with a snicker.

The gibbons had become even rowdier, a few of them were now screaming at me.

Hal took me by the arm and pulled me away from the cage. "Come," he said. "They think you're going to attack them if you stare at them like that."

After the reptiles, safely behind glass, Hal treated the boys to hot dogs, the alternative being pretzels covered with big lumps of salt. I passed but did feel called upon to take Hal aside and remark that the boys hadn't even stayed with us a full twenty-four hours and this was the third time they'd been fed hot dogs. What kind of example was that?

"You wouldn't understand," he said. "It's a man thing. Loosen up. Here!" And he held his hotdog in front of my mouth.

I took a bite. Nobody had ever accused me of not being loose enough.

We sauntered into the small theater near the center of the zoo grounds where they were continuously showing a film about the disappearing rain forests that pointed an accusatory finger at mankind. When the credits rolled, I wondered what these two little boys had to look forward to.

The animals in those cages. The forests disappearing. The naked ape wreaking havoc, wanting so much more than just to cover its nakedness. This was all so thoroughly depressing. I should have let Hal take the boys to the zoo and just stayed home. I was no fun at all. Hal gave me one of his funny looks when I suggested we plant some more trees around the house.

But Jesse and Jamey didn't seem to notice their futures were shot. On our way out, Hal bought them each a bag of popcorn. "To make sure they have a balanced meal," he said, grinning at me.

The brightly colored parrots printed on the popcorn bags reminded me that I had inherited Solo. If Lani's children weren't starving him to death. How would Moon and Mellow deal with the foul-mouthed cretin? Who would win a fur-and-feathers Armageddon? How could I get rid of him? To whom could I give a bird whose cage had to be covered whenever there was company? Maybe the zoo would take him. Hardly anyone spoke French anyway.

When we got home the boys wanted to play out in the mud. Hal and I looked at each other, but neither of us could think of any real reason why they shouldn't be allowed to do that. Mab and Dooley would look after them. Dooley drooling and Mab semi-aloof.

For the next half hour, Hal and I had some quiet time. We each grabbed a book and a couch in the living room. The wind came up and started blowing around the house, but the boys stayed outside. From the love seat, I could see them splashing in the puddles, swinging sticks, and yelling at each other. Mab was lying low under the beech trees. Dooley, unable to decide whom to adore more, kept scuttling back and forth between the two boys.

I lowered my eyes back to the book I was reading, John Irving's *A Son of the Circus,* a long and intricate tale told in Irving's usual quirky style. I realized I'd read the same paragraph about three times now without having any idea what it said, because I'd been watching the boys.

I looked over at Hal. He was nearly finished with his refresher course of *Abduction*. I'd leafed through some of those books of his. In one of them I'd found a checklist that was supposed to help identify oneself as an abductee. *Have you lost time? Do you often find bruises and cuts on your body you cannot explain? Do you find yourself in places and cannot remember how you got there? Are you ever compelled to do something that is not your own idea?*

Many of the questions had looked familiar. It had taken me some time to figure out why. They were nearly identical to the ones on the list handed to me at my first meeting of AA to help identify myself as an alcoholic. *Maybe you've made a mistake!* Denial had whispered.

"What'll we have for dinner?" I asked.

"We're out of hot dogs," Hal said without looking up from his book. "How about pizza? If you call it in, I'll get it. Combination with anchovies!"

Sounded good to me. Ben's Warme Bakkerij also prepared ready-to-bake pizzas with thick crusts made with real yeast, not that premixed baking soda stuff. I hoisted myself off the couch and phoned in the order while Hal called the boys who immediately went into a state of absolute euphoria when they heard they were going to be fed pizza. It must be another food Grace wouldn't allow in her home. Poor Grace! In one single weekend, we were undoing years of responsible child-rearing.

"How about I rent a movie, too?" Hal suggested. "The boys might like to see *Chucky*."

"You're not serious," I said. Now he was going too far. "They won't sleep for two weeks."

"You think so?" He seemed genuinely surprised, as if he'd totally forgotten what it was like to be eight years old.

"I *know* so," I said. *Chucky*, indeed! It was bad enough they'd seen Lani. But, of course, I didn't say this to Hal and hoped the boys wouldn't either.

Only Jamey wanted to join him on the trip to Londen. My motherly instincts now in full gear, I remarked that neither of the twins should be taken anywhere except to the bath tub, because they were covered with mud from head to toe, but Hal said his truck needed cleaning anyway, so Jamey hurriedly washed his hands and face, and danced after his uncle.

"Why don't you go take a bath now?" I said to Jesse.

"Aunt Fae!" Jesse whined playfully but then immediately jumped up. "OK!" On his way upstairs, he shouted, "Do I have to put my jammies on already?"

"Only if you want to," I yelled back. A few moments later I could hear the water running in the bath tub. I tried to remember if as an eight-year-old I had still needed help, but decided if he just sat in the tub for a few minutes and then dried himself off, he'd be clean enough.

As I was setting the table, Jesse's voice rose above the splashing, first hesitantly, repeating lines, then finally in full song. "All night, all day, Marianne. Down by the seaside sifting sand. Even little children love Marianne. Down by the seaside sifting sand." Over and over.

He came downstairs wearing his *Superman* pajamas, his wet hair standing out in all directions. Somehow, it didn't look too clean. I'd have to ask Hal to investigate, check his ears.

He sat down at the table and began to hum "Marianne" again.

"That's a very nice song," I said. "Did your teacher teach you that?"

He looked at me as if I had lost my mind and said, "My teacher doesn't sing. Mr. Marks teaches music!"

"Well, did Mr. Marks teach you that song?" I placed a stack of napkins in the holder at the center of the table. We would need plenty of those.

"Noooo!"

"Well then, is it a secret?"

"Nooo!" He shook his head like a valley girl. "The lady taught me the song!"

I had a sinking feeling but asked dumbly, "What lady?"

"You know, the lady in red. The one who was there yesterday, next to the barn. The one who moved in here last week."

Wait a minute! Moved in here?

"*Gadverdamme!*" I said under my breath.

"You said a bad word, aunt Fae!" He wasn't so much shocked as stating a fact.

"It was a Dutch word. You don't speak Dutch," I said.

"Nope, but you cursed!"

"I sure did," I admitted. "Just don't tell your mother!"

"*Gadverdamme!*" Jesse said in perfect Dutch.

"Will you sing that nice song for me again?" I asked.

He was still singing sweetly, and driving me a bit nuts, when Hal and Jamey came in, each carrying a box.

As we were about to attack our pizza, the distinct, huffing noise of Sasha's Volkswagen bus coming up our driveway could be heard. After a short rap on the door, Sasha made a subdued entrance. All her rings were back in place and her hair was gathered into a low pony tail, showing the shaved sides above her ears.

The boys stared at her in awe, mouths agape.

I introduced them to each other and invited her to join us. She sat down, making a funny face for the boys, arching her eyebrows and rolling her eyes.

The twins glanced at each other and, after some secret mutual go-ahead, began to laugh loudly. I thought we might have to tie them to their chairs, but soon the silliness faded and we were all munching on pizza while listening to Sasha's stories.

She told us about her adventures in Europe, where she said she'd been several times in recent years. I remembered the many stickers on her old suitcase. The boys were astounded. At each tidbit of trivia they jerked their heads around and looked at each other, bug-eyed.

"I went to this real castle outside Amsterdam, you know. They used to have a wooden shelf next to their bed, and at night they would comb out the fleas and lice, let them fall on that shelf, and then they'd smash them."

Hal and the boys munched on unperturbed, but this was more than I needed to be reminded of while eating pizza.

How had Sasha been able to afford all these European vacations?

Chapter 22

Look here, upon this picture, and on this.

After dinner, Sasha said she wanted to talk to me. I asked her to come up to my office, where we would have some privacy. She followed me upstairs and sat down in Dooley's chair, her hands grasping the armrests as if they were the sides of a roller coaster car. Shifting position, she relaxed and glanced around the room. She then cleared her throat several times and asked if it would be OK to smoke. In answer, I handed her an ashtray. But she just stared at it.

I had a notion Sasha could perhaps use a little more time to collect her thoughts and excused myself. Down in the kitchen, I started some coffee.

Hal and the boys were setting up for a game of cards. He had taught them to play poker the year before, at the tender age of seven, something his sister wouldn't appreciate if she ever found out. I was just glad it wasn't strip poker.

When I got back, Sasha was staring at the tip of her burning cigarette.

The wind was howling now, an eerie noise that made the house creak and produced knocking sounds as if someone were stomping around in the attic. Rain swept against the tall window, the reflection of the barn light making the streaks of water look like falling stars.

"It's a week ago today. Tonight," Sasha said, still gazing at her cigarette.

I could barely hear her, not only because of the wind, but because her voice was barely above a whisper. Gone was the bluster of downstairs, in front of the boys.

She glanced at me. "Since you found her."

I nodded.

"I'm really sorry about what happened at that lawyer's office. You didn't deserve that, you know."

I shrugged. *What the hell, let go and let God.* The fact was that Alicia's behavior had angered me more than I at first had wanted to admit to myself. I'd thought it was a good thing the boys were staying over to keep my mind off her accusations. But then I'd begun to wonder why I cared so much about something Alicia had said and came to the conclusion that my anger was nothing but defensiveness. Not that Alicia's behavior was all right, but the real trouble was inside myself. I was still feeling guilty.

"We never knew what Mother would do next, you know, but we expected something like this. Ali would have to admit that, if she could be honest for a few minutes. We're really messed up." She lit another cigarette. "As a family, I mean."

"Sasha, I truly had no idea about the will. As a matter of fact, I've decided to go see a lawyer next week and find out what can be done about changing it." I gestured at her package of cigarettes, and she handed it to me with her lighter.

"Well, I won't be the one to tell Ali that. Let her make fool of herself."

"You always hope a person will do the right thing, so I can understand why Alicia's disappointed, even if she did expect it." I could, although the woman had gone a bit beyond *disappointed*. But then, she'd already been malignant before the will was ever read. "Your mother, I think, was very confused."

"Mother wasn't confused, Fae. She was an MP." She looked me straight in the eyes to register my reaction.

I was lost. My confusion must have shown, for she explained, "A multiple personality."

I looked at her intently. Was she joking? She calmly returned my gaze, a bit of a twinkle in her eyes, the beginning of a smile playing around her lips. What had she called it? MP? I would never get used to the American habit of replacing proper, perfectly comprehensible words with letters.

"Would you like some coffee, Sasha? It should be done by now."

Sasha bit her lip and said that, sure, she'd like some coffee.

I went downstairs thinking, "So, MP doesn't just stand for Member of Parliament, Monty Python, or Military Police. I learn something new every day here in America."

I took my time with the coffee, trying to reconcile Lani's personality and behavior with what I'd learned during my early years at college, when I'd read quite a few articles and books about multiple personality beyond the assigned texts for my psych classes.

A coping mechanism of the mind, multiple personality disorder helps a person survive long-term severe emotional and physical abuse by developing other personalities with traits that enable the person to deal with the chaos and torture he or she is subjected to.

There is a core personality from which the others, each with particular character traits needed in different situations, splinter off. This disorder develops most often before the age of five, at which time the personality normally becomes more or less fixed.

I now wondered, as I had years ago, why it should even be called a "disorder," because it helps a person to not go totally insane. The abuse was the *dis*-order.

What had gotten me into this mini research project was the movie *The Three Faces of Eve*, whose real-life subject, Chris Sizemore, in fact had more than sixty "faces." It was at the height of my drinking career, and I was grasping at anything that might explain my own, often bizarre, behavior. I wanted desperately to know what was wrong with me.

Though my search in this direction now seemed rather peculiar to me, I'd heard countless numbers of recovering alcoholics share that they'd actually been diagnosed with this disorder by a real live psychiatrist, plaque on the wall and all, only to find out later that their alcoholism had mimicked multiple personality disorder, as it apparently can several other illnesses, such as paranoid schizophrenia and bi-polar depression. In each case, the psychiatrist had failed to probe into the drinking or drug habits of the patient. Once alcohol was taken out of the equation, the symptoms disappeared, sometimes practically overnight. These people would become normal. As normal as recovering alcoholics can become.

On the other hand, I had also met a few people who were both alcoholic and MPs, as Sasha called it. One condition didn't exclude the other but made a diagnosis extremely difficult. They had renamed it *dissociative identity disorder*.

I carried two steaming mugs of coffee upstairs and put them down on the desk.

"You didn't know, did you." There was no question in her voice.

"How did you find out she was a multiple personality, Sasha?" I asked carefully.

"She went to see a psychiatrist. That was a little over ten years ago, when I was in my early twenties. Some guy in San Francisco, you know. Willem took her there. She'd been acting very bizarre, losing time, denying that she said or did things." Sasha paused.

So far, this all sounded like the typical run-of-the-gin-mill alcoholic or like one of Hal's abductees.

"I was taking classes and was spending Thanksgiving break on the ranch," Sasha went on. "One night, I rented the movie *Sybil*. Have you seen it?"

I nodded. It had cured me forever of wanting to be a multiple personality.

"Well, just for fun, you know." She smiled apologetically. "I had no idea. I thought it was one of those fright-night movies, like *Carrie*. We watched it together. Mother, Willem, and I. When it was over, we just sat around. Nobody spoke. We kept staring at the TV. It was spooky. Then Mother suddenly began to cry hysterically. She couldn't stop. 'That's us, that's us.' She kept saying '*us*.'

"I immediately knew she didn't mean her, Willem, and me. It was the first time I ever heard her use the plural in referring to herself. I thought I was going to flip my lid, you know." Sasha took a sip of her coffee. "She was right, though. It *was* her. *Them*."

This would indeed explain some of Lani's capricious behavior Kate and Janny and the three siblings had told me about, her costume and interior decorating adventures, the marked switches in her personality. Her hair.

"So, what happened? How was she diagnosed?"

"Willem finally calmed her down and promised to take her to a doctor, a psychiatrist, the next week. He did, you know. But she only saw him maybe four times. Then she refused to go any longer."

"Why was that?"

"She got into an argument with him. Or, rather, *they* did. I mean, several of her personalities. They didn't agree with the doctor about his proposed method of treatment. He wanted to integrate all the personalities, insisted it would be the best way to go."

"Both the disease and various treatment approaches are controversial," I commented.

"You're telling me! I guess that was *their* feeling, too. The doctor wanted them to become one, *they* did not. They said it would be impossible to decide which of them would have to be killed off, and which would live. Especially the one named Karen was extremely outspoken. She raised Alicia, you know, though she wasn't her real mother. I guess the doctor got kind of pushy, so she screamed at him that she was against the death penalty, and who the hell did he think he was, playing God? Willem could hear her all the way in the waiting room, you know. She slammed the door behind her and told him to take her home. She never went back or got other treatment."

"You said Karen raised Alicia?"

"We were all born of different birth-mother personalities." Sasha smiled. "They showed up because they could deal with the pain of giving birth and then they'd disappear. Others stepped in to raise us. Karen was extremely strict and critical. *Mommy Dearest.* I think Alicia got mostly the mean ones.

"Luckily, someone else was there for me, a hippy chick named Sky. There was Jane, who would often come out in the evening and read us bedtime stories. Then there was little Mary, who wasn't any kind of mother at all. She was a kid. She played with us and let us do anything we wanted. Jump on the beds, eat ice cream for breakfast. She was really cool!"

Sasha had become more and more animated as she was talking. She was smiling a lot, even letting out a giggle here and there, as if somehow the painful chaos of her childhood had been one great party, but she kept biting her nails in between sentences.

My heart went out to her, and then I realized I was looking at my own reflection, making light of things so the weight wouldn't pull me down into a swamp of self-pity. Ours was the laughter of survival. We knew we weren't unique in our suffering and that everything was relative. Whenever I heard other people's childhood horror stories, I always felt that mine hadn't been so bad after all.

"Do you have any idea how she came to be that way?"

"She wasn't adopted by the Pochards until she was almost five. All we know is that when she was dumped at the orphanage, she was covered with bruises and couldn't make up her mind about what her name was. That's what they told the Pochards. They were good people, my grandparents. They both died in a car crash when I was twenty."

"Not long before your mother finally received that diagnosis?"

"Yes, you're right." Sasha looked surprised. "Maybe that's what made her get worse."

"So, who were friends with me?" I asked, loosely using the word *friends*.

"Several. I think Lani liked you best."

"Lani?" There had been a real Lani?

"Then there were some who couldn't stand you." She gave an embarrassed giggle.

"Really?" *I wish I'd known this earlier.*

"Yes, the one who was going with Steve, for example. Candy. She said you were snooty to him."

"She did, huh?"

"Well, she actually used another word. Candy was sort of a biker chick." Sasha raised her eyebrows in pretend disapproval. "Don't worry! Candy didn't like anybody *but* Steve. None of the others cared for him, except maybe little Mary who didn't know any better. A few weren't even aware that Steve existed."

"Wow!" I shook my head.

"Some also liked to play tricks on the others, you know. One would do something weird, disappear, and then another would be left holding the bag. Jane was often the victim of these pranks, and she'd become very upset. She was so prim and proper, you know. Even had her own set of dishes. She was the last one to decorate the living room, I think."

"How do you know all this?" I was rather confused by this flood of information. A close-up of a real-life multiple personality was so much more overwhelming than reading a book or watching a movie, in which everything was nicely organized about the subject. "I mean, how did you find out about all these different personalities, who they were, and which one was out?"

"Quite a few of them talked to me at one time or another. I guess they considered me to be *safe*. That means they felt they could trust me." She stared at me. "I thought that somehow you knew. You really had no idea?"

"Not an inkling." I shook my head. "I just thought she was ... , uh, drunk." *Why beat around the bush, Fae?*

"That's what Alicia wanted to believe, you know. That Mother was fickle and a mean drunk. She couldn't accept the idea that Mother was a multiple personality. It's kind of funny how Ali now wants to use this diagnosis to contest the will, while she refused to believe it all these years." Sasha bit her nails some more.

"That's kind of why I came over. To tell you that she's already been to the library this afternoon to get a list of psychiatrists that practice in San Francisco. See, we cannot remember the doctor's name. She wants to have Mother declared incompetent posthumously, I think. Or something like that."

"Can that be done?"

"I have no idea. Ali's going to try." An apologetic grimace.

"She should save herself the trouble," I said.

"Nah! Maybe it'll get some of the poison out if she thinks she has a mission. Give poor Chuck a break." She grinned at me and got up. "I'm going back to the house."

Downstairs, Sasha high-fived the boys, said goodbye to Hal, and gave me a hug. After letting her out, I went straight back upstairs, my head reeling as if several puzzles had been tossed out of their boxes at the same time. I had to think.

I'd read how one personality could have allergies the others didn't share. On a physical level, alcoholism was a kind of allergy. If Lani had multiple personalities, it could mean not all of them were alcoholic. Sasha had said that some liked playing tricks on the others. Could there have been some controlling temperance-movement personality among them who had taken the Boozabuse, had then disappeared, leaving one of the drunks to get deathly ill? But that would go against the mechanics and the whole purpose of multiple personality, which was to cope and survive.

On yet another level, I wondered if in the hereafter the personalities had now finally been integrated. If not, which of them were haunting me? Lani's ghost had consistently worn her red dress, even for Jesse. If Lani was only one now, which one? Who had been her core personality? Or were they all still arguing in that other realm of existence? Was she still an alcoholic—out there?

And how did that old Dutch soccer drinking song go again? "In Heaven There's No Beer, That's Why We Drink It Here."

Enough of all this. I must have looked as funny as I felt, because as soon as I walked back into the kitchen, Hal frowned at me and asked, "Is something wrong?"

Even the kids noticed I wasn't my usual self. "Aunt Fae, you look weird!" Jesse said with concern.

"You look like you've seen a ghost!" Jamey offered as a second opinion. He opened his eyes wide and spread his arms. "Boo!"

"Time for bed!" I called out with a stern face.

They rolled off their chairs in a phony fit of laughter.

"Just joking!" I rubbed Jesse's head with my knuckles. "You guys want to watch a movie?"

Hal said they first had to finish the game. Jesse was winning.

Chucky having been successfully eliminated, I went into the living room to check out our movie collection and decided on *Milo and Otis*, because it was the only childproof movie we owned. They'd watched it every time they'd come to visit for at least the past four years, so I knew they liked it.

Habits, I thought. What is familiar feels safe, even if it isn't. I could see why Lani had refused treatment. Why would she have wanted to give up the known for the unknown? And why would Alicia want to part with her familiar resentments of Lani? If she did, she could no longer blame her mother for her fairy-tale-gone-wrong life with Charles. Perhaps Alicia was afraid of the new Charles, alias Chuck.

My own resentments toward Lani had directly resulted from my habit of not setting boundaries. Someone might not like me anymore if I set limits. Although, in Lani's case, would setting boundaries have worked? If I had said stop to one personality, wouldn't another just have come tramping along? I couldn't believe I'd been so blind, hadn't been able to see that Lani had more than a drinking problem.

Hal and the boys came in for the movie, saving me from thinking more deep thoughts.

"What are we watching?" Jamey asked.

"*Milo and Otis*." I read the title off the jacket as if I didn't know, as if *they* didn't know, and stuck the DVD in the player.

"Yeah! All right!" The easily amused twosome exclaimed. Hal made a super bored face behind their backs, but he sat down with Jesse and Jamey slumped on each side against him. The three of them talked more than Dudley Moore did, and when I gave them a large bowl of popcorn they got even noisier. But before the happy ending, the twins were snoring softly. We took them upstairs and tucked them into bed under only mild and groggy protest.

"What did Sasha have to say?" Hal asked as we came back into the living room. He stretched out on the couch.

I lay down on the loveseat, my legs over the armrest, staring at the ceiling, and reported to him what Sasha had said about Lani, and how this might open up a whole new set of possibilities, and how very confusing this made everything, and how stupid I felt that I hadn't known Lani was a multiple personality.

I poured my heart out.
"What do you think?" I finally asked.
Hal didn't answer.
I looked over at him.
He was sleeping like an eight-year-old.

Chapter 23

I'll cross it, though it blast me.

Sunday morning, I was determined that for once we were going to have a real breakfast. The hotdogs were gone, and Hal, whom I'd left sleeping on the couch, had eaten the left-over pizza in the middle of the night before he'd come to bed.

While I was shaking the Brinta cereal out of the box, Jesse wanted to know if it had sugar and "perservatives." I told him no but we could add some.

"Is this really from Holland?" Jamey looked at the box, trying to decipher the language.

"Really!" I handed him the milk. He missed the bowl a bit but got enough on his cereal to make it edible.

"How did it get here?" Jesse wanted to know.

"My brothers send packages over once in a while with Dutch foods. You can also buy it at the store here." Actually, their wives sent the packages. My brothers pretended not to know enough to put a package together, except for Gert, my brother one up from me, who threw rubber spiders and snakes in with the foam peanuts, and had added a big gob of home-made slime in the last package. It had taken me half an hour to get it off my hands. Hilarious.

"You have *brothers*?" they asked in unison, looking at each other as if they'd just discovered I was human after all.

"Sure, I have brothers! Four of them, as a matter of fact." This must be a *Milo-and-Otis* thing. I'd told them all about my brothers before, thousands of times.

"Are they as *old* as you are?" Jamey With-the-Social-Graces inquired.

"No, two are older and two are younger."

"So, you're in the middle." Jesse had just figured out the root of all my problems.

Hal concurred, "She sure is! Now, eat your cereal." He was in a hurry to get out to the barn to do things to his bike. The weather was clear, and that meant his riding buddies would be coming over at noon.

"Are they all in Holland?" Jesse With-the-Spinach-Packed-Ears continued the inquest.

"Mmm!" I pointed at his bowl. They both got the idea and munched on quietly.

We were putting the dishes away when Kate called. She sounded very mysterious and wanted to know if I could meet her in town at Full of Beans. I asked if she would come to our house instead, because Hal's nephews were staying over. She said she certainly would, because she *really* had to talk to me. When I probed for a little preview, she became coy and clammed up on me. "I'll tell you when I get there. Say, about eleven?"

Hal went out to the barn with Jamey and Jesse in tow. I pretended to clean, playing my pick-up game of randomly moving things from one place to another so that when I was done, everything was in a different place and we couldn't find anything anymore. Hal spent whole days doing this in the barn. Hours after he'd disappear, I'd walk into his work area and ask, "Hi, Honey, what are you doing?" He'd say, "Oh, getting organized." And I swear it always looked the same, but I'd nod and look around as if impressed with the enormous improvement the area has just undergone. He returned the favor for me in the house, but then he'd act as if I worked for the lost-and-found booth at the county fair.

By the time Kate arrived I'd managed to build several heaps of clothes, books, and toys near the foot of the stairs in the hall way. Most of it was the boys' stuff. It amazed me how much Grace could fit in one bag and how much the duo had found in nooks and crannies, left behind from prior visits.

"Looks like you've been busy!" Kate remarked.

"Don't beat around the bush," I said. "You've come to tell me something."

"Guess!" Her Irish eyes sparkled. She looked radiant.

"They found your run-away?"

"No!"

"You're pregnant?"

"No!" She made a face as if she'd never done it. Innocent. Shocked.

"Oh, come on, just tell me!"

"Pour me a cup of coffee and sit down," she commanded. We had to go through her cream and sugar ritual, which took forever because she emptied half the sugar pot spoon by spoon in her cup, before she finally would look me in the eyes again.

"He's asked me to marry him!" She let out a deep, delighted sigh.

"Who?" I feigned total confusion.

"Fae-hae!" She sounded like one of the twins, even punched me on my arm.

I laughed and got up to give her a big hug. "That's good news, Kate!" And I meant it. I wasn't so sure about this archaic *asking* bit, though. It would never have occurred to me to wait for Hal to *ask* me to marry him, just as it would have never occurred to him to ask me. We just got married.

"You don't think it's too soon?" Worry-clouds had suddenly appeared in her eyes. "It's only been a little over five months."

"Did you set a date?"

"No ... " She hesitated. "We didn't even talk about a date." By the look on her face I could tell that this aspect of the engagement hadn't entered either's mind. What a match!

"What are you worried about?"

"We're not kids anymore!" She said, as if that was supposed to explain something I'd obviously not understood.

"Kate, is something the matter?" I asked in my trust-me voice.

"No!" She shook her head and pursed her lips. Then she said, "It's just that you're the first person I've told, and suddenly I'm scared."

I could fix that. "You can stay engaged forever, you know? It took us ten years to get married."

"But you lived together!" It sounded like an accusation.

"We did, but we talked about getting married for several years."

"I didn't know that. You suddenly took off for Reno and came back married." She still sounded miffed.

"We only talked about marriage when we were watching TV movies, for some reason. During the commercial breaks, one of us would bring up the fact that we really had no reason not to get married. The other would agree, and then the movie would start again. It never went further than that until one day I walked into the garage and Hal said, 'So, when are we getting married?' I asked, 'Do you *want* to get married?' He said, 'Why not?' I still couldn't think of a reason, so the next day we took off and got married."

"He asked you to marry him in the *garage*?"

"It was before we had a barn," I said defensively. "And he didn't *ask*."

"Are you saying we should live together first? My parents would absolutely kill me."

Getting killed already seemed pretty absolute to me. It appeared my story wasn't quite making it as a compare-and-contrast essay, and I wasn't sure what it had to do with Kate's dilemma—not knowing exactly what Kate's dilemma was—or if it had put her mind at ease at all.

"It's a big step," Kate said.

"So, what was your answer?" I asked.

"I said *yes*, of course!"

I snickered.

"You're not making any sense, Fae!"

I wasn't making sense? "If he was just *asking*, you could have answered, 'Let me think about it for a while,'" I said.

The sound of several motor cycles rattled the windows. We went out unto the porch to say *hello* to the gang.

Jesse and Jamey walked around the bikes in a complete state of stupefaction, eyes as big as flying saucers. They were absolutely ecstatic when the Judge and Bobby offered to take them for a short ride. Sam and Hal lent the boys their helmets. They looked like two little aliens.

Kate and I went back inside. "I'm going to see a lawyer this week about Lani's will," I said.

"I've been thinking about that, about you inheriting from her. I wondered if there would be a problem."

"There is. Alicia is furious. And rightfully so, although not with the right person. I had nothing to do with Lani changing her will."

"I know that. But I was thinking more about what happens if they decide it wasn't an accidental death after all. I mean, you still don't believe it was an accident, do you?"

"No, I don't. That whole Boozabuse thing is fishy. Bobby promised to look into it."

"Would they think you had something to do with her death?"

"That's exactly what Rita suggested." I frowned at Kate.

She frowned back. She still didn't like to be compared with Rita, of all people, despite their little chat at Lani's funeral. I hadn't fixed that yet.

"Not that Bobby would ever think that about you, but I mean Lani's family," Kate said.

"Alicia's already accused me of first making Lani change her will and then killing her." I raised an eyebrow to show what I thought about that. "I still need to talk to Bobby about Steve Krieger. Did you notice that bandage on his cheek at the funeral? Rita told me that Sarah scratched the rapist's face."

"Oh, my God!" Kate clapped her hand over her mouth. "You think he did it then? First killed Lani and then raped Sarah? Do you *sense* this?"

Kate had been aware of my psychic abilities since we'd met in Berkeley, when at first she'd scoffed at the idea of second sight, because she had no such experiences, she claimed. I later thought it had more to do with her upbringing and the fact that she hadn't known me well enough yet to realize I found my gifts a burden, nothing to brag about.

But then a female student had disappeared. The university community was shocked. Flyers were posted everywhere, on trees, on buildings, in coffee shops. Volunteers searched the hills. The girl seemed to have vanished into thin air. About a month after her disappearance, I had a vision of where she was and told Kate. Two days later, the student was found in a shallow grave, covered by leaves and branches, exactly as I'd seen. From the point of view of the victim, as Gwen had recently explained.

It was the first of such visions, and it happened not long after my mother passed over. I'd often thought there was a relationship between my mother appearing to me two months after her death and the sudden onset of these visions. I couldn't think of anything else that might have triggered this. It had been distressing to know that, against all our hopes, the girl wouldn't be found alive. It had filled me with intense sadness, and this had been the only reason I had said anything to Kate.

But still, after all these years of friendship, it was one thing to talk to Kate about having insights and intuitions, the mild stuff, or even visions, but it was a very different thing to talk to her about Lani inciting electrical insurrections and actually appearing to me. That's why I hadn't told her anything about Lani's afterlife behavior. I wasn't sure how she would take it.

"Sense intuitively? No, but it makes sense. I'm just putting two and two together." *Hadn't Gwen said Lani wanted to tell me something?* I looked at Kate. *Should I tell her more?* No, not unless she brought it up herself, as Janny had done. But it made me feel as if I weren't being totally honest with Kate.

"How is Sarah doing?" Kate asked.

"She's slowly recovering. Rita said Sarah was supposed to come home yesterday. I'll go for a visit tomorrow." I swallowed hard. "I'm just so glad she's alive."

Kate nodded. "I was doing some research the other day for a paper I'm presenting next month on domestic abuse. I came across a bunch of statistics that just made me sick to my stomach. Did you know that every nine seconds a woman is assaulted and beaten? One in every six women in America is a victim of rape. That doesn't even include victims under the age of twelve. They're on a separate list. Who knows how many children suffer abuse. And, you wonder how many rapes and assaults are never reported, because they happen in the home. It's probably closer to one in four women. I kept thinking about Sarah and about the kids at my school, and that behind those cold numbers are real human beings, each and every one of them suffering at the hands of another human being who considers them nothing but prey."

Kate was in deep thought for a while, a troubled look on her face. Suddenly, she raised her head and said, "I don't understand something. Remember when you called me from the hospital and told me you thought Krieger mistook Sarah for you because of the jacket you gave her?"

"Yes, and you told me to hold off on the crucifixion."

Kate ignored that. "Well, say you're right—and I'm not saying you are, but there's the jacket and the bandage ... "

I frowned. "Say what now?"

"Say Krieger thought Sarah was you. Why, if he wanted to shut you up about Lani, did he let her go?"

"Maybe he finally realized she wasn't me. She's taller and her hair is much longer. I don't know what else he thought I could say, anyway. I'd already told Bobby that Lani was supposed to go to the movies with him the night she was killed. Maybe he wanted revenge. Maybe it had nothing to do with shutting me up."

"Oh," she said. She looked disappointed that she'd have to find another way to prove me wrong. The crucifixion was still on.

"Did you know Lani was a multiple personality?" I asked, point blank.

"Yes, it occurred to me," Kate answered calmly, then she corrected herself. "I knew, kind of."

"Why didn't you ever tell me?" While I had been struggling to deal with Lani, my best friend had left me in the dark about something this crucial?

"I first noticed her memory lapses, and that she had them even when I was sure she hadn't been drinking. She would also suddenly change her body language and speech patterns. Then there was the way she dressed, as if she had several completely different wardrobes. I suspected something more than alcoholism was going on. But she never came out and told me in so many words, so I wasn't sure if she was even aware of it herself. I couldn't talk about it to you, because I was her sponsor, too, kind of."

"Oh," I said. Kate was right. Whatever I told her wouldn't go any further either.

"There's an enormous stigma attached to multiple personality disorder. We've had a few students at our school who were diagnosed MPs. These kids struggle tremendously. It's very painful. I've thought a lot about how this condition begins. In early life, at some level, these people choose to create the alternate personalities to survive what they're going through. I wonder if later, when it has outlived its initial purpose, it hasn't become a habit, a form of addiction. But by then the personality is set, and they don't know another way of being. Does that make sense?"

"Yes it does. It sounds a bit like alcoholism. Early on, we choose to drink because it makes us feel better, but then we cross a line and the choice shifts beyond our reach because the behavior has become fixed. Certain pathways in the brain are probably created and it takes some major rerouting to change this. Of course, our brains don't seem to function like those of normal people to begin with. I read that cell memory has something to do with the inability to stop."

Kate let out a snorty laugh. "I'm glad they're doing all this research finally. It supports about everything they wrote about alcoholism nearly seventy years ago. It'll be funny when some day they discover that all abnormal, antisocial behavior ultimately comes down to cell memory and brain chemistry. Thought influencing the physical world, the physical affecting the mental, like a cycle. Then sin will be no more. The preachers and priests will be out of work."

Did I have a genuine heretic on my hands? "That would only address compulsive, repetitive behaviors. But I'm hoping they get some more insight into mental illnesses."

"When did you figure it out about Lani?" Kate asked.

"I didn't. Sasha told me. In Lani's case, could one of the personalities have taken the Boozabuse without the others knowing? Sasha said they sometimes played tricks on each other."

"Your guess is as good as mine." Kate shrugged, not uncaringly.

Hal came in to announce that he and the guys were taking off and the boys would be left to play in the back. It would be a short ride, no more than a couple of hours.

I dug around in my freezer, found some chicken soup I'd made some weeks earlier, and stuck it in the microwave to defrost.

Kate took one look at the block of frozen soup and said she was going to visit Janny, who should be home from church by now.

"Does she know yet?" I asked.

"No. At least, I doubt Bobby called her early this morning to tell her."

"Men are funny that way. Hal wanted to keep our marriage a secret. For no reason other than that he thought it would be fun." I shook my head. "I told him he could keep it a secret, but I was going to organize a big party to celebrate. Then he wanted to keep it a secret *and* have a party."

"The male mystique." Kate smiled. "That was a great party."

"You must have met Bobby then for the first time. He was there."

"I did. I remember thinking how cute he was. But our paths crossed only a few times all these years, and only when one of our students was seriously out of control."

"It would be hard to get a date out of that."

After saying goodbye to the boys, Kate took off to see her future mother-in-law. I could just imagine Janny's pleased face when she heard the news. And all the advice she'd have to impart.

Life's good, I thought and poured the soup in a pan and popped some bread in the toaster. Then I realized I still hadn't talked to Kate about Matchett and my annoying fall assignment. Maybe I should draw a star on my hand to remind myself.

I turned the heat under the soup down and buttered the toast, putting two more pieces of bread in the toaster. I was glad everything was behaving now. Except for my blow dryer inexplicably turning on and off this morning, the appliance uprising had apparently been a one-time event. I wondered if Lani maybe thought she was entertaining me. What had been the purpose of all the ruckus she'd made so far?

I'd read somewhere about spirits stuck in limbo—not the Catholic but the transitional kind—because they were unaware that they were dead. That didn't make much sense. It seemed to me that it would be pretty obvious if you were dead, but then I'd never been dead. Not that I remembered, at least. If spirits could be unaware that they were dead, and if Lani was one of those, would she still be a multiple personality in the hereafter? But why was she, or were *they*, bugging me?

I had just finished setting the table and opened the door to call the boys in, when one of them screamed like an overpaid banshee.

"Aunt Fae! Aunt Fae!"

I ran out the back door. Mab was running around my car. Jamey was banging on the passenger door.

Jesse sat in the driver seat, crying hysterically, his face red with fright as he frantically tried to open the door on his side. In the back sat Dooley, a confused look on his big face, barking rhythmically as if to some inner meter.

"What happened?" I asked Jamey who ran to me as soon as he saw me. He grabbed my hand and dragged me over to the car.

"He's locked in the car! He can't get out!" Jamey let go of my hand and pulled on the door handle. The door didn't budge. "Can you help him? Can you get him out?"

"Oh, calm down!" I said and tried the handle myself. "Stop pulling on the handle inside," I instructed Jesse. He was still crying but did as I told him.

"Now, pull up that little locking button." I pointed at it. Again, he did as I told him.

I pulled the handle. The button went down. I let go of the handle. The button went up. Each time I pulled the handle the button went down, each time I quit pulling the button went up. I tried grabbing the handle quickly, but the button went down even faster.

Very funny!

"It's the lady," Jamey cried, "She won't let him out! She locked him in!"

"That's enough!" I said sternly—but not to Jamey.

Suddenly, Dooley quit barking. His head turned sideways and his eyes followed something that was leaving the car.

Something I couldn't see.

The locking button was left in the up position. I opened the door and helped Jesse out. He put his arms around my waist, holding on for dear life. I stroked his hair and murmured, "Now, now."

"She said we'd play a game!" Jesse sobbed.

"She's mean!" Jamey said indignantly.

I looked down at them. "Next time she shows up, tell her you're no longer allowed to play with her."

Although I wasn't sure it would work, my suggestion seemed to make sense to the boys. They nodded, took a deep breath, and dried their eyes.

But I had to pry their little arms off me and push them down in their chairs at the kitchen table.

Lunch was a healing event.

Chapter 24

**For this relief much thanks;
'tis bitter cold and I am sick at heart.**

With an enthusiasm born of having survived a major catastrophe, the boys took their belongings to their room. They stomped up and down the stairs, happy to perform a mindless task that required nothing more than repetitious movement. Moon and Mellow snuck off to their semi-secret hiding places to avoid the bustle.

When Hal and his buddies came roaring up the drive, the twins immediately abandoned their chore to run outside.

"Hey!" I ineffectively called out after them. Closing the door, I thought maybe I should have told them not to say anything about what happened with my car, but they seemed to have all but forgotten about the incident, their little towheads popping up all over the place between the bikes.

A strong sense of *déjà vu* came over me when a little later all the guys were sitting around the table, rolling cigarettes. But as usual when the point came when I thought I could predict what would happen next, the whole illusion fell apart and turned into *jamais vu*. The brain playing tricks. As I poured the coffee, the echo in my head subsided.

"Guess Kate told you, huh?" Bobby quietly asked when I filled his mug.

I was somewhat surprised that he would talk about it, in broad daylight!

"Told Fae what?" Hal wanted to know.

"Bobby and Kate are getting married," I said with an innocent smile.

All the guys looked silently at Bobby, who glared at me as if I'd just betrayed him. Lifting my eyebrows, I shrugged lightly and put my hand over my mouth in an oops! gesture. He shouldn't have brought it up if he didn't want it broadcast all over the county. News like this was just too good to keep to myself. "Congratulations! I'm very happy for you two!" I gave him a big smacking kiss on the cheek.

He didn't turn the other cheek but smiled and shook his head. At last, the others stopped staring and began to slap him on the shoulder, wishing him good luck, something that had always sounded rather dubious to me.

"Why do they wish the man good luck as if he's going on some perilous mission but congratulate the woman as if her mission is accomplished? When in all truth … "

"Because there's nothing 'as if' about it," Hal said, smirking.

Sam snickered. And so did Pete and Paul and John and Bobby. There was a virus going around.

"Sam will be our last man standing." Hal raised his coffee mug to toast their *pars pro toto* incarnate of bachelorhood.

I returned the pot to the coffeemaker and glowered at my husband, hands on my hips. He grinned and pulled me to him. Bobby politely looked away as Hal patted my rear.

"And when is the blessed event?" asked the Judge, dragging on his cigarette.

As I had already gathered from my conversation with Kate, Bobby had no more of an idea about *when* than she did. He looked at me as if I could provide the answer.

I could. "In about a year," I said convincingly. It seemed as good a time as any.

Bobby thought for a moment and then nodded in agreement. That kind of sounded fine to him, too. He had no clue.

"That was a surprise about Lani's will, wasn't it?" Pete van Nuys turned to me.

"How do you know about that?" I certainly didn't think Hal had had much opportunity to talk about this over the roar of bikes, if he would have thought of mentioning it at all.

"Oh, word gets around." Pete laughed. "Sandra told me, yesterday."

"But how did Sandra know?" I was going to get to the bottom of this security leak.

"I have no idea." Pete shook his head.

"My aunts told me about it," said Sam.

I raised my arms in surrender.

"How did you do it?" Sam asked.

"Do what?" I asked.

"Get her to change her will?" Sam grinned.

"Oh, now, that is *very* funny, Sam Verhoog!"

"Hey, I'm just joking!" Laughing, my colleague held up his hands as if to shield himself from attack.

"Fae's upset because that's what Lani's oldest daughter suggested. That she somehow coerced Lani into changing her will." It was Sir Hal, coming to my rescue.

"Nah!" Sam laughed even harder.

Hal's disclosure caused much merriment all around. But then they all looked at me expectantly.

Now that I had their undivided attention, I figured I might as well tell them the rest. "Actually, she suspects me of murdering her mother!" *So, stick that in your helmet! Or, wherever.*

"Oh!" the Judge sighed dismissively. "Who would believe that? That's crazy talk. Must run in that family."

I guessed that when Lani had her run-ins with Bobby, she also must have gone to court a few times. John van der Meer had been around for a long time in this county. I was glad to have him on my side and gave him a grateful look for his support.

"Come on, Fae, she didn't really mean that, did she?" Sam was still snickering.

"I'm sure she did. She was outraged." I was beginning to feel weary again now. John was wrong. Two other people had made the same suggestion, though not in the manner Alicia had. But still.

I also noticed that Bobby had been quietly looking away while this conversation was going on.

"Seen anymore of that Steve character?" Sam asked in an obvious attempt to change the subject. There it was again, *déjà vu*, and the cherry smell in the outhouse.

"He was at the funeral," Hal answered.

"He hasn't been bothering you anymore, has he, Fae?" John checked.

"Oh, no," I answered absentmindedly. I was wondering what Bobby was thinking and why he suddenly wouldn't look at me when the subject of Lani's will and possible murder had been broached. Had he found out something? Whatever it was, he was obviously not going to divulge that information right here and now, maybe not at all, but I badly wanted to talk to him. Alone.

I was just trying to figure out how I could lure Bobby away from the rest of the group, when Matt and Grace drove up. They were early, it was only four-thirty.

As soon as Hal saw that his sister had arrived, he dove into the living room. The boys ran out to meet their parents. I had forgotten to send them upstairs to finish their packing and get cleaned up. The little darlings were absolutely filthy.

Grace stood still in the doorway, fanning the smoky air, a disapproving look on her face that changed to pure dismay when *Born To Be Wild* suddenly blasted through the house. Having made his point, whatever it was, Hal turned the sound down. He returned to the kitchen trying to look as if he'd been a very good boy all his life, avoiding my attempts to catch his eye to administer an ocular chastisement.

He made general introductions, knowing they'd all met before, sat down, and then pointed at two empty chairs. I knew that as soon as he'd shed his leather, he would regain some of his manners.

Grace raised her eyebrows slightly, but I could see that despite herself she was duly impressed with my Dirty Half-Dozen. She sat down quietly next to the Judge, who immediately handed her the tobacco pouch with a deadpan look. She held the pouch between her thumb and index finger for a few moments, studying it as if it were an exotic object and then handed it to Pete, on her other side.

Matt turned his chair around and straddled it, his eyes dreamy, his forearms leaning on the back of the chair.

Jesse and Jamey jumped up and down behind their mother.

"I was locked in the car!" Jesse exclaimed.

"It was the lady, Mom!" Jamey yelled.

"What lady?" Grace asked, amused, turning to her sons.

The boys looked at each other.

"Oh, just a lady," Jesse answered weakly. Jamey glanced at me meaningfully and then quickly turned to talk to his father who was actually rolling a cigarette from the package Pete had just passed him.

Grace looked over at me.

I shrugged, raised my eyebrows the way she had done, and shook my head. *Kids!*

From behind his mother's back, Jesse eyed me. A secretive smile on his face, he put his index finger to his mouth and made the international code-of-silence sign.

Grace went upstairs to help the boys pack up their last belongings. Matt admired his handiwork, what looked like a miniature megaphone. It was obvious this man had never rolled a joint in his life. Or, maybe he was just a great pretender.

I took my coffee and went outside for some fresh air. A frosted sun stood low in the winter sky. The ground under the almond trees was white with petals, just a few blossoms remaining on the trees. The rains and winds had shortened their lifespan by nearly two weeks. There would be only a small crop this year. I looked over at the barn and noticed something was missing. It was Hal's rusty barbecue. He must have moved it into the barn, next to the other ones. If he went on collecting things like that, we might have to build an even bigger barn.

"We had to terminate the investigation," Bobby said behind me.

I turned and looked at him, dismayed.

"We checked everything. There is nothing to indicate foul play. All bottles and glasses were clean. Her stomach was empty. No sign of any Boozabuse other than the pills left in the bottle." Bobby sounded defensive. Probably because of the look I was giving him.

"But how did that bottle get in the medicine cabinet? Who put it there?"

"We questioned her family and friends. Nobody remembers putting it in that cabinet. There were no fingerprints on the bottle."

"Well, isn't that a bit strange?"

"Not really. We solved that mystery. Alicia told us that she cleaned the bathroom, including the cabinet, the night she arrived. She took everything out and placed it on the counter. Then she accidentally splashed a bottle of eau de toilette all over the place, so she rinsed all the containers off and wiped them down before putting them back in the medicine cabinet."

How terribly convenient! "Shouldn't her prints have been on all the containers then?"

"Not necessarily. She was holding them with a towel when she replaced them. She doesn't remember the Boozabuse bottle specifically."

"I think that a sole, large, brown prescription bottle would have stood out like a sore thumb among all those white and pink beauty products," I said.

"Well, you know how when you clean up, you don't usually recall every little item you pick up and put away. Besides, her mother had just suddenly died. Alicia was probably preoccupied."

Preoccupied? You can say that again! But not with her mother's death. "I simply don't think Lani took that medication knowingly. You don't take something to help you stop drinking if you don't want to stop, and especially not when it will make you very ill," I said stubbornly.

"Lani was a multiple personality and a severe alcoholic." He swished his coffee around in his cup. "Alicia told me about her mental condition. Her mother was a very troubled woman."

"It still makes no sense." I stuck my chin out.

Bobby put his cup down on the railing. He looked unconvinced. "Fae, all you have is your intuition. We need something tangible, some proof that she didn't do it herself. We couldn't find any. Believe me, we turned over every rock and looked under it. With as many personalities as Lani apparently had, it's not inconceivable that one of them took that dose of Boozabuse."

"What you're saying is that Lani could be a suspect in her own murder?"

Bobby gave me a funny look but then quickly straightened his face back out. "I wouldn't put it that way. Under the law that would be classified as a suicide." He sighed. "But there's no evidence that she committed suicide. That's why the coroner ruled it an accidental death. And I don't see a murder. Just a very confused victim of her own behavior. She took the Boozabuse, drank on top of it, lost consciousness, and suffocated in the mud."

I should save my breath. We were just talking in circles. Well, at least that got me off the hook as a suspect, if I ever was one. Now I'd have to dig around, find something "tangible" to substantiate what I knew to be true from the moment I had that vision: Lani had been murdered. I could tell that all Bobby thought I suffered from was a little female intuition, which he probably believed I got once a month.

"What's going on with Sarah's case?" I asked. I placed my hands on the banister and gazed at the orchard.

"That's not been assigned to me." He glanced over. "Why?"

I told him about Sarah scratching the rapist's face, about the turquoise jacket, about Steve Krieger's bandage.

"I'll ask them to look into it," he promised. He gently patted my hand. "I'm very sorry, Fae, about Sarah." A cold, hard look turned his eyes to steel. "We'll get the bastard." He clenched his jaws.

"I hope so, Bobby." I let go of the banister and went back inside.

Everyone left at once. Matt and Grace's Volvo drove off amid an escort of bikes, two in front and three behind, breaking all barriers of sound and sanity. Jamey and Jesse were turned around, looking out the rear window, their faces lit up in fascination with the thundering motor cycles. They didn't respond to our goodbye waves. Future bikers of America.

Suddenly, Hal and I were all alone, surrounded only by our dogs and cats. A soft orange-and-pink glow was fading in the west over the horizon. We stood silently, breathing in the frosty evening air.

I gazed at the deep dark blue sky overhead. Night skies usually have a quieting effect on me. When I look up at the stars, I am filled with awe. But sometimes when I look at the stars, I just get very dizzy. I'll wonder when gravity will finally give up on us and we all float into the universe or when the moon will veer from its orbit and collide with earth, as it has done in many of my dreams. Then, I just want to lie down flat on the ground and hug the soil for safety.

Dooley nudged my hand with his big nose. He wanted to be petted, scratched behind his ears. I complied. Mab whined for attention at Hal's side. So, Hal scratched her behind her ears. She whined even harder at that. We were all feeling abandoned.

"I think I'll go to a meeting tonight," I announced.

"That sounds like a good idea," Hal said, too kindly.

I gave him an injured look.

He laughed and playfully picked me up and deposited me in the kitchen.

"I should go over to Lani's house and … " I forgot what I was going to say, because I suddenly realized that the big canal-house-like relic was no longer Lani's house.

"And what?" Hal asked.

"I wonder if they're still there."

"Alicia and Jason left. We saw them on the freeway, going north. He must have been taking her to Sacramento Airport."

That was a relief to hear. I didn't mind Jason so much, but the bottle-wiping Alicia I could do without for a while.

"I should get Solo. He'll have to be locked up in the guest bedroom. I'll have to find a home for him somewhere."

"Moon and Mellow may go nuts even if he's out of sight." Hal picked up the newspaper he hadn't had a chance to read that morning.

"Don't you think Solo is too feisty a meal for a cat?" I asked.

"Frankly, I don't know who would do more damage to whom, but there are two of them and only one of him." He opened the paper. "And don't forget Dooley."

"Dooley's a sweetheart. He wouldn't hurt a fly."

"I wouldn't count on it. He's a retriever." Hal glanced at me. "A *bird* dog. He's a *dog*."

Sometimes Hal's professional advice was absolutely invaluable to me. "Huh?" I said and put on my coat. "See you later!" I pecked his cheek.

"Oh, yeah," he murmured.

✳✳✳

"So, do you have any ideas?" I asked. *And better ones than "pray and hope for the best."*

I was finally talking to Gwen again, face to face. She had apologized for not returning my call because she'd been out of town. I'd forgotten I'd left a message for her until she reminded me. We were standing outside, after the meeting, pow-wow dancing around a bit to stay warm. The air had gotten downright icy, and it was hard to tell the difference between the smoke I blew and the condensation of my breath. I'd just finished telling her about Lani's latest antics.

"It's not that big of a problem, Fae," she said reassuringly. "The important thing is not to get all flustered. Remember what I told you before? How Lani was a certain way here, on this side, and how she's still very much like that. I sense that she enjoys hanging around you. She likes your energy."

Darn! Tell me something else! I nodded in agreement.

"But I also still feel she has something to say to you, only she's being very playful about it." Gwen hesitated. "Well, in view of what she did with the car, *playful* may not be the right word. The way she's going about giving you her message—or rather *not* giving you her message—is part of what she wants to say. Do you understand?"

"You mean I'm supposed to infer something from her behavior?"

"Right! She's using situations as symbols. You have to figure out what they mean. I think you're the only one who *can* figure them out."

"I just would like to figure out how I can … help her go on," I said. "Get rid of her" was what I had really wanted to say, but that didn't sound politically correct in the presence of Gwendolyn Blackwaters.

"It's all about energy." Gwen laughed, fine little crinkles around her dark eyes. "But if you want to get rid of her, there are certain things you can do that speed up the process."

I might as well say what I think around Gwen.

"This kind of spiritual energy," she went on, "can be diffused by the use of sound, light, and scent. So, play music, light candles, open the curtains, and burn some incense. Then talk to her and tell her to go on to the Light."

"That's all?" It sounded a little too simple, like Hal's advice on how to deal with Matchett.

"If it doesn't help, there are other ways to solve this problem."

I wanted to hear about the other ways *first*. Frankly, I wasn't so sure Lani would be chased off by some smells and noises. She'd been producing enough of those herself. If she'd been trying to tell me something, she probably wouldn't leave until I got the message straight. Besides, any incense I'd ever tried smelled like yet another variety of molds and mildews. It made me cough, gave me a headache. It stank!

But I nodded obediently at Gwen.

"It's also important not to be afraid. Negative energy may be attracting her."

"You mean she could be hanging around purely to annoy me?" It had actually never occurred to me to be afraid of Lani's ghost.

"No, she definitely wants to tell you something. She's just being a pain about it. I'm not quite sure what is going on."

"What if I just get mad?" I asked.

"That doesn't work so well either. Both anger and fear create a kind of vacuum that draws in this energy. And, it gives her attention. Just remember, she didn't grow wings." Gwen's eyes were still crinkled in amusement. Her jet black hair was tightly braided in the back. She pulled her purple woolen scarf up over her head and opened her car door. "One other thing you could also do is write her a letter."

I'd heard about that before, writing a letter to a dearly—or not-so-dearly—departed. I thanked her and turned to leave but suddenly remembered the reason for my call to her. "Wait!"

Gwen rolled down her window.

I walked back over to her and told her what had happened to Sarah, but before I could get to my question, she said, "You're wrong, you know."

"Wrong about what?" I hadn't told her anything yet I could've been wrong about.

"About the jacket. I just saw a turquoise jacket. And you're wrong about it."

How did she know about the jacket? I hadn't said a thing about any jacket.

"I have to go now," Gwen said. "Just think about it."

On my way home, I mentally rehashed what Gwen had advised me to do about Lani and worked out a plan of attack. Or, should I call it a plan of defense? Or, the more neutral *plan de campagne*? I spent several miles pondering this issue, only to decide that it mattered absolutely nothing.

First, I would make a to-do list. Even if I never did the to-dos, the list would give me a sense of taking back control over my life. *Careful now.* If I made the list with the idea already in mind that I might not do the to-dos, I wouldn't get that sense of taking back control. Taking charge would involve first organizing information, impressions, facts, and then deciding what actions to take, one step at a time.

Suddenly, I was full of good ideas. I would do a twenty-first-century brainstorm on my computer. It occurred to me that if Moses had lived today, he would have been handed the Ten Commandments on a CD.

It felt very bright inside my head as my high beams illuminated the left-over almond blossoms on both sides of the road. I was going to lick this problem with Lani. My self-esteem rose to unprecedented levels. I congratulated myself on having laid yet another cornerstone to the vast foundation of my true self.

But then I looked to my right and nearly swerved off the road, barely missing a humongous live oak tree. I let out a loud gasp of relief.

When I looked again, she was still next to me in the passenger seat.

"What the hell do you think you're doing!" If she hadn't already been dead, I might have stopped the car and killed her.

She didn't react at all.

Driving at a snail's pace, I leaned on the steering wheel. "Lani, you scared the shit out of me!" I shouted so loudly, my throat ached. "Get out! You're not supposed to be here anymore. You're dead," I said cruelly and immediately felt guilty.

She didn't seem to hear me. Then I realized she wasn't all there.

Only her head and shoulders were showing in a kind of cameo bubble that floated in the air, and she wasn't looking at me or at anything. She had a smile on her face as if she were holding still to have her picture taken.

I pulled over to the side of the road, coming to a halt right in front of the soft-shoulder sign I'd stopped at a little over a week ago. I glanced at Lani again, thinking this must be pretty emotional for her, considering what had happened to her here, but her serene expression didn't change. Then she slowly faded until she was gone.

I returned my car to the asphalt and downed the accelerator. I had to get home fast and begin my exorcism program before the green pea soup hit the fan. Forget the list, forget the *plan de* whatever, forget organizing. Lani's interferences were endangering my life.

This had now become an emergency.

Chapter 25

Though this be madness, yet there is method in't.

To my relief, Hal was gone when I got home, which meant he had probably taken his own advice and was at a meeting, giving me the needed privacy for what I had to do.

After a perfunctory greeting, Mab returned to her vigil for her lord and master in the driveway. Dooley, who came in with me, went straight for the cat food and finished it off in a few bites. Moon and Mellow eyed him uncertainly, not knowing what to make of him, mainly because he totally ignored them. They began to parade back and forth with their tails in the air, but he acted as if they were just so much fluff. He followed me to my office and plunked down on his chair, his big front feet hanging over the arm rest, enormous head on his legs. He let out a satisfied sigh and closed his eyes.

I sat behind my desk and stared at the blank top sheet of the writing tablet in front of me. I played with my pen, tapped it on the desk. Looked around. Made faces. Stared at Dooley. Said the Serenity Prayer.

How to begin? "Lani, stop messing with my sobriety"? That might not come over too well. I chewed on my pen. Pain shot through my fillings as I rediscovered silver fountain pens were not chewable.

Dooley snored and made little yelping sounds, his feet moving rapidly. *Dream walker.*

I put my pen to paper and began to write. "Dear Lani." *Dear?* I crossed it out and wrote, "To Lani." That sounded wrong, too. I put my pen in my mouth again, careful this time not to crunch down on it with my molars.

If I was going to write a letter to Lani, beating around the bush would defeat the purpose. I should get straight to the point. What did I want? I wanted to get rid of her, for her to go on to wherever she was supposed to go. Heaven, Valhalla, an afterlife by any name. I also wanted to know who had "slipped" her the Boozabuse. By now, I really didn't care a flying fart what she was trying to tell me, but I guessed that asking her about this would not only be polite but might persuade her to get to *her* point and then move on.

On a clean sheet, I wrote:

Lani,
    Please, tell me clearly what you want. Who gave you the Boozabuse?
    I will do what I can, but I almost crashed my car tonight when you showed up.
    You need to go toward the Light.
Fae
P.S. Red is not your color.

It was a nice, little, teacherly note, except for the postscript maybe. Should I have used the word *inappropriate* somewhere? I certainly hoped there was a light for her to go to. I read the note out loud.

Oh, this is stupid! What am I doing, writing to a dead woman? I pinned the message to the cork board over my desk, so she could read it in her own sweet time. Wait, there was no time where she was. Should I have dated it?

"What's that?" Hal asked.

I almost fell off my chair. I hadn't heard his truck drive up. He had no business sneaking up behind me like that.

"Will you stop doing that!"

He laughed at me. "What is *that*?"

"Sneaking up on me!"

"No, I mean *that*!" He pointed at the note on the cork board. Mab, his co-conspirator, stood in the doorway.

"What?" I asked as if I still had no idea what he was talking about.

An exaggerated frown appeared on his face.

"It's a letter," I said defensively.

He cleared his throat. "I can see that. But why are you writing a letter to Lani?"

"It's called a *dead letter*. It's a way of communicating with someone who's passed over." I knew he was only acting as if his skeptical mind wanted to know, Hal being a real-live illustration of Herbert Spencer's observation that "contempt prior to investigation will leave a man in everlasting ignorance."

"Over where?" He asked as if he weren't familiar with the kinder expression for the word *dead*, which I'd been using for years now.

"The other side," I answered, expecting his next question to be, "What other side?"

But instead, he asked, "You think she'll pay any attention?"

Did he really want to know this time or was he being sarcastic again? I gave him an inquisitive look but saw no smirk signs on his face, so I decided to answer his question. "I don't know. It's something I haven't tried yet. I want her to stop bugging me. She keeps popping up everywhere. On the way home, she made me swerve off the road."

The muscles in his face were working overtime to keep doubt from flooding his face, but doubt won. "Fae? Don't you think you may want to see someone?"

"Hal?" I smiled sweetly. "Ask Jesse and Jamey about what happened to them today. They saw her more than once this past weekend."

"They're little boys." He stared at me.

"Yes, and they knew nothing about her. They still don't know that the woman they saw was a ghost. I didn't tell them."

"They're very impressionable."

"You're not listening to me. Hey! I just saw some little gray men run downstairs. Go after them! Leave me alone. Go watch TV, or something."

Hal shook his head and smiled. "I think I'll go check on that dog," he said.

"What dog?"

"I found a dog on my way back, a black dog. He was walking along the road. He looked lost, but he came when I called him."

"Where is he?" I asked.

"I put him in the barn. He's pretty old. Fat and slow."

"Poor thing!" I followed Hal out to the barn, Mab and Dooley on our heels.

Hal's foundling got up and slowly came over to us, tail wagging.

"Turn on the light, will you? He may be hungry. I'll put some food out." I reached out to pet what seemed a pretty sizable dog. Hal turned on the light over his work bench.

"It's a full-blooded Labrador!" I looked at the dog. Then I looked at Hal. "Honey?" I said.

"He's pretty chubby, huh? Can't have been lost too long," he said, eyeing the dog.

"Honey?" I said again to my husband, the biologist. "He is a *she*, and she is not fat but pregnant. It looks as if she's about to whelp any minute!"

Hal kneeled next to the dog and carefully felt her belly. "Oh, no! You're right! I can't believe I didn't notice."

"Well, it was dark!" I said generously. "She's quite pretty. Hi, Baby!" She licked my hand, her tail wagging faster and faster until her whole body wiggled with the exercise. Afraid that her puppies would pop out, I tried to calm her down, but then Mab and Dooley decided this was to be a tail-wagging competition, and Hal and I were surrounded by a whirl of adoring canines. With difficulty, we got back on our feet.

While Hal arranged a neat little bed under his work bench with a tarp, an old blanket, and some clean towels, I went to get a bowl out of the house and filled it with dog food.

"I guess I'll have to hammer together a whelping box." He scratched his head.

"Maybe we should first try to find out where she belongs. I can't think of anyone here on Blackberry Road who has a black Lab." I patted the doggy bed, and she immediately came over. The food was right in front of her nose, but, apparently more tired than hungry, she put her head down. A Labrador who didn't eat everything in sight? Amazing!

Hal shut the barn door behind us and we went back into the house with Mab and Dooley.

A feeling of utter exhaustion suddenly came over me. I wanted to go to bed and sleep for a long time. Without dreams.

Hal said he would have to stay up a while longer because he needed to read a report for a meeting early Monday. We kissed good night.

I dragged myself up to the bathroom, washed the make-up off my face, and sat down behind my dressing table in the bedroom. Absentmindedly, I began to brush my hair.

This day had been awfully long. I thought about the boys and their enviable supply of energy. I thought about Kate and Bobby getting married. Next year. *Something old, something new, something borrowed,* … something blue was standing behind me.

I stared in the mirror.

There she was, wearing a blue version of the dress she'd been buried in.

Well, at least she'd read my message.

I squeezed my eyes shut to make her go away.

***

The front door of Lani's house stood open. I looked up at the bathroom window and was relieved to see she wasn't there this time.

It was an overcast Monday morning, a dreary gray sky draining all the world of color. Even the normally bright mustard flowers that were sprouting up everywhere in the orchards and alongside the roads didn't look so sunny this morning.

Next to Sasha's Volkswagen van stood a new red Jeep, its cargo door up. Sasha's old, leather suitcase was stashed in the back.

"Hello!" I called out upon entering the hallway.

No answer, but upstairs was the sound of footsteps.

I walked into the living room where the object of my mission immediately greeted me with a screeching *"Bonjour!"*

"Bon matin to you, Solo!" Least I could do was be civil to the little orphan. Maybe it would rub off.

"Merde!"

"Spunky little guy, isn't he?" a deep voice behind me said.

I turned to find myself facing a tall man in his mid sixties. His hair, going from pepper to salt, offered a sharp contrast to his hazel eyes. Though he was clean shaven, his skin had a weathered out-doors appearance, tanned and lined. He looked me over for an instant. Flattering insolence.

"Jack Peterson." He held out his hand.

My heart jumped into my throat. I couldn't lift my arm to shake his hand.

"Anything wrong?" Jack gave me a quizzical look. He lowered his outstretched hand.

I couldn't very well say, "You're dead!" It would be very rude to say such a thing to this nice-looking man. He seemed so very pleasant and alive, even though he had supposedly been killed years ago, according to Lani. This was the man with the bottle by the same first name who had wrapped himself around an old oak tree.

Sasha came in. "What's the matter, Fae? You look like you've seen a ghost." She opened the curtains behind Solo. "I see you've met my dad."

With a shock I noticed she was wearing the same dress Lani had shown herself in the night before. Something blue. Forget-me-not blue. Blue bayou blue. Maybe they had bough them in bulk: buy two, get one free.

"My van conked out on me. Dad's taking me back to Berkeley. He'll come back to fix Volksy later this week."

I still hadn't said a word to either her or her "dead" father. When I finally spoke, my voice sounded a bit like Solo's. "I came to pick up the bird."

"He's all yours!" Sasha snorted. "Maybe you should give him to that Steve character. Birds of a feather, you know."

I smiled weakly and tried not to stare at Jack Peterson.

Drunks are a tricky lot, but pretending that the father of one of your children has died in a car accident is a little beyond your average drunk's bullshit. I wondered how much more rubbish Lani had fed me. And how was I supposed to find out who had caused her death—–if that's what she wanted me to do—when dead people kept showing up out of nowhere? Was this all just a wild goose chase?

I looked over at Sasha again and wondered what the meaning of the blue dress was. Was there a message or was it coincidence or was it another one of Lani's games? Where had Sasha been when her mother died? What motive could she have had to off her old lady? Why had she been so nice about my inheriting everything from her mother?

And now here was Jack, not dead at all, but alive and well. Was he another viable suspect? Not that I needed any more. But had Lani caused my near accident last night to point the finger at him? Old oak tree. Old live oak tree?

Sasha looked around the room one last time, taking in every detail. She sighed, then nodded her head as if in agreement with something someone had said and walked out.

"Well, back to Berzerkley!" Smiling, Jack held out his hand once more. This time, I shook it.

Outside, Sasha gave me a deposit slip with her address and phone number. "Come see me, will you, when you get to Berkeley?"

"Maybe this Friday. I'll call you," I said absentmindedly. I couldn't explain the intense sadness that suddenly washed over me. It made me nauseated.

"Oh, would you tell Jason when he comes back? About my van and Dad coming back?" Sasha asked.

"Jason? I thought he went back to Sacramento? He's coming back?" Hadn't the guys seen him drive off with Alicia yesterday?

"He went to drop Ali off at the airport and check up on the business. But he said he'd be back in a couple of days, because he wanted to talk to you about some of Mother's more personal belongings, you know. He'll probably call you."

"Do you need some help with that bird?" Jack asked.

"That would be nice. Thank you!" I smiled at him.

He went back inside and brought the cage out to my car. We put Solo in the backseat.

As they drove off, Sasha turned around and waved. I raised my hand in response.

I took Solo home and hauled him up to the guest room, past two very suspicious cats. I made sure the door clicked shut before I went back downstairs and then fed the two felines some extra food, just in case. Soon, Solo was at it. "Hey, Lani, Lani, La—neee!" Moon and Mellow looked stupefied.

I put a handful of cat food in my jacket pocket and went outside to check on the mother-to-be. She was scouting out the property with the help of Mab and Dooley. They trotted over as soon as I sat down on the back steps. With a new rival, Mab was a bit more affectionate to me. I had to pet all three of them at the same time.

Our newcomer looked much livelier this morning. She seemed a lot younger than she had in the dark of night. With her shiny black coat and boxy head, she looked like a smaller, short-haired version of Dooley. I checked her teeth: no major damage, or wear and tear. I felt her belly. Her sixty-three days were nearly up.

Suddenly, the Lab stuck her nose in my pocket, took a mouthful of cat food, and began to munch away. Just like Bluebelle used to do. I stared at her. I had *taught* Bluebelle to do that. When had I last seen Bluebelle? Just a few days ago.

I confined the Lab in the barn, so she wouldn't whelp all over the place, and went back inside.

Up in the guest room, Solo was screaming bloody murder. With dismay, I realized that I'd forgotten to bring along the black cloth for his cage. I went in search of a piece of material that would do the trick and finally settled on an old sheet.

"*Fou! Bête! Crétin!*" he screeched as I covered him up. A few more screams and he was quiet.

Neither the animal pound nor the Humane Society had received a report of a missing Labrador. I left information about the dog and our phone number. Maybe she'd been dumped. The shelters were full of beautiful dogs. I went to work on the poster, wondering if anyone would claim her and secretly hoping no one would come forward. I printed out ten copies of the poster, put them in a manila folder and then went downstairs to check the paper under "Lost and Found." No Labs were listed. I ran upstairs to pull the sheet off of Solo's cage and made my escape under a barrage of unpardonably foul French.

It was noon when I got to Londen. First, I went straight to the House of Variety to get food for Solo.

Pete van Nuys was standing behind the counter. "Hi, Fae!" He didn't ask if he could help me. By now, I knew his store almost better than he did.

"Hi, Pete! You know what an African Grey eats?" I asked. I'd seen Lani feed Solo seeds and nuts, but I wasn't sure if that was all he needed.

"Oh, let's see. Nuts and vegetables. They need variety." He rubbed the side of his nose and then pulled his ear. "You bought a parrot?"

"It's Lani's." I picked up a large, ceramic dog bowl that could double as a bird bath.

"Oh, Lani's!" Pete made a face.

"What?" I asked.

"Nothing," Pete said. "We'll miss her."

I suddenly had a brilliant idea. "Hey, Pete! How about putting him here in the store? He needs a new home."

"Huh?" was all Pete had to say about that. He smiled apologetically. "They're a bit noisy."

That's a bit of an understatement! "OK then. How about putting this poster in your window?" I handed him a copy of my Labrador poster.

He read it and said, "Sure!" relieved I hadn't insisted on his help with the disposal of Solo.

I couldn't blame Pete. Fleetingly, I wondered if he was just familiar with parrots in general or Lani's parrot in particular. *How well had he known Lani?*

"Papa?" a voice called from the back. A young woman appeared, carrying an infant. It was the mother from the park, the one whose baby had rendered Kate and me speechless.

"Have you met my daughter, Fae?" Pete said. He introduced her as *Anna*.

I had heard about Anna living out of state, I'd forgotten which. "Hello," I said. "We met in the park the other day."

"Anna's come to stay with us for a while." Pete took the baby over from his daughter. "And this is Mickey!" said the proud grandfather.

The little boy broke into one of the sweetest smiles I'd ever seen on a baby. My heart ached at the joy and innocence in that smile. How perfect this baby was.

Pete held his grandson high up in the air. Anna glanced out the store window and then reached out for her baby. Her father carefully handed him back to her. She gave me a quick smile and returned to the living quarters in back.

Pete got out a roll of tape and posted my sign in the window next to the door. "So, how's that?"

I nodded my approval and put the bowl on the counter. "I'd better get one of those big bags of mixed nuts then." I pointed at a basket filled with red-netted bags near the counter.

Pete grabbed a bag and put it next to the bowl.

Five pounds it said on the label. "Make it two." I had no idea how many nuts that nutcracker could crack.

Pete raised an eyebrow but added another bag after I nodded to indicate I meant business. Solo would not go the way of the dodo.

"I almost forgot! I need some incense." The only reason I didn't forget was that the rack with incense was standing right in front of my nose on the counter. *Rosemary? No, that's for remembrance. Gardenia? No, it's got something to do with love. Better not get the rose. She likes that too much. Sweet pea! For goodbye, departure. No sweet pea on the rack.* I finally picked out a bag of "Calming Lavender" scent. *If it doesn't calm her, it will at least calm me.*

"What?" Pete asked.

"Oh, nothing," I said lightly. I needed to stop talking out loud. Hal kept telling me it sounded as if I'd lost my mind, but that just showed how much he knew. I'd heard a psychologist explain once that highly intelligent people talk to themselves to order their thoughts. I should have taped that discussion for Hal. Seemed a lot of people hadn't seen that program.

"She used to come in here and take things," Pete said under his breath.

"Who?" I thought he was talking about his daughter.

"Lani! She used to put things in her pockets, her purse," Pete explained. "Then the next day she'd come back and pay for them. I never said anything. They were always small things. Figured she was a kleptomaniac, couldn't help herself helping herself."

"Really?" I said.

He looked at me intently for a few seconds as if he wanted to say something else, but his mouth opened and closed without any words having come out.

I paid Pete and walked out to put my purchases in the car.

Steve Krieger was sitting across the street in his truck, puffing on a cigarette, blowing smoke out of the window. He had his radio turned up full blast. Percy Sledge's "When a Man Loves a Woman." He tried to give me a dirty look, but I pretended not to see him.

Maybe he'd go away. If he got too close, I could always hit him over the head with a bag of nuts. How was that for *appropriate*? Without looking in Steve's direction, I crossed the street to Full of Beans.

I thought I-am-your-waiter Phil was going to burst into tears when he read my poster. He said, "I volunteer at the Humane Society."

I hadn't known, but now I realized why I'd always liked him so much: he had Dooley eyes. A dog man. He cleared some of the older announcements off the poster board and resolutely pinned my flyer down on all four corners. "There!"

After commiserating for a while on the fate of our favorite members of the animal kingdom, I ordered a double cappuccino to go, thanked Phil for his help, and continued on my mission.

Steve was gone.

The library was closed on Mondays, so I'd have to come back tomorrow, but I left flyers at Ben's Warme Bakkerij and the grocery store.

My last stop in town was Paul Smit's pharmacy. He looked up from the enormous tower of anti-flu medications he was building. "Hey, Fae! How are you doing?"

"Pretty good. And you?" I walked over to him, careful not to upset any of the other marvelous structures along the path.

"Oh, I can't complain," Paul said, smiling wickedly before adding, "It drives customers away."

I grinned. Dutch Fae understood the joke. "Do you have a place for this?" I held a flyer under his aquiline nose.

He peered at it through his half-glasses. "Sure, no problem. Do you need anything else?"

To my surprise, I asked, "Would you tell me how those anti-drinking medications work?"

"You mean disulfiram? Boozabuse?"

I nodded. "I'm doing a research project."

"On Lani Pochard?" Paul smirked at me.

"I thought you weren't supposed to talk about your patients!" I said, a bit miffed at myself for being so transparent.

"Hell, Fae, number one, everybody knows how she died, and number two, she's dead."

I rolled my eyes. "Shouldn't you put that the other way around?"

"And number three, I wasn't talking about her but about you." He lifted an eyebrow. "What are you up to?"

"I'm writing a book."

For a few seconds, his eyebrow went up even higher. "A book? Well then, why didn't you say so?"

Because it's none of your business! I smiled and shrugged, not bothering to answer because he didn't believe me anyway. That sardonic grin on his face.

"Disulfiram is a prescription medicine that produces sensitivity to alcohol. When a patient ingests even small amounts of alcohol, it causes an extremely unpleasant reaction, such as headache, nausea, vomiting, dehydration, hyperventilation, blurred vision, and confusion. In severe reactions, there may even be acute congestive heart failure, unconsciousness, convulsions, and death. That's not a complete list. The reaction varies with each individual, but it's usually proportional to the amount of disulfiram and alcohol ingested, and it lasts for as long as alcohol is being metabolized."

"Yikes!" I cried out. "Death? That sounds like a pretty complete list all by itself to me. I knew it made you sick, but I didn't know it could make you dead." In fact, when Lani had said that she wasn't going to kill herself taking Boozabuse, I'd thought she was just exaggerating.

"It's not the Boozabuse, it's the combination with alcohol that can cause death in extreme cases."

"For how long does Boozabuse stay active?"

"Again, that differs with each individual, but it builds up in the body and can remain in the system for up to two weeks after a patient stops taking it. Even if a patient doesn't take it for a day or two, it continues to work. And, the effects don't become less over time, because the more is taken, the greater the sensitivity to alcohol becomes."

Two weeks? That didn't just widen the window of opportunity, it knocked the whole wall out. "Does it have any taste or smell?"

"No, it's odorless and almost tasteless. The pills can be crushed into a powder that is water soluble. I should tell you, too, that even a small amount can almost instantaneously make a person quite sick if alcohol is ingested. That's why we warn the patient to be careful and read labels to avoid alcohol in disguise, such as in sauces, vinegars, cough and cold medicines, but also in things for on the skin like aftershave, perfume, and ointments."

As a recovered alcoholic, I knew all about being vigilant, reading labels and asking about ingredients in restaurants. I'd seen cough medicines that contained twenty percent alcohol, and I'd once left a restaurant where every item on the menu had been prepared with whiskey, because I hadn't trusted the cooks to leave it out.

I bit my lip, trying to think of anything else I should ask Paul, when he said, "The sickness lasts about thirty to sixty minutes, on average."

If you don't die! "Thanks for your help, Paul." I waved the manila folder and turned, deep in thought, toward the door.

"Good luck!" Paul called after me. "With your—book?"

Odorless. Tasteless. Powder. Water soluble.

Chapter 26

**I am but mad north-north-west; when the wind is southerly,
I know a hawk from a handsaw.**

I drove over to the church out on Wilhelmina Road and knocked on the rectory door. The Reverend Ravenstein, wearing a navy turtle neck and jeans, took his pipe out of his mouth and welcomingly smiled at me. "Mrs. Nelson!" A twinkle in his dark blue eyes.

Either my fame had preceded me or he'd asked around to find out who that horrible woman was at Lani's funeral, the one who'd yelled through the church that Lani had killed herself. (Only, I hadn't, of course.) I couldn't remember ever having been introduced to him or, except for a brief handshake as we left Lani's memorial service, meeting him in person. And now that I was, I had no idea how to address him. *Reverend? Father? Mister?*

"Hello!" I said. "Would you put this where people can see it, please?" I handed him a flyer.

Ravenstein glanced at the flyer and said, "Ah! A lost dog. No, a *found* dog. I'll find a good place for it."

"Thank you! That would be very helpful." I smiled back at him.

"Mrs. Nelson?" Ravenstein looked down at his pipe.

I waited.

"Do be careful!" The laughter had left his eyes. He stepped back from the threshold.

"I will," I said. Halfway down the mossy brick path that led to the road, I looked over my shoulder. He was still standing in the doorway, a worried frown on his face. Then he nodded at me and slowly closed the door.

I turned and stood staring at the closed door. What did he mean, "do be careful"? I was tempted to knock on the door again and ask him, but maybe he just meant the weather. The rain. Slick roads.

Although, somehow, I didn't think so.

Preoccupied with Ravenstein's inscrutable warning words—was

there such a thing as a Dutch Reformed psychic?—I passed Rita's home down the road and had to make two U-turns to park in front of her house.

As if she'd been expecting me, Rita opened the door before I was out of my car.

"How is Sarah?" I asked as soon as she was within hearing distance.

Rita tilted her hand back and forth in a so-so gesture. "She's in her room."

Sarah was sitting up in bed. Her face was a mess of many colors. The gash in her upper lip was healing though still very visible. The swelling around her eyes and mouth had disappeared. She was wearing long-sleeved pajamas, but I could see the bruises on her neck and hands. A book lay open on her lap.

I swallowed hard. "Hi, Sweetheart," I said, not wanting to ask her how she was doing so she wouldn't think she'd have to answer *fine*.

The smile she gave me caused her pain. I sat down on the chair next to her bed. "What are you reading?"

She raised the book and showed me the title. Wally Lamb's *She's Come Undone*. "From your library," she said. "It's funny … but also sad. I can't read for very long at a time, because my head hurts." She leaned back into her pillow. "What have you been doing?"

I thought of the most neutral subject to talk about. "Well, we found a dog." I told her about Hal bringing the Labrador home and how he'd believed *she* was a *he* and how she would have puppies soon and how I'd distributed flyers. I prattled on and on, trying to make the story as amusing as possible. But when I said that I hoped nobody would claim the dog, Sarah's eyes suddenly were filled with tears.

"Oh, did I upset you?" I asked, barely able to stop myself from crying.

"It's not you, Fae. I just don't understand why some people are so mean. Why would anyone leave a dog on the side of the road? A pregnant dog?"

"I don't know," I said. "Maybe it wasn't on purpose. But we'll take good care of her."

Rita walked in with a loaded tray. I thought she would order me out of her home when she saw Sarah's distress, but she smiled at the both of us, put the tray down on the bed stand, and said, "Here's a nice supper. Now, I wanna see it all gone when I get back!"

I gave Sarah a goodbye kiss and followed Rita out. "I'm sorry. I shouldn't have talked about that dog ... ," I began, but she interrupted me.

"Doesn't matter what you talk about. She cries about everything." Rita put her hand to her forehead. "Better she thinks about a dog than herself. Every time she looks in the mirror, she cries. I should throw all them damned mirrors out. Maybe she'd get outta bed then. She needs to start moving around the doctor said." Rita padded me on the back. "I'll bring her over Thursday next, when I come to clean. Don't you worry."

"I should have just talked about interior decorating," I said.

As soon as I came home, I checked on the Labrador, who was still pregnant, and then went upstairs to present Solo with his new bath, a few handfuls of nuts, and several fresh broccoli florets I'd bought a whole bag of at the grocery store. Very sweetly, he said, *"Merci beaucoup!"* Maybe there was hope. He was probably just lonely and bored, because he should be in a high traffic area like the living room or kitchen. I considered hauling him downstairs but decided he'd be safer in the guest room for now.

After opening the cage so he could have some time to play outside, I went on a search for toys the twins might have left behind. All I could find, though, was a hard-plastic ball, belonging to the cats, with star-shaped holes in it and bells inside. In fact, it found me, because as I entered the bedroom the boys usually occupied during their visits, the tinkling ball rolled from somewhere and stopped right at my feet.

Solo was sitting on the window sill when I returned. I put the ball in his cage and stayed a while to talk with him. All this sudden attention was making him shy and quiet. Since there wasn't much in the room he could wreck, I left him to roam free and went downstairs to the kitchen.

I took out the phone book and looked up *Attorneys* to find a firm that could give me advice about Lani's will. There were three full pages of lawyers listed under "Wills, Estate Planning & Probate" who did just that. I closed my eyes and stabbed my pen on a page. It landed at the firm of Brown Moore Cardiff Schiff & Litman, no commas again. The phone was answered with simply "Law offices" as if they were the only ones in the book.

The lady to whom I explained that I had inherited an estate was at first very understanding, but when I told her that I didn't want what was coming to me, she became increasingly confused. She asked me to run my predicament by her several times, and while I did, her voice became gradually louder, her speech slower, and her enunciation more exaggerated as if *I* were the one with the comprehension problem. By the time she made an appointment for me with one of the partners—namely Mr. Litman, Esquire, for Wednesday afternoon at two o'clock—she clearly thought I was quite crazy. She asked if I could come a little earlier to fill out some pa ... per ... work. I rolled my eyes and told her, very slowly, that I could.

I'd just put down the phone, when Janny van Zand drove up. Maybe I imagined it, but she seemed to be skipping to the house like a child playing hopscotch.

"Fae, did you hear? Kate and Bobby are getting married!" she yelled as she stormed into my kitchen, a broad smile lighting up her face. She nearly knocked me off my feet when she hugged me.

"And what does Papa Bert have to say about it?" I asked.

"Oh, Bert!" Janny laughed. "'It's about time,' he said. Kate's had Bert wound around her little finger ever since Bobby first brought her home. 'Now, that's the girl I'd like to see Bob marry,' he said as soon as they took off for the movies."

Janny followed me around the kitchen. "I was thinking, we should give them an engagement party to celebrate, *ja*? We could make it a surprise party at our house. We'll get all their friends together and invite Kate's family, of course. I'll have to get addresses. How would I get those without her finding out?"

"I could steal her address book," I suggested.

She seemed to seriously consider my offer for two seconds, then laughed and went on, "Oh, *ja*, we can ask that nice man from Modesto—what's his name?—to cater."

"Brandenburgh, Mark," I provided. Janny must have left before Sasha introduced that nice man as her illegitimate brother-in-law.

I put water on for tea and offered Janny the tin with her own oatmeal cookies.

She didn't recognize them. "These are very good," she said, nibbling. "What do you think? I'm sure he's very busy."

Surely, not busy enough! "Sounds like a good idea," I said.

"With a last name like Brandenburgh, do you think he cooks Dutch food?"

"You mean potatoes?" I laughed. The Dutch eat more potatoes than any other people in the world but are in vehement denial of this fact. There is something *déclassé* about potatoes being a main food staple. Perhaps Van Gogh's *Potato Eaters* had something to do with this perception. As kids, we even had a sling of derogatory potato-eating jokes directed at our southern neighbors, but the joke was on us when a study showed that the Dutch ate a lot more spuds per capita than the Belgians.

"Oh, you!" Janny pretended to be exasperated. "I was thinking more of Indonesian food. *Rijsttafel*. A rice table with all those hot vegetable and meat dishes and peanut sauce."

"That does sound good. I haven't had one of those since my last visit to Holland."

"I'll call Mr. Brandenburgh. Isn't that tea done yet? Give me a cup. I need it. You know, I can't help but worry."

I poured tea for us. "Worry? About Kate and Bobby?"

"Oh, it's almost too good to be true. Those two seem to be made for each other." Janny blew on her tea. "But marriage is difficult."

Yesterday, I'd recognized Kate's sudden case of cold feet, but I never thought I'd hear Janny say something like that. Was she unhappy? She and Bert seemed to be about the most solid couple I knew, besides my Oma and Opa, whom death had parted and then reunited some years ago.

Keeping the steaming tea her focal point, Janny said, "I prayed for Kate and Bob to get together, and now I'm scared that once they're married it won't be perfect." She finally took a sip of her tea.

We sat gazing at the same spot in the pattern of the tablecloth. *Be careful what you pray for?*

Slapping her hands on the table, Janny broke the silence. "So, have you seen anything more of Lani?"

"Yes, she was quite busy this past weekend." I told her about how Lani had entertained the boys. "I'm not sure what that was with the car. All I know is that it stopped when I yelled, 'cut it out!' and Dooley seemed to be seeing something leave the car."

"She hasn't come to visit me after that one time in the chicken coup. I'd be a nervous wreck if she did. It almost sounds as if she's bored, *niet*? Maybe there's too much harp playing up there." She pointed her index finger at the ceiling.

Looking up, I said, "Gwen gave me some ideas, things to try out." I told her what Gwen's advice had been about using scent, sound, and light to defuse Lani's energy.

"It all sounds a bit like hocus-pocus to me, but I guess Gwen knows what she's talking about." Janny finished her tea.

The phone rang.

"It's Kate," I said before picking up.

"How do you know?" Janny raised her eyebrows in amazement.

"Caller ID," I said. Kate was calling from work. Janny winked at me and got up. I pointed at the coat rack. She grabbed the poncho she'd lent me, signaled that she would call me later, and left.

"They found our lost boy up in Oregon with his grandparents. He hitch-hiked all the way. Got a ride from an interstate trucker Friday night," Kate said, relief in her voice.

"That means he was up there that Saturday," I said. "That's one less suspect. Although, he wasn't much of a suspect to begin with, because he could hardly have known about the Boozabuse, and he also probably had no idea where Lani lived."

"That's true, but his disappearance still made me nervous."

"I found myself a much more likely suspect—not that I suspect myself!"

"That's one of the advantages of not suffering from blackouts. What are you up to? Staying out of trouble?" Kate asked.

I told her I had no idea what she was talking about. Then I brought up the subject of Matchett's assignment. "I don't want to do it, Kate."

"Then tell her you'd rather stick with what you're doing."

"Yes, but how do I say that? Give me a script like Petruchio's 'Say that she rail' in *The Taming of the Shrew*."

"How about, 'Dr. Matchett, I enjoy teaching Shakespeare and drama, and I wouldn't be comfortable teaching twentieth-century writers, because it's not my area of expertise.' And then hear what she says."

"Oh!" I was so disappointed. "But that's what Hal told me to do!"

I could see Kate shaking her head on the other end. "Fae, keep it simple! Just call her and tell her. The worst that could happen is that she says the course needs to be on the fall schedule and there's no one else to teach it."

I'd have to think this strategy over.

"By the way," Kate said in a way that didn't at all sound like a real by-the-way. "What's going on with Lani?"

The word *nothing* flew out of my mouth before I knew it.

"That's not what Janny told me yesterday." An inquisitive silence followed her statement.

Why hadn't Janny told me she told Kate? This was like that old shampoo commercial. *And I told a friend, and she told a friend, and* ... Or like the way I'd announced Kate and Bobby's engagement. "Uh," I said, not sure how to ease into my tale. "It's a long story."

"I've got time."

I looked at my watch. It was three o'clock. Her students were on their way back to the group homes by this time. She did have time.

Interrupted only by Kate's frequent exclamations—"Oh, no!" and "Really?" and "You're not serious!"—I supplied her with all the grizzly details of Lani's treacherous intrusions. "So, any advice?" I asked when the tale was told.

"Well, this is definitely not my area of expertise. All I have is a premonition every so often. It sounds as if you're becoming more psychic. Your abilities are getting stronger. How funny that you met Gwen right after you had that vision about Lani. I think I've talked to her. Is she Native American? Tall, amazingly pretty?"

"Yes, that sounds like Gwen."

"Then just listen to her. She's got more time in the program than I have, and she's extremely intelligent and very together."

"I haven't told her yet, but I've adopted her as my psychic sponsor."

"Smart move! Maybe she can help you apply the program to your issues with your psychic gift."

"What 'issues'? And what do you mean, 'apply the program'?"

"Do the steps. Think about it. Why haven't you told me all this before? Because it had nothing to do with your alcoholism? But I've been your friend for much longer than I've been your sponsor, and I already knew about your paranormal abilities. Yet, you talk about it by invitation only. You need to get over your fear of disapproval and ridicule. Your own lack of acceptance may be standing in the way of other people's acceptance."

"But not everybody thinks like you do, Kate. Some people don't just disapprove or ridicule, they become downright hateful."

"I'm not suggesting you walk around with a T-shirt saying 'I Am

Psychic,' but maybe you need to come out of the closet, if only in regard to those close to you."

"You mean like Jason?"

"Now that you mention it, yes. If you look for the similarities and not the differences, you'll find yourself reflected in nearly everyone you meet."

"I don't know, Kate. I kind of like my closet. It feels safe."

"You're just telling yourself that, but you'll breathe more freely when you crack the door open. You have a talent. Don't hide your light under a shrub."

"*Bushel*," I said.

"Wherever. You get my drift." She began singing "Let the Sun Shine In" from *Hair*. On these notes, laughing, we ended our conversation.

Solo was thoroughly amusing himself in his room. He said, "*Bonjour!*" when I stuck my head in to check. All the negativity had seeped out of him with a little attention and freedom. He'd done something with the curtains. They looked different, maybe a bit shredded, but I didn't feel like investigating further. "Good boy!" I said in a high-pitched voice and closed the door. "*Au revoir!*" he said. I shook my head, surprised at his ability to assign the correct meaning to words. Even his foul language he'd used appropriately, when he'd been outraged about the treatment he'd received.

I took my writing pad downstairs, refilled my cup with the last of the tepid tea, and sat at the kitchen table. In the center of the paper, I drew a circle in which I listed what Paul Smit had told me about Boozabuse, beginning with the time frame of its effectiveness, duration of the reaction, physical properties, and underneath this the words *very sick quickly*. Around the main circle, I drew a series of smaller circles for related facts, inferences, conclusions.

There it was—the old bubble-method brainstorm. I wondered why my students often were so reluctant to use this fantastic organizational tool.

I stared at the words in the center bubble: *two weeks—thirty to sixty minutes—tasteless, odorless, powder, water soluble—very sick quickly*. Funny, how I'd assumed I knew so much about Boozabuse, when actually I'd had no idea of any of these important facts that, I sensed, completely changed the picture of when and how it could have been administered. *When* and *how*.

If taken regularly at full prescription doses, the effectiveness of Boozabuse could take up to two weeks to wear off. She'd never mentioned becoming violently ill, and she would have, because it would have made excellent material for one of her outrageous stories. So, I doubted that she'd ingested the Boozabuse over a period of time. She would have been constantly ill.

Theoretically, she could have taken the Boozabuse days before she died, but if so, she wouldn't have been able to walk all the way through the orchard, with a high level of alcohol in her bloodstream. She'd have been hanging on to the toilet, puking her guts out. But what if, on the day she died, she'd downed the Boozabuse *after* she drank? It would mean that she'd taken the medicine with her on that final walk and then had thrown up in the orchard. This would explain how she'd been able to reach the road, why her stomach was empty, the awful odor when I'd found her in the ditch.

The bottles and glasses had shown no Boozabuse, but the tasteless and odorless tablets could have been crushed and mixed into about anything. Something she might use sparingly or not every day. A staple food of some kind? But Lani had not exactly been Betty Crocker, and not only because Betty Crocker was a wholly fictitious person. What would she add to those frozen dinners? Salt and pepper. No, she hadn't walked through the orchard carrying a frozen dinner or with a set of salt and pepper shakers in her pocket.

It must have been some kind of food the killer had prepared for Lani. But what, and why hadn't it been found? Maybe they hadn't looked for it. Maybe an animal had eaten it. Should I take a walk through the orchard to see what I could find? But what if I did find it, this material evidence, wouldn't Bobby just disregard it as something one of Lani's personalities had cooked up?

I'd been scribbling notes of all these ideas in the peripheral bubbles and drawing lines to the relevant main items in the center bubble. Good grief, what a mess! The bubbles were way too small and lines crisscrossed everywhere. I bet Bobby never used the bubble method when he was detecting. I tore the sheet off and continued on the next, not bothering with bubbles this time.

Back to the timing. Whoever took the Boozabuse could have done so some time ago, but not very long. While I doubted that Lani would have checked her bottle of Boozabuse every so often to see if it were still all there, she might have noticed at some point, no matter how bleary-eyed she'd been, that half of the medication was missing. She would have known something was up. The killer would not have wanted to take that chance. But there had to have been two visits, one to steal the Boozabuse and one to deliver the food stuff. Two visits, relatively close together.

The killer had to have known Lani had Boozabuse, been familiar with the effects, and been close enough to Lani—at home in her house—to have been in her kitchen and open that cabinet. Someone who had sat at her table, someone she had broken bread with.

No, not necessarily. It could have been someone who'd been told by someone close about the medicine and where it was, and who had snuck into her house.

Oh, great! Now I was right back where I'd started from. I'd narrowed down my list of suspects to the original number: about everyone who'd known Lani.

Why wasn't my intuition kicking in? Why couldn't I just shake hands with all these people, one at a time of course, and have the truth flash in front of me as happened in *Psychic Detectives* and *Medium*? Perhaps because I was using a part of my brain that blocked my intuition. I was thinking, using logic, not sensing. I had meant to talk to Gwen about learning to access my sixth sense at will, when needed, but instead I'd been trying to deal with all the disturbances caused by Lani.

Perhaps these notes contained intuitive thoughts. I should make a complete list of suspects and outline each person's motive and opportunity.

I looked at the clock. The suspects list would have to wait. Time to burn some incense and make a stink. Hal would be home soon and that would undoubtedly inhibit my attempts at clearing Lani's energy from the house.

I took three sticks of Calming Lavender and lit them. Waving them back and forth, I walked through every room.

I was up in the attic, sneezing uncontrollably, when Hal came home.

"Fae?" he called out at the bottom of the stairs.

"I'm up here, in the attic!" I called back. I heard him come up the stairs.

After waving the last of the incense around, I turned on the faucet and doused the sticks.

"What are you doing?" Hal asked.

"Nothing!" I pretended to arrange my canvasses.

"What's that smell?" Hal, child of the sixties, inhaled deeply. "You burning incense?"

"Just a little." I looked at him. "It's to defuse energy."

"What energy?"

"Oh, just energy!" I gave him my don't-make-me-explain smile.

Chapter 27

**Why, look you now,
how unworthy a thing you make of me!**

When I came downstairs, Tuesday morning, Rita was energetically mopping the kitchen floor. Hal had left for work at the usual time. I vaguely remembered being kissed and urged to go back to sleep. I hadn't protested too much.

"Good morning, Fae!" Rita greeted me. "Almost done with the kitchen. Got here at seven. The early bird gets the worm."

"That's not what they say where I grew up," I grumbled, stumbling over to the coffeemaker. She was too chipper.

"What do they say in Holland?" She leaned on the mop.

"Birds that sing early are for the cat," I answered in the voice of doom.

"I wasn't talking about no singing, just worms. *Eating*." She grinned, unimpressed with my performance, and began mopping again.

"Well, I'm not going to fight you for the slimy creature. Mild case of *scoleciphobia*, a fear of worms. Don't go fishing much either." I poured myself a cup of coffee. "Is Sarah here?"

"No, I told her she's coming with me this Thursday. Give her some days to get used to the idea of leaving the house."

"How's she doing?"

Rita stopped dead. "She was feeling better 'til some little twit girlfriend of hers come by last night. I could've wrunged her scrawny neck. That little bitch! Got Sarah all upset." She began to mop even more furiously than before.

"What did she do?" I stepped aside to give Rita the right of way.

"Ask Sarah why she were out so late, like it was her fault it took so long to sign up for classes. She's one of them goody-two-shoes with a little voice and big blue eyes that go blink all the time. Looks so innocent and sweet, but her mind's full of garbage. Always bringing the bad news. 'Oh, Sarah, so-and-so said this and that about you! So-and-so don't like you!' That kind of thing."

"I told Sarah a hundred times, 'That girl ain't no friend! You don't need no friends like that.' She just says, 'Oh, Mom, she means well!' *Means well!* If I see the little bitch, I'll tell her what I think of her. And I'll *mean well!*" Rita dunked the mop in the bucket hard enough to punch a hole in the bottom.

"And how's Mike?" I'd better change the subject before I had to part the seas to get out the door.

"He wanted to kill the little bitch, too!" She wrung the mop out. Then, apparently realizing she hadn't answered my question, she said, "When he's not at work, he's just setting around, trying to figure what he can bring Sarah next. Can't stop asking if she needs something." Rita shook her head. "You know Mike, he does something once and it's a habit! I sent him to a couple meetings, just to get him out the house."

I thought I'd better get out of her way before she sent *me* to a meeting and snuck off to the living room with the paper and my coffee.

At the top of the front page was the no-front-teeth picture of a seven-year-old girl, missing down south. The parents pleading for her safe return. It went still inside of me as I gazed at the photo. And then I knew this little angel would be found dead. *Abandon all hope.* What an unimaginable hell for those parents. What horror.

Half-heartedly, I skimmed the other stories. A fire had gutted an apartment building in Modesto. The suspects, neighborhood teenagers, were in custody. The bright lights had been walking around covered in soot and smelling of gasoline. Next to this, the story of two cops indicted on charges of soliciting. They claimed to have been under cover, but such an operation wouldn't have included the actual services of the also-arrested prostitute. At the bottom of the page, a small piece about a woman who had, in the middle of the night, found a naked man doing calisthenics in her front yard. The officer in charge stated that the up-and-down-hopping man had mental problems. I guessed so.

What a front-page news salad: murder, arson, corruption, and, on a humorous note, mental illness. It might be a step toward improving my outlook on life if I stopped reading the paper altogether. As I tossed it in the basket next to the fireplace, I thought I'd better get dressed and go to the library to do some serious research on all the spooky stuff that had been going on.

When I was halfway up the stairs, Rita suddenly called after me, "You still fretting about that Lani?"

I stood still but didn't turn around. "It's hard not to when she won't leave me alone."

"Now what you mean by that?" she screeched.

I cringed as I heard her put the bucket down. I'd plumb forgotten she knew nothing about Lani's visits. I hadn't told her, because she always claimed to believe only in what she could see. Funny that she did drive after dark, so she must believe the road was still there beyond her headlights. She'd also said she'd seen Bluebelle, a hundred times. Maybe Kate was right, and I could practice coming out of the closet by telling Rita about Lani. Opportunity knocked.

"Oh, it's just going to take some time," I said, deliberately vague to throw her off the scent. "I need to go to town, do some stuff."

"Stuff? What stuff?" She asked, suspicious.

"Things, Rita, things!" Over my shoulder, I gave her a warning look that said not to repeat my non-explanatory noun.

She scrunched up her mouth and got very busy mopping the tile at the foot of the stairs, mumbling something about me stuffing some things somewhere as I continued up the stairs.

***

The Verhoog sisters—both dressed up as their antiquated vision of what librarians ought to look like: gray cardigans, hair in little buns, half glasses on chains, sensible crepe-soled shoes—were sitting behind twin desks in the small oak-paneled entrance hall of the library.

Agnes and Albertina had begun to volunteer at the library before it had been built. Over the years, they'd developed their own variant of the Dewey decimal system that took an algebraic formula to decode and that probably had Melville Dewey screaming on the other side. To prevent people from roaming about with a glazed look in their eyes, the sisters, blissfully unaware that they themselves were in fact the cause of such confusion, invariably pounced on anyone who entered their *sanctum sanctorum* with eager offers of assistance.

They were always so happy to help that I usually accepted, even though I'd broken their code some time ago—five years of algebra finally put to use for the first time since finishing high school. Today, however, I didn't want their help, because I didn't want it to get out what I was looking for: books on possession, and not the nine-tenths-of-the-law kind.

"Good morning Agnes, Albertina," I greeted them, careful to keep my eyes on the space in between them, so they wouldn't notice I had no idea who was who.

"Good morning, Fae. Do you need some help today?" the left twin asked with a hopeful look in her eyes.

"Oh, no, thanks! I'm going to do some research, but I think I can manage." I smiled, but seeing two faces fall, I quickly added, "But I'll let you know if I get stuck." That seemed to cheer them up a little.

Then I remembered my Labrador poster and took it out of my purse. "Could you perhaps find a place for this?"

"You lost a dog?" the right twin asked.

"She *found* a dog!" The other impatiently waved the poster under her sister's nose. "Sure, we'll put it right here in the lobby."

So far, this morning, I was the only one using the library. I walked over to the card file: four deep, narrow oak drawers pulled out of their cabinet and placed on the enormous reading table in the center of the library. Londen's complete treasury of books was stacked three rows deep on three sides of the room. The racks against the walls reached all the way to the twelve-foot high sculpted ceiling. Somewhere was a ladder on rollers to reach the upper shelves.

Beginning with the first file drawer, I started my search for titles containing the buzzwords I'd listed on a slip of paper: *apparition, clairvoyant, exorcism, ghost, haunting, medium, psychic, spirit, vision.* But most of what I found were titles of mystery novels, such as *The Case of the Casual Clairvoyant* and *The Haunting of Burbage House,* and some I clearly didn't need to look at, such as *Mediums, Mystics, and More Such Nonsense.* Come to my house, and I'll show you some real nonsense, I thought.

Discouraged, I sighed and leaned back in the chair. Perhaps I should walk by the stacks to see if my gift of scripture, finding answers in writing, would kick in. It was quite a wonderful gift that allowed me to find books, passages, lines that were a direct answer to a question, a problem. Thinking of my question, I'd pull a book off a shelf without looking or open one at random, and there would be the answer. But, right now, I felt out of tune. I'd do it the normal-people way and go through the cards first.

"How are you doing?" One of the twins had crepe-soled up to me and was looking through her half glasses over my shoulder at the card I'd pulled out, *Ghost Stories of the Wild West.* I quickly reinserted the card in its place. But not fast enough, because with barely veiled excitement Agnes—or Albertina—inquired, "Are you looking for stories about ghosts?"

Apparently taking my silence for agreement, she went on, "There's a book on the subject that's very well written. It contains explanations as well as some intriguing stories. Now what is it called again?" She looked up at the ceiling and evidently found the answer there, "*Psychic Journeys*. That's it!"

I nearly groaned in exasperation. There went my hush-hush mission.

"It should be right about there, on the wall, upper shelf," she pointed to the center of the wall behind me. "You'll have to get it down yourself, Fae. We don't go up the ladder anymore." After an encouraging nod, she trotted off back to her desk.

Wondering why our library needed any kind of cataloging system at all—the Verhoog sisters seemed to know where every book was—I went in search of the ladder. It was one of those contraptions that looked like part of a stage set, with a square base on four wheels. I found it between the first and second row on the opposite side of where my quarry was and pushed it over to the area my sweet but nosy librarian had pointed at.

Uncertainly, I climbed the ladder, wanting to stay as close to the ground as possible while at the same time needing to reach the book, with as result that I had to stretch myself to maximum capacity. I had it!

"I need to talk to you!" a voice right below me whispered.

I almost lost my balance. Clasping the book against my chest, I glanced down.

It was Steve Krieger.

In the library? I frowned and considered throwing the book at him, then jumping down and running out.

But just as I was working out my escape route, he said the magic word, "Please?"

My, are we civil today!

Steve's voice held an urgency that made me look at him more closely. There was something different about him. He looked sincere. No, it was his hair. He'd had his hair cut, and it was also very curly now. A wolf with a perm.

As if in a trance, I descended the ladder. It was a very rough haircut. Had he done it himself? A home perm? Or had he gone to the same hairdresser as Lani?

"Could we sit down and talk?" He nervously ran his left hand over his newly-acquired hairdo and then let it rest in his bare neck where once his puny pony tail had been.

I stared at him, trying to figure out what else was different about him. It was more than just his hair.

It was the bandage: it was gone. And where it had been was not a scratch but a round wound like a chafe or a burn. Could Sarah have been mistaken about having scratched her assailant and have instead hit him with something that would have caused this kind of wound?

We sat down next to each other at the reading table. I had wanted to sit across from him to put some distance between us, but the size of the table would have forced us to speak louder than was acceptable in the library and this would also have allowed us to be overheard by the Verhoog sisters, who were peering at us, curiosity mingled with concern on their faces. I nodded reassuringly, and they returned to their efforts to further corrupt Dewey's system.

Steve looked straight ahead of him out the front window.

I followed his gaze until we were both staring at the rear-end of Zwarte Jan.

"That's my great-great-grandfather," Steve said as he pointed at the statue.

I thought he must have forgotten a few *greats*, because Zwarte Jan lived in the mid-nineteenth century, but let that one pass to remark, "Your last name's *Krieger*. It's German and means *warrior, soldier*. Zwarte Jan was Dutch."

"I'm related to him on my mother's side."

It was on my tongue to ask, "You have a *mother*?" but my Higher Self kicked in. It was true then: we were all related if we went back far enough into human history. The thought of a unified mankind depressed me on this occasion, because, in this particular case, it meant that Steve Krieger was my distant cousin. Six Degrees from Fae van Dalen? I hoped there was a link missing.

"I didn't kill her. She said she was leaving everything to me. But I didn't kill her." Steve's eyes were now intent on the book I'd laid between us on the table as if he were having a conversation with it, instead of with me.

I also looked at the book.

"She wrote a new will. It's somewhere in the house. That's what I was looking for the other day. Anyway, I don't know what she did with it. I *know* she wrote it." His beady eyes shifted to the far end of the table and then to the book shelves behind me.

"Did you see her write it?" I decided to help him along.

"No, huh ... , but she told me she'd do it after Chuck came over and they got into a terrible fight. She said she wasn't going to let him waste any of her money on that potato farm."

"Potato farm? I thought he was raising beef." Hadn't Alicia said Chuck smelled of cow manure? But if he was growing potatoes, he must be an even better man than I'd already suspected. "What's wrong with growing potatoes?" I asked defensively.

Steve seemed to think deeply about my question before answering, "I don't know. Nothing, I guess." He scratched the side of his head, a confused look on his face.

I waited a few seconds and then said, "Well, go ahead, tell me what happened," as if he were the one who'd taken the conversation off track.

"Some weeks later, when I asked her about it, she told me the whole thing, what she'd written, out of her head. Verbatim!" He finally looked me in the eyes.

Verbatim? He knew the word *verbatim*? This *arse equus* knew the *meaning* of the word *verbatim*?

"I know that will is somewhere in her house!" He slapped his hand on the table.

"Steve ... " I was about to explain Lani's mental condition, although he probably wouldn't understand despite his rudimentary knowledge of Latin, but he saved me the trouble by interrupting.

"Did you find it?" He squinted at me, a devious glint in his eyes.

Squinting right back, I shook my head. The poor devil seriously believed Lani had written a new will, in favor of him. What, for Pete's sake, did he want from me? An admission that I'd somehow made off with Lani's mythical very last *Last Will and Testament*?

Lani'd had so many legal problems with men and property over the years that she'd practically been a lawyer herself. She'd known all the legal lingo and could easily have composed the so-called will in her head to recite for this doofus. Verbatim. Indeed. Doubtless, she'd made other promises to keep Steve from running off with the circus or a younger woman. Even if she had written anything down, she'd have known that such an unwitnessed document wouldn't be worth a thing. I was beginning to feel sorry for him.

"Were there any witnesses?" I asked.

"Witnesses?" He frowned, uncomprehending.

"Yes, *witnesses*." I sighed and then, unable to help myself, I added, "Other than Solo."

He sneered at me. "You know what I think? I think you took it and then you killed her!"

I stopped feeling sorry for him. Where had I heard this last bit before? Verbatim. "Well, if I did, I got away with it, because they've closed the investigation and I've inherited all her property," I said with a serious expression on my face as if I were puzzled by this—for him, unlucky—chain of events.

Glaring at me, he rolled his sleeves up, a threatening gesture, the way he did it.

I looked down. On the inside of his right forearm, near his elbow, was a black tattoo. It was a *Hakenkreuz*, a swastika.

My head jerked to one side as if I'd been hit hard in the face. My blood froze up in my arteries. I kept staring at Steve's *Hakenkreuz* while the tide of my thinking pulled out, to leave an emptiness, a great hollowness. Then, a tsunami of thoughts and feelings washed over me with so much violence that I had to close my eyes.

I saw my father point at whole rows of houses in Nijmegen and heard him say, "I must have taken over a hundred bodies out of here. No, not bodies … heads, arms, legs, and rumps." I saw the bullet holes in the red bricks of the old post office, where the Nazis had shot at my father. I saw the helmet on the grave of my seventeen-year-old uncle, Henny, a large hole where the grenade shell had blasted through. I saw my Oma's eyes filled with tears, on the day of his death, on his birthday, and on many days in between.

I opened my eyes and noticed Steve glancing from his swastika to me and back again, a speculative look on his face. I felt physically ill. Did he think he was just making some kind of fashion statement? There's nothing innocent about the *Hakenkreuz* when you've grown up in post-war Europe. It's a Fascist sign connected to bloody carnage, terrible destruction, starvation during the Hunger Winter. The unspeakable sorrows and horrors of war.

With my face turned away from him, I grabbed my book, pushed back the chair, and got up. "You have a chemical imbalance in your brain."

"I wasn't the only one who could have given her that medicine!"

For a moment, I had no idea who or what he was talking about.

He put his hand—the hand connected to the arm with the *Hakenkreuz*—on my shoulder and pushed me down on the chair. "I wasn't the only one who knew about it. The whole family knew! And what about Jason's boyfriend? What's his name? He went to see Lani that week. And Mark Brandenburgh came over a few days before it happened. He told Lani to keep her mouth shut about him and Alicia. *She* could have told Mark about it. And how about Sasha and her father, Jack? Maybe they all planned it together."

"Sure, on the Orient Express!" I hissed. "I don't give a shit!" I wrested myself free and stood up, backing into the chair, which scraped loudly over the floor.

"But you're the one who got all the money!" A triumphant look appeared in his eyes.

"Stay away from me, you little creep!" I was furious, ready to smack him with *Psychic Journeys* and give him some visions.

The Verhoog sisters, their necks craned, were still sitting behind their desks, alternately eying us and casting anxious looks at each other.

Giving Steve a wide berth, I hurried to the entrance hall and handed the book to the twin on my left. She turned it over a few times before opening it and taking the card out. Carefully, she stamped the card and the check-out leaflet on the inside cover with her purple-inked date stamp.

"There," she said while handing the book back to me. She then leaned over her desk and whispered, "You watch out for that one. He isn't all there." She rolled her eyes upward.

Giving her a weak smile, I nodded.

Finally outside, I took a deep breath. As I looked in through the window, Steve was still sitting at the table. He stared at me, slyness covering his long face like a mask.

Driving home, I tried to stay in the here and now by focusing on the trees, the clumps of new grass, the mustard flowers at the side of the road, but when the feeling of having been exposed to a foul pollutant wouldn't leave me, I allowed my mind to wander.

I hadn't known about Dean Cooper or Mark Brandenburgh visiting Lani. Had Jason sent Dean instead of coming himself? What had Dean come to talk about? But there had to have been two visits, and Jason hadn't been to his mother's house for at least a year—if I could believe the incredulous look as he commented on the Victorian living room. Or had Alicia taken the Boozabuse and given it to Mark, who was a caterer and could undoubtedly cook up a storm?

All the other possible suspects paraded through my mind, one by one, until I finally, inevitably, came back to Steve Krieger, the very person I'd tried to avoid thinking about. I'd have to check with Sarah about the scratch she put on the rapist's face. Or, Rita would know. Better talk to Rita and not upset Sarah like that nasty friend had done. The wound on Steve's cheek had looked like a chafe as if he'd fallen on asphalt. Maybe he got hit with a brick. And Gwen had said I was wrong about the jacket. But did this mean that I was wrong about Steve?

Apparently, he also didn't think the fat lady had sung yet, despite that the investigation had been closed. Why would he want to keep things going if he were guilty? Had he deliberately shown me that swastika? To intimidate me? Steve, whose language had undergone a remarkable improvement since Lani's death. Steve, who hated women, whose Mark of the Beast told me he hated whole races, whole continents. It was so easy to think of him as a rapist, a killer. *Krieger.*

Or, was he just an ignorant coward?

Chapter 28

There is nothing either good or bad, but thinking makes it so.

The fallout of Calming Lavender still lingered throughout the house. I wasn't sure which was worse, enduring Lani's antics or this musty odor, but right now I seemed to have little choice in regard to either.

The first thing I did after entering the kitchen was to pick up the phone and call Gwen.

"You're upset about something," she said, right after I told her who was calling.

"Steve Krieger followed me into the library," I said. "He still wants to get his hands on Lani's property and was really obnoxious."

"Is that all?" Gwen asked in a tone that said she knew better.

"No. He has a swastika on his arm. I found that upsetting."

"I see," she said. "But there's something else."

"What did you mean when you said I was wrong about the jacket?" I asked.

"Just that. I saw a turquoise jacket and knew something was wrong with your perception about it," she said.

"Are you sure?" I asked, urgently.

"That's what I got, at least," Gwen said. "I could try to second guess my initial impressions."

"Uhuh ... ," was all I could say to that. Been there, done that. Besides, I knew Gwen wasn't serious. "It's just that I thought that whoever killed Lani and raped Sarah was one and the same person."

"And you suspect it's this Swastika Steve?"

"Yes, but some things don't quite fit. Are you getting any impressions?"

"Wow! Yes! Too many. A lot of confusion."

"I know. There are so many other people involved. There's ... ," I was going to rattle off a list of suspects and other information, but Gwen interrupted me.

"No, no! Don't tell me any more. Right now, I only seem to be picking up *your* energy. You're acting like a filter, or maybe it's more like a wall." She laughed.

I didn't think that was funny at all. To be called a wall. Although, I did feel pretty dense not having figured everything out by now.

"The less you tell me, the more I can keep an open mind. I'm more likely to get insights that way," Gwen elaborated. "For now, you need to trust your own intuition, even if you don't think you have much at the moment. Don't live your life by other people's insights. I certainly don't. You'll be led to the solution when you're good and ready."

"But how do I get ready?"

"First, let me tell you what problems I think you're having. You're too close to the situation. It's hard to see what's going on when you're close. Things become unfocused. That's why sensitives often don't know what will happen in their own lives. Also, your emotions are clearly getting in the way. Strong sympathies and antipathies can warp your perceptions. Your own character defects can prevent you from receiving information. You'll need to clear the channel of all that chatter."

So, what she was saying was that I had this gift but wasn't quite up to it?

Gwen continued, "We need to be careful with our judgments of people. Sometimes we pick up too much—things that come from us, not from them. There are also rare instances in which people can mess with their own energy. They can project or block aspects of their personality. Have you ever met a sociopath?"

"Considering that an estimated one in twenty-five people is a sociopath, some of my family members, friends, and acquaintances are probably sociopaths. But, yes, I've been aware of a few." *Steve Krieger, for one!*

"Then you know that they often don't seem what they are. Although, for us, this usually doesn't last long and it's only possible when we're not focused or second guess our sixth sense. We need to stay centered." She paused again.

Had my notion that Steve had killed Lani and attacked Sarah come from conjecture, not from my sixth sense? Just because he was a sociopath didn't mean he was a killer and rapist.

"Do you meditate?" Gwen asked.

"Meditate?" I squeaked, put on the spot.

"Yes. Meditation would help you a lot. If you have trouble relaxing, letting go, imagine you're looking at a big white sheet," Gwen said.

Oh, no! Not The Big White Sheet again! I had tried that a few times, years ago, but my imaginary sheet had soon been stained with imaginary spots, had flapped in the imaginary wind, and then had blown clear off the imaginary line I'd had it hanging on. That usually had marked the end of my efforts to meditate.

"Yes," I said, trying to convey both comprehension and cooperation in that one little word. *Why a white sheet? Why not a green or purple sheet? Could it be a satin sheet? White satin. Nights in white satin, never reaching the end. Maybe I should hang up a real sheet.*

"Fae?"

"Yes, yes, a sheet! I mean, meditation. Thanks! I'll talk to you later. Thanks!"

Having no intention of meditating any time soon, I went into the living room and stretched out on the couch to peruse *Psychic Journeys: Travels Beyond the Obvious*, as the book was called.

The whole cover was printed in wavy lines of washed-out pink, royal blue, and lavender. On the front, puffy white clouds floated in a light-blue triangle at the center whereof was a huge eye. In its jet-black pupil sparkled a many-pointed silver star. The jacket's layout was far more mesmerizing than any imaginary sheet I'd ever gazed at.

After staring at it for a while I opened the book at its table of contents, hoping to find a chapter on trouble shooting. But, apparently, the author hadn't found it necessary to write a whole chapter on mayhem from the beyond. I checked the reference section in the back for some of my buzzwords, but found nothing curative of hauntings on any of the pages I was referred to. Exasperated, I dropped the book next to me on the floor and pushed my head deeper into the pillow.

Just as I closed my eyes, I heard what sounded like a loud and unpleasant laughter ring through the room. I sat up with a start, just in time to see Moon and Mellow roughly push each other aside at the swinging door, each trying to be the first to get out.

Had it been her? Laughing at me?

I got up, stormed into the kitchen, grabbed the package of incense, and shook five of the fattest sticks out of the container. Lighting them one at a time with my cigarette lighter, I tiptoed back into the living room. With a wide motion, I waved the sticks around several times and then planted them upright in the potted palm. Tentatively seating myself on the couch again, I picked up the book once more. There had to be some practical advice in there. *Seek and ye shall find.*

Indeed, there was a chapter on haunted houses. I skimmed through the collection of short stories about hauntings in Old England, the Colonies, and the South. For the most, the tales reflected the author's disgustingly positive attitude toward meddlesome ghosts, so that she only described what I would call *minor* hauntings. Apparitions at the top of elaborate staircases, hesitant footsteps in dark hallways, a little banging around in dusty attics. These ghosts certainly never shut one's nephew in one's car.

In a few stories, the advice given to the hauntees on how they could rid themselves of a spirit was noted, but it was no better than the suggestions Gwendolyn had made. In fact, it was the same. "And because the lady of the house was losing much sleep as a result of the nightly goings-on, her husband took counsel of a local witch who advised that the burning of sage in the home would surely clear the house of the discontented spirit."

A witch, huh?

Before I could find out what happened to the unhappy couple, I suddenly became aware that the strong smell of lavender was being replaced by a much more powerful scent.

It was the unmistakable fragrance of Lani's roses, quickly growing heavier and sweeter than any earthly rose could possibly smell, until it stank like Hal's compost pile behind the barn. What had, that first time, been a spiritual flowers greeting was now turned into an act of aggression.

Determined not to give in, I opened the French doors wide and then went over to the record player. Plan B was about to be executed.

I thumbed through my eclectic CD collection—Glenn Miller, The Stones, Tommy Dorsey, The Police, Nina Simone, Procul Harem, Elvis Presley, The Moody Blues—but finally decided to grab one of my old records. It turned out to be one of The Doors. The grey vinyl player was a left-over relic from my Berkeley days, and I had to fiddle with the knobs for a while to get both speakers to produce sound at the same time. When they finally did, *Break on Through to the Other Side*, interspersed with loud snaps, crackles, and pops, boomed through the house.

The cats, who had returned while I was reading and had, so far, first endured my aroma aversion therapy and then Lani's smelly assault with feline condescension, both began to fidget and looked quite cranky about the racket I was making.

And then the doors started.

It began with the door to the kitchen. At first, it just swung slowly to the music, but soon it was moving faster and faster, until it went back and forth so fiercely that I feared it would come off its hinges. Then, almost immediately, my home seemed to be filled with obnoxious teenagers who were slamming doors so hard that the windows rattled.

Moon and Mellow hastily made their escape through the French doors, the only ones not taking part in this revolt, and leapt off the back porch. Under the beech trees, they stopped and stared up at the house. All three dogs were barking in concert near the barn, but even Dooley, my dark hero, didn't come to the rescue.

For a brief moment, I considered becoming hysterical, running through the house screaming, my arms wildly flailing about, if only to show Lani that I could get weird, too. But, although I was somewhat unnerved by the noise, some of which of course caused by the damaged record, I knew it was just Lani kicking up her heels. I hadn't been afraid of her when she was alive and had resolved to be only annoyed with her now she was dead. If she'd just make clear what it was she wanted.

Maybe Gwen had meant for me to make a different kind of noise, to get a bunch of lids off my pans and bang them together, play modern jazz. The irony of my grabbing a record of The Doors and that first song wasn't lost on me. *Break on Through to the Other Side.* "She's having a little fun with me," I thought. Nevertheless, I didn't approve of all this negative attention-getting behavior. Plan B had definitely bombed in a big way.

I quickly thought over Plan C, Gwen's last piece of advice of filling the house with light. Should I collect all our lamps and candles? It didn't seem to be such a great idea. Lani might set the house on fire in response.

Finally, I settled for following Moon and Mellow outside. By the time I reached the barn, where concerned canines licked my hands, the house was quiet again.

I'd have to talk to Gwen about the next level of exorcism, other than causing my own house to be burned down. Maybe I'd used the wrong incense and the wrong music. I was fairly new at this and still had much to learn, as Gwen had noted.

As I was standing there, thinking of possible ways to rid myself of Lani, Mab and Dooley began to circle me, whining nervously. I noticed that the Labrador had gone into the barn.

She was on the blankets Hal and I had folded for her under the workbench, squatting and very busy having her second pup. I went down on my knees, encouragingly and admiringly cooing at her. Covered with a thin membrane, the first-born lay wet and exhausted between her legs. I picked it up and tore the membrane off. It was black. A little boy. When I put it back down in front of her, the new mother licked it carefully. Then she got busy tending the second one, which had slid out with an ease females of the human species would envy. I broke the sack around its head. Mom didn't have time to clean number two's chocolate little body all the way, because number three made its appearance.

Now we had one of each color. Black, chocolate, and yellow. So far, we were still within the Labrador breed, it looked. It was quite a bit more messy than I remembered. With a towel, I helped wipe the puppies clean. Then I placed the newborns safely in a corner, in a warm, little nest of blanket folds.

I heard Hal's truck drive up, the motor cut, the door slam. I called out to him, "In here! She's having her babies!"

Hal came in quietly and kneeled next to me on the concrete floor. He looked tired. I stood up and rubbed his shoulders. We took turns telling the new mother what a good girl she was. I wasn't sure if she really needed our encouragement, she seemed so efficient, but it was something for us to do.

"I think we ought to keep her," Hal said, looking at the three pups that had so far come into this world.

Surprised, I glanced at him, "But she's someone's dog, Hal."

"Someone who didn't take good care of her or even cared *for* her." He frowned and got up. "When I petted her yesterday, I found wounds around her neck that seemed to have been made by a chain, and when I checked her over, under the light, I found some long scars under her coat, on her sides. I'm pretty sure she was beaten."

I grimaced at this news and immediately declared, "We'll keep her!" I slid my arm around his waist. That was my Hal. He'd take the side of a helpless animal, anytime. He should be a vegetarian. Just like me, when I became one.

I didn't tell him that I'd already secretly named our foundling when he'd brought her home Sunday night. I resolved to collect my posters as soon as possible, before anyone could claim her and hurt her even more. *Promise* had come to stay with us.

There was a lull in the birthing, so I went inside to make us some coffee. I had all but forgotten about my failed attempts at exorcism.

The house was quiet. So was Lani.

By the time I came back to the barn, eight pups had been born. Four black, two chocolate, and two yellow. I handed Hal both mugs, kneeled down, and put the pups on their mother's teats. They immediately knew what to do, sucking hard and kneading with their little front feet to stimulate the milk production. I spread one of the old blankets on the floor, lay down, and gazed at them. I was in heaven.

Looking a little dreamy eyed, too, Hal handed me my mug. He said he liked the name I'd picked out for her. We toasted Promise and the puppies with the coffee and decided to move them into the warm kitchen. Hal plugged in a little space heater and then went to collect some boards to hammer together a good-sized whelping box that would contain the puppies for the first couple of weeks.

Still not wanting to be in the house by myself for too long a time, I hung around to give him some pointers. I considered telling him what had happened earlier, decided against it, and was just about to give him instructions on how to build a whelping box, when the phone rang. Divine intervention.

It was Willem de Weder. Hal talked to him for a while.

"Willem's coming over. Do we have anything for dinner? We're going to a meeting after." He directed his words at the tall board he was holding.

Looking at the house, I said, "I can hustle something up." Would she dare start something while Willem was visiting? My resolve to only be annoyed with Lani was faltering. She could do some real damage, intentionally or not.

I went back in through the French doors and closed them behind me. The record was still turning, the needle making scratchy sounds. I lifted the arm and clicked it to go off. Strangely, the lavender had won out over Lani's eau de toilet.

As I scrounged dinner together, Gwen's words went through my head. If I was wrong about the jacket, then was Sarah's rape a random act of violence? No rhyme or reason. But Gwen hadn't been able to say in what way I was wrong. Wrong for thinking the jacket had made Steve mistake Sarah for me? Wrong for feeling guilty? Did I need to ask Rita about the scratch Sarah left? For all I knew, Steve could have burned himself on purpose to cover it up. And despite his pointing the finger at everyone else, he was still at the top of my list for having killed Lani. Steve Krieger *had* to have done it! All of it. *He's a creep! He's got a* Hakenkreuz*!*

***

Willem was trying to spear a slightly undercooked potato that kept sliding around on his plate. Hal and I both stopped eating to watch him. When Willem looked up and found our eyes on him, embarrassment colored his round face to match his red nose.

We nodded encouragingly for him to continue his chase. He seemed to be enjoying having dinner with us but wasn't getting much to eat, mainly because he'd been talking in a long stream-of-consciousness manner, like Sasha had done when she'd been over.

I'd been too preoccupied with the events of the day to make much of dinner and had thrown the food together haphazardly, combining several vegetables solely for a pleasant color combination—like an extension of interior decorating—with some mushroomed pork chops. Despite my impressive heritage of potato eaters, I'd grabbed a bag of frozen new potatoes and produced a pan of glassy specimen any self-respecting Dutchwoman would have frowned upon. They looked like old-fashioned marbles when they were still made out of marble. Even Hal, who probably would eat marbles, hadn't recognized them for what they were. "Hey, what are these?" he had asked with a funny look on his face, but when I had told him, he hadn't, right in front of Willem, challenged my Dutch-ness.

I was glad Willem was taking so much pleasure in the hunt.

He looked down at Moon and Mellow, who both acted as if they were routinely fed off the table at dinnertime. "I have fish,' he said.

We nodded our approval. Fish were good.

"I heard about Alicia making such a scene in that lawyer's office." Willem shook his head in disbelief and almost caught another potato. "I don't know what got into her, to be so rude about nothing."

"I'd say a quarter million isn't nothing." I handed him the bread basket. I had done OK on that; it came from the bakery.

Willem looked at me blankly. "A quarter of a million?"

"That's what it states in her will," Hal said. He was eating with great enthusiasm.

"But that's impossible!" Willem exclaimed. "She didn't have near that kind of money!"

All three of us dropped our utensils and stared at each other, three pairs of eyebrows raised in surprise.

"You see," Willem finally continued, "she was always borrowing money from me. That was besides the monthly alimony I paid her. The kids didn't know. I didn't think it was any of their business. But how they got the idea that Lani was well off..."

"Hum," I said, "probably from Lani."

"How was she supposed to have amassed this... *fortune*?" Willem asked with a wry look on his face.

"An investment portfolio, wasn't it, Fae?" Hal asked.

"Yes, that's what it said." I nodded. I was deliberating if it were at all possible that one of Lani's personalities had been poor while another was well to do. Interesting thought!

Willem shook his head, "Well, wait until the will goes through probate. But Lani had no portfolio other than the kind with pictures in it."

"What happened to the money we paid her for this house?" Hal asked. "Didn't she inherit it from her aunt? This house was all hers then, wasn't it?"

"Yes, it was her inheritance. But, the lawyers ended up with forty percent or more of it, because of the legal challenges from her cousins. And the rest? I don't know what she did with it. Paid off debts she'd accumulated, I suppose. I never saw any of it. Three months later, she told me she needed money again. I didn't even bother asking her for an explanation."

"What about the house she lived in?" Hal turned his attention back to his food and began to eat again.

I was too excited to eat.

"She left you that, too, huh?" Willem put his hand over his mouth and swallowed hard. He then stared ahead with an odd, constipated look on his face.

"Fae's made an appointment with a lawyer to see about giving everything to the kids." Hal was too busy eating to notice Willem's look of acute distress.

"There won't be that much for them to get," Willem said quietly. "The house wasn't hers. It's mine."

Hal and I gaped at each other. My mouth had already dropped open, but now my lower jaw was practically resting on my breasts.

"I'm really sorry, Fae," Willem mumbled, gazing at me with great compassion.

He *was* really terribly sorry for me, I could tell. But an enormous relief came flooding over me. "Oh, no, you don't understand!" I exclaimed. "This is great! I didn't want it anyway!" My problems were solved. Well, maybe not all of them.

"I'm glad you're taking it that way," Willem said, sounding doubtful. "I bought that ranch before we were married the first time. That's how we met, because it was right next to her aunt's house. When we divorced, I kept the house. Lani wasn't able to handle finances very well. She had some other problems as well."

"You mean her being a multiple personality?" I asked.

"They told you about that, too?" Willem asked. "I never did understand it, even after I took her to a doctor and he explained it to me. I knew her for so many years and never could figure out how her mind worked. Her behavior was so erratic, but she'd always explain things away so beautifully. She had an answer for everything. Still, I couldn't get over the feeling that she was constantly lying about even the smallest things." He suddenly clamped his mouth shut, shocked by his own words, his face becoming even redder and his nose seemingly growing more bulbous.

I looked away from Willem thinking about the list of suspects I'd just mentally amended on my way home from the library. Willem sure didn't sound too happy. His two marriages to Lani and indefinite financial support proved he hadn't been able to cut his ties with her. Had the co-dependent Willem finally had enough? Had he been crying so hard at the funeral not because he missed her but because he was guilty of killing her? Now that I was getting to know him, he seemed rather benign, very different from how Lani had described him. I couldn't imagine this caring man stalking anyone.

But then, I thought, we're never just one thing or just one way. We can be many opposites put together. The cruelest murderer may also be a considerate husband, a loving father, caring pet owner—

even if just of fish. Could Willem be messing with his own energy? And, had I been taken in by his act of being a benevolent version of W.C. Fields?

Hal glanced at the clock. "We'd better get going," he said. He was the only one of us who'd finished his dinner, including his potatoes.

After helping clear the table, they left in Hal's truck, Willem still looking worried about the great disappointment he'd caused me.

I fed all the animals, lingering gooey eyed at the sleeping puppies. I headed upstairs to work, or rather, to see how I could get out of some of the work for my classes. Time was running out and it had been nearly a week since I'd retyped my old Shakespeare notes. Between the funeral, the reading of the will, the twins' visit, puppies, flyers, deep thinking, and my failed attempts at exorcism, I'd made little effort to find time for my professional obligations.

Sitting behind my desk, it suddenly occurred to me that I could do with my classes what I'd just done with dinner: use more of what I already had. Thaw out those frozen potatoes. Somewhere in my filing cabinets should still be the old folder of my medieval drama class, complete with notes, essay questions, and syllabus. No need to start from scratch. And, surely, there had to be more notes on plays I'd used for prior Shakespeare classes. I'd simply adjust the list of plays to what I'd find. Then, all I'd have to do was update the paperwork for both classes, change a few things and, *voilà*. Quite brilliant!

So why hadn't I thought of this before? And when had my life's calling of being a teacher deteriorated into outsmarting Matchett the Hatchet?

Sort of when I'd first met her. That brought me to the twentieth-century course she'd dumped on me and the fear that I'd be spending most of my summer putting it together. Could I have a *Ulysses*-free twentieth-century class? If I used Kate's "I'd be more comfortable teaching Shakespeare," Matchett couldn't throw too big a fit.

Things seemed to definitely be looking up. No inheritance, no major class preps, no *Ulysses*. Perhaps soon, no Lani, either.

Before beginning my excavations, I went to visit Solo. He was happy to see me, must have been lonely. He said, "I have no bananas in my pocket." Mae West meeting Vanna White?

At least, he was mine to find a good home for. Wasn't he?

Chapter 29

'Tis now the very witching time of night.

I shivered and pulled the blankets and quilt up to my chin. An icy chill had settled into my joints. The tip of my nose felt frozen. I moved over to Hal, who was sleeping peacefully on his side, facing away from me, and pressed my body against his. I lifted my head off the pillow and looked over at the clock. It glowed a greenish two-thirty, and this surely meant I should be sound asleep, but I'd been awake for the last fifteen minutes and couldn't get back to sleep because of the cold.

I'd already gotten up once to pull on a fleece jogging suit, the pants under, the top over my nightgown, but it hadn't helped. My head hurt as if something hard and heavy were pushing down on my crown. I thought of looking in my drawers for one of the woolen hats I'd knitted last winter but didn't want to leave my bed. Never had it been this cold in our bedroom. I closed my eyes, hoping that if I could fake it I could make it and actual sleep would follow.

An acute bout of nausea, swirling through my head and stomach like a dark whirlpool dragging me down, forced my eyes open. Above me, the ceiling was moving. No, it was the bed. It gently rocked back and forth. The ceiling seemed closer than normal.

I moved to the edge of the bed and looked down to check what was going on. The feet of the bed rested securely on the floor, but the rocking continued, less gently now.

My head. It was my head.

I put my hand on Hal's shoulder and shook him, "Hal? Hal!"

But Hal slept on.

The only time I'd ever felt this sick in my life was when, as a teenager, I'd hung over the railing of the ferry from Dover to Calais and barfed into the North Sea.

I rolled one hundred-and-eighty degrees toward Hal again and pushed on his back. "Hey, Hal! Wake up!" My head was swimming. I pushed him so hard that I thought he'd fall off the bed, but he still didn't show any sign of waking other than a few loud snores as I pummeled him half to death.

Suddenly, the doors to the balcony flew open wide. The sheer curtains billowed up to the ceiling like the useless sails of a ship in a hurricane. The incoming gust was warmer than the air in the room. All the while, the bed rocked back and forth, faster and faster.

"This is bullshit." I moaned, wishing I could get out of bed and make it to the bathroom and stick my head in the bowl as in the good old times. Miserable, I stared at Hal's back.

The balcony doors slammed shut with a bang.

I pulled the blankets back up to my chin, waiting for Lani's next move, because I was convinced she was showing off once again.

But nothing happened. Utter calm. Only the sound of Hal's breathing.

It was almost as if I had imagined it. And I would almost have believed this were it not that the curtains were caught at the top of the doors, hanging half outside, a wild jumble of gauze.

Slowly, the nausea subsided, and I drifted off into an unrefreshing sleep.

***

"There are ants all over the kitchen counter," Hal announced.

I was still lying in bed and my first impulse was to argue with him about the possibility of ants running amuck in our kitchen in mid-winter. But then I realized that I didn't know anything about the habits of ants and that lately stranger things had happened in our house and who was I to argue with a biologist? He'd know an ant when he saw one.

"What's with these curtains?" He opened the doors and pulled the sheers down.

"You use bay leaves," I said.

"Bay leaves?" He slapped at the curtains to straighten them out.

"Yeah, you know, those leaves ... from the bay tree."

"Does that really work?" he asked, apparently aware that I wasn't trying to be sarcastic but was still half asleep.

"Sure! It makes them go away." I turned on my side and buried my head deeper into the pillow.

"Why are you wearing a jogging suit?" He sat next to me on the bed and rubbed my arm. "Are you feeling sick?"

"Ooh-ooh!" I wanted to tell him. I wanted to cry. So, I did both.

Hal listened, wiping sticky strands of hair out of my face. When I was done blubbering, he kissed me. "Come downstairs and I'll fix you a nice breakfast. You can take a nap later."

I had wanted him to assure me that he'd take care of that big, bad Lani, that he'd stay up and watch over me in nights to come, all night long, but he seemed to be at a loss about how to react to the tale of my nightly adventure, because it wasn't an alien abduction. I should have thrown in a four-foot, ant-like creature. Now I'd have to settle for breakfast. He must think I'd just had a bad dream. After all, why hadn't *he* woken up? *Because you can sleep through a Mars attack, Hal!*

I sighed and told him to go on downstairs and I'd be there shortly.

I took a long, hot shower. After toweling myself off, I gingerly stepped on the bathroom scale, always a depressing ritual. The numbers flew by until, finally, the arrow pointed at 285 pounds. *Wait a minute!* I almost tossed my cookies, but I hadn't eaten any.

I got off the scale, but when the disk stopped rotating the arrow pointed at 150 pounds. One of Hal's pranks? I didn't want to consider the alternative, so early in the morning. I moved the little wheel until the zero was at the arrow and stood on the scale again, wiggling my feet to change the outcome. That was more like it, but I was still hauling five extra pounds around.

Last night, while looking for my old notes and typing the text in on my computer, without thinking, I'd eaten half the box of chocolates the boys had brought over. I'd hoped the calories would take at least a few days to show up.

Disgusted, I wrapped myself in my royal blue robe, noting that the coffee stains from the appliance uprising had nicely washed out. Tying the sash tightly around where my waist was supposed to be, I walked by my office, where the not-so-circumstantial evidence of my criminally insane behavior was still on the desk. Had the chocolates made me sick?

Promise and the puppies were in the whelping box in the corner behind the door between the kitchen and the hall. After Hal had come home last night, he'd hammered the four-feet-square box together. Without my input, I might add. Promise had been a little confused about what we were doing with her pups, about being allowed into the house, but she settled in before long.

I swooned over the puppies for a while. They already looked twice as big as when they were born, but maybe this was just an optical illusion. Fat, milk-filled bellies.

Hal greeted me with, "The ants are holding a pow-wow on your bay leaves." He handed me a cup of coffee. "Here!"

"Where did you find fresh bay leaves?"

"Fresh? You said 'bay leaves,' not 'fresh.'" Hal was doing something at the stove with a spatula. It smelled greasy and the splattering sound made my stomach flip-flop.

"They have to be fresh or it won't work." I sat down at the kitchen table. "What are you making?"

"Omelet!" He answered.

"What did you put in there?" I asked suspiciously.

"Oh, green onions and bell peppers and cheese and mushrooms, and ... " He stopped and looked at me with concern.

I was thinking about the ferry from Dover to Calais and was beginning to turn a whiter shade of pale again. "I'll go take the dogs for a walk."

I got dressed and took Mab and Dooley for a double stroll to the creek. Promise wouldn't leave her babies.

Lead gray clouds covered the land like a giant lid, a soft haze hung between the trees in the orchard. The air smelled crisp and clean. Dooley found a six-foot branch to carry along until he forgot it when he waded into the creek.

When we got back, Hal was ready to leave for work. "There's some omelet on the stove for you."

I swallowed hard. "Thank you, Honey."

We went through our Hal-goes-to-work routine. *Drive carefully. I'll call you. I love you.*

I fed all the children of the dog and cat variety and then went upstairs to feed Solo. He was remarkably quiet. I thought he looked a bit depressed, although, I had no idea what a depressed bird looked like. It was just a feeling I had. I talked some baby talk to him, trying to lift his spirits, but he didn't say a word. I hoped he wasn't sick. Could he be missing Lani? I left the door to his cage open.

Reluctantly, I sat down at the computer. I double clicked on the Shakespeare folder and then created a file for *Macbeth*, one of the plays I'd found some decent notes for, from a class I'd taken at Berkeley. I'd dug that deep to outmaneuver the Hatchet, all the way to my undergraduate days.

I peered at the screen. Something behind me reflected in the glass. I turned my head.

She was sitting in Dooley's chair.

"What do you want now?" I swung around on my chair.

"I see you've gained some weight," Lani said.

Confused, I stared at her lips. They hadn't moved, yet she had spoken. She had just communicated with me for the very first time. Her words had come like a thought into my head.

And she had told me I was fat!

"I see you've lost all your weight. At least, I still have a body!" I said out loud.

Her facial expression didn't change. Was she beyond insult or was she unable to hear my voice? Maybe she could only communicate through thought transference. I'd try that.

I closed my eyes and mentally asked, "Do you have anything important to tell me?" and, waiting for an answer, I kept my eyes firmly shut to increase my receptivity.

I waited a whole minute. Maybe even longer. But when nothing came, I peeked through my eyelashes at the chair.

She was gone.

I could have saved my brainwaves. Maybe I shouldn't have used the word *important*. It had probably scared her off. At least nobody had been here to see me talk to an empty chair.

I turned back to the computer and began to work, retyping my old notes and adding to them, digging into the rich ground of *Macbeth*'s plot and characters. Drama, history, intrigue, murder, psychology, and—the supernatural.

I was wondering where I could find a copy of Roman Polanski's film to show my class as a treat, when the phone rang. It was Matchett.

"I'm sorry, Fae," she began, in her customary, curt manner that conveyed she wasn't sorry at all. "But I need to speak to you."

You are speaking to me. I took a deep breath. I'd just turned a shitty day around. Was she going to spoil it? I hung my head, ready for the guillotine.

"Are you there, Fae?" she asked loudly.

"Yes, I'm here!" *Get on with it! Don't make me suffer longer than necessary!*

"There must be something wrong with your phone." She was still shouting.

I can hear you loud and clear.

"You remember our guest lecturer last spring, Dr. Thomas Chapman?"

I told her I did. *Tommy the Gun*, Sam and I had dubbed him. He was a funny looking man with a big head, in more ways than one. Came across like a mournful monk, softly spoken, but his words were laced with an acerbic humor always directed at the listener. You'd walk away from the conversation and then later you'd think, "Now what did he say?" And, there were rumors …

"Well, his specialty is twentieth-century literature, as you know. I hope you don't mind." Her intake of a deep breath brought on a loaded silence.

I hadn't known Tommy had a specialty, at least not an English literature one, but why would I mind what it was? "Well?" I asked impatiently, using her favorite interjection.

"He has agreed to join us this fall!" Ecstasy in her voice.

Just what we need: a certificated jerk on the faculty.

"We were able to shift some funds within the department and came up with enough moneys to hire another instructor. And, … he has agreed to teach the course I had assigned to you." She paused. "I truly hope you don't mind."

Mind? I wanted to whoop into the phone. I wanted to drive over to her home and kiss her little monkey face and dry clean and hand press all her little Chanel suits and restring her pearls.

"Not at all," I said with queenly coolness, meantime joyfully slapping my hand on the desk till it hurt.

"You will still have the other three courses to teach," she said in a consoling tone.

My grief over my dreadful loss went straight from the stage of denial to the stage of acceptance. "Oh, yes, I'll stay quite busy," I assured her, just in case she might feel sorry enough for me to throw another rotten plum my way.

"Yes! Yes!" I yelled as soon as I'd put down the receiver. I ran to Solo's room to share the good news. He hadn't left his cage but tilted his head sideways when I explained, "Auntie Fae is rejoicing that she doesn't have to teach Joyce!"

He stretched his wings and stepped into his cage's door opening, looking like a tiny sage about to dole out some wisdom. "*Joyeux Noël!*" he called out.

At least, that's what it sounded like. I was flabbergasted: he had congratulated me! Granted, he'd done it by wishing me a merry Christmas a good month late, but still, he'd sensed the spirit of the occasion. What a good little bird; he deserved a better home than mine.

This was altogether becoming a wonderful day. I had no idea what had made Matchett play a numbers game with the budget, but such solutions, coming seemingly out of nowhere, helped sustain my faith in a Higher Hand steering my course. Kate had told me once that someone had told her that desire is prayer. And the Great Spirit must have heard mine.

Thinking about the Great Spirit made me think of Gwen and that I should call her and tell her about Lani's overreaction to my feeble attempts at exorcism yesterday.

"She sure gives a whole new meaning to the expression, Y'all come back now!" I said, not altogether jokingly, when I'd finished my report to Gwen.

"I think you're right," she said. "Her behavior is escalating." For the first time, she sounded a little worried. "I backed off partly because I thought it would be a good learning experience for you, but I think you need some practical help. I'll ask a friend of mine to come with me to your house and help lay Lani's ghost."

"Lay Lani?" I asked. It sounded like a Bob Dylan song: *Lay, Lani, Lay.*

"It means to help the spirit to move on. Holly is an old pro at it. You'll like her. What are you doing Saturday?"

I said I had no plans that far in the future, would be going to Berkeley on Friday but come back the same night.

"I'll call her right away and let you know if she can make it Saturday."

She called back about ten minutes later and said she and Holly would be at my house at ten o'clock, Saturday morning.

I wondered what this Holly would do. *Sprinkle Holly water? Blow Holly smoke? What did she call her car? A Holly roller?* But despite my silly state of mind, I was glad that Gwen was no longer treating Lani's haunting lightly.

I turned back to *Macbeth* but found myself staring at the screen, unable to think up anymore clever additions. I must have used up all my cleverness with my Holly jokes. This would be a good time for the nap Hal had suggested.

The temperature in the bedroom was comfortable. I lay down on top of blankets, with only the quilt covering me. Soon, I was asleep. Dreaming.

I dreamed I was at a party. No, I was observing others attending a party. I was outside of the large hall where they were celebrating, looking at them. They paid no attention to me. They couldn't see me. I was invisible, out of their sphere. They were milling around, laughing, talking, sipping drinks. It was a welcoming party, and the person they were welcoming was Lani.

She stood in the center, looking bewildered by all the merry-making, overwhelmed by how many people had shown up to welcome her. Because, although I didn't recognize anyone, she knew everyone. They were all in their early thirties. As people began to talk to her, she began to relax and enjoy herself.

Then she looked in my direction. Our eyes made contact. She was able to see beyond whatever was separating me from the revelers. Her gaze was steady, calm, serene. She opened her mouth and spoke to me. But I couldn't hear a word of what she said.

Even so, I woke up finally knowing what Lani wanted.

Chapter 30

That one may smile, and smile, and be a villain.

It wasn't the first time I had dreamed the Welcoming Dream. Usually, I'd already know that the person had just died, but sometimes it was the dream that announced someone's death. The scene was always the same: a large hall, many joyful people, the confused new arrival. The stark difference between these welcoming dreams and regular dreams was that I controlled my own thinking and actions as much as if I were fully awake. The welcoming dreams did not propel me; there was nothing dream-like about these dreams. I consciously reacted to and digested what I was seeing, and nothing happened that couldn't happen on this side of life. I even knew that I was watching the scene by means of a dream.

Snuggled under the quilt, I mulled the strangeness of all this over, for, although I'd had this dream many times before, it still felt strange that I could access the other realm. But now I noticed a shift had taken place inside me—a subtle, gentle, yet enormous shift. My *Why me?* was no longer tinged with self-pity and resentment. It was as if I were meeting my own true self, who I was meant to be.

What had happened? I didn't know. As I looked around, I had a sense of my awareness expanding, of everything feeling lighter, brighter, more defined, yet softer. The light coming through the window sparkled; the sheer curtains hung with a silvery glow; the reds, greens, and blues in the quilt had taken on a jewel-like quality.

The jade numbers on the clock slowly, slowly flipped from eleven fifty-nine to twelve and the alarm went off. I listened to the beautiful harmony of the ringing for a while before I remembered why I'd set the alarm.

Last night, Hal and I had talked things over while he was hammering together the whelping box, and we'd decided that despite Willem's disclosures I should keep my appointment with Mr. Litman of Brown Moore Cardiff Schiff & Litman, no commas. For all I knew, some of Lani's personal artifacts might prove to be valuable and, whatever property there was left to give away, I wanted nothing to boomerang back to me.

I needed to get a move on; my appointment was at two o'clock and it was—still—an hour's drive to Modesto.

I let the water wash over me in the shower, careful not to let my hair get wet since I'd already shampooed it earlier, and wondered why Lani had told me what she wanted but hadn't seen fit to disclose who had served her that last lethal cocktail.

Not that it bothered me. Nothing bothered me. As I put my physical being together with eye shadow, mascara, lipstick, hairbrush, appropriate underwear, aubergine dress and pumps, earrings, faux fox fur coat, I had the serene sense of being an observer. Even when I exchanged the fox for my navy suede coat, because someone might not get the *faux* part and throw a rotten egg at me—a concern I'd picked up living in Berkeley—this did not bother me.

Peace, love, and understanding followed me all the way to Modesto. Until I parked in front of Brown Moore Cardiff Schiff & Litman and got out of the car. Then it sort of left, I suppose. Again, I wasn't sure what happened. Suddenly, I was myself again. My untrue self, complete with all baggage of personality, emotion, and thinking.

Mr. Litman and his compañeros were located in a building that looked as if it had been designed by a Lego-stacking four-year-old, only not quite so colorful. The two-story structure was totally gray, including the woodwork and reflective windows, and surrounded by a patchy strip of lawn that was absolutely pitiful, even for California. Penny-pinching gardening had allowed for a few drought-resistant miniature shrubs that seemed to be at the end of their struggle for survival, despite the many rainstorms we'd had lately.

This whole depressing picture urged me to get back into my car and drive off. I could always call later and make up a story. I couldn't very well tell them their place was too much of a downer. But I couldn't very well lie either, could I? No, not very well.

I solved my dilemma by pushing open the heavy glass door and was mildly surprised to find that the shabby outdoor motif had been carried on inside. The small lobby was sparsely furnished with only four red vinyl arm chairs that each could have used some duct tape in various places. The floor was covered with linoleum tile in an unconvincing marble pattern and polished to such a sheen that I thought I might need skates to cross it. Each of the four walls was decorated with a different Monet print in a cheap metallic poster frame.

There was no sign of the receptionist who'd made the appointment for me. The place looked abandoned. Again, I had an urge to flee.

Just as I thought "They sure don't put up much of a front" and was about to walk out, I noticed a door standing open on my left. Behind a faux-oak desk stood an outrageously good-looking young man, eagerly craning his neck in welcome.

His short-cropped blond hair, high forehead, bright blue eyes fringed with dark lashes, straight well-pronounced nose, square chin with Kirk Douglas dimple, Cupid-bowed mouth—everything about him was in the right place.

I stared at him a little longer than was strictly polite or necessary. Something was off. I couldn't tell what it was. It must be nothing.

He straightened his maroon tie and, pulling on the sleeves of his conservative, dark gray suit, he stepped from behind the desk, holding out his hand. "How are you today?" he asked in a way that made me believe he really wanted to know.

For a moment I contemplated telling him. "I'm here to meet with Mr. Litman," I said and shook his hand and smiled at him. My diva smile. *Men cannot resist me. Kingdoms have been given up for me.*

He's young enough to be your son! Guilt said.

He looked down at the desk and traced the list of appointments with his index finger. Left handed, he was. *How endearing!*

So is Hal—your husband, Guilt said.

"Ah, yes! Mrs. Nelson?"

"*Fae* Nelson," I suggested kindly, feeling suddenly quite a bit older than a minute ago.

"Would you fill this out, please?" He held out a cheap-looking, green plastic clipboard with a form on it. A white ball pen made a sudden free fall until it was stopped by a thin piece of rope. With a look of annoyance on his handsome face, he grabbed the pen and placed it back on top of the clipboard.

I took the clipboard from him.

"You can take a seat in there." He gestured at the small red-vinyl-chaired lobby. "Mr. Litman will be with you in a moment." He nodded reassuringly.

I sighed and turned. Seated in one of the uncomfortable chairs, I filled out the questionnaire, skipping some of the questions because I couldn't figure out what the answers had to do with my business here. Why did this firm want so much personal information in exchange for a little advice? And, with all those names in the firm's nomer, they should be able to afford some more comfortable chairs.

"Roger D. Litman!" A very large hand suddenly appeared between me and the offensive form on my lap. I hadn't noticed him walking up to me.

Roger Litman was about five foot eight and skinny as a stick, but with huge hands and feet and a massive head. I was amazed that his thin neck could hold up a head that gigantic. With his bushy eyebrows, enormous nose, thick lips, and immense ears that slanted forward as if he were standing in a hard wind coming from behind, he reminded me of my old Mr. Potato Head. Although, I had never ever considered sticking my Mr. Potato Head's ears in at that angle. Also, my Mr. Potato Head didn't have a crew cut, and Mr. Roger D. Litman did.

I'd once read somewhere that lawyers prefer to wear blue to court because it's a winning color. Mr. Litman wore such a magic blue suit, but it was quite rumpled, and he seemed to be hanging out in it rather than to be wearing it. If that didn't nix his chances for victory, his multi-color-dotted tie surely would.

I put the pen down, shook his hand, and adamantly introduced myself as *Mrs. Nelson*.

"You can finish that later, if you like." He smiled as he gestured at the form.

"That's OK. I'm finished," I said and quickly handed him the clipboard.

He seemed somewhat surprised, but then he smiled again, took the questionnaire, and asked if I wanted something to drink. Coffee? Tea?

I answered that a glass of water would be welcome. He instructed the extraordinary young man to bring me a glass, with ice.

I hadn't wanted ice in my water.

In his office, Mr. Litman offered me a chair opposite of his desk and then sat down hurriedly as if he were in a game of musical chairs and feared someone might grab his seat.

When I looked up he'd become a hazy outline. Behind him was a tall window through which the low winter sun made a direct appearance into my eyes.

I moved my hand in a downward motion, "Could you ... ?"

He turned his head and acted as if he were surprised that there was a window behind him. But then, he precariously leaned back in his chair and turned the blind.

The young man came in with a glass of water and placed it on the desk in front of me. I thanked him and smiled. *Kingdoms.*

After briefly studying the form I'd filled out, Mr. Litman rubbed his big nose and sniffed a few times. He then loudly cleared his throat and said, "I detect a slight accent. Where are you from?"

"I was raised in the Netherlands," I answered.

"Ah, you lived in Holland! *Sprechen Sie Deutch?*" he asked with an atrocious accent.

"I do, but my primary language is Dutch, not German." I smiled blandly at Roger Litman.

"Ah! Dutch. German." He waved one of his big hands to show it was all the same to him. Then he raised his arm and, making a fist, he cried out, "*Germanic!*"

I looked at the life-sized statues of two four-month-old Rottweiler pups standing on the floor near me and wondered what was going on.

"You are a teacher, I see." He poked at the line on the form where I had apparently written so. "Do you teach elementary?"

"I used to. I teach community college now."

"I've known a lot of teachers who quit. Such a mess. All these donkeys dragging things down."

Donkeys? I gave him a puzzled look.

"As if we didn't have problems enough," he said, pinching and rubbing his drippy nose some more. His eyes had taken on a glazed look and he spoke so forcefully that little drops of spit flew from his mouth with each word. "You know, letting in all these darkies."

Oh, darkies, *not* donkeys. *Darkies?* I leaned back in my chair to increase the distance between us. Was this guy for real?

"About the inheritance," he continued, in a tone as if he were still on the same subject, his words punctuated by the tapping of his index finger on the desk. "My secretary made some notes here. Once it's gone through probate, you can actually just turn around and give it all to whomever you want. I can handle that for you." He picked up a thin package of papers and held it out to me. "If you sign these, it establishes a contract and I'll request a copy of the will from ... what's her lawyer's name?"

I frowned at him, neither answering nor taking the papers.

He didn't seem to notice. "All that money wasted on those special programs. Let them get a job! But, no, they go on welfare!"

I contemplated the half-life of the ice cubes in my glass, thinking this must be a cosmic test of some kind. Why else had my pen landed on Litman's name in the attorney section of the yellow pages? There were no coincidences. This was my chance to show tolerance for intolerance.

I bit the inside of my cheek to keep my mouth in check. *Who is this weirdo with the wind-swept ears? Whatever gives him the idea he's found a kindred soul in me? My blue eyes?* I looked at him. *His* eyes were brown.

His face now contorted with hatred, he continued, "Those Nazis weren't dumb. They knew a problem when they saw one. They knew how to deal with these things!"

The word *cocaine* flashed in my mind. Eric Clapton began to sing. *If you wanna get down ...*

Litman finally put the package down on his desk. Sniffed again. "Ought to get rid of all of them. Hitler had it right. He just didn't go far enough."

That was it! My Dutch-German-Irish-English-Scottish-Cherokee—ah, hell!—*American* blood was boiling. I'd take my opportunity to practice tolerance next time I'd stand in line at the grocery store. "You mean when, in the Dutch town of Putten, they lined up every boy and man, from twelve years of age, shot a number of them to death and sent the others to die horrible deaths in Nazi concentration camps? More than five hundred forty men and boys never returned. We called Putten "The Town Without Men." Or when they bombed the center of Rotterdam? "The City Without a Heart." For your information, *we* were the ones who were *liberated* from the Nazis."

Litman raised his oversized eyebrows in surprise. "I thought you were ... ," he said.

I didn't want to hear what he thought. "According to your theory you should have received a much better education than you've apparently had. So, let me give you a little history lesson. Ever heard of the Moors? They were a mixture of various African peoples that conquered Spain and were there for over seven centuries. Later, the Spanish ruled much of Europe for quite a while. Where do you think your dark-brown eyes came from, Mr. Litman?"

His jaw dropped. Then he collected himself and screamed, "I am an Aryan!"

"The Aryans lived in Iran. The great Persian king Darius was an Aryan."

"You're making all this up!"

"No, I am not." Looking straight into his eyes, I lowered my voice to the ominous range and whispered, "According to your own philosophy, your blood—it's *tainted*!"

His eyes flitted across his desk as if he were looking for something to throw at me. Then he yelled, "You just hate Germans!"

"Why should I? I have nearly as much German blood as Cherokee blood."

He gaped at me. "You have blue eyes!"

"Yes, and yours are brown, don't forget that. Remember—the Moors!"

I marched toward the door and, with my back to him, sniffed three times. "Stop snorting that white stuff. Goodbye, Mr. Litman!"

In the car, I grabbed a stack of tissues from the box, wiped my face, and dabbed my eyes. My heart was pounding, blood roared in my ears. I felt contaminated, unclean. And I was angry, not at Litman but at myself.

I'd known something wasn't right before I'd met him. As I'd been standing in front of the building and again when I was in the lobby—twice—the word *Leave!* had flashed in my mind. It had been a clear and simple instruction that had meant exactly what it said. But I had looked at the environment—thirsty bushes, red vinyl chairs, a pretty, pretty boy—and tried to find a reason for the instruction. When I hadn't found one, I'd overridden the voice of intuition with logic.

Why hadn't I listened until Eric Clapton began to sing? If I ever wanted to have good use of my sixth sense, I'd have to go to work and clean up all the messes in my thinking and behavior. Stop editing the messages. Meditate, even.

With this conclusion, I came to a full stop—in my head. I hadn't gone anywhere yet. I was still parked at the curb.

I checked the side mirror but, driving off, deliberately avoided looking in my rearview mirror.

Since I was already in Modesto and my head was still swimming upstream, I decided to perform a cleansing ritual at one of the import stores off Highway 99. Baskets from Africa, pottery from South America, rugs from Asia, jewelry and foods from every continent—here, the world was one.

I was just about to knock one of the useless birdhouses off a high shelf with a pig-shaped ladle, something they expressly requested customers *not* do by means of little signs, when a pleasant, male voice behind me asked, "Would you like me to get that for you?"

Still holding the ladle over my head, I turned.

"Oh, it's you!" Mark Brandenburgh blurted out in surprise.

"I'm shopping," I explained, as if it weren't obvious. I could feel a deep blush creeping up from my neck as I stared at him. I just didn't know what to say to Alicia's lover. My little church lady—the one who always closed her eyes when I was out of line—was busy gathering first stones.

Behind Mark stood a very pretty woman in her mid thirties. She had shiny blond hair and large, dark-brown eyes. One of the seven beauties. Her white pant suit accentuated her slightly plump figure. She was holding a baby on one hip, a boy, because it was dressed in blue. Beside her, a little girl of about four, with her mother's features, looked up at me.

"This is my wife, Marlene. This is Fae Nelson," Mark said pleasantly.

I didn't think that Mark and I had been properly introduced at Lani's funeral. That scene with Alicia in the kitchen could hardly be called an introduction. Alicia must have told him my name.

"Pleased to meet you." I waved the pig ladle in the air like a fairy godmother and smiled at Mark's wife and children.

Marlene moved the baby to her other hip and smiled back shyly.

"Piggy!" said the little girl—about the ladle.

"Well, I'd better get going," I said and put the ladle back in its bin.

"Would you like me to get that down for you?" Mark offered again, gesturing at the birdhouse.

"Uh, I don't think I really need it." I scrunched up my face. "The cats, you see!"

Mark frowned. No, he didn't see.

But then, neither did I. With such a pretty wife and two sweet children, what was he doing with Alicia?

I smiled at Marlene again and was glad she couldn't read my mind.

Then I nearly ran out of the store.

All the way home I kept thinking about Roger Litman and Mark Brandenburgh and what I could learn from meeting them. Both encounters appeared to have been random events: I'd randomly picked a lawyer from the phone book; I'd randomly chosen that store to go shopping. And there it had been: random hatred, random fornication. But how *random* was random? Was there even such a thing as *random*?

Why had I met these men today?

Mirror, mirror.

I didn't like that answer one bit.

Chapter 31

Then came each actor on his ass.

Rita showed up about noon on Thursday. Sarah was with her. Thin bangs now hung in her eyes, hiding her forehead, and she was wearing a baggy turtleneck sweater on jeans in an effort to cover her bruises.

"Hi, Fae," she said timidly as she stood in the kitchen doorway, her large, hazel eyes sweeping nervously around the kitchen.

"Hi, Sweetie!" I walked over and gave her a gentle kiss on the cheek. "Come on, sit down." I put my arm around her shoulder and slowly led her to the table where I pulled out a chair for her, but when she noticed Promise and the puppies in the corner, she kept going and knelt down next to the whelping box.

"What you want done today, Fae?" Rita asked, sticking her cigar in the side of her mouth so she could talk and smoke at the same time.

"I don't know. Windows?" We looked at each other for a moment, pondering our dilemma.

"Nah!" we both said in unison.

"What are them ants doing all over the counter?" Rita asked, peering through her bottle-bottom glasses.

"I don't know. I already wiped them off once, this morning."

She moved her cigar to the other corner of her mouth. "You gotta kill them! You gotta spray them! You gotta kill them dead!" she said, sounding as if she were reciting some magic chant.

"You mean *poison*?" I wrinkled my nose.

She looked at me as if I were an imbecile. "Yeah! What else? Think I got a can somewhere from last year. You gotta do it outside, where the nest is. If you don't, it just gets worst. Them little suckers get into everything." She rattled off a list of things the army of ants would conquer and divide.

"What about using fresh bay leaves?"

"You wanna spend the rest of the winter with bay leaves all over your counter? Besides, you ain't got no bay tree anywhere near here. You want me to drive around looking for a bay tree? Maybe you want me to rent an anteater while we're at it?"

"I get the point. Do whatever it is you have to do," I said, rolling my eyes.

Giddy with excitement, she took off in search of her poison.

I made a pot of coffee and sat down at the table again. Sarah, who had silently been watching Rita and me, finally tore herself away from the puppies.

"School starts next week," she said, standing next to me, plucking at her sweater. "Could I still sign up for one of your classes, Fae?"

"Sure, just come to the first class. We'll take care of the paperwork then. Have you ever read any Shakespeare?"

"We read *Romeo and Juliet* in high school and then put it on stage. I played Juliet." She smiled, which immediately made her wince in pain. She swallowed and looked away from me.

"That's funny, I played Juliet, too, in high school. And Cleopatra. What other classes are you taking?"

"History and geology. I'm dropping math," she said softly and turned her face back to me. "It'll be fun to have you as a teacher."

"I wouldn't be so sure about that!" I said with a stern look. But my heart ached. It was so difficult to look at her and keep pity from my eyes. How could anyone hate Sarah? Even random hatred didn't explain why someone would want to destroy this sweet and beautiful young woman. What for? For what?

"Fae?"

"Yes, Honey?"

"I'm going to be all right. It may take a while, but I *am* going to be all right."

"Yes, I know," I said, and I *knew*.

We were both wiping the tears out of our eyes when Rita marched in, vigorously shaking a big can with alarmingly much red on its label. "So, what's happening with all that stuff Lani left you?" she asked.

"There isn't much of anything. The house is Willem's. Maybe I inherited absolutely nothing. *Nada! Niets!*" I said triumphantly.

"So, you killed her for nothing, huh?" Rita grinned, but then she squinted at me. "How do you know she had nothing?" she asked suspiciously.

"Willem told me. He came by this morning and showed me the deed to the house."

Willem—worried and wanting to set my mind at ease about the possibility of a legal battle with Alicia—had shown up on our doorstep and insisted that I peruse his legal documents. Besides the deed, he brought over a small stack of checks showing his payments to Lani. I was shocked to see the amounts: he had paid through the nose for his love. His business must be doing well. Before he'd left, he'd promised to talk to Alicia.

"You sure you get nothing?" Rita asked, clearly disappointed.

"Willem did ask me to come over to the house—Jason's there all day, packing up—and choose something to remember Lani by." I had tried to refuse, but Willem wouldn't hear of it. He'd almost broken into tears as he made the offer. I hadn't had the heart to tell him I already had too much to remember Lani by: Lani herself.

"Well, well, and here I was thinking I'd have a rich friend for once." Rita shook her head. "What a stinking thing to do." She pulled the cigar out of her mouth and stared at it. "Now why you think she did that?"

"I think she saw an opportunity to insult both her kids and me at the same time." I laughed. "Killing two flies in one swat, as they say in Holland."

"They say that there, huh?" She walked out the door muttering, shaking both her head and her can of poison.

"You're not mad?" Sarah asked.

"On the contrary, I'm elated! Even *if* she'd owned everything, she had no business leaving it to me." I got up and poured us some coffee.

The doorbell rang. I excused myself to see who had snuck up on the house, past our canine security. Promise was deep asleep, exhausted from taking care of her puppies. But where were my other watchdogs?

I opened the front door and took a step back in surprise. Mark Brandenburgh was standing there. A few feet behind him were Mab and Dooley, on duty, glaring at his butt.

He cast a nervous glance over his shoulder, then greeted me with a big smile plastered on his handsome face.

After giving him a lukewarm welcome, I ushered him into the living room. He declined my offer of a cup of Java, so I left him to get my coffee from the kitchen. I told Sarah to go ahead and snoop through the library if she wanted to, that I'd be back shortly, but she was practically cuddled up with the puppies in the whelping box.

Mark was sitting on the love seat and raised himself—not all the way—when I returned.

"A very nice house you have here," he said with too much animation, like an actor practicing his lines.

I wondered what his motivation was. "We like it."

We both sat down. I sipped my coffee and waited.

Mark ran his fingers through his hair, leaving his hand on top of his head, and gave me an apologetic little grimace. "I've come to talk to you about Alicia," he said. He lowered his hand and began gesturing as he talked on. "We discussed the situation and she's decided to drop her plans for a lawsuit." He looked at me with his liquid, dark eyes.

I raised my eyebrows and sipped my coffee.

He rubbed the bridge of his beautiful nose. "She decided she'll go with her mother's wishes, however painful they are. She's devastated by what Lani has done, of course."

"Of course," I repeated after him and nodded to show I really cared about Alicia's devastation. He was actually pretty good in his role as emissary for his queen.

His eyes moved from my face to my chest area somewhere.

I looked down to make sure I'd buttoned up, but there weren't any buttons on my black angora sweater.

He said, "But she thought this would be better." Again, he produced his Hollywood smile and smoothed his dark hair.

I wondered if I should assure him his hair looked fine.

He said, "We hope we can come to an understanding."

"I thought you and Alicia already had an 'understanding.'"

He had the decency to blush ever so slightly. "I mean you and us."

I lifted my head slowly, an ah-ha! expression on my face. "Mark, she'd be suing for nothing."

"What do you mean?" His face went blank.

I was going to tell him that Lani didn't own anything to leave to anybody, when the sound of a couple of shrill rings stopped me.

"Excuse me," Mark said while he took his cell phone from his pocket and flipped it open. He turned his face away as if that were enough to grant him privacy. "Yes?" He listened for a while, said "yes" twice more, gasped, and glanced at me. "I don't believe it!" He listened again for a few seconds and then nodded. "All right." He flipped the phone shut, looking utterly confused.

"That was Alicia. Willem just called and told her the house and other property are his, that Lani didn't own anything to leave to anybody," I said, putting my cup down on the coffee table.

Now, Mark seemed even more confused. "How did you know that?"

I didn't answer but tried to look my most mysterious—serene, wise, and mysterious. It wasn't easy, because I felt only very tired, which was probably how I looked.

"I don't believe it!" His voice rose to an unmanly falsetto.

I shrugged. I really didn't much care what he *believed*. "Willem should still be at the house. Go talk to him." I got up and walked to the door. His mission was over. I wanted him to leave. "It was nice meeting your wife and children," I said dryly.

He quickly walked past me into the hallway, ignoring me.

I followed him as he went out the front door, my arms folded, and watched as he walked to his white van. *Brandenburgh Catering With Care* it said in flowing, black letters on the side.

Somehow, that reminded me ... "I heard you visited Lani right before she died," I blurted out.

He stiffened for a moment, holding the door, but then, without once looking my way, he climbed into his van and drove off.

I hadn't meant to deliver that last bit like a parting shot in the back. It had just come out when I'd suddenly remembered that little fact. If it was a fact, coming from Steve Krieger.

"Now then, that went rather well, Fae," I said to myself as I closed the door. Surely, I was on my way of perfecting the art of how to make friends and influence people.

I returned to the living room, wondering why Mark had become so upset when he'd found out the inheritance was bogus. It shouldn't matter if Alicia had already decided to give up her lawsuit.

What "understanding" had Mark and Alicia wanted to propose?

Split the money, immediately popped into my head.

That was funny! I'd asked a question and received a direct answer. It hadn't been a thought, because thinking didn't feel that way, required mental effort, reasoning. *Split the money* had come in the way Knowledge always came in, with clarity and certainty.

I sensed that I'd just made a breakthrough of some kind but wasn't quite sure what exactly had happened, what I'd done differently this time. It felt as if I'd triggered something that had produced an instant response. As I pondered over this, another question came to the fore: Why had Alicia suddenly been willing—no, *eager*, because she'd sent Mark on a mission—to split the loot?

I waited, but when the little pop-up answer didn't repeat itself, I got my coffee cup and rejoined Sarah in the kitchen.

Rita had gone upstairs. I could hear the vacuum cleaner vroom-vrooming in one of the bedrooms. Promise got up and sauntered to the back door. I let her out.

Sarah was still draped over the edge of the whelping box, looking as if she'd been asleep. "I just saw Bluebelle again," she said. "She was lying down over there." She pointed to the other side of the door to the hallway, a few feet away. "I think Promise can see her, too. It's as if Bluebelle is watching over the puppies, like an extra mom. They look so much alike, Promise and Bluebelle."

"Like two drops of water," I said.

"Fae?" Sarah got up and walked over to me. "I think I want to become an elementary school teacher."

I almost spit my coffee out over the table cloth. "A *teacher*?" I said in a quivering voice.

"Yes. I've thought about it a lot." She sounded as if she were *still* thinking about it.

I hoped so. Perhaps I could still rescue her. "Well, you think about it some more, Honey!" I patted her hand, determined to be less of a role model.

"You don't like it, do you?" Sarah giggled.

"Oh, it's just that it's a very tough job." I sighed. "It's not really a job, it's a calling. It consumes your whole life. But I know some teachers who are very happy." I tried to think of some but could only come up with one: Sam Verhoog. Good old Sam, *loves to teach*. Although, Sam didn't really count as an example, because he taught college.

"Wouldn't you rather be an actress?" I asked.

Sarah laughed out loud and shook her head. "I wasn't *that* good as Juliet!"

"What about becoming a writer?"

"Remember you told me once that you became a teacher because it would allow you to do all these things—math, reading, writing, art? And that being a teacher often was like being an actress?"

"Vaguely," I said, but I remembered it quite clearly because that *had* been my main reason for wanting to become a teacher. It was difficult to argue with her when she was using my own words. I'd have to readdress this issue some other time, when I'd be better prepared.

It was nearly two o'clock and I needed to go over to Lani's—Willem's—house to select a memento. Also, there were the flyers to collect before Promise's owner could call to claim her. Although, there'd been ample time for him or her to do so since I'd distributed them on Monday. My guess was that the owner probably wasn't a local. Driving into the hills to dump dogs seemed a pastime for too many flatlanders.

I asked Sarah if she'd like to come with me, I could drop her off at home afterward, but she wanted to wait for her mother. Sensing that she wasn't ready yet to meet other people, I didn't try to persuade her. I took off, leaving her with Promise and the puppies—and Bluebelle.

I stopped at our mailbox. It was stuffed with all sorts of junk. *Final notice! Last chance! Sorry ... we will no longer be able to send you our catalog...* The four horsemen were upon us.

There was a sweet thank-you card from Matt and Grace and the boys. As I returned it to its envelope, I noticed a drawing on the back. It was a primitive representation of a woman in a long, red dress. Underneath was written "Lani."

I wasn't sure which of the boys had made the drawing, but I *was* sure that I had never mentioned Lani's name, let stand told them how to spell it. Neither had the boys ever referred to Lani by name. When and how had the little artist gotten this information?

Willem was about to take off when I arrived at the ranch, but he got back out of his car, a brand-new burgundy Mercedes, to say hello to me.

Jack Peterson was working on Sasha's Volkswagen van. Willem walked over to him and put his hand on Jack's shoulder, which looked rather funny because he was nearly a foot shorter than Jack.

"Have you and Jack met?" he asked.

Jack waved his hands at me to show they were too dirty for a handshake.

"Yes, we have," I answered and nodded at Jack.

"Jason's inside. I have to rush. I hope you don't mind." Willem walked me to the open front door and called out to Jason.

"Be down in a minute!" his son called back.

"By the way, did you send that Mark Brandenburgh over here?" Willem asked with a wide grin.

"You mean he actually came over?" I closed my left eye and raised my right eyebrow in lopsided disbelief.

"He sure did. Began to interrogate me about The Big Inheritance. I told him it was a family matter, and when that didn't shut him up, I reminded him that he wasn't family. He can discuss it with Alicia all she wants." He patted me on the shoulder in a reassuring gesture. "I don't think either of them will be bothering you again."

A sigh of relief escaped from my mouth. Two down. But how many more to go?

After Willem left, I went into the living room and sat down on the Victorian couch. The curtains were opened wide, letting in light, and much of the clutter had disappeared. Against the far wall, where the tables had stood during the French funeral, now were small towers of boxes.

"My father has decided to sell the house," Jason said as he walked in carrying a large box, which he placed on top of a stack of three others. He glanced at me. "I'm sorry for what my mother did. That was really rotten. I wish we'd known my father still owned the house." Embarrassed, he turned his face away.

"Don't worry about it. All's well that ends well." *But it hasn't ended yet.*

Jason smiled at the floor, shook his head, then looked at me again. "Well, have you decided what you want?" He made no effort to hide the sardonic smile on his angelic face.

"How about that nice painting of the shepherds couple?"

He threw his head back and let out a peal of laughter. "You're taking it off my hands?"

"It's not so bad," I said, laughing with him.

He pointed to the back of the couch. "Well, it's right over there."

Sitting on my knees, I reached down and lifted the picture from its hiding place.

"Anything else?" He took the painting from me and placed it on the easy chair.

"No, that's all I can think of." I stared at the canvas. It suddenly struck me how alike the faces of the sheep and shepherds were, as if they were related.

Gazing at the shepherds, Jason said, "She threatened to tell my father about me. It had never been an issue until she saw me with Dean. Because he's black."

"Because he's black?" I looked at Jason in surprise.

"You must have seen us in the Hungry Hungarian. We saw you. You didn't notice he's black?" His eyes were mocking me, benignly.

"Well, sure, but what I mean is, your mother was going to tell your father that you're gay because you were seeing a *black* man?" Now I'd heard everything.

"That does sound kind of funny, doesn't it? But that's what she said. Though, I'm sure it had more to do with trying to control me. About a year ago, I stopped responding to her calls. She'd call any time of the day with one crisis or another. I was tired of the games she played and told her so.

"She came up to Sacramento a couple of days after Christmas and met Dean for the first time. She probably thought he put me up to cutting the apron strings, so to speak, and she made a big scene. The garbage she threw at Dean. She'd developed a few unpleasant personalities over the years, but the one that I guess must have been dating Steve Krieger really took the cake. What a mean streak that one had! When so much calculated meanness came from her it was difficult to remember that she couldn't help herself."

He kept staring at the painting while he was talking. "She also liked keeping Dad off kilter. He never knew if he was coming or going. I would have told Dad some day. I'm not ashamed. It's just that I wanted him to get used to the idea, slowly. I now wish I'd talked to him a long time ago. He is a good father, Fae, a good man. I love him very much."

Behind his words I heard a lot of pain and a lot of tenderness. His emotions rang inside me like an echo in a canyon.

He carried the painting out to the car and carefully placed it on the backseat. We wished each other good luck and hugged each other. Then he went back into the house.

Jack strolled over, wiping his hands on a rag soaked in black grease. "Are you still going to Berkeley tomorrow?"

"That's the plan."

"Would you bring Sasha back so she can pick up her van?" Jack continued to wipe his hands on the dirty rag.

"Sure! I'll call her tonight." My eyes locked into a stare.

"You're looking at me like that again." Jack stuffed the rag in his pocket. "Like when we first met. What's the matter?"

"It's something Lani told me." I wasn't sure if I should tell him.

"What's that?" He raised one dark eyebrow, his ruggedly handsome face set in a faintly expectant smile—but not of good news.

"She told me that you had died in a drunk-driving accident." I looked into his eyes.

Jack tilted his head to one side. His eyes narrowed, the little lines around them deepened. Quietly he said, "I was in a few accidents in those days. Never *that* serious, though. The worst accident ever was my marriage to Lani. It crashed almost as soon as we got hitched. A total loss—if it hadn't been for Sasha."

"I'm sorry. I shouldn't have told you." *Watch out little mouth what you say!*

"Hey! It's okay! It got me sober." He smiled. "Been sober for thirty years. I have a lot to thank Lani for, besides my daughter."

The old attitude of gratitude cropped up in the strangest places. I smiled. "No regrets?"

He thought for a moment. "Only about leaving Sasha with Lani. It wasn't all selfishness, wanting to get away. I just didn't know if my sobriety would stick." He wiped his forehead with the rag. It left a dark smear. "But it was very hard on Sasha. By the time I figured out how bad things were, I had already remarried, and we had three kids in five years. When Sasha hit her teens, I just didn't know what to do about her. Whenever I tried tough love, Lani would throw more money her way."

After a brief pause, he said, "Oh, well, it's all water under the bridge."

I nodded. "I've got some more errands to run. Maybe we'll see each other at a meeting somewhere."

Jack's face broke into a surprised smile. "Actually, I was just thinking I should drive over to Sasha's tomorrow and bum a ride back here with you. That way I can drive this old clunker back to Berkeley for her. I'm not sure it'll make it." He sat behind the wheel of the Volkswagen and turned the key. The motor started immediately, but it sputtered and some awfully loud farting sound came from the exhaust.

I hollered my goodbye over the noisy van and took off. All the way to Londen I kept thinking about each person I'd spoken with that day and the people they'd talked about. Mark, Alicia, Willem, Jason, Dean, Steve, Jack, Sasha. What a list! Had I forgotten someone? Had one of them forgotten that Lani couldn't help herself?

At Full of Beans, Phil said he wanted to come see the puppies. I gave him directions to our house. At the library, Agnes and Albertina immediately began a good-natured argument about whether they were too old to take one of the puppies. I settled their disagreement by telling them that a Labrador pup would divide everything they owned into chewable and non-chewable, and most of it would fall in the first category.

At the House of Variety, there was no sign of Pete, but Anna van Nuys was behind the counter. I wondered why she kept her head turned toward her right shoulder until I saw the hidden side of her face reflected in a gilt-framed mirror. She had a black eye, amateurishly covered with make-up that didn't match her skin color.

Something suddenly occurred to me. Last time I'd been here, Steve Krieger had sat across the street with his radio blaring "When a Man Loves a Woman." Anna's baby, little Mickey, looked an awful lot like Steve.

I wanted to tell her to run for her life, but instead I told her I'd come to take my poster back and pulled it off the window and crumpled it up and tossed it in the garbage bin next to the door.

Fumbling with my purse, I asked "Are you all right?"

She seemed genuinely surprised at my question, at a loss for words. Then, as if remembering her manners, she said, "Oh, yes, I'm doing great!"

Great! I was glad to hear it, though I didn't believe it. I looked at her and said, "Take good care of yourself, Anna!"

What else could I say? I felt like crying.

"I will!" she promised, keeping the right side of her face turned away from me.

I collected my other flyers at the bakery and pharmacy and then drove on to the church. The Reverend Cecil Ravenstein said he was glad to see me in good health, as if he had expected otherwise. He handed me my flyer from the bulletin board and remarked, "One has to be careful with these things."

I thought of asking him *what things* but then figured he probably just meant the thumbtacks he was pushing back into the cork.

Above the bulletin board hung a wooden plaque engraved with the saying *The mens wikt, maar God beschikt.* Man proposes, but God disposes.

"Thomas à Kempis," Ravenstein said when he noticed me looking at it.

I nodded, thinking it funny that the words of a Roman Catholic priest were hanging in the entrance hall of a conservative Protestant Dutch Reformed church, which when I was growing up would have caused the second coming of John Calvin.

"It was a gift from one of our parishioners." He gave me a wicked little wink.

"Oh!" I said with an understanding grin. A gift plaque.

As soon as I got home, I took the painting out of the car and hauled it up to the attic, vaguely thinking that I'd find a place for it later.

Then I called Sasha. Her roommate answered and told me Sasha was sleeping, had been a little sick. A bit under the weather.

I asked if I should postpone my visit, but she assured me that Sasha would be fine tomorrow. Just a touch of the flu. Some bug that was going around. Perhaps.

Poor Sasha. I had suffered from that kind of flu for a bad eighteen years.

Chapter 32

Speak no more;
Thou turn'st mine eyes into my very soul.

With some stop-and-go traffic at the Tracy bottleneck and again as I neared the Bay Area, it took almost three hours before I was inching down Ashby Avenue. Remembering from my last visit that numerous streets had been blocked off or become one-way since I'd moved, I hooked around via Shattuck and parked my car in the public garage on Durant, right around the corner of Telegraph Avenue, Berkeley's *tableau très vivant*.

I grabbed my shoulder bag from the passenger seat and beeped the doors locked. As I started to walk toward the exit, a man suddenly stood in my way.

"Which do *you* like?" He was slight of built and dressed in a checkered sports shirt and khaki pants. The remnants of his silver hair were slicked back from his pleasantly wrinkled face. On his right arm, which he was holding out straight to his side, he had draped a collection of ties. He looked at the ties and then at me again, waiting for an answer.

"They're all quite nice," I said, thinking about Hal's tie.

"I took them from my son." His blue eyes twinkled. "From his office. He has so many. He's a dentist, you know." Pride in his voice and on his face.

I nodded, duly impressed.

"People give him these. His patients, I mean." He took one of the ties from his arm and held it up for me to have a closer look. "He never wears them. They're all new." He paused and frowned lightly, but his eyes still twinkled. "I didn't tell him. You think he'll mind?"

Feeling like laughing uproariously with this ornery old man, I bit my lip and shook my head. "He'll probably be glad to get rid of some."

His face brightened, as if I'd helped him solve a great moral dilemma. "That's what I was thinking." He picked the ties off his arm and held them bunched in both his hands. After taking a few steps towards the exit, he hesitated. Looking quasi-shyly at the floor, he remarked, "You're a very pretty lady." Then he quickly walked off.

"Thank you!" I called after him, purely as California Fae, because Dutch Fae knew she couldn't take credit, having only a decorative hand in what she looked like.

The encounter with the thieving ham left me feeling lighthearted. People smiled back at me on Telegraph Avenue. I walked toward Dwight and took a left there.

Suddenly, I couldn't see anything. Someone had shoved a pamphlet in front of my face, too close for me to read it.

"Do you believe?" a male voice said.

I crooked my head and looked past the pamphlet into the sun. I couldn't see, so I stepped sideways in a semicircle. So did he. Now he was looking into the sun at me.

He was in full military garb, complete with combat boots and parka, looking ready for a dangerous mission, but his purple Mohawk and dangling feather earrings probably would have to go before he'd pass muster. "Do you believe?" he repeated, an intense look on his face.

"Believe what?" I smirked.

He shook the pamphlet in my face. "Do you believe that Pizza Boy is selling their slices today for one dollar?"

I laughed and grabbed the pamphlet.

He winked and went on his way.

Yes, I was in Berserkley, all right!

I walked past People's Park, acutely feeling the lack of meaningful exercise in my legs and butt on the slightly uphill slant of the road.

Sasha's address was on one of the side streets a few blocks off Dwight. I took her partial check out of my pocket agenda to make sure I was heading in the right direction.

The front door of the coffee-brown shingled house flew open. "Out! Out, out, out!" a thirtyish Hispanic woman shouted, without much anger, as she put a large calico cat down on the scarlet front porch. The cat meowed plaintively, turned around, and ran straight back into the house.

The woman looked up and spotted me. "No manners! No manners at all. Spoiled rotten!" She smiled, exasperated, and then put her hand to her forehead in a thought-organizing gesture. "Oh! You're Fae!"

"Yes, I am," I said and walked up the steps.

"Maria Salcedo, Sasha's roommate. We spoke yesterday." She turned and pointed toward the hall where the calico sat licking one of her hind legs. "And *that* is Sasha's cat, Mancha. I can't get anything done with her around. She keeps jumping on my papers. Ah! What am I thinking? Come in, come in." She motioned for me to follow her.

Maria was about my height and built, slightly on the chubby side of slender. Her long, black hair was tied in a pony tail with a red silk scarf that trailed in the air behind her. She had ebony eyes with thick, silky lashes, and the smile on her face felt like a real smile, coming from her own stash of happiness within. Her black tunic on matching leggings and her heart-shaped golden earrings made her look a lot more conventional than her roommate.

"Sasha went shopping for some groceries," Maria said as we entered the living room. "She should be back any moment. Would you like some coffee?"

I told her that coffee was very high on my wish list after the long trip.

She pointed understandingly at the couch. "Make yourself comfortable. I'll just be minute." She disappeared into the adjoining kitchen.

I followed up on her invitation to sit on the couch and discovered it was really a Venus flytrap. When I finally stopped sinking, I was practically sitting at floor level. I tried to struggle into an upright position but soon gave up and leaned back. I heard Maria filling a pot with water, opening and closing cupboards, grinding coffee.

The room was a trip down Memory Lane. Bud vases and statues in greens, oranges, and yellows, knotted sisal wall hangings, beaded curtains, India shawls (one of which, a red one, I could have sworn Sasha wore the first time we met), and shelves and shelves—on concrete garden blocks, of course—of books. I noticed a number of Norton anthologies.

Despite the sixties clutter, the room was only sparsely furnished with the couch that had captured me and one overstuffed brown chair which looked related to the couch, more in age than appearance. Small, unfinished wooden stools, resembling overgrown mushrooms, served as tables. Everywhere—on the back and both arms of the chair, on the stools, on the book shelves—were hand-crocheted doilies, spread around like a giant, exotic virus. But the main theme of the room was distinctly Flower Power.

Maria called from the kitchen. "Would you like something to eat?"

"No, thanks. I had a pretty good breakfast," I answered. "Who reads the Nortons?"

"Oh, those are left over from Sasha's English period." Maria returned, holding two large mugs which she placed on the stool next to the couch. "That was before her French period, which was before her art period."

"Is she still taking art classes?" I asked.

"She was going to, but her mother cut off all support." Maria pointed at a small framed pen drawing of several cats—one of them looked like Mancha—playing on the branches of a tree. "She does really nice work. It seemed she'd finally found her niche. I keep telling her she ought to apply for some scholarships and go back to school. She's already halfway to getting her degree."

She got the coffee pot from the kitchen and poured, adding some cream and sugar to mine, as requested. She handed me my coffee, apparently aware that I was in no position to raise myself.

"How long have you and Sasha roomed together?" I asked, just plain curious.

"It seems like forever, but I only moved in last spring, after her other roommate left. There are just two bedrooms. On the outside the house looks like more than it is." She sat in the chair and sank to my level. "Sasha told me you're from Holland," she said.

"I grew up there, but I was born here." I took a sip of the hot coffee. It was good.

"We went to Amsterdam last summer, Sasha and I. It rained almost the whole time we were there. Pouring down in buckets and the loudest thunderstorms. But it was neat. All those canals and narrow, ancient houses. We went to the Rijksmuseum and took some day trips out into the country. You know, the old fishing towns, that castle from the 1200's—what is it called?"

Sasha had also mentioned visiting the small castle near Amsterdam that plays an important part in Dutch history, from being the site of treacherous political murder to serving as the gathering place of an important literary group. "Het Muiderslot."

"Yes, that's it! We got the guided tour."

Someone opened the front door. "Hey, Maria! Is Fae here yet?" Sasha's voice reverberated throughout the house.

"In here!" Maria called back.

Sasha came in holding two paper grocery bags in her arms. "Hi! You made it!" She said in a tone as if it were the last thing she'd expected, genuinely happy to see me.

I began to push myself off the couch.

"Oh, no, don't try to get up. I'll just put this down in the kitchen."

A few moments later she returned, smoothing her teal India skirts and holding a mug of coffee.

"Maria was just showing me some of your art work and talking about your trip to Amsterdam."

Sasha sat on the right arm of Maria's chair and looked down at her roommate with a smile.

I sensed, however, that for a brief moment her smile lacked all warmth. But when she looked at me again, her face was animated. "Are you ready for Telegraph Avenue? I'm supposing you want to go to the bookstores there."

"That's the idea," I said, wondering what that look she'd just given Maria had been about.

"Well, let's boogie on down!" Sasha walked toward the door.

I pushed myself up into a real sitting position on the edge of the couch and then finally succeeded in standing.

I noticed Sasha hadn't invited Maria to join our little excursion, but it seemed that the latter hadn't expected to be included. She told us to have a good time and leaned back in her chair, petting Mancha who had jumped into her lap.

Telegraph Avenue was bustling with the Friday crowd now. We walked on the not-yet-sunny side of the street for a short distance, until we were opposite Moe's bookstore, where we crossed.

A very tall woman—an enormous live boa constrictor hanging around her neck—stood near the entrance, in deep conversation with an anemic-looking young man dressed in black and with the face of a bat.

Sasha laughed at me when I winced at the snake. We climbed the stairs to the third floor, where I used to spend many an hour in my Berkeley days.

"Hey, Sasha!" a painfully skinny woman called out. She was Sasha's age and wore a jeans jacket over a black vintage cocktail dress and white knee-high socks in army boots. Her spiky hair was Lucy Ball red near the scalp and burgundy at the tips.

I stepped back as a hugging match ensued. After giving the redhead a final slap on the back, Sasha introduced her as Alice, her former roommate.

It was obvious that the two amigas had some catching up to do, so I excused myself and went over to browse in the New Age section. I leafed through a number of books about beliefs and philosophies that had been around since long before Christendom. I was just wondering how and when age-old had become New Age, when Sasha materialized behind me. "Find anything interesting?" She read the title of the book I was holding. "Alice was gone for almost a year, you know. Had an affair. Got real heavy. He was married. Then she found out he was cheating on her."

Didn't Alice have that backwards? "He went back to his wife, you mean?"

"No, he never dumped the wife. Some little freshman. He's a professor, you know. Lots of fresh meat coming his way. Can't keep his hands off."

I stared at the book that I had, without looking, just taken off the shelf: *Path of the Masters* by Julian Johnson. Funny. On my way up, I'd thought about my old quest for this book, still wanting it, a classic in oriental mysticism that had become rather difficult to find.

"She took off for New Mexico when she found out. Never told me where she went, never wrote. She was my roommate for three years, you know."

It took me a moment to remember who *she* was. *Alice*.

We spent another half hour looking around and met up again at the check stand, each with several books.

Our next stop was made at Sasha's request. She wanted to buy some herbal teas at the health food store. It looked like the kind of a place where they burned incense, so I told her I'd wait outside.

"Want me to read the cards for you?" a friendly voice asked. It belonged to a young man whose hair—scalp, eyebrows, lashes, mustache, and goatee—had been dyed fluorescent green.

I found this quite fascinating, and before I knew what I was doing, I was sitting opposite of him at the little card table, my hands stroking the dark-blue velvet cloth sprinkled with glittering silver stars.

He began to expertly shuffle the cards. "I don't set a fee for consultations. I just ask for a donation. Do you have a question?"

"Uh ... " I had loads of questions, but I couldn't think of one to ask or that I really wanted an answer to. "I'm not sure," I murmured.

"How about I just give you a general reading," he suggested with a reassuring smile. "The most important things will probably show up then."

"That sounds fine." I felt a little shiver run down my spine.

He fanned the cards out and looked at them.

Isn't that cheating?

He pulled one out and placed it faceup on the table. The picture was of a crowned woman sitting on an elaborately decorated throne at the edge of a body of water. She was holding an ornate chalice. "This is you. It's the Queen of Cups," the green man said, very sure of himself.

And I knew why, because what he'd just said sounded about right. *I am the Queen of Cups* did sound much better than *I am an alcoholic*.

"She is a woman of vision. Very intuitive." His green eyebrows knitted in concentration, he shuffled the cards some more and then asked me to cut them. I did.

He laid the cards on the table, facedown. "This is called the Celtic Cross. It will give a good picture of what's going on. Past, present, and future." He turned the cards over one by one.

I watched silently.

"Well, the first card is in the place that shows the atmosphere surrounding the matter you are most concerned about. It's the Ten of Swords." He frowned at the card.

It didn't look too good to me either. A man was lying face down with ten swords stuck in his back. A decidedly uncomfortable position. Or maybe not: he looked quite dead of overkill.

"The issue is very serious. There have been some major disruptions. You have gone as far as you can on this and must now find release."

His index finger rested on the next card. Another woman on a throne, but this one holding a sword in the air and with an unhappy look on her face. "The second card represents the forces influencing the situation—for good or bad. This is the Queen of Swords. She's a fickle woman. Says one thing, does another. You can never quite figure her out. She likes to manipulate people. She may be the cause of your problems as shown in the first card. Anyway, she's interfering with the solution."

I was beginning to feel cold.

Something lobster-like was crawling out of the water in the foreground of the next card. A dog and a wolf sat baying at a pensive moon. "The third card represents the basis of the matter. It's already part of your experience. This is the Moon. It's the card of intuition, psychic abilities, dreams, premonitions, but also of deception, secret enemies. Since it's next to the Queen of Swords, you may have had dreams and psychic experiences in connection with her. The Moon also emphasizes the deceptive quality of her nature."

I shifted uneasily on the metal foldout chair.

The green man tapped his finger on the next card. A woman, tied-up and blindfolded, stood surrounded by a hedge of eight swords.

"The fourth card, which is the place of matters passing out of your experience, is the Eight of Swords. There are communication problems. You're not seeing things clearly, unable to get the whole picture or to understand what you're being told. But there's also an indication that you'll be able to break free from this condition."

The pretty stained-glass windows popped up in my peripheral vision. "Is there anything *good* in here, somewhere?" I asked.

He pulled at his green goatee and looked at the last card. "Well, to quote Shakespeare: it ends well."

"Tell me about the ending!"

"You want to skip what's in between? You really should hear the whole thing. It all goes together, you know."

"Just the last card." It looked good: a row of cups forming a rainbow in the sky over a happy couple and two frolicking children.

"OK." He sighed. "That's the Ten of Cups. It's the card of contentment, harmony, and love inspired from above, friendship and peacemaking. It indicates serenity."

Serenity? I got up. I'd heard enough.

I was going to die! That was the only way I'd ever get that kind of serenity.

I tossed a five-dollar bill in his little twig basket and thanked him.

Sasha was coming out of the health food store. I quickly walked over to her.

"Hey!" the green man cried behind me.

I looked at him.

"You'll be OK!" he called out. "You'll be fine!" He waved the Ten of Cups through the air.

I sincerely hoped so.

"Are you all right?" Sasha asked. She was holding a small bag. "Did Harry read the Tarot for you?"

"Hairy?" I asked, dazed.

"Harry! You know—*Harry*," Sasha said.

"Oh, Harry! Yes," I answered absentmindedly. "Yes, Harry read me the Tarot."

"So, what did he say?" Sasha slapped the little brown bag against her thigh.

"Oh, not much." *Too much!*

We walked by the snake lady who was now standing in front of the flower stand on the corner of Durant, still, or again, in passionate conversation with her vampirish companion.

My bags felt heavy and my feet hurt. "Let's have some coffee at Caffe Roma," I suggested.

"Roma?" Sasha asked.

"Yes, Caffe Roma, on the corner of Bancroft and College."

"It's called Caffe Strada now."

I groaned. It was bad enough that they'd blocked off every damned street and made people drive in convoluted circles, but to change the name of my favorite coffee hangout ...

We sat on the terrace and sipped *lattes* sprinkled with chocolate. We didn't talk much, because each time we tried one of Sasha's numerous acquaintances stopped at our table. *Haven't seen you in a while. You look great! Where have you been? I'll come by soon. Sorry to hear about your mother.* I skimmed through the various newspapers others had left and waited for the next pal to come along.

After half an hour my feet were finally willing to become part of my body again. My stomach was rumbling for food. I suggested we have lunch somewhere, but Sasha said she had everything for a great lunch at home. We picked up our bags and tracked back to her house.

Mancha was sitting on the porch. She walked in with us, tail up proprietarily.

"Have a seat," Sasha commanded. "I'll go fix us some lunch." She disappeared into the kitchen.

Maria came down, holding a package of papers and a pencil in one hand and licking whatever it was she was holding in her other hand. "Ah, you're back." She smiled and sat down in the chair. Then she yelled toward the kitchen, "Hey, your father called!"

Sasha gave a muffled response.

I sank into the couch, on the opposite side of where I'd sat earlier, hoping in vain the springs would be more supportive here.

"Want some candy?" Maria asked.

"Sure!"

She reached in the pocket of her tunic. "Here!" She threw a small package at me.

I caught it in my lap and unwrapped it. It was hard red candy in a plastic seashell.

"It's French," Maria informed me. "Sasha made it. She calls it *doo*, or something."

I smelled it. Very cherry.

Doux. Sweet.

"She made a whole bunch." Maria continued to lick her candy.

Sasha was suddenly standing in the kitchen doorway. She was staring at me with a look of utter incredulity.

"Where did you get that?" she asked Maria, her voice hoarse. Then louder, almost yelling, "Where did you get that?"

Maria stopped licking the candy but said nothing. She looked up at Sasha with a mixture of concern and curiosity on her face.

Sasha gestured at me, waving her hand up and down, "No! Don't!"

Then I remembered that I'd seen this candy before. And where.

Chapter 33

Rest, rest, perturbed spirit.

My thoughts twirling, I stared at the plastic seashell filled with cherry candy. It was identical to the one I'd found in Lani's upstairs bathroom and put in the medicine cabinet that day Steve had ransacked the house and the three siblings had arrived at the farm. I'd mistaken it for an air freshener. Forgotten all about it.

All at once, the whole picture was clear. I looked up at Sasha again and said, "Don't worry, I have no intention of drinking." Neither did I have any intention of licking the candy.

As if by some invisible hand, the look on Sasha's face changed from disbelieving fright to desperate grief. Tears streamed down her cheeks. Her whole body shook.

"I didn't mean to kill her," she sobbed. "I just wanted her to stop. To feel for someone else besides all those selves of hers."

I patted the space next to me. She followed my directions like an obedient child. For a while she sat bent over, crying silently, her face in her hands. Maria got some paper towels out of the kitchen and quietly handed them to her.

Sasha wiped her eyes and blew her nose. "It was a mean thing to do, but I didn't know she'd die," she said with a choking voice.

An accidental overdose? "What happened?" I asked.

Sasha took a deep breath. "It began last summer when she suddenly cut off my allowance. I brought some of my art work home for her to see that I was serious about getting a degree. I'd even applied for a special scholarship to study abroad for a semester. In Italy." She paused to dab her eyes.

"Mom acted like she was happy for me. She looked at my work and said it was really good. We talked about my going to Italy. She said I should get some decent clothes so I wouldn't look like a leftover hippie." Sasha snorted, laughing and crying at the same time. "Then, two days after I got back to Berkeley, there was a short note in the mail. Three lines. She wrote, 'The check you got Sunday is going to be the last. It's time you took care of yourself. Love, your Mother.' Just like that. I called her, but she didn't pick up the phone. I left messages on her machine, but she didn't call me back.

"Finally, after a couple of weeks, I drove back home. She treated me like a stranger. I didn't know the personality that had suddenly taken over. I tried to get Jane or Mary or someone else to come out, anyone but that cold fish who called herself my *Mother*. But nothing I did worked." She shook her head. "All of a sudden, I was of no consequence to her, like a piece of garbage. I was really mad, you know. It was way too late to apply for any financial aid. I had to cancel my classes. I found a job at a flower shop on University Avenue. I didn't know much about flowers, but the owner said she'd teach me all there was to know. She was like a grandma, practically adopted me. Brought me lunch. Cookies. And then, right after Thanksgiving, she died of a heart attack." Sasha's eyes filled with sorrow. "Mrs. Grant," she whispered.

I felt guilty about Mrs. Grant's death.

"A couple of days before Christmas, I went home to visit Mom again," Sasha went on. "I hadn't seen her in months. She still acted cold, you know. Only now she was full of this new boyfriend, Steve. It was Steve this and Steve that. Then she introduced me to him and it turned out he was damned Nazi! It was obvious he was just using her. I asked her if she'd totally lost her mind. She told me to get out." Sasha took a deep breath and looked up at the ceiling.

"So, I left. But before I took off, I grabbed the bottle of Boozabuse from the kitchen cabinet. I wasn't sure what I was going to do with it exactly. Maybe use it myself. She sure wasn't taking it. She was drinking hard."

I hadn't noticed that Maria had slipped away into the kitchen. She was suddenly standing there with a pot of tea in one hand and three mugs hanging from the fingers of the other. Silently, she put the mugs down on the stool near me and began to pour.

Sasha took a mug from Maria and held it against her cheek. "A couple of weeks later, Jason called. He said Mom was behaving strangely. He said she was absolutely nasty to him and even worse to Dean. She'd threatened to tell Willem about him and Dean. She'd never been mean like that—not to Jason.

"It was then that I really had the idea that maybe I could purge this repulsive personality out of her by making her sick." She turned to me. "They do, you know, if they can't function any longer. They weaken and then they disappear. I'd heard you get really miserable from drinking on top of Boozabuse. I wanted her to be miserable enough to get rid of that new personality." Sasha closed her eyes. "I crushed a whole bunch of the tablets and put them in the candy. It's not something you eat in chunks; you just lick it a few times and then put it away. So, I didn't think she'd be getting that much of the Boozabuse." Her eyes flew open. "Oh! Jason didn't know! Nobody did."

I nodded my understanding.

"Then I mailed her a package with a silk scarf and a couple of the shells. When Jason called me and told me Mom had had an accident, I didn't connect it to my candy. When I met you that morning, at the farm, I still didn't believe Mom was gone. Forever. Not until later that evening, when Jason and I were talking, did it finally dawn on me that she was never coming back, and then I began to suspect that she'd gotten sick from my candy."

"When did you put the Boozabuse in the medicine cabinet upstairs?" I asked.

"I'd had it in my suitcase all along, so I wouldn't forget to bring it back at my next visit. Alicia was in the kitchen making supper, so I left it upstairs. I found one of the candy shells in the medicine cabinet. I couldn't figure out what it was doing in there. I took it out and put it in my suitcase."

That's why Bobby had never mentioned the candy, because it wasn't in the medicine cabinet when he looked and found the bottle of Boozabuse. The other shell, the one Lani'd taken with her into the orchard, must still be under the trees somewhere.

The three of us quietly looked at each other.

"I wanted to talk to you, Fae, but I couldn't. I felt so terrible," Sasha whispered after a while. "You knew it was me, didn't you?"

"No, I didn't know. I thought it was … " *Anyone but you.*

"Oh," Sasha said, looking surprised. "I thought you knew." She felt around for the paper towels but couldn't find them.

Maria brought the whole roll of towels in and handed it to Sasha.

Looking up at her roommate, Sasha said, "I'm sorry, Maria. I'm so sorry. I was awful to you these last few weeks."

"It's all right," Maria said with a compassionate smile.

"What should I do now?" Sasha asked. "Are you going to tell Bobby van Zand?" She looked at me with a mixture of hope and dread in her eyes.

I thought for just a moment. "No, I won't tell Bobby."

"You're right. You mean *I* should tell him," Sasha said.

I wasn't sure how to say what I had to say, so I just said it. "Your mother asked me not to tell anyone."

Leave it to Heaven had been the message I'd woken up to after the Welcoming Dream. *It*, not *her*. That was the cute part. That's why I still hadn't known if it was a *her* or a *him*.

Both women gaped at me as if I'd just sprouted—wings.

"Ahem?" Maria said, without really clearing her throat, and Sasha's face broke into a sad but triumphant smile. "I *knew* it!" she said. "You're fucking psychic, aren't you?"

I hadn't thought of putting it quite that way. "I am a *sensitive*," I said, in a deliberately prissy tone. Then, dropping the prim and proper routine, "And these last two weeks I've had one hell of a time."

"You saw my mother after she died," Sasha said.

"Yes, I did." *Again and again and again.*

They both looked at me intently, waiting for me to begin my story, so I told them about the vision I'd had on the night Lani died. I told them about the first dream, in which Lani had been on the beach—I now knew what she'd picked up: a plastic seashell with cherry candy—and disappeared through the red door. I told them about the Welcoming Dream, after which I'd known that Lani wanted me to keep whatever I'd find out to myself. (I'd tell Hal. He probably wouldn't believe it anyway.) And I told them about some of the special appearances in between: the near accident, my ferry ride on the bed, the song "Marianne" she'd taught Jesse. As I was talking, these all now began to take on a new meaning, to contain messages. It was an accident. Something made her violently ill. The line "Even little children love Marianne" and Hal's nephews adoring Sasha.

I didn't tell them about all the nasty little pranks Lani pulled, but I did want Sasha to know that Lani had asked me in more ways than one to keep quiet. That Lani had hung around to let me know her wishes. I wanted Sasha to have that one good memory of her mother.

"She did that?" Sasha asked with disbelief in her voice. A soft light entered her eyes. "She protected me?"

I nodded. I certainly hoped that was what Lani had meant. Else, all hell would break loose on my return home. I didn't think I could stand any more of that. I wasn't so sure how good Gwen's friend Holly would be at the business of exorcism.

We talked through another mug of tea and ate our late lunch. When I finally thought of looking at my watch, it was almost six o'clock and dark outside. I asked if Sasha were still planning to ride with me to pick up her Volkswagen. For a moment a cloud passed over her face. Then she answered that she'd come with me.

I called Hal. He claimed he had expected me home at six, then he changed it to four. And, what was he going to eat while his "wifey" was cavorting around? I rolled my eyes and then realized that he couldn't see me, so I said, "You know that lasagna you made? It was very good. I'm bringing Sasha over."

He made a quip about women's lib. I shut him up by telling him I loved him and that I'd eventually come home. Maybe even before ten o'clock. He laughed and told me to drive carefully.

Sasha called her father. Jack had a flu epidemic raging at his house. He thought that if she'd drive in daylight she'd be all right.

A bright, full moon cast a magic glow as we left Berkeley. We talked little.

Suddenly Sasha said, "You know, that red door Mom went through in your dream? I know what it means. Our front door here in Berkeley used to be all red. I wanted to paint it black."

I gave her a sideways glance. Surely, she was jesting?

She caught my look and smirked. "I'm serious! Just like the Stones song. Anyway, Maria didn't like it, so we compromised and I just painted the borders, left the panels red. Mom was giving you a snow job with that all-red door. She wanted you to know but not to know. Like saying, it was her business only."

Yes. And Sasha hadn't foreseen "that thing happening" to Lani. Just like in the song.

The latter part of the trip we traveled in complete silence. When we arrived home, I had to wake Sasha. Hal came out and helped with the bags. He put his arm around me and nuzzled my ear when he thought Sasha wasn't looking. I wasn't sure why this should be kept a secret and laughed at him.

Throughout dinner, we all yawned a lot. My head almost fell into my plate a few times. Instead of making lasagna, Hal had done something to a whole chicken. I wasn't sure what it was he'd done, but it was tasty, full of herbs and garlic and some other ingredients I couldn't quite identify and was too tired to ask about.

He said he'd also tried to make some vegetables.

"*Tried?*" I asked.

"Yes, *tried!* Brussels sprouts. They exploded." He opened the microwave. It looked like vegetarian diarrhea in there.

"That's disgusting!" I said.

"Expanding air pockets," Hal explained.

"Yes, I know," I said. *Nothing spooky about expanding air pockets.*

I told Sasha she should spend the night and gave her one of my one-size-fits-all flannel night gowns. She followed my command without protestations.

I fell asleep before my head touched the pillow and had my last dream of Lani. She was floating up, up, and away. Smiling, smiling. I didn't really want to talk to her anymore and watched her drift off. Then, just to be sure, I called out, "Are you coming back?" She answered, but she was too far away for me to hear her.

Saturday morning, I drove Sasha over to get her van. She insisted on taking Solo with her to Berkeley.

"What about Mancha?" I asked.

"They'll just have to get used to each other."

Maybe taking Solo was her idea of doing penance. Maybe she actually liked that mouthy bird.

Sasha became teary eyed as she looked up at her mother's old house. "I'll call Bobby van Zand as soon as I get home," she said, letting out a deep sigh that ended in a hiccup.

Something inside me did a one-hundred-eighty-degree turn. "Oh, shit, don't do that!" I had an impulse to say. *Bobby might not be so understanding.* But I nodded and said nothing.

All the same, I worried.

When she drove off, honking her horn and waving her arm out of the window, that's when I knew Sasha would be all right.

***

There was a message from Rita when I returned. I called her back.

"They got the bastard!" she yelled. "He grabbed another girls last night. At Sandhill. Some guys heard the girl scream and come to help her. Beat the crap out of the fucking bastard! Then they drug him to the nearest-by phone and called the cops." Rita began to cough. "But they beat the crap out of him first," she finally got out, gasping but with triumph in her voice.

"Are they sure it's the same guy?" I leaned against the wall.

"Got big scratches on his face. Looks like they was made by fingernails, the cops said. They're gonna do some tests." Rita wheezed.

"Good," I said. I meant that the rapist had been caught, although I wasn't too sad about him being crapless either. Might give him a bit of insight into what he'd done to Sarah, to—how many?—other women. Maybe prison would complete that lesson.

"Who is he?" I asked.

"Some student, they told us. We're gonna go to the station to find out some more. I'll call you when we get back."

I felt a bit guilty about the relief that was flooding through me. Because if it hadn't been Steve Krieger, then it hadn't been my jacket. Gwen had been right. And I had been wrong twice about Steve.

I wiped my eyes.

***

Gwen and her friend Holly arrived promptly at ten. We sat at the kitchen table and talked for a while. When Hal became aware of the subject of our conversation, he excused himself and made a beeline for the barn.

After finishing our coffee, we slowly went through the house, Holly leading the way. Going from room to room, she even opened several closet doors.

I hoped nothing would fall on her head. But then, I thought, maybe she would see that coming.

When we finally arrived in my attic art studio, Holly said, "There is nothing here." She sounded puzzled.

"Nothing?" Gwen and I asked simultaneously.

"No entity like Gwen described to me." Holly hesitated. "But there *is* an old woman sitting in that rocking chair over there. She's telling me she used to live here. She's telling me to thank you for helping her niece."

I looked at the chair. I didn't see a thing.

But then the chair began to rock—gently.

I turned and followed Bluebelle downstairs.